The Lady Chosen

D1409856

Stephanie Laurens

The Lady Chosen

A Bastion Club Novel

AVON

An Imprint of HarperCollinsPublishers

The name Stephanie Laurens is a registered trademark of Savdek Management Proprietary Ltd.

HarperCollins books may be purchased for educational, business, or sales promotional use. For information, please write: Special Markets Department, HarperCollins Publishers, 195 Broadway, New York, NY 10007.

First Avon Books paperback printing: August 2014
First Avon Books mass market printing: September 2003
First Avon Books special printing: April 2003

Library of Congress Cataloging-in-Publication Data is available upon request.

ISBN 978-0-06-233656-9

14 15 16 17 18   OV/RRD   10 9 8 7 6 5 4 3 2 1

The Lady Chosen

The Bastion Club
"a last bastion against the matchmakers of the ton"

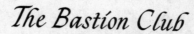

MEMBERS

Christian Allardyce,
Marquess of Dearne

Anthony Blake,
Viscount Torrington

Jocelyn Deverell,
Viscount Paignton

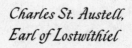

Charles St. Austell,
Earl of Lostwithiel

Gervase Tregarth,
Earl of Crowhurst

Jack Warnefleet,
Baron Warnefleet of Minchinbury

Tristan Wemyss,
Earl of Trentham

Prologue

༄ ☙❧ ༄

The Pavilion, Brighton
October 1815

"His Royal Highness's straits must be dire indeed if he needs must summon His Britannic Majesty's best simply to bask in the reflected glory."

The drawled comment contained more than a little cynicism; Tristan Wemyss, fourth Earl of Trentham, glanced across the stuffy music room, packed with guests, sycophants, and all manner of toadies, at its subject.

Prinny stood in the center of a circle of admirers. Decked out in gold braid and crimson, with epaulets high and fully fringed, their Regent was in genial and expansive good humor, retelling heroic tales of derring-do drawn from the dispatches of recent engagements, most notably that of Waterloo.

Both Tristan and the gentleman standing beside him, Christian Allardyce, Marquess of Dearne, knew the real stories; they had been there. Easing free of the throng, they'd retreated to the side of the opulent chamber to avoid hearing the artful lies.

It was Christian who'd spoken.

"Actually," Tristan murmured, "I'd viewed tonight more in the nature of a distraction—a feint, if you will."

Christian raised heavy brows. "Listen to my stories of England's greatness—don't worry that the Exchequer's empty and the people are starving?"

Tristan's lips quirked downward. "Something like that."

Dismissing Prinny and his court, Christian surveyed the others crowding the circular room. It was an all-male company primarily composed of representatives from every major regiment and arm of the services recently active; the chamber was a sea of colorful dress uniforms, of braid, polished leather, fur, and even feathers. "Telling that he chose to stage what amounts to a victory reception in Brighton rather than London, don't you think? I wonder if Dalziel had any say in that?"

"From all I've gathered, our Prince is no favorite in London, but it seems our erstwhile commander has taken no chances with those names he volunteered for the guest list tonight."

"Oh?"

They were talking quietly, out of habit disguising their communication as nothing more than a social exchange between acquaintances. Habit died hard, especially since, until recently, such practices had been vital to staying alive.

Tristan smiled vaguely, indeed *through* a gentleman who glanced their way; the man decided against intruding. "I saw Deverell at the table—he was seated not far from me. He mentioned that Warnefleet and St. Austell were here, too."

"You can add Tregarth and Blake—I saw them as I was arriving—" Christian broke off. "Ah, I see. Dalziel has only allowed those of us who have sold out to appear?"

Tristan caught his eye; the smile that was never far from his mobile lips deepened. "Can you imagine Dalziel allowing even Prinny to identify his most secret of secret operatives?"

Christian hid a smile, raised his glass to his lips, and sipped.

Dalziel—he went by no other name or honorific—was the Foreign Office taskmaster who, from his office buried in the depths of Whitehall, managed His British Majesty's foreign spy network, a network that had been instrumental in handing victory to England and her allies both in the Peninsula campaign and more recently at Waterloo. Together with a certain Lord Whitley, his opposite number in the Home Office, Dalziel was responsible for all covert operations both within England and beyond its borders.

"I didn't realize Tregarth or Blake were in the same boat as we two, and I know of the others only by repute." Christian glanced at Tristan. "Are you sure the others are leaving?"

"I know Warnefleet and Blake are, for much the same reasons as we. As for the others, it's purely conjecture but I can't see Dalziel compromising an operative of St. Austell's caliber, or Tregarth's or Deverell's for that matter, just to pander to Prinny's latest whim."

"True." Christian again looked out over the sea of heads.

Both he and Tristan were tall, broad-shouldered, and lean, with the honed strength of men used to action, a strength imperfectly concealed by the elegant cut of their evening clothes. Beneath those clothes, both bore the scars of years of active service; although their nails were perfectly manicured, it would be some months yet before the telltale signs of their unusual, often ungentlemanly erstwhile occupation faded from their hands—the calluses, the roughness, the leatherlike palms.

They and their five colleagues known to be present had all served Dalziel and their country for at least a decade, Christian for nearly fifteen years. They'd served in whatever guise had been required, from nobleman to streetsweeper, from clerk to navvy. There had, for them, been only one measure of success— discovering the information they'd been sent behind enemy lines to acquire and surviving long enough to get it back to Dalziel.

Christian sighed, drained his glass. "I'm going to miss it."

Tristan's laugh was short. "Aren't we all?"

"Be that as it may, given that we're no longer on His Majesty's payroll"—Christian set his empty glass down on a nearby side-board—"I fail to see why we need stand here talking, when we could be much more comfortable doing the same elsewhere . . ." His grey gaze met the eyes of a gentleman clearly considering approaching; the gentleman considered again and turned away. "And without running the risk of having to do the pretty for whichever toady captures us and demands to hear our story."

Glancing at Tristan, Christian raised a brow. "What say you— shall we adjourn to pleasanter surrounds?"

"By all means." Tristan handed his empty glass to a passing footman. "Do you have any particular venue in mind?"

"I've always been partial to the Ship and Anchor. It has a very cosy snug."

Tristan inclined his head. "The Ship and Anchor, then. Dare we leave together, do you think?"

Christian's lips curved. "Heads together, talking earnestly in hushed and urgent tones—if we make for the door unobtrusively but determinedly, I can see no reason we shouldn't walk straight through."

They did. Everyone who saw them assumed one had been sent to summon the other for some secret but highly significant purpose; the footmen rushed to get their coats, and then they strode out, into the crisp night.

Both paused, drew in a deep breath, clearing the stultifying stuffiness of the overheated Pavilion from their lungs, then, exchanging faint smiles, they stepped out.

Leaving the Pavilion's brightly lit entrance, they emerged onto North Street. Turning right, they walked with the relaxed gait of men who knew where they were going toward Brighton Square and the Lanes beyond. Reaching the narrow cobbled ways lined with fishermen's cottages, they dropped into single file, at every crossroads changing place, eyes always watching, searching the shadows . . . if either realized, realized they were now at home, at peace, no longer fugitives, no longer at war, neither commented nor tried to suppress the behavior that had become second nature to them both.

They headed steadily south, toward the sound of the sea, soughing in the darkness beyond the shore. Finally, they turned into Black Lion Street. At the end of the street lay the Channel, the border beyond which they'd lived most of the past decade. Halting beneath the swaying sign of the Ship and Anchor, they both paused, eyes on the darkness framed by the houses at the end of the street. The smell of the sea, the brine on the wind, the familiar tang of seaweed reached them.

Memory held them both for an instant, then, as one, they turned. Christian pushed open the door, and they went inside.

Warmth enveloped them, the sounds of English voices, the hop-infused scent of good English ale. Both relaxed, an indefinable tension falling from them. Christian walked up to the bar. "Two pots of your best."

The landlord nodded a greeting and quickly pulled the pints.

Christian glanced at the half-closed door behind the bar. "We'll sit in your snug."

The landlord glanced at him, then set the frothing tankards

on the bar. He shot a quick glance at the snug door. "As to that, sir, you're welcome, I'm sure, but there's a group o' gen'lemen in there already, and they might not welcome strangers, like."

Christian raised his brows. He reached for the flap in the counter and lifted it, stepping past as he picked up one tankard. "We'll risk it."

Tristan hid a grin, tossed coins on the counter for the ale, hoisted the second tankard, and followed on Christian's heels.

He was standing at Christian's shoulder when Christian sent the snug door swinging wide.

The group gathered about two tables pushed together looked around; five pairs of eyes locked on them.

Five grins dawned.

Charles St. Austell sat back in the chair at the far end of the table and magnanimously waved them in. "You are better men than we. We were about to take bets on how long you'd stand it."

The others stood so the tables and chairs could be rearranged. Tristan shut the door, set down his tankard, then joined in the round of introductions.

Although they'd all served under Dalziel, they'd never met all seven together. Each knew some of the others; none had previously met all.

Christian Allardyce, the eldest and longest-serving, had operated in the east of France, often in Switzerland, Germany, and the other smaller states and principalities; with his fairish coloring and facility for languages, he'd been a natural in that sphere.

Tristan himself had served more generally, often in the heart of things, in Paris and the major industrial cities; his fluency in French as well as German and Italian, his brown hair, brown eyes, and easy charm had served him and his country well.

He'd never crossed paths with Charles St. Austell, the most outwardly flamboyant of the group. With his tumbling black locks and flashing dark blue eyes, Charles was a magnet for ladies young and old. Half-French, he possessed both the tongue and the wit to make the most of his physical attributes; he'd been Dalziel's principal operative in the south of France, in Carcasonne and Toulouse.

Gervase Tregarth, a Cornishman with curling brown hair and sharp hazel eyes, had, so Tristan learned, spent much of the last decade in Britanny and Normandy. He knew St. Austell from the past, but in the field they'd never met.

Tony Blake was another scion of an English house who was also half-French. Black-haired, black-eyed, he was the most elegant of the group, yet there was an underlying sharpness beneath the smooth veneer; he was the operative Dalziel had most often used to intercept and interfere with the French spymasters' networks, a hideously dangerous undertaking centered on the northern French ports. That Tony was alive was a testament to his mettle.

Jack Warnefleet was outwardly a conundrum; he appeared so overtly English, startlingly handsome with fairish brown hair and hazel eyes, that it was hard to imagine he'd been consistently successful in infiltrating all levels of French shipping and many business deals as well. He was a chameleon even more than the rest of them, with a cheery, hail-fellow-well-met geniality few saw beyond.

Deverell was the last man Tristan shook hands with, a personable gentleman with an easy smile, dark brown hair, and greenish eyes. Despite being uncommonly handsome he possessed the knack of blending in with any group. He had served almost exclusively in Paris and had never been detected.

The introductions complete, they sat. The snug was now

comfortably full; a fire burned cheerily in one corner as in the flickering light they settled about the table, almost shoulder to shoulder.

They were all large men; they had all at some point been guardsmen in one regiment or another, until Dalziel had found them and lured them into serving through his office.

Not that he'd had to persuade all that hard.

Savoring his first sip of ale, Tristan ran his eye around the table. Outwardly, they were all different, yet they were, very definitely, brothers beneath the skin. Each was a gentleman born of some aristocratic lineage, each possessed similar attributes, abilities, and talents although the relative balance differed. Most importantly, however, each was a man capable of dicing with danger, one who would accept the challenge of a life-and-death engagement without a flicker—more, with an inbred confidence and a certain devil-may-care arrogance.

There was more than a touch of the wild adventurer in each of them. And they were loyal to the bone.

Deverell set down his tankard. "Is it true we've all sold out?" There were nods and glances all around; Deverell grinned. "Is it polite to inquire why?" He looked at Christian. "In your case, I assume Allardyce must now become Dearne?"

Wryly, Christian inclined his head. "Indeed. Once my father died, and I came into the title, any choice evaporated. If it hadn't been for Waterloo, I would already be mired in issues pertaining to sheep and cattle, and no doubt leg-shackled to boot."

His tone, faintly disgusted, brought commiserating smiles to the others' faces.

"That sounds all too familiar." Charles St. Austell looked down the table. "I hadn't expected to inherit, but while I was away, both my elder brothers failed me." He grimaced. "So now

I'm the Earl of Lostwithiel and, so my sisters, sisters-in-law, and dear mother constantly remind me, long overdue at the altar."

Jack Warnefleet laughed, not exactly humorously. "Entirely unexpectedly, I've joined the club, too. The title was expected— it was the pater's—but the houses and the blunt came via a great-aunt I barely knew existed, so now, I've been told, I rank high on the list of eligibles and can expect to be hunted until I surrender and take a wife."

"*Moi, aussi.*" Gervase Tregarth nodded to Jack. "In my case it was a cousin who succumbed to consumption and died ridiculously young, so now I'm the Earl of Crowhurst, with a house in London I haven't even seen and a need, so I've been informed, to get myself a wife and heir, given I'm now the last of the line."

Tony Blake made a dismissive sound. "At least you don't have a French mother—believe me, when it comes to hounding one to the altar, they take the cake."

"I'll drink to that." Charles raised his tankard to Tony. "But does that mean you, too, have returned to these shores to discover yourself encumbered?"

Tony wrinkled his nose. "Courtesy of my father, I've become Viscount Torrington—I'd hoped it would be years yet, but . . ." He shrugged. "What I didn't know was that over the past decade the pater had taken an interest in various investments. I'd expected to inherit a decent livelihood—I hadn't expected to succeed to great wealth. And then I discover the entire ton knows it. On my way down here I stopped briefly in town to call on my godmother." He shuddered. "I was nearly mobbed. It was horrendous."

"It's because we lost so many at Waterloo." Deverell gazed into his tankard; they were all silent for a moment, remembering lost comrades, then all lifted their cups and drank.

"I have to confess I'm in much the same straits." Deverell set down his tankard. "I'd no expectations when I left England, only to discover on my return that some distant cousin twice removed had turned up his toes, and I'm now Viscount Paignton, with the houses, the income—and just like you all, the dire need of a wife. I can manage the land and funds, but the houses, let alone the social obligations—they're a web far worse than any French plot."

"And the consequences of failing could drive you to your grave," St. Austell put in.

There were dark murmurs of assent all around. All eyes turned to Tristan.

He smiled. "That's quite a litany, but I fear I can trump all your tales." He looked down, turning his tankard between his hands. "I, too, returned to find myself encumbered—with a title, two houses and a hunting box, and considerable wealth. However, both houses are home to an assortment of females, great-aunts, cousins, and other more distant connections. I inherited from my great-uncle, the recently departed third Earl of Trentham, who loathed his brother—my grandfather—and also my late father, and me.

"His argument was we were wastrel ne'er-do-wells who came and went as we pleased, traveled the world, and so on. In all fairness, I must say that now I've met my great-aunts and their female army, I can see the old boy's point. He must have felt trapped by his position, sentenced to live his life surrounded by a tribe of doting, meddling females."

A *frisson*, a shudder, ran around the table.

Tristan's expression grew grim. "Consequently, when his own son's son died, and then his son as well, and he realized I would inherit from him, he devised a devilish clause to his will. I've inherited title, land, and houses, and wealth for a year—but if I fail to marry within that year, I'll be left with the title, the land, and the houses—all that's entailed—but the bulk of the wealth, the funds needed to run the houses, will be given to various charities."

There was silence, then Jack Warnefleet asked, "What would happen to the horde of old ladies?"

Tristan looked up, eyes narrow. "That's the devilish heart of it—they'd remain my pensioners, in my houses. There's nowhere else for them to go, and I could hardly turf them into the streets."

All the others stared at him, appreciation of his predicament dawning in their faces.

"That's a dastardly thing to do." Gervase paused, then asked, "When's your year up?"

"July."

"So you've got next Season to make your choice." Charles set his tankard down and pushed it away. "We're all in large measure in the same boat. If I don't find a wife by then, my sisters, sisters-in-law, and dear mother will drive me demented."

"It's not going to be plain sailing, I warn you." Tony Blake glanced around the table. "After escaping from my godmother's, I sought refuge in Boodles." He shook his head. "Bad mistake. Within an hour, not one, but *two* gentlemen I'd never before met approached and asked me to dinner!"

"Set on *in your club?*" Jack voiced their communal shock.

Grimly, Tony nodded. "And there was worse. I called in at the house and discovered a pile of invitations, literally a foot high. The butler said they'd started arriving the day after I'd sent word I'd be down—I'd warned my godmother I might drop in."

Silence fell as they all digested that, extrapolated, considered . . .

Christian leaned forward. "Who else has been up to town?"

All the others shook their heads. They'd only recently returned to England and had gone straight to their estates.

"Very well," Christian continued. "Does this mean that when next we each show our faces in town, we'll be hounded like Tony?"

They all imagined it. . . .

"Actually," Deverell said, "it's likely to be much worse. A lot of families are in mourning at the moment—even if they're in town, they won't be going about. The numbers calling should be down."

They all looked at Tony, who shook his head. "Don't know—I didn't wait to find out."

"But as Deverell says, it must be so." Gervase's face hardened. "But such mourning will end in good time for next Season, then the harpies will be out and about, looking for victims, more desperate and even more determined."

"*Hell!*" Charles spoke for them all. "We're going to be"—he gestured—"precisely the sort of targets we've spent the last decade *not being*."

Christian nodded, serious, sober. "In a different theater, maybe, but it's still a form of war, the way the ladies of the ton play the game."

Shaking his head, Tristan sat back in his chair. "It's a sad day when, having survived everything the French could throw at us, we, England's heroes, return home—only to face an even greater threat."

"A threat to our futures like none other, and one we haven't, thanks to our devotion to king and country, as much experience in facing as many a younger man," Jack added.

Silence fell.

"You know . . ." Charles St. Austell poked his tankard in circles. "We've faced worse before, and won." He looked up, glanced around. "We're all much of an age—there's what? Five years between us? We're all facing a similar threat, and have a similar goal in mind, for similar reasons. Why not band together—help each other?"

"One for all and all for one?" Gervase asked.

"Why not?" Charles glanced around again. "We're experienced enough in strategy—surely we can, and should, approach this like any other engagement."

Jack sat up. "It's not as if we'd be in competition with each other." He, too, glanced around, meeting everyone's eyes. "We're all alike to some degree, but we're all different, too, all from different families, different counties, and there's not too *few* ladies but too *many* vying for our attentions—that's our problem."

"I think it's an excellent idea." Leaning his forearms on the table, Christian looked at Charles, then at the others. "We all have to wed. I don't know about you, but I'll fight to the last gasp to retain control of my destiny. *I* will choose my wife—I will not have her foisted, by whatever means, upon me. Thanks to Tony's fortuitous reconnoitering, we now know the enemy will be waiting, ready to pounce the instant we appear." He glanced around again. "So how are we going to seize the initiative?"

"The same way we always have," Tristan replied. "Information is key. We share what we learn—dispositions of the enemy, their habits, their preferred strategies."

Deverell nodded. "We share tactics that work, and warn of any perceived pitfalls."

"But what we need first, more than anything," Tony cut in, "is a safe refuge. It's always the first thing we put in place when going into enemy territory."

They all paused, considered.

Charles grimaced. "Before your news, I would have imagined our clubs, but that clearly won't do."

"No, and our houses are not safe for similar reasons." Jack frowned. "Tony's right—we need a refuge where we can be certain we're safe, where we can meet and exchange information." His brows rose. "Who knows? There might be times when it would be to our advantage to conceal our connections with each other, at least socially."

The others nodded, exchanging glances.

Christian put their thoughts into words. "We need a club of our own. Not to live in, although we might want a few bedchambers in case of need, but a club where we can meet, and from which we can plan and conduct our campaigns in safety without having to watch our backs."

"Not a bolt-hole," Charles mused. "More a castle . . ."

"A stronghold in the heart of enemy territory." Deverell nodded decisively. "Without it, we'll be too exposed."

"And we've been away too long," Gervase growled. "The harpies will fall on us and tie us down if we waltz into the ton unprepared. We've forgotten what it's like . . . if we ever truly knew."

It was a tacit acknowledgment that they were indeed sailing into unknown and therefore dangerous waters. Not one of them had spent any meaningful time in society after the age of twenty.

Christian looked around the table. "We have five full months before we need our refuge—if we have it established by the end of February, we'll be able to return to town and slip in past the pickets, disappear whenever we wish . . ."

"My estate's in Surrey." Tristan met the others' gazes. "If we can decide on what we want as our stronghold, I can slip into town and make the arrangements without creating any ripples."

Charles's eyes narrowed; his gaze grew distant. "Someplace close to everywhere, but not too close."

"It needs to be in an area easily reachable, but not obvious." Deverell tapped the table in thought. "The fewer in the neighborhood who recognize us the better."

"A house, perhaps . . ."

They tossed around their requirements, and quickly agreed that a house in one of the quieter areas outside but close to Mayfair yet away from the heart of town would serve them best. A house with reception rooms and space enough for them all to congregate, with a room in which they could meet with ladies if necessary, but the rest of the house to be female-free, with at least three bedchambers in case of need, and kitchens and staff quarters—and a staff who understood their requirements . . .

"That's it." Jack slapped the table. "Here!" He grabbed up his tankard and raised it. "I give you Prinny and his unpopularity— if it weren't for him, we wouldn't be here today and wouldn't have had the opportunity to make all our futures that much safer."

With wide grins, they all drank, then Charles pushed back his chair, rose, and lifted his tankard. "Gentlemen—I give you our club! Our last bastion against the matchmakers of the ton, our secured base from which we'll infiltrate, identify, and isolate the lady we each want, then take the ton by storm and capture her!"

The others cheered, thumped the table, and rose.

Charles inclined his head to Christian. "I give you the bastion which will allow us to take charge of our destinies and rule our own hearths. Gentlemen!" Charles raised his tankard high. "I give you the Bastion Club!"

They all roared their approval and drank.

And the Bastion Club was born.

Lust and a virtuous woman—only a fool combined the two.

Tristan Wemyss, fourth Earl of Trentham, reflected that he'd rarely been called a fool, yet here he stood, gazing out of a window at an undoubtedly virtuous lady and indulging in all manner of lustful thoughts.

Understandable, perhaps; the lady was tall, dark-haired, and possessed a willowy, subtly curvaceous figure displayed to advantage as, strolling the back garden of the neighboring house, she paused here and there, bending to examine some foliage or flower in the lush and strangely riotous garden beds.

It was February, the weather as bleak and chill as in that month it was wont to be, yet the garden next door displayed abundant growth, thick leaves in dark greens and bronzes from unusual plants that seemed to thrive despite the frosts. Admittedly, there were trees and shrubs leafless and lifelorn scattered throughout the deep beds, yet the garden exuded an air of winter life quite absent from most London gardens in that season.

Not that he possessed any interest in horticulture; it was the lady who held his interest, with her gliding, graceful walk, with the tilt of her head as she examined a bloom. Her hair, the color of rich mahogany, was coiled in a coronet about her head; he couldn't from this distance divine her expression, yet her face was a pale oval, features delicate and pure.

A wolfhound, shaggy and brindle-coated, snuffled idly at her heels; it usually accompanied her whenever she wandered outside.

His instincts, well honed and reliable, informed him that today the lady's attention was perfunctory, in abeyance, that she was killing time while she waited for something. Or someone.

"M'lord?"

Tristan turned. He was standing in the bay window of the library on the first floor in the rear corner of the terrace house at Number 12 Montrose Place. He and his six coconspirators, the members of the Bastion Club, had bought the house three weeks ago; they were in the process of equipping it to serve as their private stronghold, their last bastion against the matchmakers of the ton. Situated in this quiet area of Belgravia mere blocks from the southeast corner of the park, beyond which lay Mayfair, where they all possessed houses, the house was perfect for their needs.

The library window overlooked the back garden, and also the back garden of the larger house next door, Number 14, in which the lady lived.

Billings, the carpenter in charge of the renovations, stood in the doorway studying a battered list.

"I think as we've about done all the new work, 'cepting for this set of cupboards in the office." Billings looked up. "If you

could take a look and see if we've got the idea right, we'll get it
done, then we'll start the painting, polishing, and cleaning up,
so's your people can settle in."

"Very good." Tristan stirred. "I'll come now." He cast a last
glance at the garden next door, and saw a towheaded boy racing
across the lawn toward the lady. Saw her turn, see, wait expec-
tantly . . . clearly the news she'd been anticipating.

Quite why he found her fascinating he had no idea; he preferred blonds of more buxom charms and despite his desperate
need of a wife, the lady was too old to be still on the marriage
mart; she would certainly already be wed.

He drew his gaze from her. "How long do you think it will be
before the house is habitable?"

"Few more days, p'raps a week. Belowstairs is close to done."

Waving Billings ahead, Tristan followed him out of the door.

"Miss, miss! The gentl'man's here!"

At last! Leonora Carling drew in a breath. She straightened,
spine stiffening in anticipation, then unbent to smile at the bootboy. "Thank you, Toby. Is it the same gentleman as before?"

Toby nodded. "The one as Quiggs said is one of the owners."

Quiggs was a journeyman-carpenter working on the house
next door; Toby, always curious, had befriended him. Through
that route Leonora had learned enough of the gentlemen-owners'
plans for next door to decide she needed to learn more. A lot
more.

Toby, tousle-haired, bright color in his cheeks where the wind
had nipped, jigged from foot to foot. "You'll need to look sharpish
if'n you want to catch 'im though—Quiggs said as Billings was
having a last word, and then the gentl'man'd likely leave."

"Thank you." Leonora patted Toby's shoulder, drawing him with her as she walked quickly toward the back door. Henrietta, her wolfhound, loped at their heels. "I'll go around right now. You've been most helpful—let's see if we can persuade Cook that you deserve a jam tart."

"*Cor!*" Toby's eyes grew round; Cook's jam tarts were legendary.

Harriet, Leonora's maid, who'd been with the household for many years, a comfortable but shrewd female with a mass of curling red hair, was waiting in the hall just inside the back door. Leonora sent Toby to request his reward; Harriet waited only until the boy was out of earshot before demanding, "You're not going to do anything rash, are you?"

"Of course not." Leonora glanced down at her gown; she tweaked the bodice. "But I must learn whether the gentlemen next door were those who previously wanted this house."

"And if they are?"

"If they are, then either they were behind the incidents, in which case the incidents will cease, or alternatively they know nothing of our attempted burglaries, or the other happenings, in which case . . ." She frowned, then pushed past Harriet. "I must go. Toby said the man would be leaving soon."

Ignoring Harriet's worried look, Leonora hurried through the kitchen. Waving aside the usual household queries from Cook, Mrs. Wantage, their housekeeper, and Castor, her uncle's ancient butler, promising to return shortly and deal with everything, she pushed through the swinging baize-covered door into the front hall.

Castor followed. "Shall I summon a hackney, miss? Or do you wish for a footman . . . ?"

"No, no." Grabbing her cloak, she swung it about her shoulders and quickly tied the strings. "I'm just stepping into the street for a minute—I'll be back directly."

Snatching her bonnet from the hall stand, she plonked it on her head; looking into the hall mirror, she swiftly tied the ribbons. She spared a glance for her appearance. Not perfect, but it would do. Interrogating unknown gentlemen was not something she often did; regardless, she wasn't about to quail or quake. The situation was all too serious.

She turned to the door.

Castor stood before it, a vague frown creasing his brow. "Where shall I say you've gone if Sir Humphrey or Mr. Jeremy should ask?"

"They won't. If they do, just tell them I've gone to call next door." They'd think she'd gone to visit at Number 16, not Number 12.

Henrietta sat beside the door, bright eyes locked on her, canine jaws parted, tongue lolling, hoping against hope . . .

"Stay here."

With a whine, the hound flopped to the flags and, in patent disgust, laid her huge head on her paws.

Leonora ignored her. She gestured impatiently at the door; as soon as Castor opened it, she hurried out onto the tiled front porch. At the top of the steps, she paused to scan the street; it was, as she'd hoped, deserted. Relieved, she rapidly descended into the fantasy of the front garden.

Normally, the garden would have distracted her, at least made her look and take note. Today, hurrying down the main path, she barely saw the bushes, the bright berries bobbing on the naked branches, the strange lacy leaves growing in profusion. Today, the fantastical creation of her distant cousin

Cedric Carling failed to slow her precipitate rush for the front gate.

The new owners of Number 12 were a group of lords—so Toby had heard, but who knew? At the very least they were tonnish gentlemen. Apparently they were refurbishing the house, but none of them planned to live in it—an unquestionably odd, distinctly suspicious circumstance. Combined with all else that had been going on . . . she was determined to discover if there was any connection.

For the past three months, she and her family had been subjected to determined harrassment aimed at persuading them to sell their house. First had come an approach through a local agent. From dogged persuasion, the agent's arguments had degenerated into belligerence and pugnacity. Nevertheless, she'd eventually convinced the man, and presumably his clients, that her uncle would not sell.

Her relief had been short-lived.

Within weeks, there'd been two attempts to break into their house. Both had been foiled, one by the staff, the other by Henrietta. She might have dismissed the occurences as coincidence if it hadn't been for the subsequent attacks on her.

Those had been much more frightening.

She'd told no one bar Harriet of those incidents, not her uncle Humphrey or her brother Jeremy or any other of the staff. There was no point rattling the servants, and as for her uncle and brother, if she managed to make them believe that the incidents had actually happened and weren't a figment of her untrustworthy female imagination, they would only restrict her movements, further compromising her ability to deal with the problem. To identify those responsible and their reasons, and ensure no further incidents occurred.

That was her goal; the gentleman from next door would, she hoped, get her one step further along her road.

Reaching the tall wrought-iron gate set into the high stone wall, she hauled it open and whisked through, turning to her right, toward Number 12—

And crashed into a walking monument.

"Oh!"

She cannoned off a body like stone.

It gave not an inch, but it moved like lightning.

Hard hands gripped her arms above the elbows.

Sparks flared and sizzled, struck by the collision. Sensation flashed from where his fingers grasped.

He held her steady, stopping her from falling.

Also trapping her.

Her lungs seized. Her eyes, widening, clashed, then locked with a hard hazel gaze, one surprisingly sharp. Even as she noticed, he blinked; his heavy lids descended, screening his eyes. The planes of his face, until then chiseled granite, softened into an expression of easy charm.

His lips changed the most—from a rigid, determined line into curving, beguiling mobility.

He smiled.

She hauled her gaze back up to his eyes. Blushed.

"I'm so sorry. Pray excuse me." Flustered, she stepped back, disengaged. His fingers eased; his hands slid from her. Was it her imagination that labeled the move reluctant? Her skin prickled; her nerves skittered. Oddly breathless, she hurried on, "I didn't see you coming . . ."

Her gaze flicked beyond him—to the house at Number 12. She registered the direction from which he'd been walking, and the trees along the boundary wall between Number 12 and Number

14, the only ones that could have hidden him during her earlier survey of the street.

Her fluster abruptly evaporated; she looked at him. "Are you the gentleman from Number 12?"

He didn't blink; not a flicker of surprise at such a strange greeting—almost an accusation given her tone—showed in that charmingly mobile face. He had sable brown hair, worn slightly longer than was fashionable; his features possessed a distinctly autocratic cast. An instant, brief but discernible, passed, then he inclined his head. "Tristan Wemyss. Trentham, for my sins." His gaze moved past her to the open gate. "I take it you live here?"

"Indeed. With my uncle and brother." Lifting her chin, she drew a tight breath, fixed her eyes on his, glinting green and gold beneath his dark lashes. "I'm glad I caught you. I wished to ask if you and your friends were the purchaser who attempted to buy my uncle's house last November, through the agent Stolemore."

His gaze returned to her face, studying it as if he could read far more than she would like therein. He was tall, broad-shouldered; his scrutiny gave her no opportunity to assess further, but the impression she'd gleaned was one of quiet elegance, a fashionable facade behind which unexpected strength lurked. Her senses had registered the contradiction between how he looked and how he felt in the instant she'd run into him.

Neither name nor title meant anything to her yet; she would check in Debrett's later. The only thing that struck her as out of place was the light tan that colored his skin . . . an idea stirred, but, held by his gaze, she couldn't pin down the impression. His hair fell in gentle waves about his head, framing a broad forehead above arched dark brows that now drew into a frown.

"No." He hesitated, then added, "We heard of the proposed sale of Number 12 in mid-January, through an acquaintance.

0#

Stolemore handled the sale, true enough, but we dealt directly with the owners."

"Oh." Her certainty dissipated; her belligerence deflated. Nevertheless, she felt forced to ask, "So you weren't behind the earlier offers? Or the other incidents?"

"Earlier offers? I take it someone was keen to buy your uncle's house?"

"Indeed. Very keen." They'd well-nigh driven her demented. "However, if it wasn't you or your friends . . ." She paused. "Are you sure none of your friends . . . ?"

"Quite sure. We were in this together from the first."

"I see." Determined, she drew breath, lifted her chin even higher. He was a full head taller than she; it was difficult to adopt a censorious stance. "In that case, I feel I must ask what you intend to do with Number 12, now you have bought it. I understand neither you nor your friends will be taking up residence."

Her thoughts—her suspicions—were there to be read, clear in her lovely blue eyes. Their shade was arresting, neither violet nor plain blue; they reminded Tristan of periwinkles at twilight. Her sudden appearance, the brief—all too brief—moment of collision when, against all odds, she'd run into his arms . . . in light of his earlier thoughts of her, in light of the obsession that had been building over the past weeks while, from the library of Number 12, he'd watched her walk her garden, the abrupt introduction had left him adrift.

The obvious direction of her thoughts rapidly hauled him back to earth.

He raised a brow, faintly haughty. "My friends and I merely wish for a quiet place in which to meet. I assure you our interests are in no way nefarious, illicit, or . . ." He'd been going to say "socially unacceptable"; the matrons of the ton would probably not agree. Holding her gaze, he glibly substituted, "Such as to cause any raised eyebrows even among the most prudish."

Far from being put in her place, she narrowed her eyes. "I thought that's what gentlemen's clubs were for. There are any number of such establishments only blocks away in Mayfair."

"Indeed. We, however, value our privacy." He wasn't going to explain the reasons for their club. Before she could think of some way to probe further, he seized the initiative. "These people who tried to buy your uncle's house. How insistent were they?"

Remembered aggravation flared in her eyes. "Too insistent. They made themselves—or rather the agent—into a definite pest."

"They never approached your uncle directly?"

She frowned. "No. Stolemore handled all their offers, but that was quite bad enough."

"How so?"

When she hesitated, he offered, "Stolemore was the agent for the sale of Number 12. I'm on my way to speak with him. Was it he who was obnoxious, or . . . . ?"

She grimaced. "I really can't say that it was he. Indeed, I suspect it was the party he was acting for—no agent could remain in business if he habitually behaved in such a manner, and at times Stolemore seemed embarrassed."

"I see." He caught her gaze. "And what were the other 'incidents' that occurred?"

She didn't want to tell him, was wishing she'd never mentioned them; that was clear in her eyes, in the way her lips set.

Unperturbed, he simply waited; his gaze locked with hers, he let the silence stretch, his stance unthreatening, but immovable. As many had before, she read his message arright. Somewhat waspishly replied, "There have been two attempts to break into our house."

He frowned. "Both attempts after you'd refused to sell?"

"The first was a week after Stolemore finally accepted defeat and went away."

He hesitated, but it was she who put his thoughts into words.

"Of course, there's nothing to connect the attempted burglaries with the offer to buy the house."

Except that she believed the connection was there.

"I thought," she continued, "that if you and your friends had been the mystery purchasers interested in our house, then that would mean that the attempted burglaries and"—she caught herself, hauled in a breath—"were not connected but to do with something else."

He inclined his head; her logic, as far as it went, was sound, yet it was plain she hadn't told him all. He debated whether to press her, to ask outright if the burglaries were the sum total of the reasons why she'd come barreling out to do battle with him, deliberately disregarding the social niceties. She cast a quick glance toward her uncle's gate. Questioning her could wait; at this juncture, Stolemore might be more forthcoming. When she glanced back at him, he smiled. Charmingly. "I believe you now have the better of me."

When she blinked at him, he went on, "Given we're to be neighbors of sorts, I think it would be acceptable for you to tell me your name."

She eyed him, not warily but assessingly. Then she inclined her head, held out her hand. "Miss Leonora Carling."

His smile broadening, he grasped her fingers briefly, was visited by an urge to hold on to them for longer. She wasn't married after all. "Good afternoon, Miss Carling. And your uncle is?"

"Sir Humphrey Carling."

"And your brother?"

A frown started to grow in her eyes. "Jeremy Carling."

His smile remained, all reassurance. "And have you lived here long? Is it as peaceful a neighborhood as it seems at first glance?"

Her narrowing eyes told him she hadn't been deceived; she answered only his second question. "Entirely peaceful."

Until recently. Leonora held his disturbingly sharp gaze, and added, as repressively as she could, "One hopes it will remain so."

She saw his lips twitch before he glanced down.

"Indeed." With a wave, he invited her to walk with him the few steps back to the gate.

She turned, only then realized her acquiescence was a tacit acknowledgment that she'd come racing out purely to meet him. She glanced up, caught his gaze—knew he'd seen the action for the admission it was. Bad enough. The glint she glimpsed in his hazel eyes, a flash that made her senses seize, her breath catch, was infinitely more disturbing.

But then his lashes veiled his eyes, and he smiled, as charmingly as before. She felt increasingly sure the expression was a mask.

He halted before the gate and held out his hand.

Courtesy forced her to surrender her fingers once more to his grasp.

His hand closed; his sharp, too-farseeing eyes trapped her gaze. "I'll look forward to extending our acquaintance, Miss Carling. Pray convey my greetings to your uncle; I will call to pay my respects shortly."

She inclined her head, consciously clinging to graciousness while she longed to pull her fingers free. It was an effort to keep them from fluttering in his; his touch, cool, firm, a fraction too strong, affected her equilibrium in a most peculiar way. "Good afternoon, Lord Trentham."

He released her and bowed elegantly.

She turned, went through the gate, then swung it shut. Her eyes touched his briefly before she faced the house.

That fleeting connection was enough to steal her breath once again.

Walking up the path, she tried to force her lungs to work, but could feel his gaze still on her. Then she heard the scrape of boots as he turned, the sound of firm footsteps as he headed down the pavement. She finally breathed in, then exhaled in relief. What was it about Trentham that so set her on edge?

And on the edge of what?

The feel of his hard fingers and faintly callused palm about her hand lingered, a sensual memory imprinted on her mind. Recollection niggled, but as before proved elusive. She'd never met him before, of that she was sure, yet something about him was faintly familiar.

Inwardly shaking her head, she climbed the porch steps and determinedly forced her mind to the duties she'd left waiting.

Tristan strolled down Motcomb Street toward the huddle of shops midway along that housed the office of Earnest Stolemore, House and Land Agent. His discussion with Leonora Carling had sharpened his senses, stirring instincts that, until recently, had been a critical element in his daily life. Until recently his life had depended on those instincts, in reading their messages accurately, and reacting correctly.

He wasn't sure what he made of Miss Carling—Leonora as he thought of her, only reasonable given he'd been silently watching her for three weeks. She'd been physically more attractive than he'd deduced from afar, her hair a rich mahogany in which veins of garnet glowed, those unusual blue eyes large and almond-shaped beneath finely drawn dark brows. Her nose was straight, her face finely boned, cheekbones high, her skin pale and flawless. But it was her lips that set the tone of her appearance; full, generously curved, a dusky rose, they tempted a man to take, to taste.

His instantaneous reaction, and hers, had not escaped him. Her response, however, intrigued him; it was almost as if she hadn't recognized that flash of sensual heat for what it was.

Which raised certain fascinating questions he might well be tempted to pursue, later. At present, however, it was the pragmatic facts she'd revealed that exercised his mind.

Her fears about the attempted burglaries might be simply a figment of an overactive feminine imagination aroused by what he assumed had been Stolemore's intimidatory tactics in trying to gain the sale of the house.

She might even have imagined the incidents entirely.

His instincts whispered otherwise.

In his previous occupation, reading people, assessing them, had been crucial; he'd long ago mastered the knack. Leonora Carling was, he would swear, a strong-willed, practical female with a healthy vein of common sense. Definitely not the sort to start at shadows, let alone imagine burglaries.

If her supposition was correct, and the burglaries were connected with Stolemore's client's wish to buy her uncle's house . . .

His eyes narrowed. The full picture of why she'd come out to beard him formed in his mind. He didn't, definitely didn't, approve. Face set, he strolled on.

To the green-painted frontage of Stolemore's enterprise.

Tristan's lips curved; no one viewing the gesture would have labeled it a smile. He caught sight of his reflection in the glass of the door as he reached for the handle, as he turned it, substituted a more comforting face. Stolemore, no doubt, would satisfy his curiosity.

The bell over the door jangled.

Tristan entered. The rotund figure of Stolemore was not behind his desk. The small office was empty. A doorway opposite the front door was masked by a curtain; it led into the tiny house of which the office was the front room.

Shutting the door, Tristan waited, but there was no sound of shuffling feet, of the lumbering gait of the heavily built agent.

"Stolemore?" Tristan's voice echoed, far stronger than the tinkling bell. Again he waited. A minute ticked by and still there was no sound.

None.

He had an appointment, one Stolemore would not have missed. He had the bank draft for the final payment for the house in his pocket; the way the sale had been arranged, Stolemore's commission came from this last payment.

Hands in his greatcoat pockets, Tristan stood perfectly still, his back to the door, his gaze fixed on the thin curtain before him.

Something was definitely not right.

He drew in his attention, focused it, then walked forward, slowly, absolutely silently, to the curtain. Reaching up, he abruptly drew the folds aside, simultaneously stepping to the side of the doorway.

The jingle of the curtain rings died.

A narrow, dimly lit corridor led on. He entered, keeping his shoulders angled, his back toward the wall. A few steps along he came to a stairway so narrow he wondered how Stolemore got up it; he debated but, hearing no sound from upstairs, sensing no presence, he continued along the corridor.

It ended in a tiny lean-to kitchen built onto the back of the house.

A figure lay slumped on the flags on the other side of the rickety table that took up most of the space.

Otherwise, the room was uninhabited.

The figure was Stolemore; he'd been savagely beaten.

There was no one else in the house; Tristan was certain enough to dispense with caution. From the look of the bruises on Stolemore's face, he'd been attacked some hours ago.

One chair had tipped over. Tristan righted it as he edged around the table, then went down on one knee by the agent's side. The briefest examination confirmed Stolemore was alive, but unconscious. It appeared he'd been staggering to reach the pump handle set in the bench at the end of the small kitchen. Rising, Tristan found a bowl, placed it under the spout, and wielded the handle.

A large handkerchief was protruding from the nattily dressed agent's coat pocket; Tristan took it and used it to bathe Stolemore's face.

The agent stirred, then opened his eyes.

Tension stabbed through the large frame. Panic flared in Stolemore's eyes, then he focused, and recognized Tristan.

"Oh. *Argh* . . ." Stolemore winced, then struggled to rise.

Tristan grabbed his arm and hauled him up. "Don't try to talk yet." He hoisted Stolemore onto the chair. "Do you have any brandy?"

Stolemore pointed to a cupboard. Tristan opened it, found the bottle and a glass, and poured a generous amount. He pushed the glass to Stolemore, recorked the bottle and placed it on the table before the agent.

Slipping his hands into his greatcoat pockets, he leaned back against the narrow counter. Gave Stolemore a minute to regain his wits.

But only a minute.

"Who did it?"

Stolemore squinted up at him through one half-closed eye. The other remained completely closed. He took another sip of brandy, dropped his gaze to the glass, then murmured, "Fell down the stairs."

"Fell down the stairs, walked into a door, hit your head on the table . . . I see."

Stolemore glanced up at him fleetingly, then lowered his gaze to the glass and kept it there. "Was an accident."

Tristan let a moment slip by, then quietly said, "If you say so."

At the note in his voice, one of menace that chilled the spine, Stolemore looked up, lips parting. His eye now wide, he rushed into speech. "I can't tell you anything—bound by confidentiality, I am. And it don't affect you gentlemen, not at all. I swear."

Tristan read what he could from the agent's face, difficult given the swelling and bruising. "I see." Whoever had punished Stolemore had been an amateur; he or indeed any of his ex-colleagues could have inflicted much greater damage yet left far less evidence.

But there was no point, given Stolemore's present condition, in going further down that road. He would simply lose consciousness again.

Reaching into his pocket, Tristan withdrew the banker's draft. "I've brought the final payment as agreed." Stolemore's eyes fastened on the slip of paper as he drew it back and forth between his fingers. "You have the title deed, I take it?"

Stolemore grunted. "In a safe place." Slowly, he pushed up from the table. "If you'll stay here for a minute, I'll fetch it."

Tristan nodded. He watched Stolemore hobble to the door. "No need to rush."

A small part of his mind tracked the lumbering agent as he moved through the house, identified the location of his "safe place" as under the third stair. For the most part, however, he stayed leaning against the counter, quietly adding two and two.

And not liking the number he came up with.

When Stolemore limped back, a title deed tied with ribbon in one hand, Tristan straightened. He held out a commanding hand; Stolemore gave him the deed. Unraveling the ribbon, he unrolled the deed, swiftly checked it, then rerolled it and slipped it into his pocket.

Stolemore, wheezing, had slumped back into the chair.

Tristan met his eyes. Raised the draft, held between two fingers. "One question, and then I'll leave you."

Stolemore, his gaze all but blank, waited.

"If I was to guess that whoever did this to you was the same person or persons who late last year hired you to negotiate the purchase of Number *14* Montrose Place, would I be wrong?"

The agent didn't need to answer; the truth was there in his bloated face as he followed the carefully spaced words. Only when he had to decide how to reply did he stop to think.

He blinked, painfully, then met Tristan's gaze. His own remained dull. "I'm bound by confidentiality."

Tristan let a half minute slide by, then inclined his head. He flicked his fingers; the bank draft sailed down to the table, sliding toward Stolemore. He put out a large hand and trapped it.

Tristan pushed away from the counter. "I'll leave you to your business."

Half an hour after returning to the house, Leonora escaped the demands of the household and took refuge in the conservatory. The glass-walled and -roofed room was her own special place within the large house, her retreat.

Her heels clicked on the tiled floor as she walked to the wrought-iron table and chairs set in the bow window. Henrietta's claws clicked in soft counterpoint as she followed.

Presently heated against the cold outside, the room was filled with rioting plants—ferns, exotic creepers, and strange-smelling herbs. Combining with the scents, the faint yet pervasive smell of earth and growing things soothed and reassured.

Sinking into one of the cushioned chairs, Leonora looked out over the winter garden. She should report meeting Trentham to her uncle and Jeremy; if he called later and mentioned it, it would appear odd if she hadn't. Both Humphrey and Jeremy would expect some description of Trentham, yet assembling a word picture of the man she'd met on the pavement less than an hour ago was not straightforward. Dark-haired, tall, broad-shouldered, handsome, dressed elegantly, and patently of the first stare—the superficial characteristics were simple to define.

Less certain was the impression she'd gained of a man outwardly charming and inwardly quite different.

That impression had owed more to his features, to the sharpness in his heavy-lidded eyes, not always concealed by his long lashes, the almost grimly determined set of mouth and chin before they'd softened, the harsh lines of his face before they'd eased, adopting a cloak of beguiling charm. It was an impression underscored by other physical attributes—like the fact he'd not even flinched when she'd run full tilt into him. She was taller than the average; most men would at least have taken a step back.

Not Trentham.

There were other anomalies, too. His behavior on meeting a lady he'd never set eyes on before, and could not have known anything of, had been too dictatorial, too definite. He'd actually had the temerity to interrogate her, and he'd done it, even knowing she'd noticed, without a blink.

She was accustomed to running the house, indeed, to running all their lives; she'd performed in that role for the past twelve years. She was decisive, confident, assured, in no way intimidated by the male of the species, yet Trentham . . . what was it about him that had made her, not exactly wary but watchful, careful?

The remembered sensations their physical contact had evoked, not once but multiple times, rose in her mind; she frowned and buried them. Doubtless some disordered reaction on her part; she hadn't expected to collide with him—it was most likely some strange symptom of shock.

Moments passed; she sat staring through the windows, unseeing, then shifted, frowned, and focused her mind on defining where she and her problem now were.

Regardless of Trentham's disconcerting presence, she'd extracted all she'd needed from their meeting. She'd learned the answer to what had been her most pressing question—neither Trentham nor his friends were behind the offers to buy this house. She accepted his word unequivocally; there was that about him that left no room for doubt. Likewise, he and his friends were not responsible for the attempts to break in, nor the more disturbing, infinitely more unnerving attempts to scare her witless.

Which left her facing the question of who was.

The latch clicked; she turned as Castor walked in.

"The Earl of Trentham has called, miss. He's asked to speak with you."

A rush of thoughts tumbled through her mind; a flurry of unfamiliar feelings flitted in her stomach. Inwardly frowning, she quelled them and rose; Henrietta rose, too, and shook herself. "Thank you, Castor. Are my uncle and brother in the library?"

"Indeed, miss." Castor held the door for her, then followed. "I left his lordship in the morning room."

Head high, she glided into the front hall, then stopped. She eyed the closed door of the morning room.

And felt something inside her tighten.

She paused. At her age, she hardly needed to be missish over being alone for a short time in the morning room with a gentleman. She could go in, greet Trentham, learn why he'd asked to speak with her, all in private, yet she couldn't think of anything he might have to tell her that would require privacy.

Caution whispered. The skin above her elbows pricked.

"I'll go and prepare Sir Humphrey and Mr. Jeremy." She glanced at Castor. "Give me a moment, then show Lord Trentham into the library."

"Indeed, miss." Castor bowed.

Some lions were better left untempted; she had a strong suspicion Trentham was one. With a swish of her skirts, she headed for the safety of the library. Henrietta padded behind.

Extending along one side of the house, the large library possessed windows facing both the front and back gardens. If either her brother or her uncle had been aware of the outside world, they might have noticed the large visitor walking up the front path.

Leonora assumed they'd both been oblivious.

The sight that met her eyes as she opened the door, entered, then quietly shut it, confirmed her supposition.

Her uncle, Sir Humphrey Carling, was seated in an armchair angled before the hearth, a heavy tome open on his knees, an especially strong quizzing glass distorting one pale blue eye as he squinted at the faded hieroglyphics inscribed on the pages. He had once been an imposing figure, but age had stooped his shoulders, thinned his once leonine head of hair, and drained his physical strength. The years, however, had made no discernible impact on his mental faculties; he was still revered in scientific and antiquarian circles as one of the two foremost authorities in translating obscure languages.

His white head, hair thin, straggling, and worn rather long

despite Leonora's best efforts, was bowed to his book, his mind clearly in . . . Leonora believed the present tome hailed from Mesopotamia.

Her brother, Jeremy, her junior by two years and the second of the two foremost authorities in translating obscure languages, sat at the desk nearby. The surface of the desk was awash with books, some open, others stacked. Every maid in the house knew she touched anything on that desk at her peril; despite the chaos, Jeremy always instantly knew.

He'd been twelve when, together with Leonora, he'd come to live with Humphrey after the deaths of their parents. They'd lived in Kent then; although Humphrey's wife had already passed on, the wider family had felt that the countryside was a more suitable environment for two still growing and grieving children, especially as everyone accepted that Humphrey was their favorite relative.

It was no great wonder that Jeremy, bookish from birth, had been infected with Humphrey's passion to decipher the words of men and civilizations long dead. At twenty-four, he was already well on the way to carving out a niche for himself in that increasingly competitive sphere; his standing had only grown when, six years ago, the household had moved to Bloomsbury so Leonora could be introduced to society under her aunt Mildred, Lady Warsingham's aegis.

Yet Jeremy was still her little brother; her lips curved as she took in his wide but slight shoulders, the mop of brown hair that regardless of any brushing was perennially tousled—she was sure he ran his fingers through it, yet he swore he didn't, and she'd never caught him at it.

Henrietta headed across the floor for the spot before the hearth. Leonora walked forward, unsurprised when neither man looked up. A maid had once dropped a silver epergne on the tiles outside the library door, and neither had noticed.

"Uncle, Jeremy—we have a visitor."

Both looked up, blinked in identical, blankly distant fashion.

"The Earl of Trentham has called." She continued toward her uncle's chair, patiently waiting for their brains to wander back to the real world. "He's one of our new neighbors at Number 12." Both sets of eyes followed her, both still blank. "I told you the house was bought by a group of gentlemen. Trentham is one of them. I gather he's been overseeing the renovations."

"Ah—I see." Humphrey closed his book, set it aside with his quizzing glass. "Good of him to call."

Positioning herself behind her uncle's chair, Leonora didn't miss the rather more puzzled look in Jeremy's brown eyes. Plain brown, not hazel. Comforting, not razor-sharp.

Like the eyes of the gentleman who walked into the room in Castor's wake.

"The Earl of Trentham."

Pronouncement made, Castor bowed and withdrew, closing the door.

Trentham had paused just before it, his gaze raking the company; as the latch clicked, he smiled. His charming mask very much to the fore, he walked toward the group about the hearth.

Leonora hesitated, suddenly unsure.

Trentham's gaze lingered on her face, waiting . . . then he looked at Humphrey.

Who gripped his chair's arms and, with obvious effort, started to rise. Leonora quickly stepped close to lend a hand.

"I pray you won't disturb yourself, Sir Humphrey." With a graceful gesture, Trentham waved Humphrey back. "I'm grate-

width:967px; height:1508px;

ful for your time in seeing me." He bowed, acknowledging Humphrey's formal nod. "I was passing and hoped you would forgive the informality as we are in effect neighbors."

"Indeed, indeed. Pleased to make your acquaintance. I understand you're making some changes at Number 12 prior to settling in?"

"Purely cosmetic, to make the place more habitable."

Humphrey waved at Jeremy. "Allow me to present my nephew, Jeremy Carling."

Jeremy, who had risen, reached across the desk and shook hands. Initially politely, but as his gaze met Trentham's, his eyes widened; interest flared across his face. "I say! You're a military man, aren't you?"

Leonora looked at Trentham, stared. How had she missed it? His stance alone should have alerted her, but combined with that faint tan and his hardened hands . . .

Self-preservatory instincts flared and had her mentally stepping well back.

"Ex-military." With Jeremy clearly waiting, wanting to know, Trentham added, "I was a major in the Guards."

"You've sold out?" Jeremy had what Leonora considered an unhealthy interest in the recent campaigns.

"After Waterloo, many of us did."

"Are your friends ex-Guards, too?

"They are." Glancing at Humphrey, Trentham went on, "That's why we bought Number 12. A place to meet that's more private and quieter than our clubs. We're not used to the bustle of town life anymore."

"Aye, well, I can understand that." Humphrey, never one for tonnish life, nodded feelingly. "You've come to the right pocket of London for peace and quiet."

Swiveling, Humphrey looked up at Leonora, smiled. "Nearly forgot you there, my dear." He looked back at Trentham. "My niece, Leonora."

She curtsied.

Trentham's gaze held hers as he bowed. "Actually, I encountered Miss Carling earlier in the street."

Encountered? She leapt in before Humphrey or Jeremy could wonder. "Lord Trentham was leaving as I went out. He was good enough to introduce himself."

Their gazes met, directly, briefly. She looked down at Humphrey.

Her uncle was appraising Trentham; he clearly approved of what he saw. He waved to the chaise on the other side of the hearth. "But do sit down."

Trentham looked at her. Gestured to the chaise. "Miss Carling?"

The chaise sat two. There was no other seat; she would have to sit beside him. She met his gaze. "Perhaps I should order tea?"

His smile took on an edge. "Not on my account, I pray."

"Or me," Humphrey said.

Jeremy merely shook his head, moving back to his chair.

Drawing in a breath, her head discouragingly high, she stepped from behind the armchair and crossed to the end of the chaise closer to the fire and Henrietta, sprawled in a shaggy heap before it. Trentham very correctly waited for her to sit, then sat beside her.

He didn't purposely crowd her; he didn't have to. Courtesy of the short chaise, his shoulder brushed hers.

Her lungs seized; warmth slowly spread from the point of contact, sliding beneath her skin.

"I understand," he said, as soon as he'd elegantly disposed his long limbs, "that you've had considerable interest from others in purchasing this house."

Humphrey inclined his head; his gaze shifted to her.

She plastered on an innocent smile, airily waved. "Lord Trentham was on his way to see Stolemore—I mentioned we'd met."

Humphrey snorted. "Indeed! The knuckleheaded bounder. Couldn't get it through his skull that we weren't interested in selling. Luckily, Leonora convinced him."

That last was said with sublime vagueness; Tristan concluded that Sir Humphrey had no real idea how insistent Stolemore had been, or to what lengths his niece had been forced to go to dissuade the agent.

He glanced again at the books piled on the desk, at the similar mounds heaped about Sir Humphrey's chair, at the papers and clutter that spoke eloquently of a scholarly life. And scholarly abstraction.

"So!" Jeremy leaned forward, arms folded across an open book. "Were you at Waterloo?"

"Only on the fringes." The distant fringes. Of the enemy camp. "It was a widespread engagement."

Eyes alight, Jeremy questioned and probed; Tristan had long ago mastered the knack of satisfying the usual questions without stumbling, of giving the impression he'd been a normal regimental officer when in fact he'd been anything but.

"In the end, the allies deserved to win, and the French deserved to lose. Superior strategy and superior commitment won the day."

And lost altogether too many lives in the process. He glanced at Leonora; she was staring into the fire, patently distancing herself from the conversation. He was well aware that prudent mamas warned their daughters away from military men. Given her age, she'd doubtless heard all the stories; he shouldn't have been surprised to find her pokering up, determinedly holding aloof.

Yet . . .

"I understand"—he returned his attention to Sir Humphrey—"that there've been a number of disturbances in the neighborhood." Both men looked at him, unquestionably intelligent but not connecting with his meaning. He was forced to expand, "Attempted burglaries, I believe?"

"Oh." Jeremy smiled dismissively. "Those. Just a would-be thief trying his luck, I should think. The first time, the staff were still about. They heard him and caught a glimpse, but needless to say he didn't stop to give his name."

"The second time"—Sir Humphrey took up the tale—"Henrietta here raised a fuss. Not even certain there was anyone there, heh, old girl?" He rubbed the somnolent hound's head with his shoe. "Just got the wind up—could have been anything, but roused us all, I can tell you."

Tristan shifted his gaze from the placid hound to Leonora's face, read her tight lips, her closed, noncommittal expression. Her hands were clasped in her lap; she made no move to interject.

She was too well-bred to argue with her uncle and brother before him, a stranger. And she may well have resigned the battle of puncturing their detached and absentminded confidence.

"Whatever the case," Jeremy cheerfully concluded, "the burglar's long gone. Quiet as a grave around here at night."

Tristan met his eyes, and decided to agree with Leonora's judgment. He would need more than suspicions to convince Sir Humphrey or Jeremy to heed any warning; he consequently said nothing of Stolemore in the remaining minutes of his visit.

It drew to a natural close and he rose. He made his farewells, then looked at Leonora. Both she and Jeremy had risen, too, but it was she he wished to speak with. Alone.

He kept his gaze on her, let the silence stretch; her stubborn resistance was, to him, obvious, but her capitulation came sufficiently fast for both her uncle and brother to remain transparently unaware of the battle conducted literally before their noses.

"I'll see Lord Trentham out." The glance that went with the clipped words held an arctic chill.

Neither Sir Humphrey nor Jeremy noticed. As, with an elegant nod, he turned from them, he could see in their eyes that they were already drifting back to whatever world they customarily inhabited.

Who stood at the helm of this household was increasingly clear.

Leonora opened the door and led Trentham into the front hall. Henrietta lifted her head, but for once didn't follow; she settled down again before the fire. The desertion struck Leonora as unusual, but she didn't have time to dwell on it; she had a dictatorial earl to dismiss.

Cloaked in chilly calm, she swept to the front door and halted; Castor slipped past and stood ready to open the door. Head high, she met Trentham's hazel eyes. "Thank you for calling. I bid you a good day, my lord."

He smiled, something other than charm in his expression, and held out his hand.

She hesitated; he waited . . . until good manners forced her to surrender her fingers into his clasp.

His untrustworthy smile deepened as his hand closed strongly about hers. "If you could spare me a few minutes of your time?"

Under his heavy lids, his gaze was hard and clear. He had no intention of releasing her until she acceded to his wishes. She tried to slip her fingers free; his grip tightened fractionally, enough to assure her she could not. Would not. Until he permitted it.

Her temper erupted. She let her disbelief—*how dare he?*—show in her eyes.

The ends of his lips quirked. "I have news you'll find interesting."

She debated for two seconds, then, on the principle that one shouldn't cut off one's nose to spite one's face, she turned to Castor. "I'll walk Lord Trentham to the gate. Leave the door on the latch."

Castor bowed and swung the door wide. She allowed Trentham to lead her out. He paused on the porch. The door shut behind them; he glanced back as he released her, then met her gaze and waved at the garden.

"Your gardens are amazing—who planted them, and why?"

Assuming that, for some reason, he wished to ensure they were not overheard, she went down the steps by his side. "Cedric Carling, a distant cousin. He was a renowned herbalist."

"Your uncle and brother—what's their primary interest?"

She explained as they strolled down the winding path to the gate.

Brows rising, he glanced at her. "You spring from a family of authorities on eccentric subjects." His hazel eyes quizzed her. "What's your specialty?"

Head rising, she halted. Met his gaze directly. "I believe you had some news you thought might interest me?"

Her tone was pure ice. He smiled. For once with neither charm nor guile. The gesture, strangely comforting, warmed her. Thawed her . . .

She fought off the effect, kept her eyes on his—watched as all levity faded and seriousness took hold.

"I met with Stolemore. He'd been given a thorough thrashing, very recently. From what he let fall, I believe his punishment stemmed from his failure to secure your uncle's house for his mysterious buyer."

The news rocked her, more than she cared to admit. "Did he give any indication who . . . ?"

Trentham shook his head. "None." His eyes searched hers; his lips tightened. After a moment, he murmured, "I wanted to warn you."

She studied his face, forced herself to ask, "Of what?"

His features once more resembled chiseled granite. "Unlike your uncle and brother, I don't believe your burglar has retired from the field."

He'd done all he could; he hadn't meant to do even that much. He didn't, in fact, have the right. Given the situation within the Carling ménage, he'd be well advised not to get involved.

The next morning, seated at the head of the table in the breakfast room of Trentham House, Tristan idly scanned the news sheets, kept one ear on the twitterings of the three of the six female residents who'd decided to join him for tea and toast, and otherwise kept his head down.

He should, he was well aware, be reconnoitering the social field *à propos* of identifying a suitable wife, yet he couldn't summon any enthusiasm for the task. Of course, all his old dears were watching him like hawks, waiting for any sign that he would welcome assistance.

They'd surprised him by being remarkably sensitive in not pushing their help upon him thus far; he sincerely hoped they'd hold to that line.

"Do pass the marmalade, Millie. Did you hear that Lady War-rington has had her ruby necklace copied?"

"Copied? Great heavens—are you sure?"

"I had it from Cynthia Cunningham. She swore it was true."

Their scandalized accents faded as his mind returned to the events of the day before.

He hadn't intended to return to Montrose Place after seeing Stolemore. He'd left the shop in Motcomb Street deep in thought; when next he'd looked up, he'd been in Montrose Place, outside Number 14. He'd surrendered to instinct and gone in.

All in all, he was glad he had. Leonora Carling's face when he'd told her his suspicions had remained with him long after he'd left.

"Did you see Mrs. Levacombe making eyes at Lord Mott?"

Lifting one of the news sheets, he held it before his face.

He'd shocked himself by his readiness, unquestioning and immediate, to use force to extract information from Stolemore. Admittedly, he'd been trained to be utterly ruthless in pursuit of vital information. What shocked him was that by some warping of his mind information pertaining to threats against Leonora Carling had assumed the status of vital to him. Previous to yesterday, such status had been attained only by king and country.

But he'd now done all he legitimately could. He'd warned her. And maybe her brother was right and they'd seen the last of the burglar.

"My lord, the builder from Montrose Place has sent a boy with a message."

Tristan looked up at his butler, Havers, who had come to stand by his elbow. About the table, the chatter died; he debated, then inwardly shrugged. "What's the message?"

"The builder thinks there's been some tampering, nothing

major, but he'd like you to view the damage before he repairs it."
Holding Tristan's gaze, Havers wordlessly conveyed the fact that
the message had been rather more dramatic. "The boy's waiting
in the hall if you wish to send a reply."

Premonition clanging, instincts alert, Tristan tossed his
napkin on the table and rose. He inclined his head to Ethelreda,
Millicent, and Flora, all elderly cousins many times removed. "If
you'll excuse me, ladies, I have business to attend."

He turned, leaving them agog, the room wrapped in pregnant
silence.

The twittering broke in a storm as he stepped into the corridor.

In the hall, he shrugged into his greatcoat, picked up his
gloves. With a nod to the builder's boy, standing in awe, eyes
wide with wonderment as he drank in the rich trappings of the
hall, he turned to the front door as a footman swung it wide.

Tristan strode out and down the steps into Green Street; the
builder's boy on his heels, he headed for Montrose Place.

"You see what I mean?"

Tristan nodded. He and Billings stood in the rear yard of
Number 12. Leaning down, he examined the minute scratches
on the lock of the rear window at the back of what would, within
days, be the Bastion Club. Part of the "tampering" Billings had
summoned him to see. "Your journeyman has sharp eyes."

"Aye. And there were one or two things disturbed like. Tools
we always leave just so that had been pushed aside."

"Oh?" Tristan straightened. "Where?"

Billings waved indoors. Together, they entered the kitchen.
Billings stumped through a short corridor to a dark side door; he

waved to the floor before it. "We leave our things here at night, out of sight of prying eyes."

The builder's gang was working; thumps and a steady *scritch-scratch* drifted down from the floors above. There were few tools left before the door, but the marks in the fine dust where others had lain were clearly visible.

Along with a footprint, close by the wall.

Tristan hunkered down; one close look confirmed that the print had been made by a gentleman's leather-soled boot, not the heavy working boots the builders wore.

He was the only gentleman who'd been about the house recently, certainly within the time the coating of fine sawdust had fallen, and he hadn't been anywhere near this door. And the print was too small; definitely a man's, but not his. Rising, he looked at the door. A heavy key was in the lock. He took it out, turned, and walked back to the kitchen where windows allowed light to stream in.

Telltale flecks of wax were visible, both along the key's shank and its teeth.

Billings peered around his shoulder; suspicion darkened his face. "An impression?"

Tristan grunted. "Looks like it."

"I'll order new locks." Billings was outraged. "Never had such a thing happen before."

Tristan turned the key in his fingers. "Yes, get in new locks. But don't fit them until I give you the word."

Billings glanced at him, then nodded. "Aye, m'lord. I'll do that." He paused, then added, "We're finished with the second floor if you'd like to take a gander?"

Tristan looked up. Nodded. "I'll just put this back."

He did so, carefully aligning the key precisely as it had been, so it wouldn't impede another key being inserted from the outside. Waving Billings ahead, he followed him up the kitchen stairs to the ground floor. There, the workmen were busily preparing what would be a comfortable drawing room and cosy dining room for the finishing touches of paint and polish. The only other rooms at that level were a small parlor beside the front door that the club members had agreed should be set aside for interviewing any females they might be forced to meet, a boothlike office for the club porter and another larger office toward the rear for the club's majordomo.

Climbing the stairs in Billings's wake, Tristan paused on the first floor to glance briefly at the painting and polishing going on in the library and the meeting room before heading up to the second floor where the three bedrooms were located. Billings conducted him through each room, pointing out the finishes and specific touches they'd requested, all in place.

The rooms smelled new. Fresh and clean, yet substantial and solid. Despite the winter chill, there was no hint of damp.

"Excellent." In the largest bedroom, the one above the library, Tristan met Billings's eye. "You and your men are to be commended."

Billings inclined his head, accepting the compliment with a craftsman's pride.

"Now"—Tristan swung to the window; like the library below it commanded an excellent view of the Carling's rear garden—"how long will it be before the staff quarters are habitable? In light of our nighttime visitor, I want to get someone in here as soon as possible."

Billings considered. "There's not much more we need to do in the attic bedrooms. We could finish those up by evening tomorrow. Kitchen and belowstairs will take a day or two more."

His gaze on Leonora strolling the rear garden with her hound at her heels, Tristan nodded. "That will do admirably. I'll send for our majordomo—he'll be here late tomorrow. His name's Gasthorpe."

"Mr. Billings!"

The call floated up the stairs. Billings turned. "If there's nothing else, m'lord, I should tend to that."

"Thank you, no. Everything appears most satisfactory. I'll make my own way out." Tristan nodded a dismissal; with a deferential nod in reply, Billings went.

Minutes ticked by. Hands in his greatcoat pockets, Tristan remained before the window, staring down at the graceful figure drifting about the garden far below. And tried to decide why, what it was that was driving him to act as he was about to. He could rationalize his actions, certainly, but were his logical reasons the whole truth? The real truth?

He watched the hound press close to Leonora's side, saw her look down, lift a hand to stroke the dog's huge head, lifted in canine adoration.

With a snort, he turned away; with a last glance around, he headed downstairs.

"Good morning." He turned his most beguiling smile on the old butler, adding just a hint of masculine commiseration in the face of feminine waywardness. "I wish to speak with Miss Carling. She's walking in the back garden at present—I'll join her there."

Title, bearing, and the excellent cut of his coat—and his bald-faced boldness—won through; after only the slightest hesitation, the butler inclined his head. "Indeed, my lord. If you'll step this way?"

He followed the old man down the hall and into a cosy parlor.

A fire crackled in the grate; a piece of embroidery, barely started, lay on a small sidetable.

The butler gestured to a pair of French doors standing ajar. "If you'd like to go through?"

With a nod, Tristan did, emerging onto a small paved terrace that gave onto the lawns. Descending the steps, he strolled around the corner of the house and sighted Leonora examining blooms on the opposite side of the main lawn. She was looking the other way. He headed toward her; as he approached, the hound scented him and turned, alert but waiting to judge his intentions.

Courtesy of the lawn, Leonora didn't hear him. He was still a few yards away when he spoke. "Good morning, Miss Carling."

She whirled. She stared at him, then glanced—almost accusingly—at the house.

He hid a smile. "Your butler showed me through."

"Indeed? And to what do I owe this pleasure?"

Before answering the cool and distinctly prickly greeting, he held out a hand to the hound; she inspected, accepted, nudging her head under his palm, inviting him to pat. He did, then turned to the less tractable female. "Am I right in thinking that your uncle and brother see no continuing threat arising from the attempted burglaries?"

She hesitated. A frown formed in her eyes.

He slid his hands into his greatcoat pockets; she hadn't offered her hand, and he wasn't fool enough to push his luck. He studied her face; when she remained silent, he murmured, "Your loyalty does you credit, but in this instance, might not be your wisest choice. As I see it, there's something—some action—which the two attempts to break in here are part of. They're not finite acts in themselves, but incidents in a continuing whole."

That description hit the mark; he saw the flare of connection in her eyes.

"I suspect there are incidents which already have followed, and there will almost certainly be incidents to come." He hadn't forgotten there was more, something in addition to the burglaries she'd yet to tell him. But that was the closest he dared come to pressing her; she was not the sort he could browbeat or bully. He was accomplished in both roles, but with some, neither worked. And he wanted her cooperation, her trust.

Without both, he might not learn all he needed to know. Might not succeed in lifting the threat he sensed hanging over her.

Leonora held his gaze, and reminded herself she knew better than to trust military men. Even ex-military; they were assuredly the same. One couldn't rely on them, on anything they said let alone anything they promised. Yet why was he here? What had prompted him to return? She tilted her head, watching him closely. "Nothing has happened recently. Maybe whatever"—she gestured— "whole the burglaries were part of is no longer centered here."

He let a moment elapse, then murmured, "That doesn't appear to be the case."

Turning, he faced the house, scanned its bulk. It was the oldest house in the street, built on a grander scale than the terrace houses that in later years had been constructed on either side, walls abutting on both left and right.

"Your house shares walls, presumably basement walls, too, with the houses on either side."

She followed his gaze, glancing at the house, not that she needed to to verify that fact. "Yes." She frowned. Followed his logic.

When he said nothing more, but simply stood by her side, she set her lips and, eyes narrowing, glanced up at him.

He was waiting to catch that glance. Their gazes met, locked. Not quite in a battle of wills, more a recognition of resolutions and strengths.

"What's happened?" She knew something had, or that he'd discovered some new clue. "What have you learned?"

Despite its apparent mobility, his face was difficult to read. A heartbeat passed, then he drew one hand free of his greatcoat pocket.

And reached for hers.

Slid his fingers around her wrist, slid his hand around her much smaller one. Closed it. Took possession of that much.

She didn't stop him; couldn't have. Everything within her stilled at his touch. Then quivered in response. The heat of his hand engulfed hers. Once again, she couldn't breathe.

But she was growing used to the reaction, enough to pretend to ignore it. Lifting her head, she raised a brow in distinctly haughty question.

His lips curved; she knew absolutely that the expression was not a smile.

"Come—walk with me. And I'll tell you."

A challenge; his hazel eyes held hers, then he drew her to him, laid her hand on his sleeve as he stepped closer, beside her.

Dragging in a tight breath, she inclined her head, fell into step beside him. They strolled across the lawn, back toward the parlor, her skirts brushing his boots, his hand over hers on his arm.

She was screamingly aware of his strength, sheer masculine power close, so close, by her side. There was heat there, too, the beckoning presence of flame. The arm beneath her fingers felt like steel, yet warm, alive. Her fingertips itched, her palm burned. By an effort of will, she forced her wits to work. "So?" She slanted him a glance, as chill as she could make it. "What have you discovered?"

His hazel eyes hardened. "There's been a curious incident next door. Someone broke in, but carefully. They tried to leave as little as possible to alert anyone, and nothing was taken." He paused, then added, "Nothing bar an impression of the key to a side door."

She digested that, felt her eyes widen. "They're coming back."

He nodded, his lips a thin line. He looked at Number 12, then glanced at her. "I'll be keeping watch."

She halted. "Tonight?"

"Tonight, tomorrow. I doubt they'll wait long. The house is nearly ready for occupation. Whatever they're after—"

"It would be best to strike now, before you have servants installed." She swung to face him, tried to use the movement to slip her hand free of his.

He lowered his arm, but closed his hand more firmly about hers.

She pretended to be oblivious. "You'll keep me—us—informed of what transpires?"

"Of course." His voice was subtly lower, more resonant, the sound sliding through her. "Who knows? We might even learn the reason behind . . . all that's gone before."

She kept her eyes wide. "Indeed. That would be a blessing."

Something—some hint not of laughter, but of wry acceptance—showed in his face. His eyes remained locked with hers. Then, with blatant deliberation, he shifted his fingers and stroked the fine skin over her inner wrist.

Her lungs seized. Hard. She actually felt giddy.

She would never have believed such a simple touch could so affect her. She had to look down and watch the mesmerizing caress. Realized in that instant that this would never do; she forced herself to swallow, to diguise her reaction, to turn her locked attention to good effect.

Continuing to look at his hand holding hers, she stated, "I realize you have only recently returned to society, but this really is not the done thing."

She'd intended the statement to be coolly distant, calmly censorious; instead, her voice sounded tight, strained, even to her ears.

"I know."

The tenor of those words jerked her eyes back to his face, to his lips. To his eyes. And the intent therein.

Again moving with that deliberation she found shocking, he held her stunned gaze, and raised her hand.

To his lips.

He brushed them across her knuckles, then, still holding her gaze, turned her hand, now boneless, and placed a kiss—warm and hot—in her palm.

Lifting his head, he hesitated. His nostrils flared slightly, as if he was breathing her scent. Then his eyes flicked to hers. Captured them. Held them as he bent his head again, and set his lips to her wrist.

To the spot where her pulse leapt like a startled hind, then raced.

Heat flared from the contact, streaked up her arm, slid through her veins.

If she'd been a weaker woman, she'd have collapsed at his feet.

The look in his eyes kept her upright, sent reaction rushing through her, stiffening her spine. Had her lifting her head. But she didn't dare take her eyes from his.

That predatory look didn't fade, but, eventually, his lashes swept down, hiding his eyes.

His voice when he spoke was deeper, murmurous thunder rolling in, subtly yet definitely menacing. "Tend your garden." Once again he caught her gaze. "Leave the burglars to me."

He released her hand. With a nod, he turned and strode away, over the lawn toward the parlor.

Tend your garden.

He hadn't been speaking of plants. "Tend your hearth" was the more common injunction directing women to focus their energies in the sphere society deemed proper—on their husband and children, their home.

Leonora didn't have a husband or children, and didn't appreciate being reminded of the fact. Especially on the heels of Trentham's practiced caresses and the unprecedented reactions they'd evoked.

Just what had he thought he was doing?

She suspected she knew, which only further fired her ire.

She kept herself busy through the rest of the day, eliminating any chance of dwelling on those moments in the garden. From reacting to the spur she'd felt at Trentham's words. From giving rein to her irritation and letting it drive her.

Not even when Captain Mark Whorton had asked to be released from their engagement when she'd been expecting him to set their wedding day had she permitted herself to lose control. She'd long ago accepted responsibility for her own life; steering a safe path meant keeping the tiller in her hands.

And not allowing any male, no matter how experienced, to provoke her.

After luncheon with Humphrey and Jeremy, she spent the afternoon on social calls, first to her aunts, who were delighted to see her even though she'd purposely called too early to meet any of the fashionable who would later grace her Aunt Mildred's drawing room, and subsequently to a number of elderly connections it was her habit to occasionally look in upon. Who knew when the old dears would need help?

She returned at five to oversee dinner, ensuring her uncle and brother remembered to eat. The meal consumed, they retreated to the library.

She retired to the conservatory.

To evaluate Trentham's revelations and decide how best to act.

Seated in her favorite chair, her elbows on the wrought-iron table, she ignored his edict and turned her mind to burglars.

One point was unarguable. Trentham was an earl. Even though it was February and the ton correspondingly thin on the London streets, he'd no doubt be expected at some dinner or other, invited to some elegant soirée. If not that, then doubtless he'd go to his clubs, to game and enjoy the company of his peers. And if not that, then there were always the haunts of the demimonde; given the aura of predatory sexuality he exuded, she wasn't so innocent as to believe he wasn't acquainted with them.

Leave the burglars to him? She stifled a dismissive snort.

It was eight o'clock and pitch-dark beyond the glass. Next door, Number 12 loomed, a black block in the gloom. With no light gleaming in any window or winking between curtains, it was easy to guess it was uninhabited.

She'd been a good neighbor to old Mr. Morrissey; irascible old scoundrel that he'd been, he'd nevertheless been grateful for her visits. She'd missed him when he'd died. The house had passed to Lord March, a distant connection who, having a perfectly good mansion in Mayfair, had had no use for the Belgravia house. She hadn't been surprised that he'd sold it.

Trentham, or his friends, were apparently acquainted with his lordship. Like his lordship, Trentham was probably, at that moment, preparing for a night on the town.

Leaning back in the chair, she tugged at the stiff little drawer that clung to the underside of the circular table. Wrestling it open, she considered the large, heavy key that rested within, half-buried by old lists and notes.

She reached in and retrieved the key, laid it on the table.

Had Trentham thought to change the locks?

He couldn't risk lighting a match to check his watch. Stoically, Tristan settled his shoulders more comfortably against the wall of the porter's alcove off the front hall. And waited.

About him, the shell of the Bastion Club lay silent. Empty. Outside, a bitter wind blew, sending flurries of sleet raking across the windows. He estimated it was past ten o'clock; in such freezing weather, the burglar was unlikely to dally much beyond midnight.

Waiting like this, silent and still in the dark for a contact, a meeting, or to witness some illicit event had been commonplace until recently; he hadn't forgotten how to let time slip past. How to free his mind from his body so he remained a statue, senses alert, attuned to all around him, ready to snap back to the moment at the slightest movement, while his mind roamed, keeping him occupied and awake, but elsewhere.

Unfortunately, tonight, he didn't appreciate the direction in which his mind wanted to go. Leonora Carling was certain distraction; he'd spent most of the day lecturing himself on the unwisdom of pursuing the sensual response he evoked in her—and she, correspondingly and even more strongly, evoked in him.

He was well aware she didn't recognize it for what it was. Didn't see it as a danger despite her susceptibility. Such innocence would normally have dampened his ardor; with her, for some ungodly reason, it only whetted his appetite further.

His attraction to her was a complication he definitely did not need. He had to find a wife, and that quickly; he required a sweet-tempered, biddable, gentle female who would cause him not a moment's angst, who would run his houses, keep his troop of elderly relatives in line, and otherwise devote herself to bearing and raising his children. He did not expect her to spend much time with him; he had for too long been alone—he now preferred it that way.

With the clock ticking on the outrageous terms of his greatuncle's will, he couldn't afford to be distracted by a strong-willed, independent-minded, prickly termagent, one he suspected was a spinster by design, and was, moreover, possessed of a waspish tongue and, when she chose to deploy it, a distinctly chilly hauteur.

There was no purpose in thinking of her.

He couldn't seem to stop.

He shifted, easing his shoulders, then leaned back again. What with taking up the reins of his inheritance, getting accustomed to having a tribe of old dears under his feet on a daily basis, inhabiting his houses and complicating his life, as well as considering how best to secure a wife, he'd let the small matter of a mistress or any other avenue of sexual release slide to the back of his mind.

In hindsight, not a wise decision.

Leonora had cannoned into him and set spark to tinder. Their subsequent exchanges hadn't doused the flame. Her haughty dismissiveness was the equivalent of a blatant challenge, one to which he instinctively reacted.

His morning's ruse of using their sensual connection to distract her from the burglars, while tactically sound, had been personally unwise. He'd known it at the time, yet had cold-bloodedly reached for the one weapon that had promised the greatest chance of success; his overriding aim had been to ensure her mind was fixed on matters other than the putative burglar.

Outside the wind howled. Again he straightened, silently stretched, then settled against the wall once more.

Fortunately for all concerned, he was too old, too wise, and far too experienced to allow lust to dictate his actions. During the day, he'd formulated a plan for dealing with Leonora. Given he'd stumbled onto this mystery and she was, no matter what her uncle and brother thought, threatened by it, then given his training, given his nature, it was understandable, indeed right and proper, for him to resolve the situation and remove the threat. Thereafter, however, he would leave her alone.

The distant scrape of metal on stone reached him. His senses focused, expanded, straining to catch any further evidence that the burglar was near.

A trifle earlier than he'd expected, but whoever it was was most likely an amateur.

He'd returned to the house at eight o'clock, slipping in via the rear alleyway and the shadows of the back garden. Entering through the kitchen, he'd noted that the builders had left only a few tools gathered in a corner. The side door had been as he'd left it, the key in the lock but not turned, the teeth not engaged. The scene set, he'd retreated to the porter's alcove, leaving the door at the top of the kitchen stairs propped open with a brick.

The porter's alcove commanded an uninterrupted view of the

ground floor hall, the stairs leading upward, and the door to the kitchen stairs. No one could enter from the ground or the upper floors and get access to the basement level without him seeing them.

Not that he expected anyone to come that way, but he'd wanted to leave the way clear for the burglar belowstairs. He was willing to wager the "burglar" would head for some area of the basement; he wanted to let the man settle to his task before he intervened. He wanted evidence to confirm his suspicions. And then he intended to interrogate the "burglar."

It was difficult to imagine what a real burglar would expect to steal from a vacant house.

His ears caught the soft slap of a leather sole on stone. Abruptly, he turned and faced the front door.

Against all the odds, someone was coming in that way.

A wavering outline appeared on the etched-glass panels of the door. He slipped noiselessly out of the porter's booth and merged with the shadows.

Leonora slid the heavy key into the lock and glanced down at her companion.

She'd retired to her bedchamber supposedly to sleep. The servants had locked up and retired. She'd waited until the clock had struck eleven, reasoning that by then the street would be deserted, then she'd slipped downstairs, avoiding the library where Humphrey and Jeremy were still poring over their tomes. Collecting her cloak, she'd let herself out of the front door.

There was, however, one being she couldn't so easily avoid.

Henrietta blinked up at her, long jaws agape, ready to follow her wherever she went. If she'd tried to leave her in the front hall and go out alone at this hour, Henrietta would have howled.

Leonora narrowed her eyes at her. "Blackmailer." Her whisper was lost in the strafing wind. "Just remember," she continued, more by way of bolstering her own courage than instructing Henrietta, "we're only here to watch what he does. You have to be absolutely quiet."

Henrietta looked at the door, then nudged it with her nose.

Leonora turned the key, pleased when it slid smoothly around. Removing it, she pocketed it, then drew her cloak close. Curling one hand about Henrietta's collar, she grasped the doorknob and turned it.

The bolt slid back. She opened the door just wide enough for her and Henrietta to squeeze through, then swung around to shut it. The wind gusted; she had to release Henrietta and use both hands to force the door closed—silently.

She managed it. Heaving an inward sigh of relief, she turned.

The front hall was shrouded in stygian gloom. She stood still as her eyes began to adjust, as the sense of emptiness—the strangeness of a remembered place stripped of all its furnishings—sank into her.

She heard a faint click.

Beside her, Henrietta abruptly sat, posture erect, a suppressed whimper, not of pain but excitement escaping her.

Leonora stared at her.

The air around her stirred.

The hair on her nape lifted; her nerves leapt. Instinctively, she dragged in a breath—

A hard palm clamped over her lips.

A steely arm locked about her waist.

Hauled her back against a body like sculpted rock.

Strength engulfed her, trapping her, subduing her.

Effortlessly.

A dark head bent close.

A voice in which fury was barely leashed hissed in her ear, *"What the devil are you doing here?"*

Tristan could barely believe his eyes.

Despite the gloom, he could see hers, wide with shock. Could sense the leap and race of her pulse, the panic that gripped her.

Knew absolutely that it was only partially due to surprise. Sensed his own response to that fact.

Ruthlessly reined it in.

Lifting his head, he scanned with his senses but could detect no other movement in the house. But he couldn't talk to her, even in whispers, in the front hall; devoid of furnishings, its surfaces polished and clean, any sound would echo.

Tightening his arm about her waist, he lifted her off her feet and carried her to the small parlor they'd set aside for interrogating females. Spared a moment to wonder at their farsightedness. He had to take his hand from her face to turn the knob, then they were inside, and he shut the door.

He still had her in his arm, feet off the ground, her back locked to him.

She wriggled, hissed, "Put me down!"

He debated, in the end, grim-faced, complied. Speaking face-to-face would be easier; keeping her wriggling her derriere against him was senseless torture.

The instant her feet touched the floor, she spun around.

And collided with his finger, raised to point at her nose. "I didn't tell you about the incident here so you could waltz in and put yourself in the middle of it!"

Startled, she blinked; her eyes rose to his face. Quite stunned; she'd never had any man take such a tone with her. He seized the initiative. "I told you to leave this to *me*." He spoke in a deep but furious whisper, at a level that wouldn't carry.

Her eyes narrowed. "I recall what you said, but this person, whoever he is, is *my* problem."

"It's *my* house he's going to be breaking into. And anyway—"

"Besides," she continued as if she hadn't heard him, chin lifting but like him keeping her voice low, "you're an *earl*. I naturally assumed you'd be out socializing."

The jab pricked his frustration. He spoke through his teeth. "I'm not an earl by choice, and I avoid socializing as much as I can. *But* that's neither here nor there. *You* are a woman. A female. You have no purpose here. Especially given *I'm* here."

Her mouth fell open as he grabbed her elbow and spun her to face the door.

"I'm not—!"

"Keep your voice down." He marched her forward. "And you most certainly are. I'm going to see you out of the front door, then you're going straight home and staying there come what may!"

She dug in her heels. "But what if he's out there?"

He halted, looked at her. Realized she was staring beyond the hall door toward the dark, tree-shrouded front garden. His thoughts followed hers.

"Damn!" He released her, squelched a more explicit curse.

She looked at him; he looked at her.

He hadn't checked the front door; the would-be intruder could have taken an impression of that key, too. He couldn't check now without lighting a match, and that he couldn't risk. Regardless, it was perfectly possible the "burglar" would check the front of the house before proceeding to the alley behind. Bad enough she'd come in, running the risk of scaring off the burglar or worse, encountering him, but to send her out now would be madness.

The intruder had already proved to be violent.

He drew in a deep breath. Nodded tersely. "You'll have to stay here until it's over."

He sensed she was relieved, in the dimness couldn't be sure.

She inclined her head haughtily. "As I said, this may be your house, but the burglar's my problem."

He couldn't resist growling, "That's debatable." In his lexicon, burglars were not a woman's problem. She had an uncle *and* a brother—

"It's my house—at least, my uncle's—that he's trying to gain access to. You know that as well as I."

That was unarguable.

A faint scratching reached them—from the hall door.

Saying "Damn!" again seemed redundant; with an eloquent glance at her, he opened the door. Shut it behind the shaggy heap that walked in. "Did you have to bring your dog?"

"I didn't have a choice."

The dog turned to look at him, then sat, lifting her great head in an innocent pose, as if intimating that he of all people should understand her presence.

He suppressed a disgusted growl. "Sit down." He waved Leonora to the window seat, the only place to sit in the otherwise empty room; luckily the window was shuttered. As she moved to comply, he continued, "I'm going to leave the door open so we can hear."

He could forsee problems if he left her alone and returned to his post in the hall. The scenario that most exercised his mind was what might happen when the burglar arrived; would she stay put, or rush out? This way, at least, he would know where she would be—at his back.

Opening the door silently, he set it ajar. The wolfhound slumped to the floor at Leonora's feet, one eye on the gap in the door. He moved to stand beside the door, shoulders against the wall, head turned to watch the dark emptiness of the hall.

And returned to his earlier thought, the one she'd interrupted. Every instinct he possessed insisted that women, ladies of Leonora's ilk especially, should not be exposed to danger, should not take part in any dangerous enterprises. While he acknowledged such instincts arose from the days when a man's females embodied the future of his line, to his mind those arguments still applied. He felt seriously irritated that she was there, that she'd come there, not defying so much as negating, stepping around, her uncle and her brother and their rightful roles. . . .

Glancing at her, he felt his jaw set. She probably did it all the time.

He had no right to judge—her, Sir Humphrey, or Jeremy. If he read all three arright, neither Sir Humphrey nor Jeremy possessed any ability to control Leonora. Nor did they attempt to. Whether that was because she'd resisted and browbeaten them into acquiescence, or because they simply did not care enough to insist in the first place, or alternatively, were too sensitive to her willful independence to rein her in, he couldn't tell.

Regardless, to him, the situation was wrong, unbalanced. Not how things ought to be.

Minutes ticked by, stretched to half an hour.

It had to be close to midnight when he heard a metallic scrape—a key turning in the old lock belowstairs.

The wolfhound lifted her head.

Leonora straightened, alerted both by Henrietta's sudden attention and the unfurling tension emanating from Trentham, until then apparently relaxed against the wall. She'd been conscious of his glances, of his irritation, his frowns, but had vowed to ignore them. Learning the burglar's purpose was her aim, and with Trentham present they might even succeed in catching the villain.

Excitement gripped her, escalated as Trentham motioned her to stay where she was and restrain Henrietta, then flitted, wraithlike, through the door.

He moved so silently, if she hadn't been watching, he'd have simply disappeared.

Instantly, she rose and followed, equally silent, grateful the builders had left drop sheets spread everywhere, muting the click of Henrietta's claws as the wolfhound fell in at her heels.

Reaching the hall door, she peered out. Spied Trentham as he merged with the dense shadows at the top of the kitchen stairs. She squinted as she drew her cloak about her; the servants' door seemed to be propped open.

"*Ow!* Oooof!"

A string of curses followed.

"Here! Get *orf!*"

"*What the hell are you doing here, you crazy old fool?*"

The voices came from below.

Trentham was gone down the kitchen stairs before she could blink. Grabbing up her skirts, she raced after him.

The stairs were a black void. She rushed down without thinking, heels clattering on the stone steps. Behind her, Henrietta woofed, then growled.

Reaching the landing midway down, Leonora gripped the banister and looked down into the kitchen. Saw two men—one tall and cloaked, the other large but squat and much older—

wrestling in the middle of the flags where the kitchen table used to sit.

They'd frozen at Henrietta's growl.

The taller man looked up.

In the same instant she did, he saw Trentham closing in.

With a huge effort, the taller man swung the older one around and shoved him at Trentham.

The old man lost his footing and went flying back.

Trentham had a choice; sidestep and let the old man fall to the stone flags, or catch him. Watching from above, Leonora saw the decision made, saw Trentham stand his ground and let the old man fall against him. He steadied him, would have set him on his feet and gone after the tall man, already racing toward a narrow corridor, but the old man grappled, struggling—

"Be still!"

The order was rapped out. The old man stiffened and obeyed.

Leaving him swaying on his feet, Trentham went after the tall man—

Too late.

A door slammed as Trentham disappeared down the corridor. An instant later, she heard him swear.

Hurrying down the stairs, she pushed past the old man and raced to the back of the kitchen, to the windows that looked down the path to the rear gate.

The tall man—he had to be their "burglar"—raced from the side of the house and plunged down the path. For one instant he was lit by a faint wash of moonlight; eyes wide, she drank in all she could, then he disappeared beyond the hedges bordering the kitchen garden. The gate to the alley lay beyond.

With an inward sigh, she drew back, replayed all she'd seen in her mind, committed it to memory.

A door banged, then Trentham appeared on the paving outside. Hands on his hips, he surveyed the garden.

She tapped on the window; when he looked her way, she pointed down the path. He turned, then went down the steps and loped toward the gate, no longer racing.

Their "burglar" had escaped.

Turning to the old man, now sitting at the bottom of the stairs, still wheezing and trying to catch his breath, she frowned. "What are you doing here?"

He talked, but didn't answer, mumbling a great deal of fustian by way of excuses but failing to clarify the vital point. Clad in an ancient frieze coat, with equally ancient and worn boots and frayed mittens on his hands, he gave off an aroma of dirt and leaf mold readily detectable in the freshly painted kitchen.

She folded her arms, tapped her toe as she looked down at him. "Why did you break in?"

He shuffled, mumbled, and muttered some more.

She was at the limit of her patience when Trentham returned, entering via the door down the dark corridor.

He looked disgusted. "He had the foresight to take *both* keys."

The comment wasn't made to anyone in particular; Leonora understood that the fleeing man had locked the side door against Trentham. While he halted, hands in his pockets and studied the old man, she wondered how, keyless, he had managed to get through that locked door.

Henrietta had seated herself a yard from the old man; he eyed her warily.

Then Trentham commenced his interrogation.

With a few well-phrased questions elicited the information that the old man was a beggar who normally slept in the park. The night had turned so raw he'd searched for shelter; he'd known the house was empty, so he'd come there. Trying the back windows, he'd found one with a loose lock.

With Trentham standing like some vengeful deity on one side and Henrietta, spike-toothed jaws gaping, on the other, the old codger clearly felt he had no option but to make a clean breast of it. Leonora suppressed an indignant sniff; apparently she hadn't appeared sufficiently intimidatory.

"I didn't mean no harm, sir. Just wanted to get out of the cold."

Trentham held the old man's gaze, then nodded. "Very well. One more question. Where were you when the other man tripped over you?"

"In through there." The old man pointed across the kitchen. "Farther from the windows is warmer. The bu—blighter hauled me out here. Think he was planning on throwing me out."

He'd pointed to a small pantry.

Leonora glanced at Trentham. "The storerooms beyond share basement walls with Number 14."

He nodded, turned back to the old man. "I've a proposition for you. It's mid-February—the nights will be freezing for some weeks." He glanced around. "There's dust cloths and other coverings around for tonight. You're welcome to find a place to sleep." His gaze returned to the old man. "Gasthorpe, who'll be majordomo here, will be taking up residence tomorrow. He'll bring blankets and start to make this place habitable. However, all the servants' bedrooms are in the attic."

Tristan paused, then continued, "In light of our friend's unwelcome interest in this place, I want someone sleeping down here. If you're willing to act as our downstairs nightwatchman, you can sleep here every night legitimately. I'll give orders you're to be treated as one of the household. You can stay in and be warm. We'll rig up a bell so all you need do if anyone tries to gain entry is ring it, and Gasthorpe and the footmen will deal with any intruder."

The old man blinked as if he couldn't quite take in the suggestion, wasn't sure he wasn't dreaming.

Without allowing any trace of compassion to show, Tristan asked, "Which regiment were you in?"

He watched as the old shoulders straightened, as the old man's head lifted.

"Ninth. I was invalided out after Corunna."

He nodded. "As were many others. Not one of our better engagements—we were lucky to get out at all."

The rheumy old eyes widened. "You were there?"

"I was."

"Aye." The old man nodded. "Then you'll know."

Tristan waited a moment, then asked, "So will you do it?"

"Keep watch for ye every night?" The old man eyed him, then nodded again. "Aye, I'll do it." He looked around. "Be strange after all these years, but . . ." He shrugged, and pushed himself up from the stairs.

He bobbed his head deferentially to Leonora, then moved past her, looking around the kitchen with new eyes.

"What's your name?"

"Biggs, sir. Joshua Biggs."

Tristan reached for Leonora's arm and propelled her onto the stairs. "We'll leave you on duty, Biggs, but I doubt there'll be any further disturbance tonight."

The old man looked up, raised a hand in a salute. "Aye, sir. But I'll be here if there is."

Fascinated by the exchange, Leonora returned her attention to the present as they regained the front hall. "Do you think the man who fled was our burglar?"

"I seriously doubt we have more than one man, or group of men, intent on gaining access to your house."

"Group of men?" She looked at Trentham, cursed the darkness that hid his face. "Do you really think so?"

He didn't immediately answer; despite not being able to see, she was sure he was frowning.

They reached the front door; without releasing her, he opened it, met her gaze as they stepped out onto the front porch, Henrietta padding behind them. Faint moonlight reached them.

"You were watching—what did you see?"

When she hesitated, marshaling her thoughts, he instructed, "Describe him."

Letting go of her elbow, he offered his arm; absentmindedly she laid her hand on his sleeve, and they went down the steps. Frowning in concentration, she walked beside him toward the front gate. "He was tall—you saw that. But I got the impression he was young." She slanted a glance at him. "Younger than you."

He nodded. "Go on."

"He was easily as tall as Jeremy, but not much taller, and leanish rather than stout. He moved with that sort of gangling grace younger men sometimes have—and he ran well."

"Features?"

"Dark hair." Again she glanced at him. "I'd say even darker than yours—possibly black. As to his face . . ." She looked ahead, seeing again in her mind's eye the fleeting glimpse she'd caught. "Good features. Not aristocratic, but not common, either."

She met Trentham's gaze. "I'm perfectly sure he was a gentleman."

He didn't argue, indeed, didn't seem surprised.

Emerging onto the pavement into the teeth of the wind slicing up the street, he drew her close, into the lee of his shoulders;

they put their heads down and swiftly walked the few yards to the front gate of Number 14.

She should have made a stand and left him there, but he'd swung the gate open and whisked her in before the potential difficulties of his seeing her all the way to the front door occurred to her.

But the garden, as always, soothed her, convinced her that no problem would arise. Like inverted feather dusters, a profusion of lacy fronds lined the path, here and there an exotic-looking flower head held high on a slender stalk. Bushes shaped the beds; trees accented the graceful design. Even in this season, a few starry white blooms peeked from under the protective hoods of thick, dark green leaves.

Although the night sent chill fingers sneaking along the twisting path, the wind could only batter at the high stone wall, could whip only the topmost branches of the trees.

On the ground, all was still, quiet; as always the garden struck her as a place that was alive, patiently waiting, benign in the dark.

Rounding the last bend in the path, she looked ahead, through the bushes and waving branches saw light shining from the library windows. At the far end of the house, abutting Number 16, the library was distant enough for there to be no danger of Jeremy or Humphrey hearing their footsteps on the gravel and looking out.

They might, however, hear an altercation on the front porch.

Glancing at Trentham, she saw that his eyes, too, had been drawn to the lighted windows. Halting, she drew her hand from his arm and faced him. "I'll leave you here."

He looked down at her, but didn't immediately reply.

As far as Tristan could see, he had three options. He could

accept her dismissal, turn his back, and walk away; alternatively, he could take her arm, march her up to the front door, and, with suitable and pointed explanations, hand her into her uncle and brother's keeping.

Both options were cowardly. The first in bowing to her refusal to accept the protection she needed and running away—something he'd never done in his life. The second because he knew neither her uncle nor her brother, no matter how outraged he managed to make them, was capable of controlling her, not for more than a day.

Which left him no option bar the third.

Holding her gaze, he let all he felt harden his tone. "Coming to wait for the burglar tonight was an incredibly foolhardy thing to do."

Up went her head; her eyes flashed. "Be that as it may, if I hadn't, we wouldn't even know what he looks like. You didn't see him—I did."

"And what"—his voice had taken on the icy tone he would have used to dress down a wantonly reckless subaltern—"do you think would have happened had I not been there?"

Reaction, hard and sharp, speared through him; until that moment, he hadn't allowed himself to envisage that event. Eyes narrowing as real fury took hold, he stepped, deliberately intimidating, toward her. "Let me hypothesize—correct me if I'm wrong. On hearing the fight belowstairs you would have rushed down—into the teeth of things. Into the fray. And what then?" He took another step and she gave ground, but only fractionally. Then her spine locked; her head rose even higher. She met his gaze defiantly.

Lowering his head, bringing their faces close, his eyes locked with hers, he growled, "Regardless of what happened to Biggs, and having seen the villain's efforts with Stolemore, it wouldn't have been pretty, what—just *what* do you imagine would have happened to you?"

His voice had not risen but deepened, roughened, gained in power as his words brought the reality of what she had risked home to him.

Her spine stiff, her gaze as chill as the night about them, she opened her lips. "Nothing."

He blinked. "Nothing?"

"I would have set Henrietta on him."

The words stopped him. He glanced down at the wolfhound, who sighed heavily, then sat.

"As I said, these would-be intruders are *my* problem. I'm perfectly capable of dealing with any matters that arise myself."

He shifted his gaze from the hound to her. "You hadn't intended to bring Henrietta with you."

Leonora didn't succumb to the temptation to shift her eyes. "Nevertheless, as it happened, I did. So I wasn't in any danger."

Something changed—behind his face, behind his eyes. "Just because Henrietta is with you, you aren't in any danger?"

His voice had altered again; cold, hard, but flat, as if all the passion that had invested it a moment earlier had been drawn in, compressed.

She replayed his words, hesitated, yet could see no reason not to nod. "Precisely."

"Think again."

She'd forgotten how fast he could move. How totally helpless he could make her feel.

How totally and completely helpless she was, yanked into his arms, crushed against him, and ruthlessly kissed.

The impulse to struggle flared, but was extinguished before

it took hold. Drowned beneath a tidal wave of feelings. Hers, and his.

Something between them ignited; not anger, not shock—something closer to avid curiosity.

She closed her hands in his coat, grabbed hold, held on as a rush of sensation swept her up, caught her, held her trapped. Not just by his arms but by myriad strands of fascination. By the shift of his lips, cool and hard on hers, the restless flexing of his fingers on her upper arms as if he longed to reach further, explore and touch, longed to pull her closer yet.

Spiraling thrills cascaded through her; licks of excitement teased her nerves, built her fascination. She'd been kissed before, but never like this. Never had pleasure and greedy need leapt to such a simple caress.

His lips moved on hers, ruthless, relentless, until she surrendered to the unsubtle pressure and parted them.

Her world shook when he pressed them wider yet and his tongue slid in to meet hers.

She tensed. He ignored it and caressed, then probed. Something within her rocked, teetered, then cracked. Sensation spilled down her veins, flowing steadily through her, hot, scalding, bright.

Another flash, another sharp shock of sensation. She would have gasped but he caught her to him, one steely arm sliding about her and tightening—distracting her as he deepened the kiss.

By the time her senses refocused, she was too enthralled, too enmeshed in the novel delights to think about breaking free.

Tristan sensed it, knew it in his bones, tried not to let his hunger take advantage. She'd been kissed before, but he'd stake his considerable reputation that she'd never yielded her mouth to any man.

But it, and she, were now his to enjoy, to savor, at least as far as a kiss would allow.

Madness, of course. He knew that now, but in that heated moment when she'd blithely consigned her protection to a hound—a hound who was sitting patiently by while he ravished her mistress's soft mouth—all he'd seen was red. He hadn't realized how much of that haze had been due to lust.

He knew now.

He'd kissed her to demonstrate her inherent weakness.

In doing so had uncovered his own.

He was hungry—starved; by some blessing of fate so was she. They stood in the silent garden, locked together, and simply enjoyed, took, gave. She was a novice, but that only added a piquancy, a delicate touch of enchantment to know that it was he who was leading her along paths she'd never trod.

Into realms she hadn't before explored.

The warmth of her, the supple strength, the blatantly feminine curves pressed to his chest—the fact he had her locked in his arms sank through his senses, sank evocative talons deep.

Until he knew just what he wanted, knew beyond doubt what Pandora's box he'd opened.

Leonora clung as the kiss went on, as it progressed, expanded, opening up new horizons, educating her senses. Some part of her reeling mind knew without question that she wasn't in any danger, that Trentham's arms were a safe haven for her.

That she could accept the kiss and all it brought if not with impunity, then at least without risk.

That she could grasp the brief glimpse of passion he offered, seize the moment and, starved, ease her hunger at least that much, own to wanting more without fear, knowing that when it ended she would be able—would be allowed—to step back. To remain herself, locked away and safe.

Alone.

So she made no move to end it.

Until Henrietta whined.

Trentham lifted his head instantly, looked down at Henrietta, but he didn't let her go.

Blushing, very glad of the darkness, she pushed back, felt his chest, warm rock, beneath her hands. Still frowning, glancing around at the shadows, he eased his hold on her.

Clearing her throat, she stepped back, out of his arms, putting clear distance between them. "She's cold."

He looked at her, then at Henrietta. "Cold?"

"Her coat's wiry hair, not fur."

He looked at her; she met his gaze, and suddenly felt terribly awkward. How did one part from a gentleman who'd just . . .

She looked down, snapped her fingers at Henrietta. "I'd better take her in. Good night."

He said nothing as she turned and started for the front steps. Then suddenly she sensed him shift.

"Wait."

She turned, raised a brow, as haughty as she could make it.

His face had hardened. "The key." He held out a hand. "To the front door of Number 12."

Heat rushed to her cheeks again. Reaching into her pocket, she drew it out. "I used to visit old Mr. Morrissey. He had terrible trouble doing his household accounts."

He took the key, weighed it in his palm.

She glanced up; he caught her gaze.

After a moment, very quietly he said, "Go inside."

It was too dark to read his eyes, yet caution whispered, told her to obey. Inclining her head, she turned to the front steps. She climbed them, opened the door she'd left on the latch, slipped in, and quietly closed it behind her, conscious all the while of his gaze on her back.

Sliding the key into his pocket, Tristan stood on the path amid the waving fronds and watched until her shadow disappeared into the house. Then he swore, turned, and walked away into the night.

CHAPTER

Four

&❦&

It wasn't the first time in his career that he'd made a tactical blunder. He needed to put it behind him, pretend it hadn't happened, and stick to his strategy of rescuing the damn woman, then moving on, getting on with the fraught business of finding himself a wife.

The next morning, as he strode up the front path to the door of Number 14, Tristan kept repeating that litany, along with a pointed reminder that an argumentative, willful, trenchantly independent lady of mature years was assuredly not the sort of wife he wanted.

Even if she tasted like ambrosia and felt like paradise in his arms.

How old was she anyway?

Nearing the front porch, he thrust the question out of his mind. If this morning went as he planned, he'd be much better placed to adhere to his strategy.

Pausing at the bottom of the steps, he looked up at the front door. He'd tossed and turned all night, not only with the inevitable effects of that unwise kiss, but even more because, stirred by the earlier events of the night, his conscience wouldn't settle. Whatever the truth about the "burglar," the matter was serious. Experience insisted it was so; his instincts were convinced of it. Even though he had no intention of leaving Leonora to deal with it on her own, he didn't feel comfortable in not alerting both Sir Humphrey and Jeremy Carling to the danger.

He'd come determined to make a real attempt to bring home to them the true tenor of the situation. It was their right to protect Leonora; he couldn't in all honor usurp their role while leaving them in ignorance.

Straightening his shoulders, he went up the steps.

The ancient butler answered his knock.

"Good morning." Charm to the fore, he smiled. "I'd like to speak to Sir Humphrey, and also Mr. Carling, if they're available."

The man's starchy demeanor eased; he opened the door wide. "If you'll wait in the morning room, my lord, I'll inquire."

He stood in the middle of the morning room and prayed Leonora didn't hear of his arrival. What he wanted to achieve would be easier accomplished between gentlemen, without the distracting presence of the object central to their discussion.

The butler returned and conducted him to the library. He entered and found Sir Humphrey and Jeremy alone, and heaved a small sigh of relief.

"Trentham! Welcome!" Seated as he had been on Tristan's earlier visit, in the armchair by the fire with—Tristan was almost certain—the same book open on his knee, Humphrey waved him to the chaise. "Sit down, sit down, and tell us what we can do for you."

Jeremy, too, looked up and nodded a greeting. Tristan returned the nod as he sat. Again, he got the impression little had changed on Jeremy's desk except, perhaps, the particular page he was studying.

Catching his glance, Jeremy smiled. "Indeed, I'll be grateful for a respite." He waved at the book before him. "Deciphering this Sumerian script is deuced hard on the eyes."

Humphrey snorted. "Better that than this." He indicated the tome on his knees. "More than a century later, but they weren't any neater. Why they couldn't use decent quills—" He broke off, then grinned engagingly at Tristan. "But you've not come to hear about that. You mustn't let us get started, or we can talk scripts for hours."

Tristan's mind boggled.

"So!" Humphrey closed the tome on his lap. "How can we help you, heh?"

"It's not so much a matter of help." He was feeling his way, unsure of his best approach. "I thought I should let you know that there was an attempted burglary at Number 12 last night."

"Good God!" Humphrey was as taken aback as Tristan could have wished. "Dashed bounders! Getting a great deal too above themselves these days."

"Indeed." Tristan grabbed back the reins before Humphrey could bolt. "But in this case, the builders noticed that some tampering had occurred on the previous night, so we mounted a watch last night. The felon returned and entered the house—we would have caught him but for some unexpected obstacles. As things fell out, he escaped, but it appeared he was . . . let us say not the expected low-class villain. Indeed, he bore all the signs of being a gentleman."

"A gentleman?" Humphrey was astounded. "A *gentleman* breaking into houses?"

"So it seems."

"But what would a gentleman be after?" Frowning, Jeremy met Tristan's gaze. "It seems quite nonsensical to me."

Jeremy's tone was dismissive; Tristan squelched his exasperation. "Indeed. Even more amazing is that a burglar would bother breaking into a completely empty house." He looked at Humphrey, then Jeremy. "There's literally nothing in Number 12, and given the builders' paraphernalia and presence throughout the day, that fact must be patently obvious."

Both Humphrey and Jeremy only looked more puzzled, as if the entire subject was completely beyond them. Tristan knew all about deceptiveness; he was starting to suspect he was watching a practiced performance. His voice hardened. "It occurred to me that the attempt to gain access to Number 12 might be linked to the two attempted burglaries here."

Both faces turned to him remained blank and vague. Too blank and vague. They understood everything, but were steadfastly refusing to react.

He deliberately let the silence grow awkward. Eventually, Jeremy cleared his throat. "How so?"

He nearly gave up; only a trenchant determination fueled by something very like anger that they shouldn't be allowed so easily to abdicate their responsibilities and retreat into their long-dead world, leaving Leonora to cope by herself in this one, had him leaning forward, with his gaze capturing theirs. "What if the burglar *isn't* your usual run of thief, and all evidence suggests that's so, but instead he's after something specific—some item that has value to him. If that item is here, in *this* house, then—"

The door opened.

Leonora swept in. Her eyes found him; she beamed. "My lord! How delightful to see you again."

Rising, Tristan met her eyes. She wasn't delighted—she was in a flat panic. She glided up; inwardly disgusted with how poorly things had gone, he seized the inherent advantage and held out his hand.

She blinked at it, but after only the slightest hesitation surrendered her fingers. He bowed; she curtsied. Her fingers quivered in his.

The courtesies satisfied, he drew her to sit beside him on the chaise. She had no option but to do so. As, tense and on edge, she sank onto the damask, Humphrey said, "Trentham's just told us there was a burglary next door—just last night. Blackguard escaped, unfortunately."

"Indeed?" Eyes wide, she turned to Tristan as he sat again, angling herself so she could watch his face.

He caught her eye. "Just so." His dry tone wasn't wasted on her. "I was just suggesting that the attempt to gain access to Number 12 might be connected to the previous attempts to gain entry here."

She, he knew, had arrived at the same conclusion, and that sometime ago.

"I still don't see any real link." Jeremy leaned on his book and fixed Tristan with a steady but still dismissive gaze. "I mean, burglars try their hand wherever they might, don't they?"

Tristan nodded. "Which is why it seems odd that this 'burglar'—and I think we can safely assume all the attempts have been by the same party—continues to push his luck in Montrose Place despite his failures to date."

"Hmm, yes, well, perhaps he'll take the hint and go away, given he couldn't get into either of our houses?" Humphrey raised his brows hopefully.

Tristan hung on to his temper. "The very fact he's tried three times suggests he won't go away—that whatever he's after he's driven to get."

"Yes, but that's just it, don't you see." Sitting back, Jeremy spread his hands wide. "What on earth could he want here?"

"That," Tristan retorted, "is the question."

Yet every suggestion that the "burglar" might be after something contained in their researches, some information, concealed or otherwise, or some unexpectedly valuable tome, met with denials and incomprehension. Other than speculating that the villain might be after Leonora's pearls, something Tristan found difficult to believe—and from the look on her face, so did Leonora—neither Humphrey nor Jeremy had any ideas to advance.

It was patently clear they had no interest in solving the mystery of the burglar, and were both of the opinion that ignoring the matter entirely was the surest route to getting it to disappear.

At least for them.

Tristan didn't approve, but he recognized their type. They were selfish, absorbed in their own interests to the exclusion of all else. Over the years, they'd learned to leave anything and everything to Leonora to deal with; because she always had, they now viewed her efforts as their right. She haggled with the real world while they remained engrossed in their academic one.

Admiration for Leonora—exceedingly reluctant for it was definitely something he didn't want to feel—along with a deeper understanding and a niggling sense that she deserved better bloomed and slid through him.

He could make no headway with Humphrey or Jeremy; eventually he had to concede defeat. He did, however, exact a promise that they would bend their minds to the question and inform him immediately if they thought of any item that could be the burglar's goal.

Catching Leonora's eye, he rose. Throughout, he'd been conscious of her tension, of her watching him like a hawk ready to jump in and deflect or confuse any comment that might reveal her part in the previous night's activities.

He held her gaze; she read his message and rose, too.

"I'll see Lord Trentham out."

With easy smiles, Humphrey and Jeremy bade him farewell. Following Leonora to the door, he paused on the threshold and looked back.

Both men were already head down, back in the past.

He looked at Leonora. Her expression stated she knew what he'd seen. One brow rose quizzically, as if she was wryly amused that he'd thought he could change things.

He felt his face harden. Waving her on, he followed, closing the door behind them.

She led him to the front hall. Drawing level with the door to the parlor, he touched her arm.

Met her gaze when she looked at him. "Let's walk in the back garden." When she didn't immediately acquiesce, he added, "I want to talk to you."

She hesitated, then inclined her head. She led him through the parlor—he noticed the piece of embroidery still precisely as it had been previously—out through the French doors and down onto the lawn.

Head high, she walked on; he fell in beside her. And said nothing. Waited for her to ask what he wished to talk about, grasping the moment to work on a strategy for convincing her to leave the matter of the mysterious burglar to him.

The lawn was lush and well tended, the beds circling it thick with odd plants he'd never seen before. The late Cedric Carling must have been a collector as well as an authority on herbal horticulture . . . "How long ago did your cousin Cedric die?"

She glanced at him. "Over two years ago." She paused, then continued, "I can't see that there'd be anything valuable in his papers, or we would have heard long ago."

"Most likely." After Humphrey and Jeremy, her open acuity was refreshing.

They'd walked across the width of the lawn; she halted where a sundial was set on a pedestal standing just within the boundary of a deep bed. He stopped beside and a little behind her. Watched as she put out a hand, with her fingertips traced the engraving in the bronze face.

"Thank you for not mentioning my presence in Number 12 last night." Her voice was low but clear; she kept her gaze on the sundial. "Or what happened on the path."

She drew breath, lifted her head.

Before she could say more—tell him the kiss hadn't meant anything, had been a silly mistake, or some similar nonsense he'd feel forced to prove wrong—he raised his hand, set one fingertip to her nape, and traced slowly, deliberately, down her spine, all the way down to below her waist.

Her breath caught, then she swung to face him, periwinkle blue eyes wide.

He trapped her gaze. "What happened last night, especially those moments on the path, is between you and me."

When she continued to stare at him, searching his eyes, he elaborated, "Kissing you and telling anyone is not within my code, and definitely not my style."

He saw the flash of reaction in her eyes, saw her consider asking, waspishly, just what his style was, but caution caught her tongue; she raised her head, haughtily inclined it as she looked away.

The moment was going to turn awkward, and he still hadn't thought of any approach likely to deflect her from the burglaries. Casting about in his mind, he looked past her. And saw the house beyond the garden wall, the house next door, which also, like Number 12, shared a wall with Number 14.

"Who lives there?"

She glanced up, followed his gaze. "Old Miss Timmins."

"She lives alone?"

"With a maid."

He looked down into Leonora's eyes; they were already filled with speculation. "I'd like to call on Miss Timmins. Will you introduce me?"

She was only too happy to do so. To leave the disconcerting moment in the garden—her thudding heart had yet to slow to its normal rhythm—and plunge instead into further investigations. By Trentham's side.

Quite why she found his company so stimulating Leonora didn't know. She wasn't even sure she approved, or that her Aunt Mildred, let alone her Aunt Gertie, would either, if they knew. He was, after all, a military man. Young girls might have their heads turned by broad shoulders and a magnificent uniform, but ladies such as she were supposed to be too wise to fall victim to such gentlemen's wiles. They were invariably second sons, or sons of second sons, looking to make their way in the world through an advantageous marriage . . . except Trentham was now an earl.

Inwardly, she frowned. Presumably that excused him from the general prohibition.

Regardless, as she walked briskly down the street beside him,

her gloved hand on his sleeve, the sense of his strength engulf-
ing her, the excitement of the hunt simmering in her veins, there
was no question in her mind but that she felt immeasurably more
alive when with him.

When she'd heard he'd called, she'd panicked. She'd felt sure
he had come to complain of her infraction in going into Number
12 last night. And possibly, even worse, to mention—in whatever manner—their indiscretion on the path. Instead, he'd made
not the slightest allusion to her part in the night's activities; even
though she was sure he'd sensed her agitation, he'd said and done
nothing to tease her.

She'd expected a lot worse from a military man.

Reaching the gate of Number 16, Trentham swung it wide,
and they went through, walking up the path and climbing the
steps to the small front porch side by side. She pulled the bell,
heard it ring deep within the house, smaller than Number 14, a
terrace similar in style to Number 12.

Footsteps pattered, approaching, then came the sound of bolts
being drawn back. The door opened a little way; a sweet-faced
maid peeped out.

Leonora smiled. "Good morning, Daisy. I know it's a trifle
early, but if Miss Timmins can spare a few minutes, we have a
new neighbor, the Earl of Trentham, who'd like to make her acquaintance."

Daisy's eyes had grown round as she took in Trentham, standing blocking the sunlight at Leonora's side. "Oh, yes, miss. I'm
sure she'll see you—she always likes to know what's going on."
Opening the door fully, Daisy waved them in. "If you'll wait in
the morning room, I'll tell her you're here."

Leonora led the way into the morning room and sat on the
chaise.

Trentham didn't sit. He paced. Prowled. Looking at the windows.

Examining the locks.

She frowned. "What—"

She broke off as Daisy hurried back in. "She says as she'll be delighted to receive you." She bobbed to Trentham. "If you'll come this way, I'll take you up to her."

They climbed the stairs, following Daisy; Leonora was aware of the glances Trentham directed this way and that. If she didn't know better, she'd think *he* was the burglar looking for the best way in. . . .

"Oh." Halting at the top of the stairs, she swung to face him. Whispered, "Do you think the burglar might try here next?"

He frowned, waved her on. With Daisy sailing ahead, she had to turn and hurry to catch up. Trentham merely lengthened his stride. With him on her heels, she glided into Miss Timmins's drawing room.

"Leonora, my dear." Miss Timmins's voice quavered. "How sweet of you to call."

Miss Timmins was old and frail and rarely ventured outside. Leonora often called; over the past year, she'd noticed the brightness in Miss Timmins's soft blue eyes fading, as if a flame were burning low.

Smiling in return, she pressed Miss Timmins's clawlike hand, then stepped back. "I've brought the Earl of Trentham to call. He and some friends have bought the house beyond ours, Number 12."

Gently vague, her prim grey curls neatly brushed and dressed, her pearls looped about her throat, Miss Timmins shyly gave Trentham her hand. Nervously murmured a greeting.

Trentham bowed. "How do you do, Miss Timmins. I hope you've been keeping well through these cold months?"

Miss Timmins flustered, but still clung to Trentham's hand. "Yes, indeed." She seemed caught by his eyes. After a moment, she ventured, "It's been such a shocking winter."

"More sleet than usual, certainly." Trentham smiled, all charm. "May we sit?"

"Oh! Yes, of course. Please do." Miss Timmins leaned forward. "I heard you're a military man, my lord. Tell me, were you at Waterloo?"

Leonora sank into a chair and watched, amazed, as Trentham—a self-confessed military man—charmed old Miss Timmins, who wasn't, generally, comfortable with men. Yet Trentham seemed to know just what to say, just what an old lady thought appropriate to talk about. Just what snippets of gossip she'd like to hear.

Daisy brought tea; as she sipped, Leonora cynically wondered just what goal Trentham was pursuing.

Her answer came when he set down his cup and assumed a more serious mien. "Actually, I had a purpose in calling beyond the pleasure of meeting you, ma'am." He caught Miss Timmins's gaze. "There have been a number of incidents in the street lately, of burglars trying to gain entry."

"Oh, dear me!" Miss Timmins rattled her cup onto its saucer. "I must tell Daisy to be doubly sure she locks every door."

"As to that, I wonder if you would mind if I look around the ground floor and belowstairs, to make sure there's no easy way inside? I would sleep much more soundly if I knew your house, with only you and Daisy here, was secure."

Miss Timmins blinked, then beamed at him. "Why, of course, dear. So thoughtful of you."

After a few more comments of a more general nature, Trentham rose. Leonora rose, too. They took their leave, with Miss Timmins instructing Daisy that his-lordship-the-earl would be looking around the house to make sure all was safe.

Daisy beamed, too.

In parting, Trentham assured Miss Timmins that should he discover any less than adequate lock, he would take care of its replacement—she wasn't to bother her head.

From the look in Miss Timmins's old eyes as she pressed his hand in farewell, his-lordship-the-earl had made a conquest.

Disturbed, when they reached the stairs and Daisy had gone ahead, Leonora paused and caught Trentham's eye. "I hope you intend making good on that promise."

His gaze was steady and remained so; eventually he replied, "I will." He studied her face, then added, "I meant what I said." Stepping past her, he started down the stairs. "I *will* sleep more soundly knowing this place is secure."

She frowned at the back of his head—the man was a complete conundrum—then followed him down the stairs.

She trailed after him as he systematically checked every single window and door on the ground floor, then descended to the basement and did the same there. He was thorough and, to her eyes, coolly professional, as if securing premises against intruders had been a frequent task in his erstwhile occupation. It was increasingly difficult to dismiss him as "just another military man."

In the end, he nodded to Daisy. "This is better than I expected. Has she always been worried about intruders?"

"Oh, yes, sir, m'lord. Ever since I came here to do for her, and that's going on six years, now."

"Well, if you lock every lock and shoot every bolt, you'll be as safe as you could be."

Leaving a grateful and reassured Daisy, they walked down the garden path. Reaching the gate, Leonora, who'd been pursuing her own thoughts, glanced at Trentham. "Is the house truly secure?"

He looked at her, then held the gate open. "As secure as it can be. There's no way to stop a determined intruder." He fell into step beside her as they paced along the pavement. "If he uses force—breaking a window or forcing a door—he'll get in, but I don't think our man is likely to be so direct. If we're right in thinking it's Number 14 he wants access to, then to get that via Number 16, he'll have to have a few nights undetected to tunnel through the basement walls. He won't get that if he's too obvious about how he gets in."

"So as long as Daisy is vigilant, all should be well."

When he didn't say anything, she looked at him. He sensed her glance, caught her eye. Grimaced. "On our way in, I was wondering how to introduce some man into the household, at least until we've laid this burglar by the heels. But she's frightened of men, isn't she?"

"Yes." She was astonished he'd been so perceptive. "You're one of the few I've ever known her to talk to beyond the barest commonplace."

He nodded, looked down. "She'd be too uncomfortable with a man under her roof, so it's lucky those locks are so sound. We'll have to put our faith in them."

"And do everything we can to catch this burglar soon."

Her determination rang in her voice.

They'd reached the gate of Number 14. Tristan halted, met her gaze. "I suppose there's no point insisting you leave the matter of the burglar in my hands?"

Her periwinkle blue eyes hardened. "None."

He exhaled, looked away down the street. He wasn't above lying for a good cause. Wasn't above using distractions, either, despite their inherent danger.

Before she could shift away, he caught her hand. Turned his head and trapped her gaze. Held it while with his fingers he sought, then flicked the opening in her glove wide, then raised her wrist, the inner face now exposed, to his lips.

Felt the quiver that raced through her, watched her head lift, her eyes darken.

He smiled, slowly, intently. Softly decreed, "What's between you and me remains between you and me, but it hasn't gone away."

Her lips set; she tugged, but he didn't release her, instead, with his thumb, languidly caressed the spot he'd kissed.

She caught her breath, then hissed, "I'm not interested in any dalliance."

Eyes on hers, he raised a brow. "No more am I." He was interested in distracting her. They'd both be better off with her concentrating on him rather than on the burglar. "In the interests of our acquaintance"—in the interests of his sanity—"I'm willing to make a deal."

Suspicion glowed in her eyes. "What deal?"

He chose his words carefully. "If you promise to do no more than keep your eyes and ears open, to do no more than watch and listen and report all to me when next I call, I'll agree to share with you all I discover."

Her expression turned haughtily dismissive. "And what if you don't discover anything?"

His lips remained curved, but he let his mask slide, let his true self show briefly. "Oh, I will." His voice was soft, faintly menacing; its tone held her.

Again, slowly, deliberately, he raised her wrist to his lips. Holding her gaze, kissed.

"Do we have a deal?"

She blinked, refocused on his eyes, then her breasts swelled as she drew in a deep breath. And nodded. "Very well."

He released her wrist; she all but snatched it back.

"But on one condition."

He raised his brows, now as haughty as she. "What?"

"I'll watch and listen and do no more if you promise to call and tell me what you've discovered *as soon* as you discover it."

His gaze locked with hers, he considered, then let his lips ease. He inclined his head. "As soon as practicable, I'll share any discovery."

She was mollified, and surprised to be so. He hid a grin and bowed. "Good day, Miss Carling."

She held his gaze for a moment longer, then inclined her head. "Good day, my lord."

Days passed.

Leonora watched and listened, but nothing of any moment occurred. She was content with their bargain; there was in truth little else she could do beyond watch and listen, and the knowledge that if anything did occur, Trentham expected to be involved in dealing with it was unexpectedly heartening. She'd grown used to acting alone, indeed eschewed the help of others who in general were more likely to get in her way, yet Trentham was undeniably able—with him involved, she felt confident of resolving the issue of the burglaries.

Staff started to appear at Number 12; Trentham occasionally called in there, as duly reported by Toby, but did not venture to knock on the Carlings' front door.

The only factor that disturbed her equanimity was her recollections of that kiss in the night. She'd tried to forget it, simply put it from her mind, an aberration on both their parts, yet forgetting the way her pulse leapt whenever he came near was much harder. And she had absolutely no idea how to interpret his comment that what lay between them hadn't gone away.

Did he mean he intended to pursue it?

But then he'd declared he wasn't interested in dalliance any more than she was. Despite his past occupation, she was learning to take his words at face value.

Indeed, his tactful dealings with the old soldier Biggs, his discretion in not speaking of her nighttime adventures, and his unprecedented charming of Miss Timmins, going out of his way to reassure and see to the old lady's safety, had in large part ameliorated her prejudice.

Perhaps Trentham was one of those whose existence proved the rule—a trustworthy military man, one who could be relied on, at least in certain matters.

Despite that, she wasn't entirely certain she could rely on him to tell her all and anything he discovered. Nevertheless, she would have allowed him a few more days' grace if it hadn't been for the watcher.

At first, it was simply a sensation, a prickling of her nerves, an eerie feeling of being observed. Not just in the street, but in the back garden, too; that last unnerved her. The first of the earlier attacks on her had occurred just inside the front gate; she no longer walked in the front garden.

She began taking Henrietta with her wherever she went, and if that wasn't possible, a footman.

With time, her nerves would doubtless have calmed, steadied. But then, strolling in the back garden late one afternoon as the abbreviated February twilight closed in, she glimpsed a man standing almost at the rear of the garden, beyond the hedge that bisected the long plot. Framed by the central arch in the hedge, a lean, dark figure swathed in a dark cloak, he stood among the vegetable beds—and watched her.

Leonora froze. He wasn't the same man who had accosted her in January, the first time by the front gate, the second time in the street. That man had been smaller, slighter; she'd been able to fight back, to break free.

The man who now watched her looked infinitely more menacing. He stood silent, still, yet it was the stillness of a predator waiting for his moment. There was only a stretch of lawn between them. She had to fight the urge to raise a hand to her throat, had to battle an instinct to turn and flee—battle the conviction that if she did he'd be on her.

Henrietta ambled up, saw the man, and growled low in her throat. The rumbling warning continued, subtly escalating. Hackles rising, the hound placed herself between Leonora and the man.

He remained still for an instant longer, then whisked around. His cloak flapped; he disappeared from Leonora's sight.

Heart thudding uncomfortably, she looked down at Henrietta. The wolfhound remained alert, senses focused. Then a distant thud reached Leonora's ears; an instant later, Henrietta wuffed and relaxed from her stance, turning to calmly continue their progress back to the parlor doors.

A chill swept Leonora's spine; eyes wide, scanning the shadows, she hurried back to the house.

The next morning at eleven o'clock—the earliest hour at which it was acceptable to call—she rang the doorbell of the elegant house in Green Street that the urchin sweeping at the corner had told her belonged to the Earl of Trentham.

An imposing but kindly-looking butler opened the door. "Yes, ma'am?"

She drew herself up. "Good morning. I am Miss Carling, from Montrose Place. I wish to speak with Lord Trentham, if you please."

The butler looked genuinely regretful. "Unfortunately, his lordship is not presently in."

"Oh." She'd assumed he would be, that like most fashionable men he was unlikely to set foot beyond his door before noon. After a frozen moment in which nothing—no other avenue of action—occurred to her, she lifted her gaze to the butler's face. "Is he expected to return soon?"

"I daresay his lordship will be back within the hour, miss." Her determination must have shown; the butler opened the door wider. "If you would care to wait?"

"Thank you." Leonora let a hint of approval color the words. The butler had the most sympathetic face. She stepped across the threshold and was instantly struck by the airiness and light in the hall, underscored by the elegant furnishings. As the butler closed the door, she turned to him.

He smiled encouragingly. "If you'll come this way, miss?"

Insensibly reassured, Leonora inclined her head and followed him down the corridor.

Tristan returned to Green Street at a little after noon, no further forward and increasingly concerned. Climbing his front steps, he fished out his latch key and let himself in; he had still not grown accustomed to waiting for Havers to open the door, relieve him of his cane and coat, all things he was perfectly capable of doing himself.

Setting his cane in the hall stand, tossing his coat across a chair, he headed, soft-footed, for his study. Hoping to slip past the arches of the morning room without being spotted by any of the old dears. An exceedingly faint hope; regardless of their occupations, they always seemed to sense his flitting presence and glance up just in time to smile and waylay him.

Unfortunately, there was no other way to reach the study; his great-uncle who'd remodeled the house had, he'd long ago concluded, been a glutton for punishment.

The morning room was a light-filled chamber built out from the main house. A few steps below the level of the corridor, it was separated from it by three large arches. Two hosted huge flower arrangements in urns, which gave him some cover, but the middle arch was the doorway, open country.

As silent as a thief, he neared the first arch and, just out of sight, paused to listen. A babble of female voices reached him; the group was at the far end of the room, where a bow window allowed morning light to stream over two chaises and various chairs. It took a moment to attune his ear to pick out the individual voices. Ethelreda was there, Millie, Flora, Constance, Helen, and yes, Edith, too. All six of them. Chattering on about knots—French knots?—what were they?—and gross-something and leaf-stitch . . .

They were discussing embroidery.

He frowned. They all embroidered like martyrs, but it was the one arena in which real competition flourished between them; he'd never heard them discussing their shared interest before, let alone with such gusto.

Then he heard another voice, and his surprise was complete.

"I'm afraid I've never been able to get the threads to lie just so."

Leonora.

"Ah, well, dear, what you need to do—"

He didn't take in the rest of Ethelreda's advice; he was too busy speculating on what had brought Leonora there.

The discussion in the morning room continued, Leonora inviting advice, his old dears taking great delight in supplying it.

Vivid in his mind was that piece of embroidery lying discarded in the parlor in Montrose Place. Leonora might have no talent for embroidery, but he'd have sworn she had no real interest in it, either.

Curiosity pricked. The nearest flower arrangement was tall enough to conceal him. Two swift steps and he was behind it. Peering between the lilies and chrysanthemums, he saw Leonora seated in the middle of one of the chaises surrounded on all sides by his collection of old dears.

Winter sunlight poured through the window at her back, a glimmering wash spilling over her, striking garnet glints from her coronet of dark hair yet leaving her face and its delicate features in faint and mysterious shadow. In her dark red walking dress, she looked like a medieval madonna, an embodiment of feminine virtue and passion, of feminine strength and fragility.

Head bowed, she was examining an embroidered antimacassar laid across her knees.

He watched her encourage her elderly audience to tell her more, to participate. Also saw her step in, swiftly tamping down a sudden spurt of rivalry, soothing both parties with tactful observations.

She had them captivated.

And not only them.

He heard the words in his mind.

Inwardly humphed.

Yet he didn't turn away. Silent, he simply stood, watching her through the screen of flowers.

"Ah—my lord!"

With incomparable reflexes, he stepped forward and turned, his back to the morning room. They'd be able to see him, but the movement would make it seem he'd just walked by.

He viewed his butler with a resigned eye. "Yes, Havers?"

"A lady has called, my lord. A Miss Carling."

"Ah! Trentham!"

He turned as Ethelreda called.

Millie stood and beckoned. "We have Miss Carling here."

All six beamed at him. With a nod of dismissal to Havers, he stepped down and crossed toward the group, not quite certain of the impression he was receiving—almost as if they believed they'd been keeping Leonora there, trapped, cornered, some special delight just for him.

She rose, a light blush in her cheeks. "Your cousins have been very kind in keeping me company." She met his gaze. "I came because there have been developments in Montrose Place that I believe you should know."

"Yes, of course. Thank you for coming. Let's repair to the library, and you can tell me your news." He held out his hand; inclining her head, she surrendered hers.

He drew her from the midst of his elderly champions, nodded to them. "Thank you for entertaining Miss Carling for me."

He had no doubt of the thoughts behind their brilliant smiles.

"Oh, we enjoyed it."

"So delightful . . ."

"Do call again, dear."

They beamed and bobbed; Leonora smiled her thanks, then let him place her hand on his sleeve and lead her away.

Side by side they climbed the steps to the corridor; he didn't need to glance back to know six pairs of eyes were still avidly watching.

As they passed into the front hall, Leonora glanced at him. "I didn't realize you had such a large family."

"I haven't." He opened the library door and ushered her in. "That's the problem. There's just me, and them. And the rest."

Drawing her hand from his sleeve, she turned to look at him. "Rest?"

He waved her to the chairs angled to the blaze roaring in the hearth. "There's eight more at Mallingham Manor, my house in Surrey."

Her lips twitched; she turned and sat.

His smile faded. He dropped into the opposite chair. "Now cut line. Why are you here?"

Leonora lifted her gaze to his face, saw within it all she'd come to find—reassurance, strength, ability. Drawing breath, she leaned back in the chair, and told him.

He didn't interrupt; when she'd finished he asked questions, clarifying where and when it was she'd felt under observation. At no point did he seek to dismiss her intuitive certainty; he treated all she reported as fact, not fancy.

"And you're sure it was the same man?"

"Positive. I caught only a glimpse as he moved, but he had that same loose-limbed motion." She held his gaze. "I'm sure it was he."

He nodded. His gaze drifted from her as he considered all she'd said. Eventually, he glanced at her. "I don't suppose you told your uncle or brother about any of this?"

She raised her brows, mock-haughtily. "I did, as it happens."

When she said nothing more, he prompted, "And?"

Her smile wasn't as lighthearted as she would have liked. "When I mentioned the feeling of being watched, they smiled and told me I was overreacting to the recent troubling events. Humphrey patted my shoulder and told me I shouldn't worry my head about such things, that there really was no need—it would all blow over soon enough.

"As for the man at the bottom of the garden, they were sure I was mistaken. A trick of the light, the shifting shadows. An overactive imagination. I really shouldn't read so many of Mrs. Radcliffe's novels. Besides, as Jeremy pointed out—in the manner of one stating an absolute proof—the back gate is always kept locked."

"Is it?"

"Yes." She met Trentham's hazel eyes. "But the wall is covered on both sides with ancient ivy. Any reasonably agile man would have no difficulty climbing over."

"Which would account for the thud you heard."

"Precisely."

He sat back. Elbow on one chair arm, chin propped on that fist, one long finger idly tapping his lips, he looked past her. His eyes glinted, hard, almost crystalline sharp beneath his heavy lids. He knew she was there, wasn't ignoring her, but was, at present, absorbed.

She hadn't before had such a chance to study him, to take in the reality of the strength in his large body, appreciate the width of his shoulders disguised though they were by the superbly tailored coat—Shultz, of course—or the long, lean legs, muscles delineated by tightly fitted buckskins that disappeared into glossy Hessians. He had very large feet.

He was always elegantly dressed, yet it was a quiet elegance; he did not need or wish to draw attention to himself—indeed, eschewed all opportunity to do so. Even his hands—she might dub them his best feature—were adorned only by a plain gold signet ring.

He'd spoken of his style; she felt confident in defining it as quiet, elegant strength. Like an aura it hung about him, not something derived from clothes or manner, but something inherent, innate, that showed through.

She found such quiet strength unexpectedly attractive. Comforting, too.

Her lips had eased into a gentle smile when his gaze shifted back to her. He raised a brow, but she shook her head, remained silent. Their gazes held; relaxed in the chairs in the quiet of his library, they studied each other.

And something changed.

Excitement, an insidious thrill, slid slowly through her, a subtle flick, a temptation to illicit delight. Heat blossomed; her lungs slowly seized.

Their eyes remained locked. Neither moved.

It was she who broke the spell. Shifted her gaze to the flames in the hearth. Breathed in. Reminded herself not to be ridiculous; they were in his house, in his library—he would hardly seduce her under his own roof with his servants and elderly cousins standing by.

He stirred and sat up. "How did you get here?"

"I walked through the park." She glanced at him. "It seemed the safest way."

He nodded, rose. "I'll drive you home. I need to look in at Number 12."

She watched while he tugged the bellpull, gave orders to his butler when that worthy arrived. When he turned back to her, she asked, "Have you learned anything?"

Tristan shook his head. "I've been investigating various avenues. Searching for any whispers of men seeking something from Montrose Place."

"And did you hear anything?"

"No." He met her gaze. "I didn't expect to—that would be too easy."

She grimaced, then rose as Havers returned to say his curricle was being brought around.

While she donned her pelisse and he shrugged into his greatcoat and dispatched a footman to fetch his driving gloves, Tristan racked his brains for any avenue he'd left unexplored, any door open to him he hadn't been through. He'd tapped any number of ex-servicemen, and some who were still serving in various capacities, for information; he was now certain that what they were dealing with was something peculiar to Montrose Place. There had been no whispers of gangs or individuals behaving in like manner anywhere else in the capital.

Which only added weight to their supposition that there was something in Number 14 the mystery burglar wanted.

As they bowled around the park in his curricle, he explained his deductions.

Leonora frowned. "I've asked the servants." Lifting her head, she tucked back a strand of hair whipping in the breeze. "No one has any idea of anything that might be particularly valuable." She glanced at him. "Beyond the obvious answer of something in the library."

He caught her glance, then looked to his horses. After a moment, asked, "Is it possible your uncle and brother would hide something important—for instance if they made a discovery and wanted to keep it secret for a time?"

She shook her head. "I often act as hostess for their learned dinners. There's a great deal of competition and rivalry in their field, but far from being secretive about any discoveries, the usual approach is to shout any new finding, no matter how minor, from the rooftops, and that as soon as possible. By way of claiming rights, if you take my meaning."

He nodded. "So that's unlikely."

"Yes, but . . . if you were to suggest that Humphrey or Jeremy might have stumbled across something quite valuable, and simply not seen it for what it was—or rather they would recognize it but not attribute an accurate value to it"—she looked at him— "I'd have to agree."

"Very well." They'd reached Montrose Place; he drew rein outside Number 12. "We'll have to assume something of the sort is at the heart of this."

Tossing the reins to his tiger who'd jumped from the back and come running, he climbed down to the pavement, then handed her down.

Linking their arms, he walked her to the gate of Number 14.

At the gate, she drew back and faced him. "What do you think we should do?"

He met her gaze directly, without any hint of his usual mask. An instant passed, then he said, softly, "I don't know."

His hard gaze held hers; his hand found hers, his fingers twined with hers.

Her pulse leapt at his touch.

He raised her hand, brushed his lips across her fingers.

Held her gaze over them.

Then, lingeringly, touched his lips to her skin again, blatantly savoring.

Dizziness threatened.

His eyes searched hers, then he murmured, deep and low, "Let me think things through. I'll call on you tomorrow, and we can discuss how best to go on."

Her skin burned where his lips had brushed. She managed a nod, stepped back. He let her fingers slide from his. Pushing the iron gate, she stepped through, shut it. Looked at him through it. "Until tomorrow, then. Good-bye."

Her pulse thrumming through her veins, throbbing in her fingertips, she turned and walked up the path.

"Is this the place?"

Tristan nodded to Charles St. Austell and reached for the doorknob of Stolemore's establishment. By the time he'd dropped by one of his smaller clubs, the Guards, the previous evening, he'd already decided to call on Stolemore and be rather more persuasive. Encountering Charles, up from the country on business, also taking refuge at the club, had been too good a stroke of fortune to overlook.

Either of them could be menacing enough to persuade almost anyone to talk; together, there was no doubt Stolemore would tell them all Tristan wished to know.

He'd only had to mention the matter to Charles, and he'd agreed. Indeed, he'd leapt at the chance to help, to once again exercise his peculiar talents.

The door swung inward; Tristan led the way in. This time, Stolemore was behind the desk. He looked up as the bell tinkled, his gaze sharpening as he recognized Tristan.

Tristan strolled forward, his gaze trained on the hapless agent.

Stolemore's eyes widened. His gaze deflected to Charles. The agent paled, then tensed.

Behind him, Tristan heard Charles move; he didn't look around. His senses informed him Charles had turned the wooden sign on the door to CLOSED, then came the rattle of rings on wood; the light faded as Charles drew the curtains across the front windows.

Stolemore's expression, eyes filled with apprehension, said he understood their threat very well. He grasped the edge of his desk and eased his chair back.

From the corner of his eye, Tristan watched Charles cross soft-footed to lounge, arms folded, against the edge of the curtained doorway leading deeper into the house. His grin would have done credit to a demon.

The message was clear. To escape the small office Stolemore would have to go through one or other of them. Although the agent was a heavy man, heavier than either Tristan or Charles, there was no doubt in any of their minds that he would never make it.

Tristan smiled, not humorously yet gently enough. "All we want is information."

Stolemore licked his lips, his gaze flicking from him to Charles. "On what?"

His voice was rough, underlying fear grating.

Tristan paused as if savoring the sound, then softly replied, "I want the name and all the details you have on the party who wished to purchase Number 14 Montrose Place."

Stolemore swallowed; again he edged back, his gaze shifting between them. "I don't go talking about my clients. Worth my reputation to give out information like that."

Again Tristan waited, his eyes never leaving Stolemore's face.

When the silence had stretched taut, along with Stolemore's nerves, he softly inquired, "And what do you imagine it's going to cost you not to oblige us?"

Stolemore paled even more; the lingering bruises from the beating administered by the very people he was protecting were clearly visible beneath his pasty skin. He turned to Charles, as if gauging his chances; an instant later, he looked back at Tristan. Puzzlement flowed behind his eyes. "Who are you?"

Tristan replied, his tone even, uninflected, "We're gentlemen who do not like seeing innocents taken advantage of. Suffice to say the recent activities of your client do not sit well with us."

"Indeed," Charles put in, his voice a dark purr, "you could say he's rattling our cages."

The last words were laden with menace.

Stolemore glanced at Charles, then quickly looked back at Tristan. "All right. I'll tell you—but on condition you don't tell him it was me gave you his name."

"I can assure you that when we catch up with him, we won't be wasting time discussing how we found him." Tristan raised his brows. "Indeed, I can guarantee he'll have much more pressing claims on his attention."

Stolemore smothered a nervous snort. He reached for a drawer in the desk.

Tristan and Charles moved, silent, deadly; Stolemore froze, then glanced nervously at them, now positioned so he was directly between them. "It's just a book," he croaked. "I swear!"

A heartbeat passed, then Tristan nodded. "Take it out."

Barely breathing, Stolemore very slowly withdrew a ledger from the drawer.

The tension eased a fraction; the agent placed the book on the desk and opened it. He fumbled, hurriedly shuffling pages, then he ran his finger down one, and stopped.

"Write it down," Tristan said.

Stolemore obliged.

Tristan had already read the entry, committed it to memory. When Stolemore finished and pushed the slip of paper with the address across the desk, he smiled—charmingly, this time—and picked it up.

"This way"—he held Stolemore's gaze as he tucked the paper into his inner coat pocket—"if anyone should ask, you can swear with a clear conscience that you told no one his name or address. Now—what did he look like? There was just one man, I take it?"

Stolemore nodded in the direction in which the slip of paper had disappeared. "Just him. Nasty piece of work. Looks gentlemanly enough—black hair, pale skin, brown eyes. Well dressed but not Mayfair quality. I took him for a nob from the country; he behaved arrogantly enough. Youngish, but he's got a mean streak and a hasty temper." Stolemore raised a hand to the bruises about one eye. "If I never see him again, it'll be too soon."

Tristan inclined his head. "We'll see what we can do to arrange it."

Turning, he walked to the door. Charles followed on his heels.

Outside on the pavement, they paused.

Charles grimaced. "Much as I would love to come and cast an eye over our stronghold"—his devilish grin dawned—"and over our delectable neighbor, I have to hie back to Cornwall."

"My thanks." Tristan held out his hand.

Charles grasped it. "Anytime." A hint of self-deprecation tinged his smile. "Truth to tell, I enjoyed it, minor though it was. I feel like I'm literally rusting in the country."

"The adjustment was never going to be easy, even less so for us than for others."

"At least you've got something to keep you occupied. All I have is sheep and cows and sisters."

Tristan laughed at Charles's patent disgust. He clapped him on the shoulder, and they parted, Charles heading back to Mayfair while Tristan headed in the opposite direction.

To Montrose Place. It was not quite ten o'clock. He would check with Gasthorpe, the ex–sergeant major they'd hired as the Bastion Club's majordomo who was overseeing the final stages of preparing the club for its patrons, then he'd call on Leonora as he'd promised.

As he'd promised, discuss how to go on.

At eleven o'clock, he knocked on the door of Number 14. The butler showed him to the parlor; Leonora rose from the chaise as he entered.

"Good morning." She bobbed a curtsy as he bowed over her hand.

The sun had managed to struggle free of the clouds; the beams of sunshine playing over the foliage in the back garden drew Tristan's gaze.

"Walk with me in the garden." He retained possession of her hand. "I'd like to see this back wall of yours."

She hesitated, then inclined her head; she would have led the way, but he didn't free her fingers. Instead, he curved his hand more definitely about hers. She threw him a brief glance as side by side they walked to the French doors. Opening them, they passed through; as they went down the steps, he drew her hand through his arm.

Aware of the skittering of her pulse, the way it quivered beneath his fingers.

She lifted her head. "We need to go through that arch in the hedges." She pointed. "The wall is at the back of the kitchen gardens."

Which gardens were extensive. With Henrietta ambling behind, they strolled down the central path, past rows of cabbages followed by endless rows lying fallow, long mounds covered with leaves and other debris waiting, slumbering, until spring returned.

He halted. "Where was he standing when you saw him?"

Leonora glanced around, then pointed to a spot just a little way ahead, about twenty feet inside the back wall. "It must have been about there."

He released her, turning to look back up the path, through the archway to the lawn. "You said he whisked out of your sight. In which direction did he go? Did he turn and walk back toward the wall?"

"No—he went sideways. If he'd turned and run back down the path, I would have been able to see him for longer."

He nodded, surveying the ground in the direction she'd indicated. "That was two evenings ago." It hadn't rained since. "Has your gardener been working here?"

"Not in the last few days. There's not much to do here in winter."

He put a hand on her arm, pressed briefly. "Stay here." He continued down the path, treading carefully along the edge. "Tell me when I get to where he was standing."

She watched, then said, "About there."

He circled the area, eyes on the ground, then moved between

the beds away from the path in the direction the man had gone.

He found what he was looking for a foot from the base of the wall, where the man had stepped heavily before jumping onto the thick creeper. He crouched down; Leonora came bustling up. The footprint was clearly delineated.

"Hmm . . . yes."

He glanced up to find her bending near, studying the impression.

She caught his eye. "That looks about right."

He rose; she straightened. "It's the same size and shape as the print I found in the dust by the side door of Number 12."

"The door the burglar came in through?"

He nodded and turned to the creeper-covered wall. He scanned it carefully, but it was Leonora who found the evidence.

"Here." She lifted a broken twig, then let it fall.

"And here." He pointed higher, where the creeper had been dislodged from the wall. He glanced at the heavy gate. "I don't suppose you have the key?"

The look she threw him was coolly superior. She drew an old key from her pocket.

He swiped it from her fingers. Pretended not to see the flare of irritation in her eyes. Moving past her, he fitted the key to the huge old lock and turned it. The gate groaned protestingly as he hauled it open.

There were two clear prints in the alley running behind the houses, in the accumulated dirt covering the rough flags. A brief glance was enough to confirm they were from the same boot, made as the man jumped down from the wall. Thereafter, however, there were no clear traces.

"That's conclusive enough." He took Leonora's arm, urged her back to the gate.

They reentered the garden, Leonora shooing Henrietta before them. Tristan closed and relocked the gate. Leonora was the only one who walked in the garden; he'd been watching long enough to be certain of that. That the burglar had singled her out worried him. Reminded him of his earlier conviction that she hadn't told him all.

Turning from the gate, he held out the key. She took it, looked down to slip it into her pocket.

He glanced around. The gate lay to one side of the path, not in line with the archway in the hedge; they were out of sight of the lawn and the house. Courtesy of the fruit trees lining the side walls, they were also screened from any neighbors.

He looked down as Leonora raised her head.

He smiled. Infused all the art of which he was capable into the gesture.

She blinked, but, somewhat to his chagrin, seemed less addled than he'd hoped.

"Those earlier attempts to break in here—the burglar didn't see you, did he?"

She shook her head. "The first time, only the servants were about. The second time, when Henrietta raised the alarm, we all came tumbling down, but he was long gone by then."

She offered nothing more. Her periwinkle blue eyes remained clear, unclouded. She hadn't stepped back; they were close, her face turned up so she could look into his.

Attraction flared, raced over his skin.

He let it. Let it flow and build, didn't try to suppress it. Let it show in his face, in his eyes.

Hers, locked on his, widened. She cleared her throat. "We were going to discuss how best to go on."

The words were breathless, uncharacteristically weak.

He paused for a heartbeat, then leaned closer. "I've decided we should play it by ear."

"By ear?" Her lashes fluttered down as he leaned closer yet.

"Hmm. Just follow our noses."

He did precisely that, lowered his head and set his lips to hers. She stilled. She'd been watching, skittish, but had not anticipated such a direct attack.

He was too experienced to signal his intentions. Not on any battlefield.

So he didn't immediately take her in his arms, instead simply kissed her, his lips on hers, subtly tempting.

Until she parted hers and let him in. Until he cradled her face, sank deep and drank, savored, took.

Only then did he reach for her, and draw her to him, unsurprised, as his tongue tangled with hers, that she stepped toward him without thought. Without hesitation.

She was caught in the kiss.

As was he.

Such a simple thing—it was just a kiss. Yet as Leonora felt her breasts meet his chest, felt his arms close around her, there seemed to be so much more. So much she'd never before felt, never before even realized existed. Like the warmth that raced through them—not just through her but through him, too. The sudden tension, not of rejection, not of reining back, but of wanting.

Her hands had risen to rest against his shoulders. Through the contact, she sensed his reaction, both his ease in this sphere, his expertise, and beneath that a deeper yearning.

His hand on her back, strong fingers splayed over her spine, urged her closer; she acquiesced, and his lips turned demanding. Commanding. She met them, gave her mouth and felt the first lick of glory in his hunger. Against her, his body felt like oak, strong and unbending, yet the mobile lips that held hers, that played, teased and made her want, were so alive, so assured.

So addictive.

She was about to sink against him, about to willingly slide deeper under his spell, when she sensed him ease back, felt his hands slide to her waist and grip lightly.

He broke off the kiss and lifted his head.

Looked into her eyes.

For a moment, she could only blink at him, wondering why he'd stopped. Regret flashed through his eyes, superceded by resolve, a hard glint in the hazel. As if he hadn't wanted to stop but felt he must.

A fleeting madness gripped her—a strong urge to reach her hand to his nape and draw him, and those fascinating lips, back to her.

She blinked again.

He set her back on her feet, steadying her.

"I should go."

Her wits snapped back into place, back into the real world. "How have you decided to proceed?"

He looked at her; she could have sworn a frown crossed behind his eyes. His lips thinned. She waited, her gaze steady.

Eventually, he replied, "I called on Stolemore this morning." He grasped her hand, wound her arm in his, and steered them back along the path.

"And?"

"He consented to tell me the name of the purchaser so intent on buying this house. One Montgomery Mountford. Do you know him?"

She looked ahead, mentally running through all her and her family's acquaintances. "No. He's not one of Humphrey's or Jeremy's colleagues, either—I help with their correspondence, and that name hasn't arisen."

When he said nothing more, she glanced at him. "Did you get an address?"

He nodded. "I'll go there and see what I can learn."

They'd reached the archway. She halted. "Where is it?"

He met her gaze; again she got the impression he was irritated. "Bloomsbury."

"Bloomsbury?" She stared. "That's where we used to live."

He frowned. "Before here?"

"Yes. I told you we moved here two years ago, when Humphrey inherited this house. For the four years before that, we lived in Bloomsbury. In Keppell Street." She caught his sleeve. "Perhaps it's someone from there, who for some reason . . ." She gestured. "Who knows why, but there must be a connection."

"Perhaps."

"Come on!" She set off for the parlor doors. "I'll come with you. There's plenty of time before lunch."

Tristan swallowed a curse and set off after her. "There's no need—"

"Of course there is!" She flicked him an impatient glance. "How will you know if this Mr. Mountford is in some odd way connected with our past?"

There was no good answer to that. He'd kissed her with the connected aims of further arousing her sensual curiosity and thus distracting her enough to allow him to pursue the burglar on his own, and had apparently failed on both counts. Swallowing his irritation, he followed her up the steps.

And through the French doors.

Exasperated, he halted. He wasn't used to following another's lead, let alone tripping on a lady's heels. "Miss Carling!"

She halted before the door. Head rising, spine stiffening, she faced him. Her eyes met his. "Yes?"

He struggled to mask his glare. Intransigence glowed in her fine eyes, invested her stance. He debated for an instant, then, like all experienced commanders when faced with the unexpected, adjusted his tactics.

"Very well." Disgusted, he waved her on. Giving way on a relatively minor point might well strengthen his hand later.

She sent him a beaming smile, then opened the door and led the way into the hall.

Lips compressed, he followed. It was only Bloomsbury, after all.

Indeed, being Bloomsbury, her presence on his arm proved a bonus. He'd forgotten that in the middle-class neighborhood into which Mountford's address took them, a couple attracted less attention than a single, well-dressed gentleman.

The house in Taviton Street was tall and narrow. It proved to be a lodging house. The landlady opened the door; neat and severe in dull black, she narrowed her eyes when he asked for Mountford.

"He's gone. Left last week."

After the foiled attempt at Number 12. Tristan affected mild surprise. "Did he say where he was going?"

"No. Just handed me my shillings on the way out." She sniffed. "I wouldn't have got them if I hadn't been right here."

Leonora edged in front of him. "We're trying to find a man who might know something of an incident in Belgravia. We're not even sure Mr. Mountford's the right man. Was he tall?"

The landlady considered her, then thawed. "Aye. Medium-tall." Her eyes flicked to Tristan. "Not as tall as your husband here, but tallish."

A faint blush tinged Leonora's fine skin; she hurried on. "Lightly built rather than heavy?"

The landlady nodded. "Black-haired, a bit too pale to be healthy. Brown eyes but a cold fish, if you ask me. Youngish in looks but in his middle twenties, I'd say. Thought a lot of himself, he did, and kept to himself, too."

Leonora glanced up, over her shoulder. "That sounds like the man we're searching for."

Tristan met her gaze, then looked at the landlady. "Did he have any visitors?"

"No, and that was strange. Usually, young gentlemen like that, I have to have a strong word about visitors, if you take my meaning."

Leonora smiled weakly. He drew her back. "Thank you for your help, ma'am."

"Aye, well, I hope you catch up with him and he can help you."

They stepped back off the tiny front porch; the landlady started to close the door, then stopped.

"Wait a minute—I just remembered." She nodded at Tristan. "He did have a visitor, once, but he didn't come in. Stood on the pavement just like you're doing and waited until Mr. Mountford came out to join him."

"What did this visitor look like? Did you get a name?"

"He didn't give one, but I remember thinking as I went up to fetch Mr. Mountford that I wouldn't need one. I just told him the gentleman was foreign, and sure enough, he knew who it was."

"Foreign?"

"Aye. He had an accent you couldn't miss. One of those that sounds like they're growling at you."

Tristan stilled. "What did he look like?"

She frowned, shrugged. "Just like any spic-and-span gentle-man. Very neat he was—I do remember that."

"How did he stand?"

The landlady's face eased. "Now that's something I can tell you—he stood like he had a poker strapped to him. He was that stiff, I thought as how he'd break if he bowed."

Tristan smiled charmingly. "Thank you. You've been a great help."

The landlady turned a soft shade of pink. She bobbed a curtsy. "Thank you, sir." After an instant, she shifted her gaze to Le-onora. "I wish you good luck, ma'am."

Leonora inclined her head graciously and allowed Trentham to steer her away. She half wished she'd asked the landlady what she was wishing her good luck with—finding Mountford, or keeping Trentham to his supposed wedding vows?

The man was a menace with that lethal smile.

She glanced up at him, then tucked the thought away along with the rest the day had brought. Better not to dwell on them while he was beside her.

He was pacing along, his expression impassive.

"What do you make of Mountford's visitor?"

Tristan glanced at her. "Make?"

Her eyes narrowed, her lips thinned; the look she bent on him told him she was more than seven. "What nationality do you think he is? You clearly have some idea."

The woman was annoyingly acute. Still, there was no harm in telling her. "German, Austrian, or Prussian. That peculiarly stiff stance plus the diction suggests one of the three."

She frowned, but said no more. He hailed a hackney and helped her in. They were bowling back to Belgravia when she asked, "Do you think the foreign gentleman could be behind the burglaries?" When he didn't immediately answer, she went on, "What possible thing could attract a German, Austrian, or Prussian to Number 14 Montrose Place?"

"That," he admitted, his voice low, "is something I'd dearly like to know."

She glanced sharply at him, but when he volunteered nothing more, she surprised him by looking ahead and keeping her counsel.

He handed her down outside Number 14; she waited while he paid the jarvey, then linked her arm in his as they turned to the gate. She kept her gaze down as he swung it open, and they passed through.

"We're giving a small dinner party tonight—just a few of Humphrey's and Jeremy's friends." She glanced briefly up at him, faint color in her cheeks. "I wondered if you would care to join us? It would give you a chance to form an opinion of the sort of secrets Humphrey or Jeremy might have stumbled upon."

He hid a cynical smile. Raised his brows in innocent consideration. "That's not a bad idea."

"If you're free . . . ?"

They'd reached the porch steps. Taking her hand, he bowed. "I would be delighted." He met her gaze. "At eight?"

She inclined her head. "Eight." As she turned away, her eyes touched his. "I'll look forward to seeing you then."

Tristan watched her climb the steps, waited until, without looking back, she disappeared through the door, then he turned and let his lips curve.

She was as transparent as glass. She wanted to question him over his suspicions regarding the foreign gentleman. . . .

His smile faded; his face resumed its customary impassive mien.

German, Austrian, or Prussian. He knew enough for those options to set warning bells clanging, but he didn't have enough information yet to do anything decisive—other than delve deeper.

Who knew? Mountford's acquaintance with the foreigner might be pure coincidence.

As he reached the front gate and swung it wide, a familiar sensation spread across the back of his shoulders.

He knew better than to believe in coincidence.

Leonora spent the remainder of the day in restless anticipation. Once she'd given her orders for dinner and airily informed Humphrey and Jeremy of their extra guest, she took refuge in the conservatory.

To calm her mind and decide on her best tack.

To revisit all she'd learned that morning.

Such as that Trentham was not averse to kissing her. And she was not averse to responding. That was certainly a change, for she'd never before found anything particularly compelling in the act. Yet with Trentham . . .

Sinking back against the cushions of the wrought-iron chair, she had to admit she would have happily followed wherever he led, at least within reason. Kissing him had proved quite pleasurable.

Just as well he'd stopped.

Eyes narrowing on a white orchid bobbing gently in the draft, she replayed all that had happened, all she'd felt. All she'd sensed.

He'd stopped not because he'd wished to, but because he'd

planned to. His appetite had wanted more, but his will had decreed he should end the kiss. She'd seen that brief clash in his eyes, caught the hard hazel gleam as his will had triumphed.

But why? She shifted again, very conscious of the way the brief interlude had remained, a nagging abrasion in her mind. Perhaps the answer lay there—the curtailing of the kiss had left her . . . dissatisfied. On some level she hadn't previously been aware of, unfulfilled.

Wanting more.

She frowned, absentmindedly tapped a finger on the table. With his kisses, Trentham had opened her eyes and engaged her senses. Teased them with a promise of what might be—and then left it at that.

Deliberately.

After telling her they should follow their noses.

She was a lady; he was a gentleman. Theoretically, it wouldn't be proper for him to press her further, not unless she invited his attentions.

Her lips curved cynically; she suppressed a soft snort. She might be inexperienced; she wasn't foolish. He hadn't curtailed their kiss because of any obedience to social mores. He'd stopped deliberately to entice, to build her awareness, to provoke her curiosity.

To make her want.

So that when next he wanted, and wanted more, wanted to take the next step along the path, she would be eager to accede.

Seduction. The word slipped into her mind, trailing the promise of illicit excitement and fascination.

Was Trentham seducing her?

She'd always known she was handsome enough; catching men's eyes had never been difficult. Yet she'd never before been interested enough to pay attention, to play any of the accepted games. Hadn't seen anything to enthuse her.

So now she was twenty-six, the despair of her aunt Mildred, definitely past her last prayers.

Trentham had come along and teased her senses awake, then left them alert and hungry for more. Anticipation of a sort she'd never before known had gripped her, but she wasn't yet sure what she wanted—what *she* wished their interaction to be.

Drawing a breath, she slowly exhaled. She didn't have to make any decisions yet. She could afford to wait, watch, and learn—to follow her nose and then make up her mind whether she approved of where that took her; she hadn't discouraged him, nor led him to believe she wasn't interested.

Because she was. Very interested.

She'd thought that aspect of life had passed her by, that circumstances had left those thrills beyond her reach.

For her, marriage was no longer an option—perhaps fate had sent Trentham as consolation.

When she turned and saw him crossing the drawing room toward her, her words echoed in her mind.

If this was consolation, what was the prize?

His broad shoulders were clothed in evening black, the coat a masterpiece of understated elegance. His grey silk waistcoat shone softly in the candlelight; a diamond pin winked from his cravat. As she was learning to expect, he'd avoided any intricacy; the cravat was tied in a simple style. Dark hair neatly brushed and sheening, framing his strong features, every element of his appearance—clothes, assurance, and manners—all proclaimed him a gentleman of the haut ton, accustomed to rule, accustomed to obedience.

Accustomed to his own way.

She curtsied and gave him her hand. He took it and bowed, lifted a brow at her as he straightened and raised her.

Challenge gleamed in his eyes.

She smiled, content to meet it, knowing she looked well in her apricot silk gown. "Permit me to introduce you, my lord."

He inclined his head, and anchored her hand on his sleeve, leaving his hand over hers.

Possessively.

Serene, with no hint of awareness showing, she led him to where Humphrey and his friends, Mr. Morecote and Mr. Cunningham, were already deep in discussion. They broke off to acknowledge Trentham, to exchange a few words, then she led him on, introducing him to Jeremy, Mr. Filmore, and Horace Wright.

She'd intended to pause there, to let Horace, the liveliest of their scholarly acquaintances, entertain them while she played the part of demure lady, but Trentham had other ideas. With his usual assumption of command, he eased her out of the conversation and guided her back to their initial position by the hearth.

None of the others, engrossed in their arguments, noticed.

Prompted by caution, she drew her hand from his sleeve and turned to face him. He caught her eye. His lips curved in a smile that showed white teeth, along with appreciation. Of her intention, but also of her—of her shoulders rising from the wide neckline of her gown, of her hair dressed in curls that tumbled about her ears and nape.

Watching his eyes drift over her, she felt her lungs tighten, fought to suppress a shiver—not of cold. Heat rose in her cheeks; she hoped he'd imagine it was due to the fire.

Lazily his gaze ambled upward and returned to hers.

The expression in his hard hazel eyes jolted her, made her breath seize. Then his lids swept down, thick lashes screening that disturbing gaze.

"Have you kept house for Sir Humphrey for long?"

His tone was the usual social drawl, languid and apparently bored. Managing to drag in a breath, she inclined her head and answered.

She used the opening to deflect their conversation into a description of the area in Kent in which they'd previously lived; paeans on the joys of the countryside seemed much safer than courting the fell intent in his eyes.

He responded with mention of his estate in Surrey, yet his eyes told her he was playing with her.

Like a very large cat with a particularly succulent mouse.

She kept her chin high, refused to acknowledge her awareness by the slightest sign. She breathed a sigh of relief when Castor appeared and announced the meal—only to realize that as the only lady present, Trentham would naturally lead her in.

Meeting his gaze directly, she placed her hand on his proffered sleeve and allowed him to steer her through the doors into the dining room.

He seated her at the end of the table, then took the chair on her right. Under cover of the jocular exchanges as the other gentlemen sat, he met her gaze, arched a brow.

"I'm impressed."

"Indeed?" She glanced around, as if to check that everything was in order, as if it was the table that had motivated his comment.

His lips curved dangerously. He leaned closer. Murmured, "I expected you to break before now."

She met his gaze. "Break?"

His eyes widened. "I felt certain you'd be determined to wring from me just what our next step should be."

His expression remained innocent; his eyes were anything but. Every utterance had two meanings, and she couldn't tell which he meant.

After a moment, she murmured, "I'd thought to restrain myself until later."

Looking down, she shook out her napkin as Castor placed her soup plate before her. Picking up her spoon, she coolly—much more coolly than she felt—met Trentham's eyes.

He held her gaze as the footman served him, then his lips curved. "That would no doubt be wise."

"My dear Miss Carling, I had meant to ask—"

Horace, on her other side, claimed her attention. Trentham turned to Jeremy with some inquiry. As usually occurred at such gatherings, the conversation rapidly turned to ancient writings. Leonora ate, sipped, and watched, surprised to see Trentham joining in, until she realized he was subtly probing for any suggestion of a secret find among the group.

She pricked up her ears; when the opportunity presented, she threw in a question, opening up yet another avenue of possibility among the ruins of ancient Persia. But no matter in which direction she or Trentham steered them, the six scholars were patently unaware of any potentially precious find.

Finally, the covers were removed and she rose. The gentlemen did, too. As was their habit, her uncle and Jeremy intended taking their friends to the library to consume port and brandy while poring over their latest research; normally, she retired at this point.

Naturally, Humphrey invited Trentham to join the male congregation.

Trentham's eyes met hers; she held his gaze, willing him to decline and allow her to conduct him to the door . . .

His lips curved; he turned to Humphrey. "Actually, I noticed you have a large conservatory. I've been thinking of adding one to my town house and wondered if I might prevail upon you to allow me to inspect yours."

"The conservatory?" Humphrey beamed genially and looked to her. "Leonora knows most about that—I'm sure she'll be pleased to show you around."

"Yes, of course. I'll be happy to . . ."

The tenor of Trentham's smile was pure seduction; he moved toward her. "Thank you, my dear." He looked back at Humphrey. "I will need to leave soon, however, so in case I don't see you again, I do thank you for your hospitality."

"It was entirely our pleasure, my lord." Humphrey shook hands.

Jeremy and the others exchanged farewells.

Then Trentham turned to her. Raised a brow and waved to the door. "Shall we?"

Her heart was beating faster, but she inclined her head calmly. And led him out.

The conservatory was her domain. Other than the gardener, no one else came there. It was her sanctuary, her refuge, her place of safety. As she led the way down the central aisle and heard the door click behind her, for the first time within the glass walls, she felt a *frisson* of danger.

Her slippers slapped softly on the tiles; her silk skirts swished. Lower yet came Trentham's soft tread as he followed her down the path.

Excitement and something sharper gripped her. "Through the winter, the room's heated by steam piped from the kitchen." Reaching the end of the path, halting in the deepest curve of the bow windows, she dragged in a breath. Her heart was thudding so loudly she could hear it, feel the pulse in her fingers. She reached out, touched one fingertip to the glass pane. "There are two layers of glass to help keep the heat in."

The night outside was black; she focused on the pane, and saw Trentham approaching, his image reflected in the glass. Two lamps burned low, one on either side of the room; they threw enough light to see one's way, to gain some idea of the plants.

Trentham closed the distance between them, his stride slow, a large, infinitely predatory figure; not for an instant did she doubt he was watching her. His face remained in shadow, until, halting close behind her, he lifted his gaze and met hers in the glass.

His eyes locked with hers.

His hands slid around her waist, closed, held her.

Her mouth was dry. "Are you really interested in conservatories?"

His gaze drifted down. "I'm interested in what this conservatory contains."

"The plants?" Her voice was a thread.

"No. You."

He turned her, and she was in his arms. He bent his head and covered her lips, as if he had the right. As if in some strange way she belonged to him.

Her hand came to rest on his shoulder. Gripped as he parted her lips and surged in. He held her anchored before him as he savored her mouth, unhurriedly, as if he had all the time in the world.

And intended taking it.

The engagement made her head spin. Pleasurably. Warmth spread beneath her skin; the taste of him—hard, male, dominant—sank into her.

For long moments, they both simply took, gave, explored. While something within them both tightened.

He broke the kiss, lifted his head, but only enough to draw her closer yet. His hand, spread across her back, burned through the fine silk of her gown. He looked into her eyes from beneath heavy, almost slumbrous lids.

"What was it you wanted to talk to me about?"

She blinked, valiantly struggled to reassemble her wits. Watched him watch her attempt it. Requesting enlightenment on what his next step would be would assuredly be tempting fate; he was waiting for the question.

"Never mind." Boldly, she reached up and drew his lips back to hers.

They were curved as they met hers, but he obliged; together they sank back into the exchange, let it draw them deeper. He drew back again.

"How old are you?"

The question feathered across her senses, into her mind. Her lips throbbed, hungry still; she brushed them across his.

"Does it matter?"

His lids lifted; their gazes touched. A moment passed. "Not materially."

She licked her lips, looked at his. "Twenty-six."

Those wicked lips curved. Once again, danger tickled her spine. "Old enough."

He drew her to him, against him; once again he bent his head. Once again she met him.

Tristan sensed her eagerness, her enthusiasm. That much, at least, he'd won. She'd handed him the situation on a platter; it had been too good to pass up—another chance to build her awareness, to expand her horizons. Enough at least so that next time he sought to distract her sensually he'd have some chance of success.

She'd snapped out of his hold too easily that afternoon, evaded his snare, shaken free of any lingering fascination far too readily for his liking.

His nature had always been dictatorial. Tyrannical. Predatory.

He came from a long line of hedonistic males who had, with few exceptions, always taken what they'd wanted.

He definitely wanted her but in a way that was somehow different, to a depth that was unfamilar. Something within him had changed, or perhaps more correctly emerged. Some part of him he'd never before had reason to wrestle with; never before had any woman called it forth.

She did. Effortlessly. But she had no idea of what she did, far less of what she tempted.

Her mouth was a delight, a cavern of honeyed sweetness, warm, beguiling, infinitely alluring. Her fingers tangled in his hair; her tongue dueled with his, quick to learn, eager to experience.

He gave her what she wanted, yet reined his demons back. She pressed closer, all but inviting him to deepen the kiss. An invitation he saw no reason to decline.

Slender, supple, subtly curvaceous, her softer limbs and softer flesh were a potent feminine prod to his totally masculine need. The feel of her in his arms fed his desire, stoked the sensual fires that had sprung up between them.

Play it by ear. Follow their noses. The simplest way forward.

She was so unlike the wife he'd imagined—the wife some part of him, was still stubbornly insisting was the sort he should be searching for—he wasn't yet ready to resign that position completely, at least not openly.

He sank deeper into her mouth, drew her closer still, savoring her warmth and its age-old promise.

Time enough to examine where they were once they'd got there; letting matters develop as they would while he dealt with the mysterious burglar was only wise. Regardless of whatever was growing between them, his priorities at this point were unwaveringly clear. Removing the threat hanging over her was his primary and overriding concern; nothing, but nothing, would deflect him from that goal—he was too experienced to permit any interference.

Time enough once he'd accomplished that mission and she was safe, secure, to turn his mind to dealing with the desire that some benighted fate had sown between them.

He could feel it welling, growing in strength, in intent, more ravenous with every minute she spent in his arms. It was time to call a halt; he had no compunction in shutting his demons in, in gradually drawing back from the exchange.

He lifted his head. She blinked dazedly up at him, then drew in a sharp breath and glanced around. He eased his hold and she stepped back, her gaze returning to his face.

Her tongue came out, traced her upper lip.

He was suddenly conscious of a definite ache. He straightened, drew breath.

"What—" She cleared her throat. "What are your plans in relation to the burglar?"

He looked at her. Wondered what it would take to totally strip her wits away. "The new Registry they're compiling at Somerset House. I want to learn who Montgomery Mountford is."

She thought for only a moment, then nodded. "I'll come with you. Two people looking will be faster than one."

He paused as if considering, then inclined his head. "Very well. I'll call for you at eleven."

She stared at him; he couldn't read her eyes but knew she was surprised.

He smiled. Charmingly.

Her expression turned suspicious.

His smile deepened into a genuine gesture, cynical and amused. Capturing her hand, he raised it to his lips. "Until tomorrow."

She met his eyes. Her brows rose haughtily. "Shouldn't you take some notes on the conservatory?"

He held her gaze, turned her hand, and placed a lingering kiss in her palm. "I lied. I already have one." Releasing her hand, he stepped back. "Remind me to show it to you sometime."

With a nod and a final challenging glance, he left her.

She was still suspicious when he arrived to take her up in his curricle the next morning.

He met her gaze, then handed her up; she stuck her nose in the air and pretended not to notice. He climbed up, took the reins, and set his greys pacing.

She looked well, striking in a deep blue pelisse buttoned over a walking gown of sky-blue. Her bonnet framed her face, her fine features touched with delicate color as if some artist had taken his brush to the finest porcelain. As he guided his skittish pair through the crowded streets, he found it hard to understand why she'd never married.

All the tonnish males in London couldn't be that blind. Had she hidden herself away for some reason? Or had her managing disposition, her trenchant self-reliance, her propensity to take the lead, proved too much of a challenge?

He was perfectly aware of her less-than-admirable traits, yet for some unfathomable reason, that part of him that she and only she had tempted forth insisted on seeing them as, not even anything so mild as a challenge—more a declaration of war. As if she was an opponent blatantly defying him. All nonsense, he knew, yet the conviction ran deep.

It had, in part, dictated his latest tack. He had agreed to her request to accompany him to Somerset House; he would have suggested it if she hadn't—there would be no danger there.

While with him, she was safe; if out of his sight, left to her own devices, she would undoubtedly try to come at the problem— *her* problem as she'd so trenchantly declared—from some other angle. Ordering her to cease investigating on her own, forcing her to do so, was beyond his present powers. Keeping her with him as much as possible was unquestionably the safest course.

Tacking down the Strand, he mentally winced. His rational arguments sounded so logical. The compulsion behind them— the compulsion he used such arguments to excuse—was novel and distinctly unsettling. Disconcerting. The sudden realization that the well-being of a lady of mature years and independent mind was now critical to his equanimity was just a tad shocking.

They arrived at Somerset House; leaving the curricle in the care of his tiger, they entered the building, footsteps echoing on the cold stone. An assistant peered at them from behind a counter; Tristan made his request and they were directed down a corridor to a cavernous hall. Regimented rows of wooden cabinets filled the space; each cabinet possessed multiple drawers.

Another assistant, advised of their search, pointed to a particular set of cabinets. The letters "MOU" were inscribed in gold on the polished wooden fronts. "I would suggest you start there."

Leonora walked briskly to the cabinets; he followed rather more slowly, thinking of what the drawers must contain, estimating how many certificates might be found in each drawer . . .

His conjecture was borne out when Leonora pulled open the first drawer. "Good Lord!" She stared at the mass of paper crammed into the space. "This could take days!"

He pulled open the drawer beside her. "Just as well you invited yourself along."

She made a sound suspiciously like a suppressed snort and started checking the names. It wasn't as bad as they'd feared; in short order they located the first Mountford, but the number of people born in England with that surname was depressingly large. They persevered, and ultimately discovered that yes, indeed, there was a Montgomery Mountford.

"But"—Leonora stared at the birth certificate— "this means he's seventy-three!"

She frowned, then pushed the certificate back, looked at the next, and the next. And the next.

"Six of them," she muttered, her exasperated tone confirming what he'd expected. "And not one of them could possibly be him. The first five are too old, and this one is thirteen."

He put a hand briefly on her shoulder. "Check carefully on either side in case a certificate's been misfiled. I'll check with the assistant."

Leaving her frowning, flicking through the certificates, he walked to the supervisor's desk. A quiet word and the supervisor sent one of his assistants scurrying. Three minutes later a dapper individual in the sober garb of a government functionary arrived.

Tristan explained what he was looking for.

Mr. Crosby bowed. "Indeed, my lord. However, I do not believe that name is one of those protected. If you'll allow me to verify?"

Tristan waved, and Crosby walked down the room.

Dispirited, Leonora shut the drawers. She returned to his side, and they waited until Crosby reappeared.

He bowed to Leonora, then looked at Tristan. "It is as you suspected, my lord. Unless there's a certificate missing—which

I very much doubt—then there is no Montgomery Mountford of the age you're searching for."

Tristan thanked him and steered Leonora outside. They paused on the steps and she turned to him.

Met his gaze. "Why would someone use an assumed name?"

"Because," he pulled on his driving gloves, felt his jaw set, "he's up to no good." Retaking her elbow, he urged her down the steps. "Come—let's go for a drive."

He took her into Surrey, to Mallingham Manor, now his home. He did so impulsively, he supposed to distract her, something he felt was increasingly necessary. A felon using an assumed name boded no good at all.

From the Strand, he headed across the river, immediately alerting her to the change in direction. But when he explained he needed to attend to business at his estate so he could return to town free to pursue the question of Montgomery Mountford, phantom burglar, she accepted the arrangement readily.

The road was direct and in excellent condition; the greys were fresh and eager to stretch their legs. He turned the curricle in between the elegant wrought-iron gates in good time for luncheon. Setting the pair pacing up the drive, he noted Leonora's attention was fixed on the huge house ahead, standing amid manicured lawns and formal parterres. The gravel drive swept up to a circular forecourt before the imposing front doors.

He followed her gaze; he suspected he saw the house as she did, for he'd yet to grow used to the idea that this was now his, his home. A manor house had stood on the spot for centuries, but his great-uncle had renovated and refurbished with zeal. What now faced them was a Palladian mansion built of creamy sandstone with pediments over every long window and mock battlements above the long line of the facade.

The greys swept into the forecourt. Leonora exhaled. "It's beautiful. So elegant."

He nodded, allowing himself to acknowledge it, permitting himself to admit that his great-uncle had got something right.

A stable lad came running as he stepped to the ground. Leaving the curricle and pair to his tiger's care, he helped Leonora down, then led her up the steps.

Clitheroe, his great-uncle's butler, now his, opened the doors before they reached them, beaming in his usual genial way. "Welcome home, my lord." Clitheroe included Leonora in his smile.

"Clitheroe, this is Miss Carling. We'll be here for luncheon, then I'll tend to business before we return to town."

"Indeed, my lord. Shall I inform the ladies?"

Shrugging out of his greatcoat, Tristan suppressed a grimace. "No. I'll take Miss Carling to meet them. I assume they're in the morning room?"

"Yes, my lord."

He lifted Leonora's pelisse from her shoulders and gave it to Clitheroe. Placing her hand on his sleeve, with his other hand he gestured down the hall. "I believe I mentioned that I had various females—family and connections—resident here?"

She glanced at him. "You did. Are they cousins like the others?"

"Some, but the two most notable are my great-aunts Hermione and Hortense. At this time of day, the group are invariably to be found in the morning room." He met her eyes. "Gossiping."

He paused and threw open a door. As if to prove his point, the flurry of feminine chatter within immediately ceased.

As he conducted her into the long room filled with light courtesy of a succession of windows along one wall, all looking out over a pastoral scene of gentle lawns leading down to a distant lake, Leonora found herself subjected to wide-eyed, unblinking stares. His ladies—she counted eight—were positively agog.

They were not, however, disapproving.

That was instantly apparent as Trentham, with his usual polished grace, introduced her to his eldest great-aunt, Lady Hermione Wemyss. Lady Hermione beamed and bade her a sincere welcome; Leonora curtsied and responded.

And so it went around the circle of lined faces, all exhibiting various degrees of joy. Just as the six old ladies in his London house had been sincerely thrilled to meet her, so, too, were these women. Her first thought, that perhaps, for whatever reason, they did not venture into society and so were starved for visitors, and therefore would have been delighted with whoever had come to call, died a quick death; as she sank onto the chair Trentham placed for her, Lady Hortense launched into an account of their latest round of visits and the excitement surrounding the local church fete.

"Always something happening around here, you know," Hortense confided. "Not dull at all."

The others nodded and eagerly chimed in, telling her of the local sights and the amenities of the estate and village before inviting her to tell them something of herself.

Completely assured in such company, she responded easily, telling them of Humphrey and Jeremy and their endeavors, and Cedric's gardens—all the sorts of things older ladies liked to know.

Trentham had remained standing by her chair, one hand on its back; now he stepped back. "If you'll excuse me, ladies, I'll rejoin you for luncheon."

They all beamed and nodded; Leonora glanced up and met

his gaze. He inclined his head, then his attention was claimed by Lady Hermione; he bent to listen to her. Leonora couldn't hear what was said. With a nod, Trentham straightened, then walked from the room; she watched his elegant back disappear through the door.

"My dear Miss Carling, do tell us—"

Leonora turned back to Hortense.

She might have felt deserted, but that proved impossible in the present company. The old ladies quite plainly set themselves to entertain her; she couldn't help but respond. Indeed, she found herself intrigued by the myriad snippets they let fall of Trentham and his predecessor, his great-uncle Mortimer. She put together enough to understand the route by which Trentham had inherited, heard from Hermione of her brother's sour disposition and disaffection with Trentham's side of the family.

"Always insisted they were wastrels." Hermione snorted. "Nonsense, of course. He was just jealous they could jaunter all over while he had to stay at home and mind the family acres."

Hortense nodded sagely. "And Tristan's behavior these past months has proved how wrong Mortimer was." She caught Leonora's eye. "Very sound man, Tristan. Not one to shirk his duties, whatever they might be."

This pronouncement was greeted with wise nods all around. Leonora suspected it had some significance beyond the obvious, but before she could think of any way to inquire tactfully, a colorful description of the vicar and the rectory household distracted her.

Some part of her liked, even reveled in the simple gossip of country life. When the butler arrived to announce that luncheon awaited them, she rose with an inward start, realizing how much she'd enjoyed the unexpected interlude.

Although the ladies had been pleasant and gentle companions, it was the subject matter that had held her, the talk of Trentham and the general round of country events.

She had, she realized, missed it.

Trentham was waiting in the dining room; he pulled out a chair and seated her by his side.

The meal was excellent; the conversation never flagged, yet neither was it strained. Despite its unusual composition, the household seemed relaxed and content.

At the end of the meal, Tristan caught Leonora's eye, then pushed back his chair and glanced around the table. "If you'll excuse us, there are a few last matters I need to attend to, and then we must return to town."

"Oh, indeed."

"Of course—so nice to meet you, Miss Carling."

"Do get Trentham to bring you down again, my dear."

He rose, taking Leonora's hand, helping her to her feet. Conscious of impatience, he waited while she exchanged farewells with his tribe of old dears, then led her out of the room and into his private wing.

By mutual agreement, the resident ladies did not intrude into his private domain; conducting Leonora through the archway and into the long corridor in some irrational way soothed him.

He'd left her with the group knowing they'd keep her amused, reasoning he'd be able to concentrate on his business affairs and deal with them more expeditiously if spared her physical presence. He hadn't reckoned with his irrational compulsion—the one that needed to know not just where she was, but how she was faring.

Throwing open a door, he ushered her into his study. "If you'll take a seat for a few minutes, I have a few matters to deal with, then we can be on our way."

She inclined her head and walked to the armchair angled before the hearth. He watched her settle comfortably, eyes on the blaze. His gaze rested on her for a moment, then he turned and crossed to his desk.

With her in the room—safe, content, and quiet—he found it easier to concentrate; he quickly approved various expenditures, then settled to check a number of reports. Even when she rose and walked to the window to stand looking out on the vista of lawns and trees, he barely glanced up, just enough to register what she was doing, then returned to his work.

Fifteen minutes later, he'd cleared his desk sufficiently to be able to remain in London for the next several weeks, and single-mindedly devote his attention to her phantom burglar. And, subsequently, if matters continued to head in that direction, to her.

Pushing back his chair, he looked up—and found her leaning against the window frame, watching him.

Her periwinkle blue gaze was steady. "You don't appear the least like one of society's lions."

He held her gaze, equally direct. "I'm not."

"I thought all earls—especially unmarried ones—were by definition."

He lifted a brow as he rose. "This earl never expected the title." He crossed toward her. "I never imagined having it."

She raised a brow back, eyes quizzing as he reached her. "And the unmarried?"

He looked down at her, after a moment said, "As you've just noted, that adjective only gains status when attached to the title."

She studied his face, then looked away.

He followed her gaze out of the window to the peaceful scene beyond. He glanced down at her. "We have time for a stroll before starting back."

She glanced at him, then looked back at the gently rolling landscape. "I was just thinking how much I've missed country pleasures. I would like a stroll."

He led her into an adjoining parlor and out through French doors onto a secluded terrace. Steps led down to the lawn, still green despite winter's harshness. They started to amble; his gaze on her, he asked, "Would you like your pelisse?"

She looked at him, smiled, shook her head. "It's not that cold in the sunshine, weak though it is."

The bulk of the house protected them from the breeze. He glanced back at it, then faced forward. And found her watching him.

"It must have been a shock to discover you'd inherited all that"—her wave indicated more than the roof and walls—"given you hadn't expected it."

"It was."

"You seem to have managed quite well. The ladies seem thoroughly content."

A smile touched his lips. "Oh, they are." His bringing her here had ensured that.

He looked ahead to the lake. She followed his gaze. They walked to the shore, then idled along the bank. Leonora spotted a family of ducks. She stopped, shading her eyes with her hand to better see them.

Pausing a few steps away, he studied her, let his gaze dwell on the picture she made standing by his lake in the dappled sunshine, and felt a content he hadn't before experienced warm him.

It seemed senseless to pretend that the impulse to bring her here hadn't been driven by a primitive instinct to have her safe behind walls that were his.

Seeing her here, being with her here, was like discovering another piece of a still scattered jigsaw.

She fitted.

How well left him uneasy.

He was normally impatient of inaction, yet was content to walk by her side, doing essentially nothing. As if being with her made it permissible for him to simply be, as if she was sufficient reason for his existence, at least in that moment. No other woman had had that effect on him. The realization only escalated his need to nullify the threat to her.

As if sensing his suddenly hardening mood, she glanced at him, wide eyes searching his face. He slipped on his mask and smiled easily.

She frowned.

Before she could ask, he took her arm. "Let's go this way."

The rose garden even in hibernation distracted her. He led her on into the extensive formal shrubbery, slowly circling back toward the house. A small marble temple, austerely classical, stood at the center of the shrubbery.

Leonora had forgotten just how pleasant walking in a large, well-designed and well-tended garden could be. In London, Cedric's fantastical creation lacked the soothing vistas, the magnificent sweeps that could only be achieved in the country, and the parks were too limited in view and too crowded. Certainly not soothing. Here, walking with Trentham, peace slid like a drug through her veins, as if a well that had been almost dry was refilling.

Placed at the junction of the shrubbery paths, the temple was simply perfect. Lifting her skirts, she climbed the steps. Inside, the floor was a delicate mosaic in black, grey, and white. The Ionic columns that supported the domed roof were white veined with grey.

Turning, she looked back at the house, framed by the high hedges. The perspective was superb. "It's magnificent." She smiled at Trentham as he halted beside her. "No matter any difficulties, you can't be sorry that this is yours."

She extended her arms, her hands, including the gardens, the lake, and the surrounding countryside in the statement.

He met her gaze. Held it for a long moment, then quietly said, "No. I'm not sorry."

She caught his tone, the existence of some deeper meaning in his words. She let her frown show.

His lips, until then straight, as serious as his expression, curved, she thought a touch wryly. Reaching out, he shackled her wrist, then slid his hand down to close about hers.

He lifted it, raised her wrist to his lips. Eyes holding hers, he kissed, let his lips linger as her pulse leapt, then throbbed.

As if that had been a signal he'd been waiting for, he reached for her, drew her closer. She permitted it, went into his arms, more than curious, openly eager.

He bent his head and her lashes fluttered down; she lifted her lips and he took them. Smoothly slid between, took possession of her mouth, and her senses.

She yielded them readily, totally unafraid; she was more than confident in her reading of him—he would never harm her. But where he was heading with his intoxicating kisses—what came next, and when—she still didn't know; she had no experience on which to draw.

She'd never been seduced before.

That that was his ultimate aim she accepted; she could see no other reason for his actions. He'd asked her age, stated she was old enough. At twenty-five, she'd been deemed on the shelf; now twenty-six, she was—clearly to his mind as well as hers— her own woman. A spinster whose life was no one's business but her own; her actions would impinge on no one else, her decisions were her own to make.

Not that she was necessarily going to accede to his wishes. She would make up her mind if and when the time came.

It wouldn't come today, not in an open temple visible from his house. Free of any prospect of having to think, she sank into his arms and kissed him back.

Dueled with him, let herself flow into the exchange, felt heat rise between them, along with that fascinating tension—a tense-ness that sent excitement rippling along her nerves, sent anticipa-tion coursing beneath her skin.

Her body tightened; heat welled and pooled.

Emboldened, she pushed her hands up, over his shoulders, slid them to his nape. Splaying her fingers, she speared them slowly through his dark locks. Thick and heavy, they slid through and over her fingers, even as his tongue slid deeper.

He angled his head and drew her nearer, until her breasts were crushed to his chest, her thighs brushing his, her skirts tangling around his boots. His arms locked around her, lifting her against him; his strength captured her. The kiss deepened into a melding of mouths, a far more intimate exchange. She half expected to be shocked—felt she should be—yet instead all she knew was that burgeoning heat, a certain assuredness both in him and her, and a dizzying hunger.

That escalating hunger was theirs—not hers, not his, but something growing between them.

It beckoned.

Enticed.

Fed Tristan's need.

But it was her need that he played to, that he watched and gauged, that ultimately had him easing his hold on her, gathering her in one arm while he raised a hand to her face. To trace her cheek, frame her jaw, hold her still while he methodically plundered. Yet at no stage did he seek to overwhelm her; that, he knew, was not the route to ensnare her.

To seduce her was an instinct he no longer sought to fight. He eased his fingers from the delicate curve of her jaw and sent them lower, flirting with her senses until her lips turned demanding, then caressing lightly, enough to educate her imagination, enough to feed her hunger, not enough to sate it.

Her breasts swelled beneath his tracing touch; he ached to take more, to claim more, but held back. Strategy and tactics were his strong suit; in this as in all things, he was playing to win.

When her fingers clenched on his skull, he consented to palm her breast, to fondle, still lightly, still inciting rather than satisfying. He felt her senses leap, sensed her nerves tightening. Felt her nipple pebble against his palm.

Had to drag a breath deep and hold it, then, gradually, step by step, he eased back from the kiss. Gradually unclenched the muscles locking her to him. Gradually let her surface from the kiss.

But he didn't take his hand from her breast.

When he released her lips and lifted his head, he was still lightly tracing, back and forth across the swell, teasingly circling her nipple. Her lashes fluttered, then she opened her eyes, looked into his.

Her lips were lightly swollen, her eyes wide.

He looked down.

She followed his gaze.

Her lungs locked.

He counted the seconds before she remembered to breathe, knew she had to be dizzy. But she didn't step back.

It was he who shifted his caressing hand to her upper arm, grasped gently, then slid his hand down to hers. He lifted it to his lips, met her eyes as, faint color in her cheeks, she looked up at him.

He smiled, but hid the true tenor of the gesture. "Come." Setting her hand on his sleeve, he turned her to the house. "We need to start back to town."

The journey was a godsend. Leonora took full advantage of the hour during which Trentham was engrossed with his cattle, smoothly tacking through the traffic that grew heavier as they entered the capital, to calm her mind. To try to restore—reclaim—her customary assurance.

She glanced at him often, wondering what he was thinking, but other than an occasional enigmatic glance—leaving her certain he was partly amused but still quite intent—he said nothing. Aside from all else, his tiger was up behind them, too close to allow any private words.

Indeed, she wasn't sure she wanted any. Any explanation. Not that he'd shown any sign of giving her one, but that seemed to be part of the game.

Part of the building exhilaration, the excitement. The craving.

That last she hadn't expected, but she certainly felt it—could now understand what she never had before—what caused women, even ladies of eminent sense, to cater to a gentleman's physical demands.

Not that Trentham had made any real demands. Yet. That was her point.

If she could know when he would, and what those demands might be, she'd be better placed to plan her response.

As matters were . . . she was left to speculate.

She was sunk in that endeavor when the curricle slowed. She blinked and looked around, and discovered they were home. Trentham drew the curricle up before Number 12. Handing the reins to the tiger, he climbed down, then lifted her to the pavement.

Hands about her waist he looked down at her.

She looked back, and made no attempt to move away.

His lips curved. He opened them—

Footsteps crunched on gravel nearby. They both turned to look.

Gasthorpe, the majordomo, a thickset man with crisp salt-and-pepper hair, came hurrying down the path from Number 12. Reaching them, he bowed. "Miss Carling."

She'd made a point of meeting Gasthorpe the day after he'd taken up residence. She smiled and inclined her head.

He turned to Trentham. "My lord, forgive the interruption, but I wanted to make sure you called in. The carters have delivered the furniture for the first floor. I would be grateful if you would cast your eye over the items, and advise me if you approve."

"Yes, of course. I'll be in in a moment—"

"Actually"—Leonora gripped Trentham's arm, drawing his gaze to her face—"I would love to see what you've done to Mr. Morrissey's house. May I come in while you check the furniture?" She smiled. "I would be happy to help—a lady's eye is often quite different in such matters."

Trentham looked at her, then glanced at Gasthorpe. "It's rather late. Your uncle and brother—"

"Won't have noticed I left the house." Her curiosity was rampant; she kept her eyes wide, fixed on Trentham's face.

His lips twisted, then set; again he glanced at Gasthorpe. "If you insist." She took his arm and he turned toward the path. "But only the first floor has been furnished as yet."

She wondered why he was being so uncharacteristically diffident, then put it down to being a gentleman more or less in charge of fitting out a house. Something he no doubt felt ill equipped to do.

Ignoring his reticence, she swept up the path beside him. Gasthorpe had gone ahead and stood holding the door. She stepped over the threshold and paused to look around. She'd last glimpsed the hall in the shadows of night, when the painters' cloths had been down, the room stripped and bare.

The transformation was now complete. The hall was surprisingly light and airy, not dark and gloomy—an impression she associated with gentlemen's clubs. However, there was not a single item of delicacy to soften the austere, starkly elegant lines; no sprigged wallpaper, not even any scrollwork. It was rather cold, almost bleak in its eschewing of all things feminine, yet she could see men—men like Trentham—gathering there.

They wouldn't notice the softness that was missing.

Trentham didn't offer to show her the downstairs rooms; with a gesture, he directed her to the stairs. She climbed them, noting the high gloss on the banister, the thickness of the stair carpet. Clearly expense had not been a consideration.

On the first floor, Trentham moved past her and led the way to the room at the front of the house. A large mahogany table stood in the middle of the floor, eight matching chairs upholstered in ocher velvet surrounding it. A sideboard stood against one wall, a long bureau against another.

Tristan glanced around, swiftly surveying their meeting room. All was as they'd envisaged it; catching Gasthorpe's eye, he nodded, then with a wave, directed Leonora back across the landing.

The small office with its desk, bank of drawers, and two chairs, need no more than a cursory glance. They moved on to the room at the back of the house—the library.

The merchant from whom they'd purchased the furniture, Mr. Meecham, was overseeing the siting of a tall bookcase. He glanced briefly their way, but immediately returned his attention to directing his two assistants, waving first one way, then that, until they had the heavy bookcase positioned to his satisfaction. They set it down with audible grunts.

Meecham turned to Tristan with a wide smile. "Well, my lord." He bowed, then looked around with patent satisfaction. "I flatter myself you and your friends will be excellently comfortable here."

Tristan saw no reason to argue; the room looked inviting, clean, and uncluttered yet with plenty of deep armchairs dotted about and numerous side tables waiting to support a glass of fine brandy. There were two bookcases, presently empty. Although the room was the library, it was unlikely they would retire here to read novels. News sheets assuredly, periodicals and reports, and sporting magazines; the library's primary function would be as a place of quiet relaxation where if any words were spoken, they would be in a deep murmur.

Glancing around, he could see them all here, private, quiet, but companionable in their silence. Returning his gaze to Meecham, he nodded. "You've done well."

"Indeed, indeed." Gratified, Meecham waved his two workers from the room. "We'll leave you to enjoy what we've thus far wrought. I'll have the rest of the items delivered within the week."

He bowed low; Tristan nodded a dismissal.

Gasthorpe caught his eye. "I'll see Mr. Meecham out, my lord."

"Thank you, Gasthorpe—I won't need you again. We'll see ourselves out."

With a nod and a speaking look, Gasthorpe left.

Tristan inwardly winced, but what could he do? Explaining to Leonora that females were not supposed to be inside the club, not beyond the small front parlor, would inevitably lead to questions he—and his fellow club members—would much rather were never asked. Answering would be too risky, akin to tempting fate.

Much better to give ground when it didn't really matter and couldn't really hurt than explain what was behind the formation of the Bastion Club.

Leonora had drifted from his side. After trailing her fingers along the back of one armchair, noting the amenities, he thought with approval, she'd wandered to the window and now stood looking out.

At her own back garden.

He waited, but she didn't return. Heaving an inward, somewhat resigned sigh, he crossed the room, the rich Turkish carpet muffling his steps. He stopped by the side of the window, leaned against the frame.

She turned her head and met his gaze.

"You used to stand here and watch me, didn't you?"

He considered every option before replying, "At times."

Her eyes remained steady on his, then she looked back at the garden. "That's how you knew who I was when I ran into you that first day."

To that he said nothing, then was left wondering what track her mind was taking.

After a long moment, her gaze fixed beyond the glass, she murmured, "I'm not very good at this business." She gestured briefly, her hand waving between them. "I haven't had any real experience."

He inwardly blinked. "So I'd assumed."

She turned her head, met his gaze. "You'll have to teach me."

As she faced him, he straightened. She closed the distance between them. He frowned, his hands instinctively circling her waist. "I'm not certain—"

"I'm perfectly willing to learn." Her gaze dropped to his lips; hers curved, innocently sensual. "Even eager."

Lifting her gaze to his eyes, she stretched upward, palms to his chest, lifted her lips to his. Softly murmured, "But you know that."

And kissed him.

The invitation was so blatant it captured him utterly. Temporarily suspended his wits, left him at his senses' mercy.

And his senses were merciless. They wanted more.

More of her, of the soft, luscious haven of her mouth, of her pliant, innocently beguiling lips. Of her body, tentatively yet determinedly pressing against his much harder frame.

That last shook him, shook enough of his wits into place for him to take control. What she was thinking he didn't know, but with her lips on his, her mouth all his, her tongue dueling increasingly hotly with his, he couldn't spare enough of his mind to follow the contortions of hers.

Later.

Now . . . all he could do—all he could force his body and senses to do—was follow her lead.

And teach her more.

He let her press close, gathered her fully into his arms. Let her feel his body hardening against hers, let her sense what she invoked, the response her body, supple, curvaceous and blatantly tempting, all female softness and feminine heat, provoked.

During their wanderings through the house, she'd opened her pelisse. Sliding a hand beneath the heavy wool, he set his palm to her breast. Not lightly tracing as he had before, but claiming possessively. Giving her now what their earlier interlude had teasingly promised, tauntingly foretold.

She gasped, clung, but not once did she waver; her lips cleaved to his, innocently demanding. Unfrightened, unshocked. Determined. Enthralled. She was caught, totally fascinated. He deepened the kiss, touched, caressed.

Felt the flames start to smolder. Felt desire slowly rise, stretch languidly, then reach out in hunger.

Leonora felt it, too, although she couldn't name it, that wash of heated emptiness deep within. It infused her, and him, intrigued and beckoned. Ensnared. She had to get closer, somehow deeper into the exchange; sliding her hands up, she twined them about his neck, sighed when the movement pressed her breast firmly into his hard palm.

His hand closed and her senses rocked. His fingers shifted, seeking, finding, and her wits, her very being, stilled.

Then fractured, shattered, as those knowing fingers tightened, tightened . . . until she gasped through their kiss.

His fingers eased and heat flooded her, a rushing tide she'd never felt before. Her breasts swelled; the bodice of her walking dress was suddenly too tight. The thin film of her chemise chafed.

He seemed to know; he dealt with her bodice's tiny buttons with practiced ease, and she could breathe again. Only to catch her breath on a rush of pleasure, on a spike of anticipation when he boldly slid his hand beneath the gaping gown to caress, to fondle. His touch screened by fine silk, to build her yearning once again, so that she ached for more definite contact. Burned to feel his skin against hers, desperate to feel still more.

Her lips were hungry, her demands clear. Tristan couldn't resist. Didn't try.

Two quick tugs and her chemise was loose; hooking one finger between her full breasts he drew the fine fabric down.

Then set his hand to her bounty.

Felt the deep shudder that racked her in his soul.

He closed his hand, hungrily possessive, and her heart leapt. His followed.

Into a furnace of greedy, eager giving, of sensual taking, of appreciation, and a dawning recognition of mutual need.

Hands and lips fed the hunger, eager, inciting. Enthralled.

There was a change in their interaction. He sensed it, surprised to find himself, although still in control, no longer dictating their play. Her developing assurance, her interest and understanding, invested her lips, directed the way she met him, the slow sensuous stroking of her tongue against his, the seductive caress of her fingers in his hair, the openly confident, determinedly fascinated way she sank against him, all supple limbs and soft heat, bathing in the flames of a mutual conflagration he'd never imagined sharing with an innocent woman.

Lust and a virtuous woman.

The thought echoed in his brain even while she filled his senses. She was more than he'd expected even while he was something other than she'd thought. Something beyond her experience, yet she was something beyond his.

The flames between them were definite, real, scorching, firing thoughts of passion, of greater intimacy, of the satiation of that mutual need.

It hadn't occurred to him that they might travel this far so soon. He in no way regretted it, yet . . .

Deeply entrenched instincts had him drawing back, easing her back. Slowing their caresses, lightening them. Letting the flames gradually subside to a simmer.

He lifted his head, looked at her eyes. Watched her lashes rise, then met her clear, startlingly blue gaze.

Read in it not shock, not the slightest hint of retreat or fluster, but instead an awakened interest. A question.

What next?

He knew, but this was not, yet, the time to explore that

avenue. He recalled where they were, what his mission was. He felt his face harden. "It's getting dark. I'll see you home."

Leonora inwardly frowned, but then her gaze slipped past his shoulder to the window; night had indeed fallen. She blinked, stepped back as he released her. "I hadn't realized it was so late."

Naturally not; her wits had been in a whirl. A pleasurable whirl, one that had opened her eyes considerably more. Ignoring her chemise, doggedly refusing to let her mind dwell on what had just occurred—later, when he wasn't around to see her blushes—she adjusted and refastened her bodice, then buttoned her pelisse.

His gaze, sharp as ever, hadn't left her. She lifted her head and met it directly. He searched her eyes, then raised a brow. "I take it"—his gaze shifted from her to sweep the room—"you approve of the decor?"

She raised a haughty brow back. "I daresay it's eminently suitable for your purpose." *Whatever that might be.*

Head high, she swung toward the door. She felt his gaze on her back as she crossed the room, then he stirred and followed.

She had very little experience of men. Especially not men like Trentham. That, Leonora felt, was her greatest weakness, one that left her at an unfair disadvantage whenever she was with him.

Stifling a humph, she dragged her silky quilt about her and climbed into the old armchair before the fire blazing in her room. It was icy outside, too cold even to sit in the conservatory and think. Besides, a quilt and an armchair before the fire seemed much more suitable given the issues she was determined to think about.

Trentham had escorted her home and requested an interview with her uncle and Jeremy. She'd taken him to the library, listened while he questioned them as to whether they'd stumbled onto any possibility that might be the burglar's aim. She could have told him that neither of them would have spared a thought for the burglar let alone his objective since he, Trentham, had last mentioned the matter—and so it had proved. Neither had any ideas or suggestions; the puzzled look in their eyes clearly stated they were surprised he was still intersted in the affair at all.

He saw it as well as she; his jaw set, but he thanked them and politely enough took his leave.

Only she had sensed his disapproval; her uncle and brother had remained, as ever, determinedly oblivious.

With Henrietta padding beside her, canine appreciation for Trentham transparent, she'd walked with him to the front hall. She'd dismissed Castor earlier; they'd been alone in the soft lamplight, in a place in which she'd always felt secure.

Then Trentham had looked at her, and she hadn't felt safe at all. She'd felt hot. Warmth had spread beneath her skin; a light flush rose to her cheeks. All in response to the look in his eyes, to the thoughts she could see behind them.

They'd been standing close. He'd lifted a hand, traced her cheek, then slid one finger beneath her chin and tipped up her face. Set his lips to hers in a swift, unfulfilling kiss.

Raising his head, he'd caught her gaze. Held it for a moment, then murmured, "Take care."

He'd released her just as Castor came hurrying from the nether regions. He'd departed without a backward glance, leaving her to wonder, to speculate. To plan.

If she dared.

That, she decided, snuggling into the quilt's warmth, was the crucial question. Did she dare satisfy her curiosity? It was, in truth, more than curiosity; she had a burning desire to know, to experience all that could lie between a man and a woman physically and emotionally.

She'd always *expected* to learn those facts at some point in her life. Instead, fate and society had conspired to keep her ignorant, the commonly accepted decree holding that only married ladies could participate, experience, and thus know.

All well and good if one was a young girl. At twenty-six, she no longer fitted that description; to her mind, the proscription no longer applied.

No one had ever advanced any explanation of the moral logic behind society's acceptance that married ladies, once they'd presented their husbands with an heir, could indulge in affairs as long as they remained discreet.

She intended to be the very soul of discretion, and she had no vows to break.

If she wished to avail herself of Trentham's offer to introduce her to the pleasures she'd thus far been denied, there were, in her view, no social conventions she need consider. As for the somewhat indefinite quibble of her falling with child, there had to be some way around such things or London would be awash with by-blows and half the ton's matrons perpetually pregnant; she was sure Trentham would know how to manage.

Indeed, it was in part his experience, that air of competence and expertise, that attracted her, that had made it possible that afternoon for her to grasp the invitation he'd offered.

Clearly, she'd read that invitation correctly; the subtle, step-by-step advancement of their engagement, from touch, to kiss, to sensual caress confirmed it. Now she'd taken the first step into his arms, he'd shown her enough for her to have some inkling of what she'd missed, of what lay ahead.

He'd introduced her to a degree of intimacy that was clearly the prelude to all she wished to know. He was willing to be her partner in adventure, her mentor in that sphere. To guide her, teach her, show her. In return, of course . . . but she understood that and, after all, who was she saving herself for?

Marriage and its attendant dependency was a yoke that simply didn't fit her. Having accepted that years ago, her only real regret, a silent and somewhat suppressed regret, had been that she would never experience physical intimacy or that particular brand of sensual pleasure.

Now Trentham had appeared, dangling temptation before her.

Eyes on the flames glowing hotly in the hearth, she considered reaching for it.

If she didn't act now and grab the chance fate had finally consented to allow her, who knew for how long his interest, and therefore his offer, would stand? Military gentlemen were not renowned for their constancy; she had firsthand experience of that.

Her mind slid away, assessing the possibilities, distracted by them. The fire slowly died to red-hot embers.

When the chill in the air finally penetrated her absorption, she realized she'd made her decision. Her mind had been engrossed, had been for some time, with two questions.

How was she to convey that decision to Trentham?

And how could she manage their interaction so that the reins remained in her hands?

Tristan received the letter by the first post the next morning.

After the customary salutations, Leonora had written:

With respect to the item the burglar seeks, I have decided it would be wise to search my late cousin Cedric's workshop. The room is quite extensive, but has been closed up for some years, indeed, since before we took possession of the house. It may be that a determined search will turn up some item of real but esoteric value. I will commence my search immediately after luncheon; should I discover anything of note, I will of course inform you.

Yours, etc.

Leonora Carling

He read the letter three times. His well-honed instincts assured him there was more to it than the superficial meaning of the words, yet her hidden agenda eluded him. Deciding he'd been a covert operative for too long and was now seeing plots where there patently were none, he set the letter aside and put his mind determinedly to business.

His, and hers.

He dealt with hers first, listing the various avenues available for identifying the man masquerading as Montgomery Mountford. After considering the list, he wrote a summons and sent a footman to deliver it, then settled to write a series of letters the recipients would prefer not to receive. Nevertheless, debts were debts, and he was calling them in in a good cause.

An hour later, Havers conducted a nondescript, rather shabby individual into the study. Tristan sat back and waved him to a chair. "Good morning, Colby. Thank you for coming."

The man was wary, but not servile. He ducked his head and sat in the chair, glancing quickly around as Havers closed the door, then looking back at Tristan. "Mornin', sir—beggin' your pardon, it's m'lord, ain't it?"

Tristan merely smiled.

Colby's nervousness increased. "What can I help you with, then?"

Tristan told him. Despite his appearance, Colby was the recognized underworld baron of the patch of London that included Montrose Place. Tristan had made his acquaintance, or rather made sure Colby knew of him, when they'd settled on Number 12 for the club.

On hearing of the strange goings-on in Montrose Place, Colby sucked his teeth and looked severe. Tristan had never believed that the attempted burglaries were the handiwork of the local louts; Colby's reaction and subsequent assurance confirmed that.

His eyes narrowed, Colby now looked more like the potentially dangerous specimen he was. "I'd like to meet this fine gentleman of yours."

"He's mine." Tristan made the statement blandly.

Colby glanced at him, assessing, then nodded. "I'll put the word around you're wanting a word with 'im. If any of the boys hear of 'im, I'll be sure to let you know."

Tristan inclined his head. "Once I lay hands on him, you won't see him again."

Colby nodded, once, bargain accepted. Information in exchange for removal of a competitor. Tristan rang for Havers, who saw Colby out.

Tristan finished the last of his requests for information, then gave them to Havers with strict instructions for delivery. "No livery. Use the heaviest footmen."

"Indeed, my lord. I apprehend we wish to make a show of strength. Collison would be best in that regard."

Tristan nodded, fighting a smile as Havers withdrew. The man was a godsend, dealing with the myriad demands of the old dears, yet with equal aplomb accommodating the rougher side of Tristan's affairs.

Having accomplished all he could regarding Montgomery Mountford, Tristan gave his attention to the day-to-day business of keeping his head above water with the details and demands of the earldom. While the clock ticked and time passed without his making any real headway in the matter of making said earldom secure.

For one of his temperament, that last irked.

He had Havers bring him luncheon on a tray and continued to whittle down the stack of business letters. Scrawling a note to his steward on the last, he sighed and pushed the completed pile aside.

And turned his mind determinedly to marriage.

To his wife-to-be.

Telling that he didn't think of her as a bride, but as his wife. Their association was not based on social superficialties, but on practical, ungilded day-to-day interactions. He could easily picture her by his side, as his countess dealing with the demands of their future life.

He should, he supposed, have considered a range of candidates. If he asked, his resident gossipmongers would be thrilled to provide him with a list. He'd toyed with the notion, or at least had told himself he was, yet appealing to others for assistance in such a personal and vitally crucial decision was simply not his style.

It was also redundant, a waste of time.

To the right of the blotter lay Leonora's letter. His gaze locking on it, on the delicate script reminiscent of the writer, he sat and brooded, turning his pen end over end between his fingers.

The clock struck three. He looked up, then threw the pen down, pushed back his chair, stood and headed for the hall.

Havers met him there, helped him into his greatcoat, handed him his cane, then swung the door wide.

Tristan walked out, went quickly down the steps, and headed for Montrose Place.

He found Leonora in the workshop, a large chamber tucked into the basement of Number 14. The walls were solid stone, thick and cold. A row of windows high along one wall looked out at ground level toward the front of the house. They would have admitted reasonable light once, but were now fogged and cracked.

They were, Tristan instantly noted, too small for even a child to crawl through.

Leonora hadn't heard him walk in; she had her nose buried in some musty tome. He scraped a sole on the flags. She looked up—and smiled in delighted welcome.

He smiled back, let the simple gesture warm him; he strolled in, looking about. "I thought you said this place had been closed up for years?"

There were no cobwebs, and all surfaces—tables, floors, and shelves—were clean.

"I sent in the maids this morning." She met his gaze as he turned to her. "I'm not particularly partial to spiders."

He noticed a pile of dusty letters stacked on the bench beside her; his levity faded. "Have you found anything?"

"Nothing specific." She closed the book; a cloud of dust puffed out from the pages. She gestured to the wooden rack, a cross between bookshelves and pigeonholes covering the wall behind the bench. "He was neat, but not methodical. He seems to have kept everything, stretching back over the years. I've been sorting bills and accounts from letters, shopping lists from drafts of learned papers."

He picked up the old parchment topping the pile. It was a letter inscribed in faded ink. He initially thought the script a woman's, but the contents were clearly scientific. He glanced at the signature. "Who's A. J.?"

Leonora leaned closer to check the letter; her breast brushed his arm. "A. J. Carruthers."

She moved away, lifting the old tome back to the shelf. He squelched a flaring urge to draw her back, to reestablish the sensual contact.

"Carruthers and Cedric corresponded frequently—it seems they were working on some papers before Cedric died."

With the tome safely stored, Leonora turned. He continued flicking through the letters. Her gaze on the pile of parchments, she moved closer. Misjudged and moved too far—she brushed, shoulder to thigh, against him.

Desire ignited, flamed between them.

Tristan tried to breathe in. Couldn't. The letters slipped from his fingers. He told himself to step back.

His feet wouldn't move. His body craved the contact too much to deny it.

She glanced fleetingly up at him through her lashes, then, as if embarrassed, eased fractionally back, creating a gap of less than an inch between them.

Too much, yet not enough. His arms were rising to haul her back, when he realized and lowered them.

She reached quickly for the letters and spread them out.

"I was"—her voice was husky; she paused to clear her throat—"going to sort through these. There might be something in them that will point to a discovery."

It took longer than he liked for him to refocus on the letters; he'd clearly been celibate for too long. He breathed in, exhaled. His mind cleared. "Indeed—they might allow us to decide if it's something Cedric discovered that Mountford's after. We shouldn't forget he wanted to buy the house—it's something he expected would be left behind."

"Or something he could gain access to by virtue of being the purchaser, before we moved out."

"True." He fanned the letters over the bench top, then looked up at the large pigeonholes. Stepping away from temptation, he turned down the room, following the bench, scanning the shelves above it, searching for more letters. He pulled out all he saw, leaving them on the bench top. "I want you to go through every letter you can find, and collect all those written in the year preceding Cedric's death."

Following him, Leonora frowned at his back, then tried to peer around at his face. "There'll be hundreds."

"However many, you'll need to study them all. Then make a list of the correspondents, and write and ask each one if they know of anything Cedric was working on that could have commercial or military significance."

She blinked. "Commercial or military significance?"

"They'll know. Scientists may be as absorbed in their work as your uncle and brother, but they usually recognize the possibilities in what they're working on."

"Hmm." Gaze fixed between his shoulder blades, she continued following at his heels. "So I'm to write to each contact he made in his last year."

"Every last one. If there was anything of significance, someone will know."

He reached the end of the room and swung around. She looked down—and walked into him. He caught her; she looked up, feigning surprise.

Didn't have to fabricate her leaping pulse, her suddenly thudding heart.

He'd focused on her lips; her gaze fell to his.

Then he glanced at the door.

"All the staff are busy." She'd made sure of that.

His gaze returned to her face. She met it but briefly; when he didn't immediately move, she wriggled her hands free and reached up, sliding one to his nape, curling the fingers of the other into his lapel.

"Stop being so stuffy and kiss me."

Tristan blinked. Then she shifted in his arms, unintentionally teasing that part of his anatomy most susceptible to her nearness.

Without another thought, he bent his head.

He escaped nearly an hour later, feeling distinctly bemused. It had been years—decades—since he'd indulged in any such mildly illicit behavior, yet far from boring him, his senses were smugly content, luxuriating in the stolen pleasures.

Striding down the front path, he raked his hand through his hair and hoped it would pass muster. Leonora had developed a penchant for thoroughly mussing his normally elegant cut. Not that he was complaining. While she'd been mussing, he'd been savoring.

Her mouth, her curves.

Lowering his arm, he noticed a smear of dust on his sleeve. He brushed it off. The maids had dusted all surfaces; they hadn't dusted the letters. When they'd finally separated, he'd had to brush telltale streaks off both himself and Leonora. In her case, not just from her clothes.

The image of how she'd appeared at that point swam across his mind. Her eyes had been bright but darkened, her lids heavy, her lips swollen from his kisses. Drawing his attention even more to her mouth—a mouth that increasingly evoked mental images not generally associated with virtuous gentlewomen.

Closing the front gate behind him, he suppressed a wholly masculine smirk—and ignored the effect such thoughts inevitably had. The afternoon's discoveries had improved his mood significantly. Reviewing the day, he felt he'd gained on a number of fronts.

He'd come to view Cedric's workshop determined to move the investigation into the burglaries forward. Impatience was sharpening its spurs; it was his duty to marry, thus protecting his tribe of old dears from destitution, but before he could marry Leonora, he had to nullify the threat to her. Eliminating that threat was his top priority; it was too immediate, too definite to give second place. Until he successfully completed his mission, he'd remain focused first and always on that.

So having escalated his own investigations through the various layers of the underworld, he'd come to assess what avenues for advancement Cedric's workshop might suggest.

Cedric's letters would indeed be useful. First in eliminating his works as a potential target for the burglar, second in keeping Leonora amused.

Well, perhaps not amused, but certainly busy. Too busy to have time to embark on any other avenue of attack.

He'd accomplished a great deal for one day. Satisfied, he strode on, and turned his mind to the morrow.

Devising her own seduction, or at least actively encouraging it, was proving more difficult than Leonora had thought. She'd expected to get rather further in Cedric's workshop, but Trentham had failed to close the door when he'd entered. Crossing the room and closing it herself would have been too blatant.

Not that matters hadn't progressed; they just hadn't progressed as far as she'd wished.

And now he'd lumbered her with the task of going through Cedric's correspondence. At least he'd restricted their search to the last year of Cedric's life.

She'd spent the rest of the day reading and sorting, squinting at faded writing, deciphering illegible dates. This morning, she'd brought all the relevant letters up to the parlor and spread them on the occasional tables. The parlor was the room in which she conducted all household business; sitting at her escritoire, she dutifully inscribed all the names and addresses onto a list.

A long list.

She then composed a letter of inquiry, advising the recipient of Cedric's death and requesting they contact her if they had any information regarding anything of value, discoveries, inventions, or possessions, that might reside in her late cousin's effects. Instead of mentioning the burglar's interest, she stated that, due to space constraints, it was intended that all nonvaluable papers, substances, and equipment would be burned.

If she knew anything of experts, should they know of anything the least valuable, the idea of it being burned would have them reaching for their pen.

After luncheon, she commenced the arduous task of copying her letter, addressing each copy to one of the names on her list.

When the clock chimed and she saw it was three-thirty, she set down her pen and stretched her aching back.

Enough for today. Not even Trentham would expect her to get through the inquiries all in one day.

She rang for tea; when Castor brought the tray, she poured and sipped.

And thought of seduction.

Hers.

A distinctly titillating subject, especially for a twenty-six-year-old reluctant-but-resigned virgin. That was a reasonable description of what she'd been, but she was resigned no more. Opportunity had beckoned, and she was determined to play.

She glanced at the clock. Too late to call at Trentham House for afternoon tea. Besides, she didn't want to find herself surrounded by his old ladies; that would not advance her cause.

But losing a whole day in inaction wasn't her style, either. There had to be some way, some excuse she could use to call on Trentham—and get him to herself in appropriate surrounds.

"Would you like me to show you around, miss?"

"No, no." Leonora crossed the threshold of the Trentham House conservatory and cast a reassuring smile at Trentham's butler. "I'll just amble about and await his lordship. If you're sure he'll return soon?"

"I'm certain he'll arrive home before dark."

"In that case . . ." She smiled and gestured about her, moving deeper into the room.

"Should you require anything, the bellpull is to the left." Serene and unperturbed, the butler bowed and left her.

Leonora looked around. Trentham's conservatory was much larger than theirs; indeed, it was monstrous. Recalling his supposed need of information on such rooms, she humphed. His was not just larger, it was better, the temperature much more even, the floor beautifully tiled in blue-and-green mosaics. A small fountain tinkled somewhere—she couldn't see through the artfully arranged, lush and verdant growth.

A path led on; she strolled down it.

It was four o'clock; outside the glass-paned walls the light was fading fast. Trentham clearly wouldn't be long, but why he would feel impelled by falling night to return to his house she couldn't fathom. The butler, however, had been quite definite on the point.

She reached the end of the path and stepped into a clearing ringed by high banks of shrubs and flowering bushes. It contained a circular pond set into the floor; the small fountain at its center was responsible for the tinkling. Beyond the pond, a wide window seat, heavily cushioned, followed the curve of the windowed wall; sitting on it, one could either view the garden outside, or look inward, contemplating the pond and the well-stocked conservatory.

Crossing to the window seat, she sank onto the cushions. They were deep, comfortable—perfect for her needs. She considered, then stood and walked on, along another path following the curved outer wall. Better she meet Trentham standing; he towered over her as it was. She could lead him back to the window seat—

A flash of movement in the garden caught her eye. She stopped, looked; she couldn't see anything unusual. The shadows had deepened while she'd been ambling; gloom now gathered beneath the trees.

Then, out of one such pocket of darkness, a man emerged. Tall, dark, lean, he wore a tattered coat and stained corduroy breeches, a battered cap pulled low on his head. He glanced furtively around as he strode rapidly for the house.

Leonora sucked in a breath. Wild thoughts of yet another burglar flooded her mind; recollection of the man who twice had attacked her stole her breath. This man was much larger; if he got his hands on her, she wouldn't be able to break free.

And his long legs were carrying him straight to the conservatory.

Sheer panic held her motionless in the shadow of the massed

plants. The door would be locked, she told herself. Trentham's butler was excellent—

The man reached the door, reached for the handle, turned it.

The door swung inward. He stepped through.

Faint light from the distant hallway reached him as he closed the door, turned, straightened.

"*Good God!*"

The exclamation exploded from Leonora's tight chest. She stared, unable to believe her eyes.

Trentham's head had snapped around at her first squeak.

He stared back at her, then his lips thinned and he frowned— and recognition was complete.

"Sssh!" He motioned her to silence, glanced toward the corridor, then, soft-footed, approached. "At the risk of repeating myself, what the damn hell are you doing here?"

She simply stared at him—at the grime worked into his face, at the dark stubble shading his jaw. A smudge of soot ran upward from one brow and disappeared beneath his hair, now hanging lank and listless under that cap—a worn tartan monstrosity that looked even worse at close range.

Her gaze drifted down to take in his coat, tattered and none too clean, to his breeches and knitted stockings, and the rough work boots he had on his feet. Reaching them, she paused, then ran her gaze all the way back up to his eyes. Met his irritated gaze.

"Answer my question and I'll answer yours—what in all Hades are you supposed to be?"

His lips thinned. "What do I look like?"

"Like a navvy from the most dangerous slum in town." A definite aroma reached her; she sniffed. "Perhaps down by the docks."

"Very perceptive," Tristan growled. "Now what brought you here? Have you discovered something?"

She shook her head. "I wanted to see your conservatory. You said you'd show it to me."

The tension—the apprehension—that had flashed through him on seeing her there leached away. He looked down at himself, and grimaced. "You've called at a bad time."

She frowned, her gaze once more on his disreputable attire. "But what *have* you been doing? Where have you been, dressed like that?"

"As you so perceptively guessed, the docks." Searching for any clue, any hint, any whisper of one Montgomery Mountford.

"You're a trifle old to be indulging in larks." She looked up and caught his gaze. "Do you frequently do such things?"

"No." Not anymore. He had never expected to don these clothes again, but on doing so that morning, had felt peculiarly justified in his refusal to throw them out. "I've been visiting the sort of dens that would-be burglars haunt."

"Oh. I see." She looked up at him with now openly eager interest. "Did you learn anything?"

"Not directly, but I've passed the word—"

"Oh, is she in here, then, Havers?"

Ethelreda. Tristan swore beneath his breath.

"We'll just keep her company until dear Tristan arrives."

"No need for her to mope about all alone."

"Miss Carling? Are you there?"

He swore again. They were all there—coming this way. "For God's sake!" he muttered. He went to grab Leonora, then remembered his hands were filthy. He kept his palms away from her. "You'll have to distract them."

It was an outright plea; he met her eyes, infused every ounce of beseeching candor of which he was capable into his expression.

She looked at him. "They don't know you go out masquerading as a lout, do they?"

"No. And they'll have fits if they see me like this."

Fits would be the least of it; Ethelreda had a horrible tendency to swoon.

They were casting about along the paths, drawing inexorably nearer.

He held out his hands, begging. *"Please."*

She smiled. Slowly. "All right. I'll save you." She turned and started toward the source of feminine twittering, then glanced back over her shoulder. Caught his eye. "But you owe me a favor."

"Anything." He sighed with relief. "Just get them out of here. Take them to the drawing room."

Her smile deepening, Leonora turned and went on. Anything, he'd said. An excellent outcome from an otherwise useless exercise.

Eight

Arranging to be seduced, Leonora was perfectly sure, wasn't supposed to be this difficult. The next day, while sitting in the parlor copying her letter, copy after copy, doggedly working through Cedric's correspondents, she reevaluated her position and considered all avenues for advance.

The previous afternoon she'd dutifully deflected Trentham's cousins to the drawing room; he'd joined them fifteen minutes later, clean, spotless, his usual debonair self. Having used her interest in conservatories to explain her visit to the ladies, she'd duly asked him various questions to which he'd denied all knowledge, instead suggesting he have his gardener call on her.

Asking him to conduct her on a tour would have been fruitless; his cousins would have accompanied them.

Regretfully, she'd crossed his conservatory off her mental list of suitable venues for seduction; an appropriate time could be managed, and the window seat provided an excellent location, but their privacy could never be assured.

Trentham had summoned his carriage, helped her into it, and

sent her home. Unfulfilled. Even hungrier than when she'd left. Even more determined.

Still, the excursion had not been without gain; she now had one trump card in hand. She intended to use it wisely. That meant clearing the time, location, and privacy hurdles simultaneously. She had no idea how rakes managed it. Perhaps they simply waited for opportunity to arise, then pounced.

After waiting patiently all these years, and having finally made up her mind, she wasn't inclined to sit back and wait any longer. The right opportunity was what was required; if necessary, she'd have to create it.

All well and good, but she couldn't think how.

She racked her brain throughout the day. And the next. She even considered taking up her Aunt Mildred's permanent offer to take her about within the ton. Despite her disinterest in society's balls and parties, she was aware such events provided venues in which gentlemen and ladies could meet privately. However, from snippets Trentham's cousins had let fall, as well as his own caustic comments, she'd gathered he had little enthusiasm for the social round. No point making such an effort herself if he wasn't likely to be present to be met, privately or otherwise.

When the clock struck four, she tossed down her pen and stretched her arms over her head. She was almost at the end of her letter-writing exercise, but when it came to venues in which to be seduced, her mind remained stubbornly blank.

"There has to be somewhere!" She pushed up from her chair, irritated and impatient. Frustrated. Her gaze went to the window. The day had been fine, but breezy. Now the wind had eased; evening was closing in, benign if cool.

She headed for the front hall, grabbed her cloak, didn't bother with her bonnet; she wouldn't be out long. She glanced around, expecting Henrietta, then realized the hound was out for her constitutional in the nearby park, led on a lead by one of the footmen.

"Damn!" She wished she'd been in time to join them.

The gardens, both front and back, were protected; she wanted—*needed*—to walk in the open air. She needed to breathe, to let the coolness refresh her, to blow away her frustration and reinvigorate her brain.

She hadn't walked outside alone for weeks, yet the burglar could hardly be watching all the time.

With a swish of her skirts, she turned, opened the front door, and walked outside.

She left the door on the latch and went down the steps, then followed the path to the gate. Reaching it, she peered out. The light was still good; in both directions the street, always a quiet one, lay empty. Safe enough. Pulling open the gate, she walked through, tugged it closed behind her, then set off walking briskly along the pavement.

Passing Number 12, she glanced in, but saw no sign of movement. She'd heard via Toby that Gasthorpe had now hired a full staff, but most were not yet in residence. Biggs, however, returned there every night, and Gasthorpe himself rarely left the house; there had been no further felonious activity there.

Indeed, since she'd last seen the man at the bottom of their garden, and he'd run off, there'd been no further incidents of any kind. The sense of being watched had receded; although occasionally she still felt under observation, the feeling was more distant, less threatening.

She walked on, pondering that, considering what it might mean in terms of Montgomery Mountford and whatever it was he was so intent on removing from her uncle's house. While arranging to be seduced was certainly a distraction, she hadn't forgotten Mr. Mountford.

Whoever he was.

The thought evoked others; she recalled Trentham's recent searches. Direct and to the point, decisive, active, yet try as she might, she couldn't imagine any other gentleman masquerading as he had done.

He'd appeared very comfortable in his disguise.

He'd looked even more dangerous than he usually did.

The image teased; she remembered hearing of ladies who indulged in passionate affairs with men of distinctly rougher background than their own. Could she—would she later—be susceptible to such longings?

She honestly had no idea, which only confirmed how much she'd yet to learn, not just of passion, but of herself, too.

With every day that passed, she became more aware of that last.

She reached the end of the street and stopped on the corner. The breeze was stronger there; her cloak billowed. Holding it down, she looked toward the park, but saw no gangling hound returning with footman in tow. She considered waiting, but the breeze was too chilly and strong enough to unravel her hair. Turning, she retraced her steps, feeling considerably restored.

Her gaze on the pavement, she determinedly turned her mind to passion, specifically how to sample it.

The shadows were lengthening; dusk was approaching.

She'd reached the boundary of Number 12 when she heard footsteps striding quickly up behind her.

Panic flared; she whirled, backing against the high stone wall even while her intellect calmly pointed out the unlikelihood of any attack.

One look at the face of the man rushing toward her, and she knew intellect lied.

She opened her mouth and screamed.

Mountford snarled and grabbed her. Hands locking cruelly about both arms, he dragged her to the middle of the wide pavement and shook her.

"*Hey!*"

The shout came from the end of the street; Mountford paused. A heavyset man was running their way.

Mountford swore. His fingers bit viciously into her arms as he swung to look the other way.

He swore again, a vulgar expletive, a hint of fear showing. His lips curled in a snarl.

Leonora looked, and saw Trentham closing fast. Some way behind him came another man, but it was the look on Trentham's face that shocked her—and momentarily transfixed Mountford.

He shook free of that killing look, glanced at her, then hauled her to him—and flung her forcefully back. Into the wall.

She screamed. The sound cut off when her head hit the stone. She was only vaguely aware of sliding slowly down, crumpling in a mass of skirts on the pavement.

Through a white fog, she saw Mountford racing across the street, avoiding the men running in from either end. Trentham didn't give chase, but came straight for her.

She heard him swear, distantly noted he was swearing at her, not Mountford, then she was wrapped in his strength and hoisted to her feet. He held her against him, supporting her; she was standing, yet he was taking most of her weight.

She blinked; her vision cleared. Leaving her staring into a face in which some primitive emotion akin to fury warred with concern.

To her relief, concern won.

"Are you all right?"

She nodded, swallowed. "Just a trifle dazed." She put up a hand to the back of her head, gingerly felt, then smiled, albeit tremulously. "Only a small bump. No serious damage."

His lips thinned, his eyes narrowed on hers, then he glanced in the direction Mountford had fled.

She frowned and tried to ease from his hold. "You should have followed him."

He didn't let her go. "The others are after him."

Others? Two and two . . . "Have you had people watching the street?"

He glanced at her briefly. "Of course."

No wonder she hadn't felt threatened by the continuing observation. "You might have told me."

"Why? So you could stage some witless act like this?"

She ignored that and stared across the street. Mountford had raced into the garden of the house opposite; the two other men, both heavier and slower, had followed.

No one reappeared.

Trentham's lips were a grim line. "Is there an alley behind those houses?"

"Yes."

He bit back a sound; she suspected it was another curse. He looked at her assessingly, then consented to ease the arm he'd locked about her. "I'd credited you with more sense—"

She raised a hand, stopped his words. "I had absolutely no reason to think Mountford would be out here. Come to that, if you had men watching from both ends of the street, why did they let him past them?"

He glanced again in the direction his men had gone. "He must have spotted them. Presumably he reached you in the same way he left, via an alley and someone's garden."

His gaze returned to her face, searched it. "How are you feeling?"

"Reasonable." Better than she'd expected; Mountford's rough handling had shaken her more than the collision with the wall. She drew breath, let it out. "Just a bit shaky."

He nodded curtly. "Shock."

She focused on him. "What are you doing here?"

Accepting that his men weren't about to return, Mountford between them, Tristan released her and took her arm. "The furniture for the third floor was delivered yesterday. I'd promised Gasthorpe I'd check and approve it. Today is his day off—he's gone to Surrey to visit his mother and won't be back until tomorrow. I'd thought to kill two birds by checking the house as well as the furniture."

He studied her face, still too pale, then turned her along the pavement. Pacing slowly, he led her along the wall of Number 12 toward Number 14 beyond. "I left it later than I'd intended. Biggs should be inside by now, so all will no doubt be well until Gasthorpe returns."

She nodded, walking by his side, leaning on his arm. They drew level with the gate of Number 12, and she stopped.

She drew in a deep breath, then met his eyes. "If you don't mind, perhaps I could come in and help you check the furniture." She smiled, definitely tremulously, then looked away. Somewhat breathlessly added, "I'd prefer to stay with you for a little while longer, to catch my breath before going in to face the household."

She ran her uncle's household; there'd no doubt be people waiting to speak to her as soon as she went in.

He hesitated, but Gasthorpe wasn't around to disapprove. And on the list of activities likely to lift a woman's spirits, viewing new furniture probably ranked high. "If you wish." He steered her through the gate and up the path to the door. While she was viewing, he'd use the time to think of how better to protect her. He couldn't, unfortunately, expect her to remain a prisoner within doors.

Taking the key from his pocket, he unlocked the front door. Frowned as he handed her over the threshold. "Where's your hound?"

"She's being taken for a walk in the park." She glanced back at him as he closed the door. "The footmen take her—she's too strong for me."

He nodded, noting that once again she'd followed his thought—that if she walked at all, then she should walk with Henrietta. But if the dog was too strong, then beyond the garden that wasn't a viable option.

She led the way to the stairs; he followed. They'd reached the first steps when a cough drew their attention to the door to the kitchens.

Biggs stood in the opening. He saluted. "On watch here, m'lud."

Tristan smiled his charming smile. "Thank you, Biggs. Miss Carling and I are just taking stock of the new furniture. We'll let ourselves out later. Carry on."

Biggs bobbed to Leonora, snapped off another salute, then turned and descended into the kitchens. The faint aroma of a pie drifted to their nostrils.

Leonora met his gaze, a smile in her eyes, then she turned, grasped the banister, and went on.

He watched, but she didn't falter. However, when they reached the second-floor landing, she glanced at him and drew in a tight breath.

Frowning anew, he took her arm. "Here." He urged her into the largest bedroom, the one over the library. "Sit down." A large armchair sat angled to the window; he led her to it.

She subsided into the chair with a little sigh. Smiled weakly up at him. "I don't faint."

He narrowed his eyes at her; she was no longer pale, but there was an odd tenseness about her. "Just sit there and study the furniture you can see. I'll check the other rooms, then you can give me your verdict."

Leonora nodded, closed her eyes, and let her head rest against the chair's back. "I'll wait here."

He hesitated, looking down at her, then he turned and left her.

When he was gone, she opened her eyes and studied the room. The large bow window looked over the back garden; during the day it would let in ample light, but now, with night encroaching, the room was gathering shadows. A fireplace stood in the center of the wall opposite her chair; a fire was set but not lit.

A chaise was positioned at an angle to the fireplace; beyond it, in the far corner of the room, stood a massive armoire in dark polished wood.

The same polished wood adorned the even more massive four-poster bed. Staring at the expanse of ruby silk coverlet, she thought of Trentham; presumably his friends were similarly large. Dark red brocade curtains were looped back about the carved posts at the head of the bed. The last light lingered on the curves and twists in the ornately carved headboard, repeated on the turned posts at the bed's foot. With its thick mattress, the bed was a substantial piece, solid, stable.

The central feature of the room; the focus of her senses.

It was, she decided, the perfect venue for her seduction.

Far better than his conservatory.

And there was no one to interrupt, to interfere. Gasthorpe was in Surrey and Biggs in the kitchens, too far away to hear anything—provided they closed the door.

She turned to look at the solid oak door.

The encounter with Mountford had only deepened her determination to press ahead. She wasn't so much shaky as tense; she needed to feel Trentham's arms around her to convince herself she was safe.

She wanted to be in his arms, wanted to be close to him. Wanted the physical contact, the shared sensual pleasure. Needed the experience, now more than ever.

Two minutes later, Trentham strolled back in.

She waved to the door. "Close that so I can see the tallboy."

He turned and did as she asked.

She dutifully studied the tall chest of drawers thus revealed.

"So"—ambling up, he halted beside the chair and looked down at her—"do the amenities meet with your approval?"

She looked up at him, slowly smiled. "Indeed, they appear quite perfect."

Rakes undoubtedly had it right; when opportunity presented, one had to pounce.

She held up her hand.

Tristan grasped it and smoothly drew her to her feet. He'd expected her to step away; instead, she'd shifted her feet—she straightened directly in front of him, so close her breasts brushed his coat.

She looked into his face, then moved closer still. Reached up and drew his head down to hers. Pressed her lips to his in a blatant, openmouthed kiss, one he only just stopped himself from falling headfirst into.

His control uncharacteristically quaked. He gripped her waist—hard—to stop himself from devouring her.

She ended the caress and drew back, but only a fraction; she lifted her lids and met his gaze. Her eyes glinted vibrantly blue beneath her lashes. Holding his gaze, she reached for the ties of her cloak, tugged, then let the garment fall to the floor. "I wanted to thank you."

Her voice was husky, low; its timbre slid through him. His body clenched, recognizing her meaning; he was pulling her closer, tight, body to body, lowering his head, before the echo had died.

She stopped him with one finger, sliding the tip across his lower lip. Her gaze followed the motion; instead of moving away, she moved closer yet—let herself sink against him. "You were there when I needed you."

Unthinking, he gathered her to him; her lids lifted, and she met his eyes. Slid her hand up to his nape again. Her lids drifted down, and she stretched upward against him. "Thank you."

He took her mouth as she offered it. Sank deep and drank, felt not just pleasure but reassurance slide through his veins. It seemed only right that she thanked him like this; he saw no reason to refuse the moment, to do anything other than sate his senses with the tribute she surrendered.

Her arms slid up, twined about his neck; she pressed close, her body a promise of bliss.

Between them, the embers they'd left smoldering flared, then flames leapt beneath their skins. He felt the fire ignite; confident he had her measure, he let it burn.

Let his fingers find their way to her breasts; when the sweet mounds were tight and straining, he reached for her laces. Dealt with them and the ribbons of her chemise with practiced ease.

Her breasts spilled into his hands; she gasped through the kiss. Possessively kneading, he held her, drew her on, urged the flames higher.

He broke from the kiss, nudged her head up, set his lips to the taut tendon in her throat. Traced it down to where her pulse beat frantically, then licked, laved. Sucked.

She gasped; the sound echoed in the silence, drove him on. Steering her around, he sank onto the chair's arm, drawing her with him, pressing her gown and chemise to her waist.

So he could feast.

She'd offered her bounty; he accepted. With lips and tongue, took and claimed. Traced the full curves. Pressed hot kisses to the tightly ruched peaks. Listened to her fractured breathing. Felt her fingers tightening on his skull as he teased.

Then he took one pebbled nipple into his mouth, rasped it lightly, and she tensed. He sucked gently, then soothed the taut nubbin with his tongue. Waited until she'd relaxed before drawing it deep and suckling.

She cried out, her body bowing in his arms.

He showed no mercy, suckling voraciously first at one breast, then the other.

Her fingers spasmed, holding him to her. He slid his hands down from her waist, back and over her hips, and captured her bottom; spreading his thighs, he drew her hips to him. Wedged her close so her stomach rode against him, both easing and teasing the fiery ache.

Closing his hands, he kneaded, and felt more than heard her gasp. He didn't stop but explored more intimately, holding her at his mercy, his lips taunting and teasing her swollen breasts while he evocatively shifted her lower body, molding hips, stomach, and thighs to him as he wished.

Then she dragged in a breath and bent her head. He released her breasts, looked up, and she captured his mouth. Slid in, caressed and heated him, stole his breath, gave it back.

He felt her fingers at his throat, then she flicked his cravat loose. Their mouths melded; they took and gave while her fingers slid down his chest.

Opening his shirt.

Tugging it free of his waistband. Trailing her fingertips over his chest, taunting, feather-light. Maddening.

"Take off your coat."

The words whispered through his brain. His skin was burning; it seemed a good idea.

He released her for a second, stood, shrugged.

Cravat, coat, and shirt fell back across the chair.

Bad move.

The instant her naked breasts touched his bare chest, he knew that was so.

Didn't care.

The sensation was so erotic, so blissfully attuned to some deeper need that he shrugged aside the warning as easily as he had the shirt. He gathered her to him, sank into her welcoming mouth, aware to his bones of the light touch of her hands on his skin, innocent, tentatively exploring.

Aware of the rush of pleasure her touch evoked, of the answering heat flaring within her.

He didn't press but let her feel and learn as she wished, his ego pleased beyond belief by her eager desire. He held her close;

hands splayed over her naked back, he traced the fine muscles bracketing her spine.

Delicate, supple yet with their own feminine strength, an echo of all she was.

He'd never been with a woman he wanted more, one who promised so completely to sate him. Not just sexually, but at some deeper level, one he didn't, in his present state, recognize or understand. Whatever it was, the compulsive need she evoked was strong.

Stronger than any lust, any mere desire.

His control had never had to cope with such a feeling.

It cracked, shattered, and he didn't even know.

Didn't even have the sense to pull back when her questing fingers wandered lower. When she traced, tantalizingly, in open wonderment, he only groaned.

Startled, she drew her hand away; he grabbed it. His hand locked around hers he guided it back, urged her to learn him as he intended to learn her. Drew back from the kiss and watched her face as she did.

Gloried in her innocence, and even more in her awakening.

His lungs constricted until he was giddy. He continued to watch her, kept his senses focused on her, away from the conflagration she was causing, from the urgent need pulsing through him.

Only when she glanced up beneath her lashes, lips parted, rosy from his kisses, did he move to draw her to him again, to again take her mouth and sweep her deeper into the magic.

Deeper under his spell.

When he finally released her lips, Leonora could barely think. Her skin was on fire; so was his. Everywhere they touched, flames leapt, singed. Her breasts ached, brushed to excruciating sensitivity by the coarse dark hair across his chest.

That chest was a sculpted wonder of hard muscle over heavy bone. Her spread fingers found scars, nicks here and there; the light tan of his face and neck extended over his chest, as if he occasionally worked outside without a shirt. Inside without a shirt he was a wonder, appearing to her senses like a god come to life. She'd only seen male bodies like his in books of ancient sculptures, yet his was alive, real, utterly male. The feel of his skin, the resilience of his muscles, the sheer strength he possessed overwhelmed her.

His lips, his tongue, teased hers, then he lifted his head and brushed a kiss to her temple.

Whispered in the heated dark, "I want to see you. Touch you."

He drew back just enough to catch her eyes. His were dark pools, compellingly intent.

His strength surrounded her, caged her; his hands stroked her bare skin. She felt them slide to her sides, then tense to press her gown and chemise lower.

"Let me."

Command and question both. She breathed slowly out, infinitesimally nodded.

He pushed her gown down. Once past the swell of her hips, both gown and chemise fell of their own accord.

The soft silken swoosh was audible in the room.

Darkness had closed in, yet enough light still lingered. Enough for her to study his face as he looked down, as, still holding her within the circle of one arm, with his other hand he traced from her breast to her waist, to her hip, flaring outward, then inward across her upper thigh.

"You are so beautiful."

The words fell from his lips; he didn't even seem to notice, as if he hadn't consciously said them. His features were set, the harsh planes austere, his lips a hard line. There was no softness in his face, no hint of his charm.

All lingering reservations of the rightness of her actions were cindered in that moment. Turned to ashes by the stark emotion in his face.

She didn't know enough to name it, but whatever that emotion was it was what she wanted, what she needed. She'd lived her life longing to be looked at by a man in just such a way, as if she were more precious, more desirable than his soul.

As if he'd willingly trade his soul for what she knew would happen next.

She reached for him as he reached for her.

Their lips met, and the flames roared.

She would have been frightened if he hadn't been there, solid and real for her to hold on to, her anchor in the maelstrom that swirled through them, around them.

His hands slid down and around, closed over her bare bottom; he kneaded, and heat raced across her skin. Fever followed, a hot urgent ache that swelled and grew as he evocatively plundered her mouth, as he held her close, lifted her hips against him, and suggestively molded her softness to the rigid line of his erection.

She moaned, hot, hungry and wanting.

Wanton. Eager. Determined.

He hoisted her higher; instinctively she wrapped her arms about his shoulders, her long legs about his hips.

Their kiss turned incendiary.

He broke from it only to demand, "Come. Lie with me."

She answered with a scorching kiss.

Tristan carried her to the side of the bed, and tumbled them both onto it. They bounced, and he angled over her, pressing her down, wedging one leg between hers.

Their lips locked, melded. He sank into the kiss, letting his wandering senses luxuriate in the heavenly delight of having her under him, naked and wanting. Some primitive, wholly male part of his soul rejoiced.

Wanted more.

He let his hands roam, shaping her breasts, then sliding lower, caressing her hips, then pressing beneath to cup her bottom and squeeze. He nudged her thighs wider, freed one hand, and placed it on her stomach.

Felt the feminine muscles beneath his palm jump, contract.

He slid his fingers lower, tangling in the dark curls at the apex of her thighs. Reaching through them, he stroked the soft, sweet flesh they concealed. Felt her shudder.

Easing her thighs wider he cupped her. Sensed the quick intake of her breath. He opened her mouth and kissed her more deeply, then eased back from the kiss, leaving their lips brushing, touching, letting her senses surface sufficiently for her to know and feel.

Their breaths mingled, heated and urgent; from beneath heavy lids, their eyes met, held.

Locked as he shifted his hand and touched her. Stroked, caressed, intimately traced. Her breasts rose and fell; her teeth closed on her lower lip as he opened her. As he teased, glorying in the slick heat of her body, then slowly, deliberately, slid one long finger into her.

Her breathing fractured; her eyes closed. Her body rose beneath his.

"Stay with me." He stroked slowly, in, out, letting her grow accustomed to his touch, to the sensation.

Her breathing ragged, she forced open her eyes; gradually, her body unclenched.

Slowly, gradually, flowered for him.

He watched it happen, watched the sensual delight rise and sweep her away, watched her eyes darken, felt her fingers tense, nails sinking into his muscles.

Then her breathing broke. Spine bowing, head pressing back, she closed her eyes. "Kiss me." A desperate plea. "Please— kiss me." Her voice broke on a gasp as sensation built, coiled, tightened.

"No." Eyes locked on her face, he pushed her on. "I want to watch you."

She was fighting for breath, clinging to sanity.

"Lie back and let it happen. Let go."

He caught a glimpse of brilliant blue from beneath her lashes. He slipped another finger in with the first, thrust deeper, faster.

And she fractured.

He watched her climax take her, listened to the soft cry that fell from her swollen lips, felt her sheath contract, powerful and tight, then relax, aftershocks rippling through the velvet heat.

His fingers still inside her, he leaned down, and kissed her.

Long, deep, giving her all he could, letting her taste his desire, see his wanting, then, step by step, drawing back.

When he withdrew his fingers, stroked them through her wet curls, then lifted his head, her fingers, tangled in the hair at his nape, closed, clutched. She opened her eyes, studied his, his face, read his decision.

He tried to ease back, to let her breathe; to his surprise, she tightened her grip, held him to her.

Held his gaze, then licked her lips. "You owe me a favor." Her voice was a hoarse whisper; it strengthened with her next words. "Anything, you said. So promise you won't stop."

He blinked. "Leonora—"

"No. I want you with me. Don't stop. Don't pull away."

He gritted his teeth. She'd blindsided him. Naked, spread beneath him, her body pliant in aftermath . . . and she was begging him to take her. "It's not that I don't want you—"

She shifted one sleek thigh.

He sucked in a breath.

Groaned. Shut his eyes. Couldn't shut off his senses. Grimly resolved, he placed his palms on the bed and pushed up, away from her heat.

Opened his eyes.

And stopped.

Hers were swimming.

Tears?

She blinked hard, but didn't shift her gaze from his. "*Please.* Don't leave me."

Her voice broke on the words.

Something inside him did, too.

His resolve, his certainty, shattered.

He wanted her so much he could barely think, yet the last thing he should do was sink into her soft heat, take her, claim her, like this, now. But he wasn't proof against the need in her eyes, a need he couldn't place, but knew he had to fill.

About them, the house was silent, still. Outside the window, night had fallen. They were alone, draped in shadows, naked on a wide bed.

And she wanted him inside her.

He drew a deep breath, bowed his head, then abruptly pulled back and sat up.

"All right."

One part of his mind was bellowing: *"Don't do it!"* The thunder in his blood, and even more a wave of emotional conviction drowned it out.

He unfastened his trousers, then stood to strip them off. Glanced back at her as he straightened, met her eyes. "Just remember this was your idea."

She smiled a soft madonna's smile, but her eyes remained wide, watchful. Waiting.

He looked at her, then looked around, stalked to where her clothes had fallen and swiped up her gown. Shaking it out, turning the skirts inside out, he returned to the bed. Dropping beside her, he scooped her hips up in one arm and spread the skirts beneath her.

Glanced at her face in time to see one delicate brow arch upward, but she made no comment, simply settled back again.

Met his eyes. Still waiting.

Read his thoughts as she often did. "I'm not going to change my mind."

He felt his face harden. Felt desire rip through him. "So be it."

She had cooled; he hadn't. He seriously doubted she had any idea of what she did to him, to what level she called to him, especially with them naked in the dappled dark, alone in an essentially empty house.

It was impossible to shake the aura of illicit danger; it was so much a part of him, he didn't even try. She wanted this, knowingly. As he stretched beside her, propped on one elbow and reached for her, he didn't try to hide anything, any part of him, from her.

Least of all the dark, primitive desire she evoked.

Their eyes had adjusted long ago; they could see each other's faces and expressions, even, given they were so close, the emotions in each other's eyes. He sensed the trepidation that quivered through her as he drew her to him. At the same time read the determination in her face, and didn't pause.

He kissed her, not as he had before but as a lover who had been given free rein. He entered like a conqueror, laid claim as he wished, laid waste to her senses.

Initially passive, waiting to see, Leonora instinctively rose to his challenge. Her body stirred, came alive once more; she lifted one hand, and speared her fingers once more into his hair.

And clung tight as, once again, the flames erupted between them. This time, he made no effort to hold them, contain them; instead, he let them rage. Deliberately sent them raging with each possessive sweep of his hard palms as he shaped her body beneath his, as he claimed every inch of her softness, explored at will, even more intimately.

She shuddered, and let him. Let him sweep her into the fiery sea, the conflagration of desire, passion and simple, unavoidable need.

He touched her in ways she had never imagined, until she clung and sobbed. Until she was awash with heat and longing, with desire burning so fiercely she felt literally on fire. He shifted over her, spread her thighs, and settled between. In the deepening darkness, he was literally a god, powerful and intent as, braced above her, he looked down on her. Then he bent his head and took her mouth again, and his sheer vitality—the fact he was all hard muscle and bone, and hot, heated blood—captured her.

The crinkly roughness of his haired skin chafed, abraded, reminded her how soft her own skin was, how sensitive. Reminded her how vulnerable and defenseless she was against his strength.

He shifted, reached down, caught one of her knees, and lifted her leg to his hip. Set it there, then traced back with his palm, around, until he found her slick and swollen, hot and ready.

And then he was pressing into her, hard, hot, and much larger than she'd realized. Her lungs seized. She felt her body stretching. He pressed inexorably in.

She gasped, tried to pull away from the kiss.

He didn't let her.

Instead, he held her down, held her trapped, and slowly, slowly filled her.

Her body arched as he did, bowed, tightened, tensed against his invasion. She felt the restriction, felt the pressure build, but he didn't stop; he pressed deeper, deeper, until the barrier simply gave, and he surged through. And on.

Until she was so full of him she could barely breathe, until she felt him throbbing high and deep inside her. She felt her body give, surrender, then accept.

Only then did he stop, hold still, the solid reality of him buried deep within her.

He drew back from the kiss, opened his eyes, looked down into hers from two inches away. Their breaths, ragged and broken, hot and heated, mingled.

"Are you all right?"

The words reached her, deep and gravelly; she considered how she felt with the hot weight of him holding her down, his muscled hardness trapping her spread and so vulnerable beneath him. With his erection buried intimately within her.

She nodded. Her lips were hungry for his; she touched them to his, tasted him, then sent her tongue exploring, savoring the unique flavor. She felt more than heard him groan, then he moved within her.

At first just a little, rocking his hips against her.

But soon that wasn't enough, not for either of them.

What followed was a journey of discovery. She hadn't imagined intimacy would be this consuming, this demanding, this fulfilling. This hot, this sweaty, this involving. He didn't speak again, didn't ask what she thought, asked for no permission as he took her. As he filled her, sank into her body, sheathed himself in her heat.

Yet throughout, again and again his eyes touched hers, checking, reassuring, encouraging. They communicated without words, and she followed him eagerly. Wantonly.

Into a landscape of passion.

It rolled on, unfolding, scene upon scene, and she realized just how much the simple act of joining could be.

How enthralling. How fascinating.

How demanding. How addictive.

How, at the very end as they tumbled through space and she felt him with her, fulfilling.

Given his expertise, she'd expected him to withdraw from her before he spilled his seed. She didn't want that; instinct drove her to sink her nails into his flexing buttocks and hold him to her.

He looked at her; almost blindly, their eyes met. Then he closed his eyes on a groan, and let it happen, let the last powerful surge take him even deeper into her, locking them together as he spent himself within her.

She felt his warmth flood her.

Her lips curved in a satisfied smile, and she finally let go, and let oblivion take her.

Slumped across the bed, Tristan tried to make sense of what had happened.

Leonora lay across him, still intimately entwined. He felt no urge to disengage. She was half-asleep; he hoped she'd remain so until he found his mental feet.

He'd collapsed on top of her, sated literally out of his mind. A novel occurrence. Later, he'd roused enough to roll to the side, taking her with him. He'd pulled the coverlet over them to protect her cooling limbs from the chill invading the room.

It was full dark, but not that late. No one would be unduly worried by her absence, not yet. Experience suggested that despite what had seemed a journey to the stars, it would not even be six o'clock; he had time to consider where they were now, and how best to go forward.

He was too experienced not to understand that going forward usually meant understanding where one had been.

That was his problem. He was not at all sure he understood all that had just taken place.

She'd been attacked; he'd arrived in time to rescue her, and they'd come in here. All seemed straightforward to that point.

Then she'd wanted to thank him. He'd seen no reason not to let her.

It was after that that matters had become complicated.

He vaguely recalled thinking that indulging her was a perfectly sensible way of taking her mind off the attack. True enough, but her thanks, rendered in the manner she'd chosen, had both soothed and invoked a darker need of his own, a reaction to the incident, a compulsion to put his mark on her, to make her irrevocably his.

Put like that, it seemed a primitive, somewhat uncivilized response, yet he couldn't deny that was what had driven him to strip her, to touch her, to know her intimately. He hadn't understood enough to fight it, hadn't seen the danger.

He glanced down at Leonora's dark head, at her hair, tumbled and jumbled, warm against his shoulder.

He hadn't intended this.

This, he now realized, increasingly so as his brain caught up with the ramifications, with the full extent of what all *this* now meant to him—*this* was a major complication in a plan that hadn't been running all that smoothly to begin with.

He felt his face harden. His lips thinned. If he hadn't been wary of waking her, he would have sworn.

It didn't take much thinking to know that now there was only one way forward. No matter what options his strategist's mind devised, his instinctive, deeply entrenched reaction never wavered.

She was his. Absolutely. In incontrovertible fact.

She was in danger, under threat.

There was only one option left.

Please . . . don't leave me.

He hadn't been able to resist that plea, knew he wouldn't, even now, were she to make it again. There'd been some need so deep, so vulnerable in her eyes, it had been impossible for him to deny. Despite the upheaval it was going to cause, he couldn't, didn't, regret anything.

In reality, nothing had changed, only the relative timing.

What was required was a restructuring of his plan. On a significant scale, admittedly, but he was too much a tactician to waste time grumbling.

Reality seeped slowly into Leonora's mind. She stirred, sighed, luxuriating in the warmth that surrounded her, enveloped her, engulfed her. Filled her.

Lashes fluttering, she opened her eyes, blinked. Realized what the source of all that comforting warmth was.

A blush—she prayed it was a blush—suffused her. She shifted enough to look up.

Trentham glanced down at her. A frown, rather vague, filled his eyes. "Just lie still."

Beneath the covers, one large palm closed about her bottom and he shifted her, settled her more comfortably on him. About him.

"You'll be sore. Just relax and let me think."

She stared at him, then looked down—at her hand spread on his naked chest. Relax, he said. They were naked, limbs tangled, and he was still inside her. No longer filling her as he had, but still definitely there . . .

She knew men were generally unaffected by their own nakedness, yet this seemed—

Dragging in a breath, she stopped thinking about it. If she did, if she started letting herself dwell on all she'd learned, all she'd experienced, stunned amazement and wonder would keep her here for hours.

And her aunts were coming to dinner.

She'd dwell on the magic later.

Lifting her head, she looked at Trentham. He was still vaguely frowning. "What are you thinking about?"

He glanced at her. "Do you know any bishops?"

"Bishops?"

"Hmm—we need a special license. I could apply to—"

She braced her hands on his chest, pushed up, and got his immediate attention. Eyes wide, she stared down at him. "Why do we need a special license?"

"Why . . ." He stared, bemusedly, back at her. Eventually said, "That's the very last thing I expected you to say."

She frowned at him. Clambered up and off him, twisting to sit in the coverlet. "Stop teasing." She looked around. "Where are my clothes?"

Silence reigned for a heartbeat, then he said, "I'm not teasing."

His tone had her looking, very quickly, back at him. Their eyes locked; what she saw in his set her heart thumping. "That's not . . . funny."

"I didn't think any of this was 'funny.' "

She sat and looked at him; her spurt of panic receded. Her brain started to function again. "I don't expect you to marry me."

His brows rose; she dragged in a breath. "I'm twenty-six. Past marriageable age. You don't have to feel that because of this"—her wave encompassed the coverlet cocoon and all it contained—"you have to make any honorable sacrifice. You don't need to feel you seduced me and so must make amends."

"As I recall, you seduced me."

She blushed. "Indeed. So there's no reason you need to find a bishop."

It was definitely time to get dressed. She spied her chemise on the floor and turned to crawl out of the cocoon.

Steely fingers closed like a manacle about her wrist.

He didn't tug or restrain her; he didn't have to. She knew she couldn't break free until he consented to let her go.

She sank back into the coverlet. He was staring up at the ceiling; she couldn't see his eyes.

"Let's just see if I've got this straight."

His voice was even, but there was an edge to it that left her wary.

"You're a twenty-six-year-old virgin—I beg your pardon, ex-virgin. You have no other entanglements, romantic or otherwise. Correct?"

She would have loved to tell him this was pointless, but from experience she knew humoring difficult males was the fastest way to deal with their megrims. "Yes."

"Am I also correct in stating that you set out deliberately to seduce me?"

She pressed her lips together, then conceded, "Not immediately."

"But today. That"—his thumb had started to draw distracting little circles on the inside of her wrist—"was intended. Deliberate. You were set on having me . . . what? Initiate you?"

He turned his head and looked at her. She blushed, but forced herself to nod. "Yes. Just that."

"Hmm." He went back to staring at the ceiling. "And now, having accomplished your goal, you expect to say: 'Thank you, Tristan, that was very nice,' and carry on as if it never happened."

She hadn't thought that far. She frowned. "I assumed, eventually, we'd go our separate ways." She studied his profile. "There's no consequences to this, no reason we need do anything because of it."

The corner of his lips lifted; she couldn't tell which of the possible moods the gesture reflected.

"Except," he stated, his voice still even, but with the accents increasingly clipped, "you've miscalculated."

She really didn't want to ask, especially given his tone, but he simply waited, so she had to. "How?"

"*You* may not expect me to marry you. However, as the one who was seduced, *I* expect *you* to marry *me*."

He turned his head, met her gaze—let her read in the blazing hazel of his eyes that he was absolutely serious.

She stared—read the message twice. Her jaw actually slackened, then she snapped her lips shut. "*That* is nonsensical! You don't want to marry me—you *know* you don't. You're simply being difficult." With a twist and a tug, she wrenched her wrist free, aware she managed only because he let her. She scrambled from the bed. Anger, fear, irritation, and trepidation were a heady mix. She made for her chemise.

Tristan sat up as she left the bed, his gaze locking on the

bruises circling her upper arms. Then he remembered the attack, and breathed again. Mountford had marked her, not him.

Then she bent and swiped up her chemise, and he saw the smudges on her hips, the faint bluish marks his fingers had left on the alabaster skin of her bottom. She turned, struggling into the chemise, and he saw similar marks on her breasts.

Softly swore.

"What?" She yanked her chemise down and glared at him.

Lips compressed, he shook his head. "Nothing." He stood, and reached for his trousers.

Something dark, something powerful and dangerous was churning inside him. Burgeoning, struggling to break free.

He couldn't think.

He grabbed her dress from the bed and shook it out; there was only the slightest stain, and a small red spot. The sight rattled his control. He blocked it out, and carried the gown to her.

She took it, conveying her thanks with a haughty inclination of her head. He nearly laughed. She thought he was letting her walk free.

He shrugged into his shirt, quickly buttoned it, tucked it into his waistband, then quickly and expertly knotted his cravat. All the while he watched her. She was used to having a maid; she couldn't do up her gown on her own.

When he was fully dressed, he picked up her cloak. "Here. Let me." He handed her the cloak; she glanced at him, then took it. And turned, presenting him with her back.

He quickly laced up her gown. As he tied off the laces, his fingers slowed. He hooked one finger beneath the laces, anchoring her before him. Leaning down, he spoke softly in her ear. "I haven't changed my mind. I intend to marry you."

She stood poker straight, looking ahead, then she turned her head and met his eyes. "I haven't changed my mind either. I don't want to get married." She held his gaze, then added, "I never truly did."

He hadn't been able to shift her.

The argument had raged all the way down the stairs, reduced to hissed whispers as they crossed the ground floor because of Biggs, only to escalate again when they reached the relative safety of the garden.

Nothing he'd said had swayed her.

When, driven to complete and total exasperation by the notion that a lady of twenty-six whom he'd just very pleasurably initiated into the delights of intimacy should refuse to wed him, title, wealth, houses, and all, he'd threatened to march straight up her garden path and demand her hand from her uncle and her brother, revealing all if she made that necessary, she'd gasped, halted, turned to him—and nearly slain him with a look of horrified vulnerability.

"You said what was between us would remain between us."

There'd been real fear in her eyes.

He'd backed down.

In real disgust had heard himself gruffly assuring her that of course he wouldn't do any such thing.

Hoisted with his own petard.

Worse, hoisted with his honor.

Late that night, slumped before the fire in his library, Tristan tried to find a way through the morass that had, without warning, appeared around his feet.

Slowly sipping French brandy, he replayed all their exchanges, tried to read the thoughts, the emotions, behind her words. Some he couldn't be certain of, some he couldn't define, but of one thing he felt reasonably sure. She honestly didn't think she—a twenty-six-year-old ape-leader—her words—was capable of attracting and holding the honest and honorable attentions of a man like him.

Raising his glass, eyes on the flames, he let the fine liquor slide down his throat.

Admitted, quietly, to himself, that he didn't truly care what she thought.

He had to have her—in his house, within his walls, in his bed. Safe. Had to; he no longer had any choice. The dark, dangerous emotion she'd stirred to life and now unleashed would not permit any other outcome.

He hadn't known he had it in him, that degree of feeling. Yet that evening, when he'd been forced to stand on the garden path and watch her—let her—walk away from him, he'd finally realized what that roiling emotion was.

Possessiveness.

He'd come very close to giving it free rein.

He'd always been a protective man, witness his erstwhile occupation, and now his tribe of old dears. He'd always understood that much of himself, but with Leonora his feelings went far beyond any protective instinct.

Given that, he didn't have much time. There was a very definite limit to his patience; there always had been.

Rapidly he mentally scanned all the arrangements he'd put in place in pursuit of Mountford, including those he'd initiated that evening after returning from Montrose Place.

For the moment, that line would hold. He could turn his attention to the other front on which he was engaged.

He had to convince Leonora to marry him; he had to change her mind.

How?

Ten minutes later he rose and went to seek his old dears. Information, he'd always maintained, was the key to any successful campaign.

The dinner with her aunts, a not-infrequent event in the weeks leading up to the Season when her aunt Mildred, Lady Warsingham, would come to try and convince Leonora to cast her hat into the matrimonial ring, was a near disaster.

A fact directly attributable to Trentham, even in his absence.

The next morning, Leonora was still having trouble subduing her blushes, still battling to keep her mind from dwelling on those moments when, panting and heated, she'd lain beneath him and watched him above her, moving in that deep, compulsive rhythm, her body accepting the surges of his, the rolling, relentless physical fusion.

She'd watched his face, seen passion strip away all his charm and leave the harsh angles and planes etched with something far more primitive.

Fascinating. Enthralling.

And utterly distracting.

She threw herself into sorting and rearranging every scrap of paper in her escritoire.

At twelve, the doorbell pealed. She heard Castor cross the hall and open the door. The next instant Mildred's voice rang out. "In the parlor, is she? Don't worry—I'll see myself in."

Leonora pushed her piles of papers into the escritoire, closed it, and rose. Wondering what had brought her aunt back to Montrose Place so soon, she faced the door and patiently waited to find out.

Mildred swept in, stylishly turned out in black and white.

"Well, my dear!" She advanced on Leonora. "Here you sit, all by yourself. I wish you would consent to come with me on my visits, but I know you won't, so I won't bother bemoaning that."

Leonora dutifully kissed Mildred's scented cheek, and murmured her gratitude.

"Dreadful child." Mildred subsided onto the chaise and settled her skirts. "Now, I had to come because I have simply *wonderful* news! I have tickets for Mr. Kean's new play for this very evening. The theater is already sold out for weeks ahead—it's going to be the play of the Season. But by a fabulous stroke of magnanimous fate, a dear friend gave me tickets, and I have a spare. Gertie will come, of course. And you will come, too, won't you?" Mildred looked at her beseechingly. "You know Gertie will mutter all through the performance otherwise—she always behaves when you're there."

Gertie was her other aunt, Mildred's older, unmarried sister. Gertie had strong views about gentlemen, and while she refrained from voicing these in Leonora's presence, deeming her niece still too young and impressionable to hear such caustic truths, she had never spared her sister from her blistering observations, blessedly delivered *sotto voce.*

Sinking into the armchair opposite Mildred, Leonora hesitated. Visiting the theater with her aunt generally meant meeting at least two gentlemen Mildred had decided were eligible partis for her hand. But such a visit also meant watching a play, during which no one would dare talk. She would be free to lose herself in the performance. With luck, it might succeed in distracting her from Trentham and *his* performance.

And a chance to see the inimitable Edmund Kean was not to be lightly refused.

"Very well." She refocused on Mildred in time to see triumph fleetingly light her aunt's eyes. She narrowed her own. "But I refuse to be paraded like a well-bred mare during the interval."

Mildred dismissed the quibble with a wave. "If you wish, you may remain in your seat throughout the break. Now, you will wear your midnight blue silk, won't you? I know you care nothing for your appearance, so you may do it to please me."

The hopeful look in Mildred's eyes was impossible to deny; Leonora felt her lips curve. "As such a sought-after opportunity comes through you, I can hardly refuse." The midnight blue gown was one of her favorites, so appeasing her aunt cost her nothing. "But I warn you—I won't put up with any Bond Street beau whispering sweet nothings in my ear during the performance."

Mildred sighed. She shook her head as she rose. "When we were girls, having eligible gentlemen whisper in our ears was the highlight of the night." She glanced at Leonora. "I'm due at Lady Henry's, then Mrs. Arbuthnot's, so I must away. I'll call for you in the carriage around eight."

Leonora nodded her agreement, then saw her aunt to the door.

She returned to the parlor more pensive. Perhaps going out into the ton, at least for the few weeks before the Season proper commenced, might be wise.

Might distract her from the lingering effects of her seduction.

Might help her recover from the shock of Trentham offering to marry her. And the even greater shock of him insisting that she should.

She didn't understand his reasoning, but he'd seemed very set on it. A few weeks in society being exposed to other men would no doubt remind her why she'd never wed.

She suspected nothing. Not until the carriage drew up before the theater steps and a harried groom opened the door did the faintest glimmer of a suspicion cross her mind.

And by then it was too late.

Trentham stepped forward and calmly held out his hand to assist her from the carriage.

Jaw slack, she stared at him.

Mildred's elbow dug into her ribs; she started, then threw a swift, fulminating glance at her aunt before haughtily reaching out and placing her fingers in Trentham's palm.

She had no choice. Carriages were banking up; the steps of the theater hosting the most talked-about play was not the place to create a scene—to tell a gentleman what one thought of him and his machinations. To inform her aunt that this time she'd gone too far.

Cloaked in chilly hauteur, she allowed him to help her down, then stood, feigning icy indifference, idly surveying the fashionable hordes streaming up the theater steps and through the open doors while he greeted her aunts and assisted them to the pavement.

Mildred, resplendent in her favorite black and white, forcefully linked her arm in Gertie's and forged her way up the steps.

Coolly, Trentham turned to her and offered his arm.

She met his gaze, to her surprise saw no triumph in his hazel eyes, but rather a careful watchfulness. The sight mollified her somewhat; she consented to lay the tips of her fingers on his sleeve and allow him to guide her in her aunts' wake.

Tristan considered the angle of Leonora's chin and preserved his silence. They joined her aunts in the foyer, where the crush had brought them to a standstill. He took the lead and with no great difficulty cleared a path to the stairs upward, drawing Leonora with him; her aunts followed close behind. Once on the stairs the press of bodies eased; covering Leonora's hand on his sleeve, he led his party up to the semicircular corridor leading to the boxes.

He glanced at Leonora as they neared the door of the box he'd hired. "I've heard that Mr. Kean is the best actor of the day, and tonight's play a worthy showcase for his talents. I thought you might enjoy it."

She met his eyes briefly, then inclined her head, still haughtily aloof. Reaching the box, he held aside the heavy curtain screening the doorway; she swept in, her head high. He waited for her aunts to pass him, then followed, allowing the curtain to fall closed behind him.

Lady Warsingham and her sister bustled to the front of the box and disposed themselves in two of the three seats along the front. Leonora had paused in the shadows by the wall; her narrowed gaze was fixed on Lady Warsingham, who was busy noting all the notables in the other boxes, exchanging nods, determinedly not looking Leonora's way.

He hesitated, then approached.

Her attention swung to him; her eyes flared. "How did you manage this?" She spoke in a hissed whisper. "I never told you she was my aunt."

He raised a brow. "I have my sources."

"And the tickets." She glanced out at the boxes, quickly filling with those lucky enough to have secured a place. "Your cousins told me you never go out in society."

"As you can see, that's not strictly true."

She glanced back at him, expecting more.

He met her gaze. "I've little use for society in general, but I'm not here to spend my evening with the ton."

She frowned, somewhat warily asked, "Why are you here then?"

He held her gaze for a heartbeat, then murmured, "To spend my evening with you."

A bell clanged in the corridor. He reached for her arm and guided her to the remaining chair at the front of the box. She threw him a skeptical glance, then sat. He drew the fourth chair around, set it to her left, angled toward her, and settled to watch the performance.

It was worth every penny of the small fortune he'd paid. His eyes rarely strayed to the stage; his gaze remained on Leonora's face, watching the emotions flitting across her features, delicate, pure; and, in this setting, unguarded. Although initially aware of him, Edmund Kean's magic quickly drew her in; he sat and watched, content, perceptive, intrigued.

He had no idea why she'd refused him—why, according to her, she had no interest in marriage at all. Her aunts, subjected to his most subtle interrogation, had been unable to shed any light on the matter, which meant he was going into this battle blind.

Not that that materially affected his strategy. As far as he'd ever heard, there was only one way to win a reluctant lady.

When the curtain came down at the end of the first act, Leonora sighed, then remembered where she was, and with whom. She glanced at Trentham, was unsurprised to find his gaze steady on her face.

She smiled. Coolly. "I'd very much like some refreshment."

His eyes held hers for a moment, then his lips curved and he inclined his head, accepting the commission. His gaze went past her and he rose.

Leonora swiveled and saw Gertie and Mildred on their feet, gathering their reticules and shawls.

Mildred beamed at her and Trentham; her gaze settled on his face. "We're off to parade in the corridor and meet everyone. Leonora hates to be subjected to the crush, but I'm sure we can rely on you to entertain her."

For the second time that evening, Leonora's jaw fell slack. Stunned, she watched her aunts bustle out, watched Trentham hold the heavy curtain aside for them to escape. Given her earlier insistence on avoiding the ritual parade, she could hardly complain, and there was nothing the least improper in her and Trentham remaining in the box alone; they were in public, under the gaze of any number of the ton's matrons.

He let the curtain fall and turned back to her.

She cleared her throat. "I really am quite parched . . ." Refreshments were available by the stairs; reaching the booth and returning would keep him occupied for a good portion of the interval.

His gaze rested on her face; his lips were lightly curved. A tap sounded by the doorway; Trentham turned and held the curtain aside. An attendant ducked past, carrying a tray with four glasses and a bottle of chilled champagne. He placed the tray on the small table against the back wall.

"I'll pour."

The attendant bowed to her, then Trentham, and disappeared through the curtain.

Leonora watched as Trentham eased the cork from the bottle, then poured the delicately fizzy liquid into two of the long flutes. She was suddenly very glad she'd worn her midnight blue gown—suitable armor for this type of situation.

Picking up both glasses, he crossed to where she still sat, swiveled on her chair so she sat sideways to the pit.

He handed her one glass. She reached for it, somewhat surprised that he made no move to use the moment, to touch her fingers with his. He released the glass, caught her gaze as she glanced up.

"Relax. I won't bite."

She arched a brow at him, sipped, then asked, "Are you sure?"

His lips quirked; he glanced out at the patrons milling in the other boxes. "These surrounds are hardly conducive."

He looked back at her, then reached for Gertie's chair, turned it so its back was to the throng, and sat, stretching his long legs out before him, elegantly at ease.

He sipped, his gaze on her face, then asked, "So tell me. Is Mr. Kean really as good as they say?"

She realized he would have no notion; he'd been away with the army for the last several years. "He's an artist without peer, at least at the moment." Deeming the topic a safe one, she related the highlights of Mr. Kean's career.

He put a question here and there. When the subject had run its course, he let a moment pass, then quietly said, "Speaking of performances . . ."

She met his eyes, and nearly choked on her champagne. Felt a slow blush rise to her cheeks. She ignored it, lifted her chin. Met his gaze directly. She was, she reminded herself, an experienced lady now. "Yes?"

He paused, as if considering not what to say but how to say it. "I wondered . . ." He raised his glass, sipped, his lashes screening his eyes. "How much of an actress are you?"

She blinked, let her frown show in her eyes, let her expression convey her incomprehension.

His lips quirked self-deprecatingly. His eyes returned to hers. "If I were to say you'd enjoyed our . . . last interlude, would I be wrong?"

Her blush intensified but she refused to look away. "No." Remembered pleasure flooded her, gave her strength to waspishly state, "You know perfectly well I enjoyed . . . all of it."

"So that didn't contribute to your aversion to marrying me?"

It suddenly occurred to her what he was asking. "Of course not." The idea he might think such a thing . . . she frowned. "I told you—my decision was reached long ago. My stance has nothing to do with you."

Could a man like him really need reassurance on such a point? She could tell nothing from his eyes, his expression.

Then he smiled, gently, yet the gesture was more predatory than charming. "I just wanted to be sure."

He hadn't resigned the battle to get her to accept him—*that* message she read with ease. Determinedly ignoring the effect of all that lounging masculinity mere feet away, she fixed him with a polite look and asked after his cousins. He replied, allowing the change of subject.

The audience started returning to their seats; Mildred and Gertie rejoined them. Leonora was aware of the sharp glances both her aunts cast her; she kept her expression calm and serene, and gave her attention to the stage. The curtain went up; the play recommenced.

To his credit, Trentham made no move to distract her. She was once again aware his gaze remained primarily on her, but refused to acknowledge the attention in any way. He couldn't force her to marry him; if she held to her refusal, he'd eventually go away.

Just as she'd imagined he would.

The notion of being proved right for once brought her no joy. Inwardly frowning at such a hint of susceptibility, she forced herself to concentrate on Edmund Kean.

When the curtain came down, tumultuous applause filled the theater; after Mr. Kean had taken countless bows, the audience, finally satisfied, turned to leave. Swept away by the drama, Leonora smiled easily and gave Trentham her hand, paused beside him as he lifted the curtain to allow Mildred and Gertie to pass out, then let him guide her in their wake.

The corridor was too crowded to allow any private conversation; the jostling crowd, however, gave plenty of scope for any gentleman wishing to tease a lady's senses. To her surprise, Trentham made no move to do so. She was highly conscious of him, large, solid, and strong beside her, protecting her from the pressure of shifting bodies. From his occasional glances, she knew he was aware of her, yet his attention remained focused on steering them efficiently through the throng and out into the street.

Their carriage drew up as they gained the pavement.

He handed Gertie and Mildred up, then turned to her.

Met her gaze. Lifted her hand from his sleeve.

Holding her gaze, he raised her fingers to his lips, kissed—the warmth of the lingering caress spread through her.

"I hope you enjoyed the evening."

She couldn't lie. "Thank you. I did."

He nodded and handed her up. His fingers slid from hers with only the faintest hint of reluctance.

She sat; he stepped back and closed the door. He signaled to the coachman. The carriage lurched, then rumbled off.

The impulse to sit forward and peer back out of the window to see if he stood watching nearly overcame her. Hands clasped in her lap, she stayed where she was and stared across the carriage.

He might have refrained from any illicit caress, any attempt to ruffle her senses, but she'd seen—experienced—enough to appreciate the reality behind his mask. He hadn't given up yet.

She told herself he would. Eventually.

Seated opposite, Mildred stirred. "Such polished manners— so masterful. You have to admit there are few gentlemen about these days who are so . . ." Lost for words, she gestured.

"Manly," Gertie supplied.

Both Leonora and Mildred looked at her in surprise. Mildred recovered first. "Indeed!" She nodded. "You're quite right. He behaved just as he ought."

Shaking free of the shock of hearing Gertie, the gentleman-hater, approve of any male—then again, this was Trentham, the charmer—she should have expected it—Leonora asked, "How did you meet him?"

Mildred shifted, settling her skirts. "He called this morning. Given you were already acquainted, accepting his invitation seemed perfectly sensible."

From Mildred's point of view. Leonora refrained from reminding her aunt that she'd said an old friend had given her the tickets; she'd long known what lengths Mildred would go to to get her into the presence of an eligible gentleman. And there was no doubt Trentham was eligible.

The thought brought him once more to mind—not as he'd been in the theater, but as he'd been in the golden moments they'd shared in the upstairs bedroom. Each moment, each touch, were imprinted on her memory; just the thought was enough to evoke again, not just the sensations but all the rest—all she'd felt.

She'd tried hard to keep the memories from her, not to think or dwell on the emotion that had filled her when she'd realized he intended drawing back from consummation—the emotion that had driven her to utter her plea.

Please . . . don't leave me.

The words haunted her, the memory alone enough to make her feel acutely vulnerable. Exposed.

Yet his response . . . despite all, regardless of what else she knew of him, how she judged his character, his machinations, she owed him for that.

For giving her all she'd wanted.

For being hers to command in that moment, for giving himself to her as she'd wished.

She let the memory slide from her; it was still too evocative to wrap herself in. Instead, she turned to the evening, considered all that had and hadn't been. Including the way she'd reacted to him, to his nearness. That had changed. No longer did her nerves leap and jump. Now, when he was close, when they touched, her nerves glowed. It was the only word she could find for the sensation, for the warm comfort it brought. Perhaps an echo of remembered pleasure. Regardless, far from being on edge, she'd felt comfortable. As if rolling naked together on a bed indulging in the act of intimacy had fundamentally changed her responses to him.

For the better, as she saw it. She no longer felt at such a disadvantage, no longer felt physically tense, keyed up in his presence. Curious, but true. Their time alone in the box had been comfortable, pleasant.

If she was honest, totally enjoyable despite his probing.

She sighed, and leaned back against the squabs. She could hardly upbraid Mildred with any sincerity. She'd enjoyed the evening far more, and in quite a different way, than she'd expected.

When he called to take her driving in the park the next morning, she was stunned. When she tried to refuse, he simply looked
at her.

"You've already admitted you don't have any engagements."

Only because she'd thought he wanted to tell her about his
investigations.

His hazel eyes remained fixed on hers. "You should tell me
about the letters you sent to Cedric's acquaintances. You can tell
me just as well in the park as here." His gaze sharpened. "Besides, you must be longing to get out in the fresh air. Today is not
the sort of day to let slip by."

She narrowed her eyes at him; he was seriously dangerous. He
was right, of course; the day was glorious, and she'd been toying
with the idea of a brisk walk, but after her last excursion hesitated to go out alone.

He was too wise to press further, but simply waited . . . waited
for capitulation as he was wont to do.

She pulled a face at him. "Very well. Wait while I get my pelisse."

He was waiting in the hall when she came down the stairs. As she walked by his side to the gate, she told herself she really should not allow this ease she felt with him to develop much further. Being with him was altogether too comfortable. Too pleasant.

The drive did nothing to break the spell. The breeze was fresh, tangy with the promise of spring; the sky was blue with wispy clouds that merely flirted with the sun. The warmth was a welcome relief from the chill winds that had blown until recently; the first swelling buds were visible on the branches beneath which Trentham steered his greys.

On such a day, the ladies of the ton were out and about, but the hour was still early, the Avenue not overly crowded. She nodded here and there to those of her aunts' acquaintances who recognized her, but largely gave her attention to the man beside her.

He drove with a light touch she knew enough to admire, and an unthinking confidence that told her more. She tried to keep her eyes off his hands, long fingers expertly managing the ribbons, and failed.

A moment later, she felt heat rise in her cheeks and forced her gaze away. "I sent the last letters off this morning. With luck someone will reply within a week."

Tristan nodded. "The more I think of it, the more likely it seems that whatever Mountford is after, it's something to do with your cousin Cedric's work."

Leonora glanced at him; wisps of her hair had come loose and flirted about her face. "How so?"

He looked to his horses—away from her mouth, her soft luscious lips. "It had to be something a purchaser would get with the house. If your uncle had been willing to sell, would you have cleared out Cedric's workshop?" He glanced at her. "I got the impression it had been forgotten, dismissed from everyone's minds. I hardly think that applies to anything in the library."

"True." She nodded, trying to tame her wayward locks. "I wouldn't have bothered going into the workshop if it hadn't been for Mountford's efforts. However, I think you're overlooking one point. If *I* was after something and had a reasonable idea where it might be, I might arrange to buy the house, not intending to complete the sale, you understand, and then ask to visit to measure up rooms for furnishings or remodeling." She shrugged. "Easy enough to get time to look around and perhaps remove things."

He considered, imagined, then reluctantly grimaced. "You're right. That leaves us with the possibility that it, whatever it is, could be just about anything secreted anywhere in the house." He glanced at her. "A house full of eccentrics."

She met his gaze, raised her brows, then tipped her nose in the air and looked away.

He called the next day and swept aside her reservations with invitations to a special preview of the latest exhibition at the Royal Academy.

She cast him a severe glance as he ushered her through the gallery doors. "Do all earls get such special privileges?"

He met her gaze. "Only special earls."

Her lips curved before she looked away.

He hadn't expected to gain all that much from the excursion, to his mind a minor exercise in his wider strategy. Instead, he found himself engrossed in a spirited discussion on the merits of landscapes over portraiture.

"People are so alive! They're what life's about."

"But the scenes are the essence of the country, of England—the people are a function of the place."

"Nonsense! Just look at this costermonger." She pointed to an excellent line drawing of a man with a barrow. "One glance and you'd know exactly where he came from—even what borough of London. The people personify the place—they're a representation of it, too."

They were in one of the smaller rooms in the labyrinthine gallery; from the corner of his eye, he saw the other group in the chamber move on through the door, leaving them alone.

Leaning on his arm, studying a busy river scene populated with half a regiment of dockworkers, Leonora hadn't noticed. Obedient to his tug, she strolled on to the next work—a plain and simple landscape.

She humphed, glanced back at the river scene, then up at him. "You can't expect me to believe you'd rather have an empty landscape than a picture of people."

He looked into her face. She stood close; her lips, her warmth, beckoned. Her hand lay trustingly on his arm.

Desire and more unexpectedly surfaced.

He didn't try to mask it, to screen it from his face or his eyes.

"People in general don't interest me." He met her gaze, let his voice deepen. "But there's one picture of you I'd like to see again, to experience again."

She held his gaze. A soft blush slowly rose in her cheeks, but she didn't look away. She knew exactly what image he was thinking of—of her naked and wanting beneath him. She drew a brief breath. "You shouldn't say that."

"Why not? It's the truth."

He felt her quiver.

"It's not going to happen—you won't see that picture again."

He studied her, felt both humble and amazed that she didn't see him for what he was—that she believed, not naively but with simple conviction, that if she stood firm, he wouldn't step beyond the bounds of honor and seize her.

She was wrong, but he valued her trust, treasured it too much to unnecessarily shake it.

So he raised a brow, smiled. "On that I fear we're unlikely to agree."

As he'd anticipated, she sniffed, put her nose in the air, and turned to the next work of art.

He let one day go by—a day he spent checking with his various contacts, all those whom he'd set the task of locating Montgomery Mountford—before returning to Montrose Place and inveigling Leonora to accompany him on a drive to Richmond. He'd done his forward planning; the Star and Garter was apparently the place to see and be seen.

It was the "be seen" aspect he required.

Leonora felt curiously lighthearted as she walked beneath the trees, her hand locked in Trentham's. Not precisely *de rigueur*, but when she'd pointed that out, he'd merely raised a brow and continued holding her hand.

Her mood was due to him; she couldn't imagine feeling this way with any other gentleman she'd known. She knew it was dangerous, that she would miss the unexpected closeness, the totally unanticipated sharing—the subtle thrill of walking beside a wolf—when he finally gave in and bade her adieu.

She didn't care. When the time came, she'd mope, but for now she was determined to grasp the moment, a fleeting interlude as spring bloomed. Not in her wildest dreams had she imagined such a state of ease could arise from intimacy, from one simple act of physical sharing.

There wouldn't be any repetition. Despite what she'd thought, he hadn't intended it to happen in the first place, and no matter what he said, he wouldn't precipitate another encounter against her wishes. Now that she knew he felt honor-bound to marry her, she knew better than to lie with him again. She wasn't such a fool as to tempt fate further.

No matter how she felt when with him.

No matter how much fate tempted her.

She slanted him a glance.

He caught it, raised a brow. "A penny for your thoughts."

She laughed, shook her head. "My thoughts are much too precious." *Much* too dangerous.

"What are they worth?"

"More than you can possibly pay."

When he didn't immediately reply, she glanced at him.

He met her gaze. "Are you sure?"

She was about to dismiss the question with a laugh, then she read his true meaning in his eyes. Realized on a rush of understanding that, as so often seemed to occur, his thoughts and hers were very much in tune. That he knew what she'd been thinking—and quite literally meant he'd pay anything she asked . . .

It was all there in his eyes, engraved in crystalline hazel, sharp and clear. He rarely adopted his mask with her now, not when they were private.

Their steps had slowed; they halted. She dragged in a tight breath. "Yes." Regardless of the price he was prepared to pay, she couldn't—wouldn't—accept.

They stood facing each other while a long moment passed.

It should have turned awkward, but, as in the gallery, a deeper understanding—an acceptance each of the other—prevented it.

Eventually, he simply said, "We'll see."

She smiled, easily, companionably, and they resumed their walk.

After inspecting the deer and ambling under the oaks and beeches, they returned to his curricle and repaired to the Star and Garter.

"I haven't been here for years," she admitted as she took her seat at a table by the window. "Not since the year I came out."

She waited while he ordered tea and crumpets, then said, "I have to admit I have difficulty seeing you as a young man on the town."

"Probably because I never was one." He settled back, held her gaze. "I went into the Guards at twenty, more or less straight from Oxford." He shrugged. "It was the accepted route in my branch of the family—we were the military arm."

"So where were you stationed? You must have attended balls in the nearest town?"

He kept her entertained with tales of his exploits, and that of his peers, then turned the table and drew out her memories of her first Season. She had enough she could say to make a decent showing; if he realized her accounts were edited, he gave no sign.

They'd moved on to her observations of the ton and its present inhabitants when a party at a nearby table, all standing to leave, tipped over a chair. She glanced around—and realized, from the fixed stares of the three girls and their mother that the reason for the commotion was that all attention had been locked on them.

The mother, an overdressed matron, cast a supercilious, purse-lipped glance their way, then moved to gather her chicks. "Come, girls!"

Two moved to obey; the third stared for a moment longer, then turned and hissed, her whisper clearly audible, "Did Lady Mott say when the wedding would be?"

Leonora continued to stare at the retreating backs. Her wits were tumbling, shooting off in all directions; as scene after scene replayed in her mind, she felt chilled, then overheated. Temper—an eruption more powerful than any she'd known—overtook her. Slowly, she turned her head, and met Trentham's gaze.

Read in the hard hazel not an ounce of contrition, not even a hint of exculpation, but simple, clear, and unequivocal confirmation.

"You *fiend*." She breathed the word. Her fingers tightened on the handle of her teacup.

His eyes didn't so much as flicker. "I wouldn't advise it."

He hadn't shifted from his lounging pose, but she knew how fast he could move.

She suddenly felt dizzy, giddy; she couldn't breathe. She pushed up out of her chair. "Let me out of here."

Her voice wavered but he acted; she was dimly aware that he was watching her closely. He got her outside, swept aside all hurdles; she was too overwrought to stand on pride and not take advantage of the escape he arranged.

But the instant her half boots touched the grass in the park, she jerked her hand from his arm and strode out. Away from him. Away from the temptation of hitting him—trying to hit him; she knew he wouldn't let her.

Gall burned her throat; she'd thought him out of his depth in the ton, but it was she who had had her eyes closed. Lulled into doe-eyed trust by a wolf—who hadn't even bothered to wear wool!

She gritted her teeth against a scream, one directed against

herself. She'd known what he was like from the first—a remarkably ruthless man.

Abruptly, she came to a halt. Panic would get her nowhere,
especially with a man like him. She had to think, had to act—in
the right way.

So what had he done? What had he actually accomplished?
And how could she negate or reverse it?

She stood still as her wits slowly realigned. A measure of calm
descended; it wasn't—couldn't be—as bad as she'd thought.

She spun around and wasn't the least surprised to discover
him two feet away, watching her.

Carefully.

She locked her eyes on his. "Have you said anything to anyone
about us?"

His gaze didn't waver. "No."

"So that girl was simply . . ." She gestured with both hands.

"Extrapolating."

She narrowed her eyes. "As you knew everyone would."

He didn't reply.

She continued to look daggers at him as the realization that all
was not lost—that he hadn't created a social snare she couldn't
simply step out of—seeped through her. Her temper subsided;
her annoyance did not. "This is not a game."

A moment went by before he said, "All life is a game."

"And you play to win?" She infused the words with something
close to contempt.

He stirred, then reached out, took her hand.

To her utter surprise, he jerked her to him.

She gasped as she landed against his chest.

Felt his arm lock her to him.

Felt smoldering embers burst into flame.

He looked down at her, then carried the hand he'd trapped to his lips. Slowly brushed his lips to her fingers, then across her palm, lastly pressed them to her wrist. Holding her gaze, holding her captive all the while.

His eyes burned, reflecting all she could sense flaring between them.

"What's between you and me remains between you and me, but it hasn't gone away." He held her gaze. "And it won't."

He lowered his head. She dragged in a breath. "But I don't want it."

From under his lashes, his eyes met hers, then he murmured, "Too late."

And kissed her.

She'd called him a fiend, and she'd been right.

By noon the next day, Leonora knew what it felt like to be under siege.

When Trentham—damn his arrogant hide—had finally consented to release her, she'd been left in no doubt whatsoever that they were locked in combat.

"I am not going to marry you." She'd made the declaration with as much strength as she'd been able to muster, in the circumstances not as much as she'd have liked.

He'd looked at her, growled—actually growled—then grabbed her hand and marched off to his curricle.

On the way home, she'd preserved a frigid silence, not because various pithy phrases hadn't been burning her tongue, but because of his tiger, perched behind them. She'd had to wait until Trentham handed her to the pavement before Number 14 to fix him with a narrow-eyed glare, and demand, "Why? Why me? Give me one sane reason why you want to marry me."

Hazel eyes glinting, he'd looked down at her, then bent closer and murmured, "Do you remember that picture we spoke of?"

She'd quelled a sudden urge to step back. Searched his eyes briefly before asking, "What of it?"

"The prospect of seeing it every morning and every night constitutes an eminently sane reason to me."

She'd blinked; a blush had risen to her cheeks. For an instant, she'd stared at him, her stomach clenching tight, then she'd stepped back. "You're crazed."

She'd spun on her heel, pushed open the front gate, and stalked up the garden path.

The invitations had started arriving with the first post that morning.

One or two she could have ignored; fifteen by lunchtime, and all from the most powerful hostesses, were simply impossible to dismiss. How he had managed it she didn't know, but his message was clear—she could not avoid him. Either she met him on neutral ground, meaning within the social round of the ton, or . . .

That implied "or" was seriously worrisome.

He was not a man she could easily predict; her failure to foresee his objectives to date was what had got her into this mess in the first place.

"Or . . ." sounded far too dangerous, and when it came down to it, no matter what he did, as long as she adhered to the simple word "No" she would be perfectly safe, perfectly secure.

Mildred, with Gertie in tow, arrived at four o'clock.

"My dear!" Mildred sailed into the parlor like a black-and-white galleon. "Lady Holland called and insisted I bring you to her soirée this evening." Subsiding with a silken swish onto the chaise, Mildred turned eyes filled with zeal upon her. "I had no idea Trentham had such connections."

Leonora suppressed a growl of her own. "Nor had I." Lady Holland, for heaven's sake! "The man's a fiend!"

Mildred blinked. "Fiend?"

She resumed her activity—pacing before the hearth. "He's doing this to"—she gestured wildly—"flush me out!"

"Flush you . . ." Mildred looked concerned. "My dear, are you feeling quite the thing?"

Turning, she looked at Mildred, then switched her gaze to Gertie, who had paused before an armchair.

Gertie met her eyes, then nodded. "Very likely." She lowered herself into the chair. "Ruthless. Dictatorial. Not one to let anything stand in his way."

"Exactly!" The relief of having found someone who understood was great.

"Still," Gertie continued, "you do have a choice."

"Choice?" Mildred looked from one to the other. "I do hope you're not going to encourage her to fly in the face of this unlooked-for development?"

"As to that," Gertie responded, entirely unmoved, "she'll do as she pleases—she always has. But the real question here is, is she going to let him dictate to her, or is she going to make a stand?"

"Stand?" Leonora frowned. "You mean ignore all these invitations?" Even she found the thought a trifle extreme.

Gertie snorted. "Of course not! Do that, and you'll dig your own grave. But there's no reason to let him get away with thinking he can force you into anything. As I see it, the most telling response would be to accept the most sought-after invitations with delight, and attend with the clear aim of enjoying yourself. Go and meet him in the ballrooms and if he dares press you there, you can give him his congé with half the ton looking on."

She thumped her cane. "Mark my words, you need to teach

him he's not omnipotent, that he won't get his way by such machinations." Gertie's old eyes gleamed. "Best way to do that is to give him what he thinks he wants, then show him that it isn't what he really wants at all."

The look on Gertie's face was unashamedly wicked; the thought it evoked in Leonora's mind was definitely attractive.

"I take your point . . ." She stared into the distance, her mind juggling possibilities. "Give him what he's angled for, but . . ." Refocusing on Gertie, she beamed. "Of course!"

The number of invitations had grown to nineteen; she felt almost giddy with defiance.

She swung to Mildred; she'd been watching Gertie, a rather bemused expression on her face. "Before Lady Holland's, perhaps we should attend the Carstairs's rout?"

They did; Leonora used the event as a refresher to dust off and buff up her social skills. By the time she walked into Lady Holland's elegant rooms, her confidence was riding high. She knew she looked well in her deep topaz silk, her hair piled high, topaz drops in her ears, pearls looped about her throat.

Following in Mildred's and Gertie's wake, she curtsied before Lady Holland, who shook her hand and uttered the usual pleasantries, all the while observing her through shrewd and intelligent eyes.

"I understand you've made a conquest," her ladyship remarked.

Leonora raised her brows lightly, let her lips curve. "Entirely unintentionally, I assure you."

Lady Holland's eyes widened; she looked intrigued.

Leonora let her smile deepen; head high, she glided on.

From where he'd retreated to lounge against the drawing-room wall, Tristan watched the exchange, saw Lady Holland's surprise, caught the amused glance she shot him as Leonora moved into the crowd.

He ignored it, fixed his gaze on his quarry, and pushed away from the wall.

He'd arrived unfashionably early, uncaring that her ladyship, who had always taken an interest in his career, would correctly guess his reasons. The past two hours had been ones of inaction, of unutterable boredom, reminding him why he'd never felt he'd missed anything in joining the army at twenty. Now Leonora had consented to arrive, he could get on with things.

The invitations he'd arranged through his own offices and those of his town-bound old dears would ensure that for the next week he'd be able to come up with her every night, somewhere in the ton.

Somewhere conducive to furthering his goal.

Beyond that, even if the damn woman still held firm, society being what it was, the invitations would continue of their own accord, creating opportunities for him to exploit until she surrendered.

He had her in his sights; she wouldn't escape.

Closing the distance between them, he came up alongside her as her aunts sank onto a chaise by one side of the room. His appearance preempted a number of other gentlemen who had noticed Leonora and thought to test the waters.

He'd discovered that Lady Warsingham was by no means unknown within the ton; nor was her niece. The prevailing view of Leonora was that she was a willful lady stubbornly and intractably opposed to marriage. Although her age placed her beyond the ranks of the marriageable misses, her beauty, assurance, and behavior cast her in the light of a challenge, at least in the eyes of men who viewed challenging ladies with interest.

Such gentlemen would no doubt take note of *his* interest and look elsewhere. If they were wise.

He bowed to the older ladies, both of whom beamed at him.

He turned to Leonora and encountered an arch and distinctly chilly glance. "Miss Carling."

She gave him her hand and curtsied. He bowed, raised her, and set her hand on his sleeve.

Only to have her lift it off and turn to greet a couple who'd strolled up.

"Leonora! I declare we haven't seen you for an age!"

"Good evening, Daphne. Mr. Merryweather." Leonora touched cheeks with the brown-haired Daphne, a lady of bounteous charms, then shook hands with the gentleman whose coloring and features proclaimed him Daphne's brother.

She shot Tristan a glance, then smoothly included him, introducing him as the Earl of Trentham.

"I say!" Merryweather's eyes lit. "I heard you were in the Guards at Waterloo."

"Indeed." He uttered the word as repressively as he could, but Merryweather failed to take the hint. He babbled on with the usual questions; inwardly sighing, Tristan gave his practiced answers.

Leonora, more attuned to his tones, shot him a curious glance, but then Daphne claimed her attention.

His hearing acute, Tristan quickly realized the tenor of Daphne's inquiries. She assumed Leonora had no interest in him; although married, it was clear Daphne did.

From the corner of his eye, he saw Leonora cast him an assessing glance, then she leaned closer to Daphne, lowered her voice . . .

He suddenly saw the danger.

Reaching out, he very deliberately closed his fingers about Leonora's wrist. Smiling charmingly at Merryweather, he shifted, including Daphne in the gesture as, entirely unsubtly, he drew Leonora to him—away from Daphne—and linked her arm with his. "I do hope you'll excuse us—I've just sighted my erstwhile commander. I really should pay my respects."

Both Merryweather and Daphne smiled and murmured easy farewells; before Leonora could gather her wits, he inclined his head and drew her away, into the crowd.

Her feet moved; her gaze was locked on his face. Then she looked ahead. "That was rude. You're not a serving officer—there's no reason you need make your bow to your ex-commander."

"Indeed. Especially as he's not present."

She shot him a narrowed-eyed look. "Not just a fiend but a lying fiend."

"Speaking of fiendish, I think we should set some rules for this engagement. For however long we spend fencing within the ton—a length of time entirely in your control, I might add—you will refrain from setting any harpies such as the lovely Daphne on me."

"But why are you here if not to sample and select among the fruits of the ton?" She gestured about them. "It's what all tonnish gentleman do."

"God knows why—I don't. I, as you very well know, am here for only one purpose—in pursuit of you."

He paused to lift two glasses of champagne from a footman's tray. Handing one to Leonora, he guided her to a less congested area before a long window. Positioning himself so he could keep the room in view, he sipped, then continued, "You may play the game between us in any way you like, but if you possess any self-preservatory instincts at all, you will keep the game between us and not involve any others." He lowered his gaze, met her eyes. "Female, or male."

She considered him; her brows lightly rose. "Is that a threat?" She calmly sipped, apparently unperturbed.

He studied her eyes, serene and untroubled. Confident.

"No." Raising his glass, he clinked the edge to hers. "That's a promise."

He drank and watched her eyes flare.

But she had her temper firmly in hand. She forced herself to sip, to appear to be surveying the crowd, then lowered her glass. "You can't simply come along and take me over."

"I don't want to take you over. I want you in my bed."

That earned him a faintly scandalized glance, but no one else was near enough to hear.

Her blush subsiding, she held his gaze. "That is something you can't have."

He let the moment stretch, then raised a brow at her. "We'll see."

She studied his face, then raised her glass. Her gaze went past him.

"Miss Carling! By Jove! A delight to see you—why it must be years."

Leonora smiled, and held out her hand. "Lord Montacute. A pleasure—and yes, it has been years. Can I make you known to Lord Trentham?"

"Indeed! Indeed!" His lordship, ever genial, shook hands. "Knew your father—and your great-uncle, too, come to that. Irascible old blighter."

"As you say."

Remembering her aim, Leonora brightly asked, "Is Lady Montacute here tonight?"

His lordship waved vaguely. "Somewhere about."

She kept the conversation rolling, foiling all Trentham's attempts to dampen it—dampening Lord Montacute was beyond even Trentham's abilities. Simultaneously, she scanned the crowd for further opportunities.

It was pleasing to discover she hadn't lost the knack of summoning a gentleman with just a smile. In short order, she'd collected a select group, all of whom could hold their own conversationally. Lady Holland's gatherings were renowned for their wit and repartee; with a gentle prod here, a verbal poke there, she started the ball rolling—after that, their discourses took on a life of their own.

She had to suppress a too-revealing smile when Trentham, despite himself, was drawn in, becoming engaged with Mr. Hunt in a discussion of suppression orders as pertaining to the popular press. She stood by his side and presided over the group, ensuring the talk never flagged. Lady Holland drifted up, paused beside her, then nodded and met her eye.

"You have quite a talent, my dear." She patted Leonora's arm, her gaze sliding briefly to Trentham, then archly back to Leonora before she moved on.

A talent for what? Leonora wondered. Keeping a wolf at bay?

Guests had started leaving before the discussions waned. The group broke up reluctantly, the gentlemen drifting off to find their wives.

When she and Trentham once more stood alone, he looked at her. His lips slowly set, his eyes hardened, glinted.

She arched a brow, then turned toward where Mildred and Gertie stood waiting. "Don't be a hypocrite—you enjoyed it."

She wasn't sure, but she thought he growled. She didn't need to look to know he prowled at her heels as she crossed the room to her aunts.

He behaved, if not with joyous charm, then at least with perfect civility, escorting them down the stairs and out to their waiting carriage.

Tristan handed her aunts up, then turned to her. Deliberately stepping between her and the carriage, he took her hand, met her eyes.

"Don't think to repeat that exercise tomorrow."

He shifted and handed her to the carriage door.

One foot on the step, she met his gaze, and arched a brow. Even in the dimness, he recognized the challenge.

"You chose the field—I get to choose the weapons."

She inclined her head serenely, then ducked and entered the carriage.

He closed the door with care—and a certain deliberation.

Over breakfast the next morning, Leonora considered her social calendar; the evenings were now much fuller than they had been three days ago.

"You choose," Mildred had told her as she'd descended from the carriage last night.

Munching her toast, Leonora weighed the possibilities. Although the Season proper was some weeks distant, there were two balls that evening to which they'd been invited. The major event was the ball at Colchester House in Mayfair, the more minor and assuredly less formal, a ball at the Masseys' house in Chelsea.

Trentham would expect her to attend the Colchester affair; he'd wait for her to appear there, as he had last night at Lady Holland's.

Pushing away from the table, Leonora rose and headed for the parlor to dash off a note to Mildred and Gertie that she fancied visiting the Masseys that evening.

Sitting at her escritoire, she wrote the brief note, inscribed her aunts' names, then rang for a footman. It was her hope that, in this instance, absence would make the heart grow *less* fond; quite aside from the fact her nonappearance at Colchester House would annoy Trentham, there was also the definite possibility that, if left alone in such an arena, he might find his eye drawn to some other lady, perhaps even become distracted with one of Daphne's ilk . . .

Inwardly frowning, she looked up as the footman entered, and handed over the note for delivery.

That done, she sat back and determinedly turned her mind to more serious matters. Given her stubborn refusal of his suit, she was perhaps naive in thinking Trentham would continue to aid her in the matter of Montgomery Mountford, yet when she tried to imagine him losing interest, removing the men he had watching the house, she couldn't. Regardless of their personal interactions, she knew he wouldn't leave her to deal with Mountford alone.

Indeed, in light of what she'd learned of his character, the notion seemed laughable.

They would remain in undeclared partnership until the riddle of Mountford was solved; it therefore behooved her to push as hard as she could on that front. Keeping clear of Trentham's snares while dealing with him on a daily basis would not be easy; prolonging the danger was senseless.

She couldn't expect any answers to her letters for at least a few days more. So what else could she do?

Trentham's suggestion that Cedric's work was most likely Mountford's target had struck a chord. Besides Cedric's letters, the workshop had contained more than twenty ledgers and journals. She'd brought them up to the parlor and stacked them in a corner. Eyeing them, she recalled her late cousin's fine, faded, cramped writing.

Rising, she went upstairs and inspected Cedric's bedroom. It was inches deep in dust and strewn with cobwebs. She set the maids the task of cleaning the room; she'd search it tomorrow. For today . . . she descended to the parlor and settled to work through the journals.

By the time evening arrived, she'd uncovered nothing more exciting than the recipe for a concoction to remove stains from porcelain; it was difficult to believe Mountford and his mysterious foreigner were interested in that. Setting aside the ledgers, she went upstairs to change.

The Masseys' house was centuries old, a rambling villa built on the riverbank. The ceilings were lower than now fashionable; there was a wealth of dark wood in beams and paneling, but the shadows were dispersed by lamps, candelabra, and sconces liberally scattered through the rooms. The large interconnecting chambers were perfect for less formal entertaining. A small orchestra scraped away at the river end of the dining room, for the occasion converted into an area for dancing.

After greeting their hostess in the hall, Leonora entered the drawing room, telling herself she'd enjoy herself. That the boredom caused by lack of purpose that customarily afflicted her would not affect her tonight because she did indeed have a purpose.

Unfortunately, enjoying herself with other gentlemen if Trentham was not there to see . . . it was difficult to convince herself there was all that much to be gained from the evening. Nevertheless, she was there, gowned in silk of a deep turbulent blue no young unmarried lady could ever wear. As she didn't particularly want to chat, she might as well dance.

Leaving Mildred and Gertie with a group of their cronies, she made her way down the room, stopping to exchange greetings here and there, but always moving on. A dance had just ended when she stepped through the doors into the dining room; quickly scanning those present, she considered which of the gentlemen—

Hard fingers, a hard palm, closed about her hand; her senses reacted, informing her who stood at her shoulder even before she turned and met his gaze.

"Good evening." His eyes on hers, Trentham raised her hand to his lips. Searched her eyes. Raised a brow. "Would you care to dance?"

The look in his eyes, the tenor of his voice—just like that, he made her come alive. Made her nerves tighten, her senses sing. Sent a rush of pleasurable anticipation sliding through her. She drew breath, her imagination eagerly supplying what dancing with him would feel like. "I . . ." She looked away, across the sea of dancers waiting for the next measure to begin.

He said nothing, simply waited. When she glanced back at him, he met her gaze. "Yes?"

His hazel eyes were sharp, watchful; behind them lurked faint amusement.

She felt her lips set, lifted her chin. "Indeed—why not?"

He smiled, not his charming smile but in predatory appreciation of her meeting his challenge. He led her forward as the opening strains of a waltz began.

It would have to be a waltz. The instant he drew her into his arms, she knew she was in trouble. Valiantly battling to dampen her response to having him so near, to feeling his strength engulf her again, his hand spread over the silk at her back, she cast about for distraction.

Let a frown form in her eyes. "I thought you would attend the Colchesters' affair."

The ends of his lips lifted. "I knew you'd be here." His eyes quizzed her—wicked, dangerous. "Believe me, I'm perfectly content with your choice."

If she'd harbored any doubt as to what he was alluding, the turn at the end of the room explained all. If they'd been at the Colchesters, waltzing in their huge ballroom, he wouldn't have been able to hold her so close, to curl his fingers so possessively about her hand, to draw her so tight through the turn their hips brushed. Here, the dance floor was crowded with other couples all absorbed with each other, immersed in the moment. There were no matrons lining the walls, watching, waiting to disapprove.

His thigh parted hers, all restrained power as he swung her through the turn; she couldn't suppress a reactive shiver— couldn't stop her nerves, her whole body responding.

Tristan watched her face, wondered if she had any idea of just how responsive she was, of what seeing her eyes flare, then darken, seeing her lashes sweep down, her lips part, did to him.

He knew she didn't know.

That only made it worse, only heightened the effect, and left him in even greater pain.

The insistent ache had been escalating over the past days, a nagging aggravation he'd never before had to contend with. Before, the itch had been a simple one to scratch. This time . . .

His every sense was focused on her, on the sway of her supple body in his arms, on the promise of her warmth, the elusive, teasing torment of the passion she seemed intent on denying.

That last was something he wouldn't permit. Shouldn't permit.

The music ended, and he was forced to halt, forced to release her, something he did reluctantly, a fact her wide eyes said she realized.

She cleared her throat, smoothed her gown. "Thank you." She looked around. "Now——"

"Before you waste time planning anything else—like attracting another gentleman to dance with you—while I'm with you, you'll dance with no one else."

Leonora turned to face him. "I beg your pardon?"

She honestly couldn't believe her ears.

His eyes remained hard. He raised a brow. "Do you want me to repeat it?"

"No! I want to forget I ever heard such an outrageous piece of impertinence."

He seemed totally unaffected by her increasing ire. "That would be unwise."

She felt her temper rise; they'd kept their voices low, but there was no doubt which way the discussion was heading. Drawing herself up, drawing every ounce of haughtiness she possessed about her, she inclined her head. "If you'll excuse me——"

"No." Steely fingers closed about her elbow; he nodded across the room. "See that door over there? We're going to go through it."

She drew in a huge breath, held it. Carefully enunciated, "I realize your experience of the ton——"

"The ton bores me to death." He glanced down at her, started unobtrusively but effectively steering her toward the closed door. "I'm therefore unlikely to pay much attention to its strictures."

Her heart was thumping. Looking into his eyes—hard, faceted hazel—she realized she wasn't playing with just a wolf, but a *wild* wolf. One who didn't acknowledge any rules beyond his own. "You *cannot* simply . . ."

Abduct me. Ravish me.

The intent in his eyes left her breathless.

His gaze remained on her face, gauging, judging, as he expertly herded her across the crowded room. "I suggest we repair to a place where we can discuss our relationship in private."

She'd been private with him any number of times; there was no need for her senses to leap at the word. No need for her imagination to run riot. Irritated that it had, she made a firm bid to take charge again. Lifting her head, she nodded. "Very well. I agree. Clearly we need to address our differing views and set matters straight."

She wasn't going to marry him; that was the point he needed to accept. If she emphasized that fact, clung to it, she'd be safe.

They reached the door and he opened it; she stepped through into a corridor running alongside the reception rooms. The passage was wide enough for two to walk abreast; one side was lined with carved paneling in which doors were set, the other was a wall of windows looking out over the private gardens.

In late spring and summer the windows would be opened and the corridor would become a delightful venue in which guests could stroll. Tonight, with a raw wind blowing and the promise of frost in the air, all the doors and windows were closed, the passage deserted.

Moonlight streamed in providing light enough to see. The walls were stone, the doors solid oak. Once Trentham shut the door behind them they stood in a silvered, private world.

He released her arm, offered his; she pretended not to notice. Head high, she paced slowly along. "The pertinent point we need to address—"

She broke off when his hand closed about hers. Possessively. She halted, looked down at her fingers swallowed in his palm.

"That," she said, her gaze fixed on the sight, "is a perfect example of the issue we need to discuss. You cannot go around grabbing my hand, seizing me as if I in some way belonged to you—"

"You do."

She looked up. Blinked. "I beg your pardon?"

Tristan looked into her eyes; he wasn't averse to explaining. "You. Belong. To me." It felt good to state it, reinforcing the reality.

Her eyes widened; he continued, "Regardless of what you imagined you were doing, you gave yourself to me. *Offered* yourself to me. I accepted. Now you're mine."

Her lips thinned; her eyes flashed. "That is not what happened. You're deliberately—God alone knows why—misconstruing the incident."

She said nothing more but glared up at him belligerently.

"You're going to have to work a lot harder to convince me that having you naked beneath me on the bed in Montrose Place was a figment of my imagination."

Her jaw firmed. "*Misconstruing*—not imagining."

"Ah—so you admit that you did, indeed—"

"What *happened*," she snapped, "as you very well know, is that we enjoyed"—she gestured—"a pleasant interlude."

"As I recall, you begged me to . . . 'initiate you' was, I believe, the term we agreed on."

Even in the poor light, he could see her blush. But she nodded. "Just so."

Turning, she walked along the corridor; he kept pace beside her, her hand still locked in his.

She didn't immediately speak, then she drew in a deep breath. He realized he was going to get at least part of an explanation.

"You have to understand—and accept—that I don't wish to marry. Not you, not anyone. I have no interest in the state. What happened between us . . ." She lifted her head, looked down the long corridor. "That was purely because I wanted to know. To experience . . ." She looked down, walked on. "And I thought you were a sensible choice to be my teacher."

He waited, then prompted, his tone even, nonaggressive, "Why did you think that?"

She waved between them, slipping her hand from his to do so. "The attraction. It was obvious. It was simply there—you know it was."

"Yes." He was starting to see . . . he halted.

She stopped, too, and faced him. Met his gaze, searched his face. "So you do understand, don't you? It was just so I would know . . . that's all. Just once."

Very carefully, he asked, "Done. Finished. Over?"

She lifted her head. Nodded. "Yes."

He held her gaze for a long moment, then murmured, "I did warn you, on the bed at Montrose Place, that you'd miscalculated."

Her head rose another notch, but she evenly stated, "That was when you felt you had to marry me."

"I *know* I have to marry you, but that isn't my point."

Exasperation flared in her eyes. "What is your point?"

He could feel a grim, definitely cynical, totally self-deprecatory smile fighting for expression; he kept it from his face, kept his features impassive. "That attraction you mentioned. Has it died?"

She frowned. "No. But it will—you know it will. . . ." She stopped because he was shaking his head.

"I know no such thing."

Wary irritation crept into her face. "I accept that it hasn't faded *yet*, but you know perfectly well gentlemen do not remain attracted to women for long. In a few weeks, once we've identified Mountford and you'll no longer be meeting me on a daily basis, you'll forget me."

He let the moment stretch while assessing his options. Eventually asked, "And if I don't?"

Her eyes narrowed. She opened her lips to reiterate that he would.

He cut her off by stepping nearer, closer, crowding her against the windows.

Immediately, heat bloomed between them, beckoning, enticing. Her eyes flared, her breathing caught, then continued more rapidly. Her hands rose, fluttered to rest lightly against his chest; her lashes lowered as he leaned closer.

"Our *mutual* attraction hasn't faded in the least—it's grown stronger." He breathed the words along her cheek. He wasn't touching her, holding her, other than with his nearness. "You say it'll fade—I say it won't. I'm sure I'm right—you're sure you are. You want to address the matter—I'm willing to be party to an agreement."

Leonora felt giddy. His words were dark, forceful, black magic in her mind. His lips touched, butterfly light, to her temple; his breath fanned her cheek. She dragged in a tight breath. "What agreement?"

"If the attraction fades, I'll agree to release you. Until it does, you're mine."

A shiver slithered down her spine. "Yours. What do you mean by that?"

She felt his lips curve against her cheek.

"Exactly what you're thinking. We've been lovers—are lovers." His lips drifted lower to caress her jaw. "We remain so while the attraction lasts. If it continues, as I'm sure it will, beyond a month, we marry."

"A month?" His nearness was sapping her wits, leaving her dizzy.

"I'm willing to indulge you for a month, no more."

She struggled to concentrate. "And if the attraction fades— even if it doesn't completely die but *fades* within a month, you'll agree that a marriage between us is not justified?"

He nodded. "Just so."

His lips cruised over hers; her unruly senses leapt.

"Do you agree?"

She hesitated. She'd come out here to address what lay between them; what he was suggesting seemed a reasonable way forward . . . she nodded. "Yes."

And his lips came down on hers.

She mentally sighed with pleasure, felt her senses unfurl like petals under the sun, wallowing, glorying, absorbing the delight. Savoring the urge—their mutual attraction.

It would fade—she knew it, absolutely beyond doubt. It might be waxing stronger at the moment simply because, at least for her, it was so new, yet ultimately, inevitably, its power would wane.

Until then . . . she could learn more, understand more. Explore further. At least a little bit further. Sliding her hands up, she wound her arms about his neck and kissed him back, parted her lips for him, surrendered her mouth, felt the addictive warmth blossom between them when he accepted the invitation.

He shifted closer, pinning her against the window; one hard hand closed about her waist, holding her steady while their mouths melded, while their tongues dueled and tangled, caressed, explored, claimed anew.

Hunger flared.

She felt it in him—a telltale hardening of his muscles, self-restraint imposed, desire harnessed—and felt her own response, a rising tide of heated longing that welled and washed through her. That had her pressing closer, sliding a hand to trace his jaw, tempting him to deepen the kiss.

He did, and for a moment the world fell away.

Flames flared, roared.

Abruptly he drew back. Broke the kiss enough to murmur against her lips, "We need to find a bedchamber."

She was giddy, wits whirling. She tried, but couldn't concentrate. "Why?"

His lips returned to hers, taking, needing, giving. He drew away, his breathing not quite steady. "Because I want to fill you—and you want me to. It's too dangerous here."

The gravelly words shocked her, thrilled her. Shook a few of her wits into place. Enough so she could think beyond the heat coursing her veins, the pounding in her blood.

Enough to realize.

It was too dangerous anywhere!

Not because he was wrong, but because he was absolutely right.

Just hearing him say the words had escalated her need, deepened that heated longing, the emptiness she knew he could and would fill. She wanted, desperately, to know again the pleasure of having him join with her.

She pulled out of his arms. "No—we can't."

He looked at her. Blinked dazedly. "Yes, we can." The words were uttered with simple conviction, as if he was assuring her they could walk in the park.

She stared at him. Realized she had no hope of arguing convincingly against it; she'd never been a good liar.

Before he could seize her wrist—as he usually did—and haul her off to a bed, she whirled and fled.

Down the corridor. She sensed him behind her; swerved and flung open one of the many doors. Rushed through.

Her mouth fell open in a silent O. She stopped, teetering on her toes just inside a large linen press. They were alongside the dining room; tablecloths and napkins were neatly stacked on shelves on either side. At the end of the tiny chamber, filling the gap between the shelves, was a bench for folding.

Before she could turn, she felt Trentham behind her. Filling the doorway, blocking her escape.

"Excellent choice." His voice purred, deep and dark. His hand curved around her bottom; he pushed her forward, stepping in behind her.

Shutting the door.

She swung around.

Tristan swept her into his arms, brought his lips down on hers, and let his reins loose. Kissed her witless, let desire rule, let the pent-up passions of the last week pour through him.

She sank against him, caught up in the maelstrom. He drank in her response. Felt her fingers tense, then her nails sank into his shoulders as she met him, appeased him, then tormented him.

Urged him on.

Why she'd taken against a bed he had no idea; perhaps she

wanted to expand her horizons. He was only too willing to accommodate her, to demonstrate all that could be accomplished even in such surroundings.

A narrow fanlight above the door let in a shaft of moonlight, enough for him to see. Her gown reminded him of a storm-wracked sea from which her breasts rose, heated and swollen, aching for his touch.

He closed his hands about them and heard her moan. Heard the entreaty, the urgency in the sound.

She was as heated, as needy, as he. With his thumbs, he circled her nipples, hard pebbles beneath the silk, tight and hot and wanting.

Sinking deeper into her mouth, plundering evocatively, deliberately presaging what was to come, he released her breasts and swiftly dealt with her laces, let the dark gown collapse about her waist while he found and unfastened the tiny buttons down the front of her chemise.

He pushed the straps from her shoulders, bared her to the waist; without breaking the kiss, he fastened his hands about her waist and lifted her, sat her on the bench, cupped her breasts one in each hand, broke from the kiss, and bent his head to pay homage.

She gasped, fingers tightening on his skull, spine bowing as he feasted. Her breathing was fractured, desperate; he pushed her ruthlessly on, laving, then suckling, until she sobbed.

Until his title fell from her lips on a pleading gasp.

"Tristan." He licked a tortured nipple, then raised his head. Took her lips again in a searing kiss.

Lifted her skirts, frothed the soft petticoats up about her waist, spreading her knees as he did, stepping between.

He clamped one hand about her naked hip.

Trailed the fingers of the other up the silky inner face of one thigh, and cupped her.

The shudder that wracked her nearly brought him to his knees. Forced him to break from the kiss, drag in a huge breath, and reach desperately for some small measure of control.

Enough to hold back from ravishing her.

He stepped nearer, pressing her knees wider, opening her to his touch. Her lids fluttered; her eyes glinted through the screen of her lashes.

Her lips were swollen, parted, her breathing ragged, her breasts alabaster mounds rising and falling, her skin pearly in the silvery light.

He caught her gaze, trapped it, held her with him as he eased a finger into her tight sheath. Her breath hitched, then rushed out as he reached deeper. Her fingers sank into his upper arms. She was slick, wet, so hot she scalded him. He wanted nothing more than to sink his aching erection into that beckoning heat.

Their gazes locked, he readied her, pressing deep, working his hand so she was fully prepared, releasing her hip to unbutton his trousers, then guiding himself to her entrance. Gripping her hip, he held her, and nudged in.

Watched her face, watched her watching him watch her as he pressed deeper. Releasing her hip, he spread his hand over her bottom, and eased her forward. With his other hand lifted her leg.

"Wrap your legs about my hips."

She dragged in a breath and did. Cradling her bottom in both hands, he drew her to the edge of the bench, and pressed in, inch by inch deeper, feeling her body give, accept and take him in.

Her eyes remained locked on his as their bodies came together; when he finally thrust the last inch, embedding himself inside her, she caught her breath. Her lashes swept down, her eyes closed, her face passion blank as she savored the moment.

He was with her, watching, knowing, feeling.

Only when her lashes fluttered up, and she again met his gaze did he move.

Slowly.

His heart was thundering, his demons raging, desire pounding in his veins, but he kept a tight rein—the moment was too precious to lose.

The startling intimacy as he drew slowly back, then filled her again, and watched her eyes darken even more. He repeated the movement, attuned to her heartbeat, to her need, to the urgency in her—not a hard, driving need like his but a softer, more feminine hunger.

One he needed to sate even more than his own.

So he kept the pace slow, and watched her rise, watched her eyes glaze, heard her breath strangle—watched her come apart in his arms. Listened to her cries until he had to kiss her to mute the telltale sounds, the sweetest symphony he'd ever heard.

He held her, sunk deep in her body, deep in her mouth, when she shuddered, fractured, and climaxed about him. Knew only a fleeting surprise when she took him with her.

Into bliss.

The slow, hot, deeply fulfilling dance slowed, halted. Left them locked together, breathing hard, foreheads touching. The thudding of their hearts filled their ears. Their lashes lifted, gazes touched.

Lips brushed, breaths mingled.

Their warmth held them.

He was sheathed to the hilt in her clinging heat and had no desire to move, to break the spell. Her arms locked about his neck, her legs locked about his hips, she made no effort to shift, to edge away—to leave him.

She seemed even more dazed, more vulnerable, than he.

"Are you all right?"

He whispered the words, watched her eyes focus.

"Yes." The reply came on a soft exhalation. She licked her lips, looked briefly at his. Cleared her throat. "That was . . ."

Leonora couldn't find any word that sufficed.

His lips kicked up at the end. "Stupendous."

She met his gaze, knew better than to nod. Could only wonder at the madness that had gripped her.

And the hunger, the raw need that had gripped him.

His eyes were dark, but softer, not sharp as they usually were. He seemed to sense her wonder; his lips curved. He touched them to hers.

"I want you." His lips brushed hers again. "In every possible way."

She heard the truth, recognized its ring. Had to wonder. "Why?"

He nudged her head back, set his lips cruising her jaw. "Because of this. Because I'll never have enough of you."

She could sense the power of his hunger rising again. Felt the sensation of him within her grow more definite.

"Again?" She heard the stunned amazement in her voice.

He answered with a low growl that might have been a very male chuckle. "Again."

She never should have agreed—acquiesced—to that heated second mating among the tablecloths.

Sipping her tea at the breakfast table the next morning, Leonora made a firm resolution not to be so weak in future—during the rest of the month that was left to them. Trentham—Tristan as he'd insisted she call him—had finally escorted her back to the reception rooms with a smug, wholly male, proprietory air she'd found irritating in the extreme. Especially given she suspected his smugness derived from his entrenched belief that she would find his lovemaking so addictive she'd blindly agree to marry him.

Time would teach him his error. In the meantime, it behooved her to exercise some degree of caution.

She hadn't, after all, intended to acquiesce to even a first mating, let alone the second.

Nevertheless . . . she had learned more, had definitely added to her store of experience. Given the terms of their agreement, she had nothing to fear—the impulse, the physical need that brought them together *would* gradually wane; an occasional indulgence was no great matter.

Except for the possibility of a child.

The notion floated into her mind. Reaching for another slice of toast, she considered it. Considered, surprised, her initial impulsive reaction to it.

Not what she'd expected.

A frown growing in her eyes, she waited for common sense to reassert itself.

Eventually acknowledged that her interaction with Trentham was teaching her, revealing to her, things about herself she'd never known.

Never even suspected.

Through the following days, she kept herself busy, studying Cedric's journals and dealing with Humphrey and Jeremy and the customary round of daily life in Montrose Place.

In the evenings, however . . .

She started to feel like the perennial Cinderella, going to ball after ball and night after night inevitably ending in the arms of her prince. An exceedingly handsome, masterful prince who never failed, despite her firm resolve, to sweep her off her feet . . . and into some private place where they could indulge their senses, and that flaring need to be together, to share their bodies and be one.

His success was startling; she had no idea how he managed it. Even when she avoided the obvious choice of entertainment, guessing which event he would expect her to attend and attending some other, he never failed to materialize at her side the instant she walked into the room.

As for his knowledge of their hostesses' houses, that was beginning to border on the bizarre. She had spent far more time than he in the ton, and that more recently, yet with unerring accuracy he would lead her to a small parlor, or a secluded library or study, or a garden room.

By the end of the week she was starting to feel seriously hunted.

Starting to realize she might have underestimated the feeling between them.

Or, even more frightening, had totally misjudged its nature.

There was very little Tristan didn't know about establishing a network of informers.

Lady Warsingham's coachman saw no difficulty in providing the local streetsweeper with news of whither he'd been instructed he would be heading each evening; one of Tristan's footmen would go strolling at noon to meet with the streetsweeper and return with the news.

His own household staff were proving exemplary sources, intrigued and eager to supply him with details of the houses Leonora chose to grace with her presence. And Gasthorpe had exercised his own initiative and handed Tristan a vital contact.

Toby, the Carlings's bootboy, inhabited the kitchen of Number 14 and therefore was privy to his masters' and mistress's intended directions. The lad was always eager to hear the ex–sergeant major's tales; in return, he innocently provided Tristan with intelligence on Leonora's daytime activities.

That evening, she'd elected to attend the Marchioness of

Huntly's gala. Tristan sauntered in a few minutes before he estimated the Warsingham party would arrive.

Lady Huntly greeted him with a twinkle in her eye. "I understand," she said, "that you have a particular interest in Miss Carling?"

He met her gaze, wondering . . . "Most particular."

"In that case, I should warn you that a number of my nephews are expected to attend tonight." Lady Huntly patted his arm. "Just a word to the wise."

He inclined his head and moved into the crowd, wracking his brains for the relevant connection. Her nephews? He was about to go and look for Ethelreda or Millicent, both of whom were somewhere in the room, to request clarification, when he recalled Lady Huntly had been born a Cynster.

Muttering a curse, he executed an immediate about-face and took up a position close by the main doors.

Leonora entered a few minutes later; he claimed her hand the instant she was free of the receiving line.

She raised her brows at him; he could see a comment regarding overt possessiveness forming in her mind. Placing his hand over hers, he squeezed her fingers. "Let's get your aunts settled, then we can dance."

She met his eyes. "Just a dance."

A warning, one he had no intention of heeding. Together, they escorted her aunts to a group of chaises where many of the older ladies had gathered.

"Good evening, Mildred." A bedezined old dame nodded regally.

Lady Warsingham nodded back. "Lady Osbaldestone. I believe you'll remember my niece, Miss Carling?"

The old dame, still handsome in her way but with terrifyingly sharp black eyes, surveyed Leonora, who curtsied. The old harridan snorted. "Indeed I remember you, miss—but you've no business being a miss still." Her gaze moved on to Tristan. "Who's this?"

Lady Warsingham performed the introductions; Tristan bowed.

Lady Osbaldestone humphed. "Well, one can hope you'll succeed in changing Miss Carling's mind. The dancing's through there."

With her cane, she waved toward an archway beyond which couples were whirling. Tristan seized the implied dismissal. "If you'll excuse us?"

Without waiting for further permission, he whisked Leonora away.

Pausing beneath the archway, he asked, "Lady Osbaldestone—who's she?"

"A *bona fide* terror of the ton. Pay her no heed." Leonora surveyed the dancers. "And I warn you, tonight we are *only* going to dance."

He made no reply; taking her hand, he led her onto the floor and whirled her into a waltz. A waltz he used to maximum effect, unfortunately, given the limitations of a half-empty dance floor, not as great an effect as he would have liked.

The next dance was a cotillion, an exercise he had little use for; it provided too few opportunities to tweak his partner's senses. It was too early yet to inveigle her away to the tiny salon overlooking the gardens; when she admitted to being parched, he left her by the side of the room and went to fetch two glasses of champagne.

The refreshment room gave off the ballroom; he was only absent for a moment, yet when he returned he discovered Leonora in conversation with a tall, dark-haired man he recognized as Devil Cynster.

His internal curses were vitriolic, but when he approached, neither Leonora nor Cynster, who was not thrilled at the interruption, would have detected anything beyond urbanity in his expression.

"Good evening." Handing Leonora her glass, he nodded to Cynster, who returned the nod, his pale gaze sharpening.

One aspect that was instantly apparent was that they were very much alike, not just in height, in the width of their shoulders, in their elegance, but also in their characters, their natures—their temperaments.

An instant passed while both assimilated that fact, then Cynster held out his hand. "St. Ives. My aunt mentioned you were at Waterloo."

Tristan nodded, shook hands. "Trentham, although I wasn't that then."

He mentally scrambled for the best way to answer the inevitable questions; he'd heard enough of the Cynsters' involvement in the recent campaigns to guess that St. Ives would know enough to detect his usual sliding around the truth.

St. Ives was watching him closely, assessingly. "What regiment were you in?"

"The Guards." Tristan met the pale green gaze, deliberately omitting any further definition. St. Ives's gaze narrowed; he held it, murmured, "You were in the heavy cavalry, as I recall. Together with some of your cousins, you relieved Cullen's troop on the right flank."

St. Ives stilled, blinked, then a wry, quite genuine smile curved his lips. His gaze returned to Tristan's; he inclined his head. "As you say."

Only someone with a very high level of military clearance would know of that little excursion; Tristan could almost see the connections being made behind St. Ives's clear green eyes.

He noted St. Ives's quick, reassessing glance before, with an almost indiscernible movement they both saw and understood, he drew back.

Leonora had been looking from one to the other, sensing a communication she could not follow, irritated by it. She opened her lips—

St. Ives turned to her and smiled with devastating, purely predatory force. "I was intending to sweep you off your feet, but I believe I'll leave you to Trentham's tender mercies. Not the done thing to cross a fellow officer, and there seems little doubt he deserves a clear shot."

Leonora's chin came up; her eyes narrowed. "I am not some enemy to be captured and conquered."

"That's a matter of opinion." Tristan's dry comment brought her gaze swinging his way.

St. Ives's smile grew, unrepentant; he sketched a bow and withdrew, saluting Tristan from behind Leonora's back.

Tristan saw that last with relief; with luck, St. Ives would warn off his cousins, and any others of their ilk.

Leonora cast a frowning glance at St. Ives's retreating back. "What did he mean by you 'deserving a clear shot'?"

"Presumably because I sighted you first."

She swung back, her frown deepening. "I am not some form of"—she gestured, glass and all—"*prey*."

"As I said, that's a matter of opinion."

"Nonsense." She paused, eyes on his, then continued, "I sincerely hope you're not thinking in such terms, for I warn you I have no intention of being captured, conquered, let alone tied up."

Her diction had grown more definite with every word; her last phrase had nearby gentlemen turning to view her.

"This"—Tristan caught her hand and wound her arm in his— "is not the place to discuss my intentions."

"Your *intentions?*" She lowered her voice. "As far as I'm concerned, you have none *vis à vis* me. None that have any likelihood of coming to fruition."

"I'm desolate to have to contradict you, of course. However . . ." He kept talking, fencing with her as he steered her to a side door. But as he reached to open it, she realized. And dug in her heels.

"No." She narrowed her eyes at him even more. "Just dancing tonight. There's no reason we need be private."

He raised a brow at her. "Retreating in disarray?"

Her lips thinned; her eyes were mere slits. "Nothing of the sort, but you won't catch me with such an obvious lure."

He heaved an exaggerated sigh. In point of fact, it was too early—the rooms insufficiently crowded—for them to risk slipping away. "Very well." He turned her back into the room. "That sounds like a waltz starting up."

Lifting her glass from her fingers, he handed both glasses to a passing footman, then swept her onto the dance floor.

Leonora relaxed into the dance, let her senses free; at least here, in the presence of others, it was safe to do so. In private, she trusted neither him nor herself. Experience had taught her that once in his arms, she couldn't rely on her intellect to guide her. Rational logical arguments never seemed to win when pitted against that warm rush of needy yearning.

Desire. She knew enough now to name it, the passion that drove them, that fired their attraction. She'd acknowledged it as such to herself, but knew better than to allow her understanding to show.

However, as she whirled through the dance in Trentham's arms, relaxed but with her senses exhilaratingly alive, it was a different aspect of their interaction that concerned her.

An aspect Devil Cynster's words and their ensuing discussion had brought into sharper focus.

She held her tongue until the dance ended, but then they were joined by two other couples, and conversation became general. When the musicians struck up the opening bars to a cotillion, she met Trentham's gaze in fleeting warning, then accepted Lord Hardcastle's hand.

Trentham—Tristan—let her go with no reaction beyond a hardening of his gaze. Heartened, she returned to his side once the dance ended, but when the next measure proved to be a country dance, she again accepted an offer from another—young Lord Belvoir, a gentleman who might one day be of Tristan's and St. Ives's ilk, but was now merely an entertaining companion much of her own age.

Again, Tristan—she'd started to think of him by his given name—he'd teased it from her often enough under circumstances sufficiently unique and memorable that she was unlikely to forget it—bore her defection with outwardly stoic calm. Only she was near enough to see the hardness, the possessiveness, and, more than anything else, the watchfulness in his eyes.

It was that last that underscored her thoughts of how he viewed her, and finally had her throwing caution to the wind in an attempt to reason with her wolf. Her wild wolf; she didn't forget, but sometimes it was necessary to take risks.

She bided her time until the small group they were a part of dispersed. Before others could join them, she placed her hand on Tristan's arm and nudged him toward the door he'd previously headed for.

He glanced at her, raised his brows. "Have you had second thoughts?"

"No. I've had other thoughts." She met his eyes fleetingly, and continued toward the door. "I want to talk—just *talk*—to you, and I suppose it had better be in private."

Reaching the door, she paused and met his gaze. "I presume you do know of somewhere in this mansion we can be assured of being alone?"

His lips curved in a wholly male grin; opening the door, he handed her through. "Far be it from me to disappoint you."

He didn't; the room he led her to was small, furnished as a sitting room in which a lady of the house could sit in comfortable privacy and look out over the manicured gardens. Reached through a maze of intersecting corridors, it was some distance from the reception rooms, a perfect venue for private conversation, verbal or otherwise.

Inwardly shaking her head—how did he do it?—she went straight to the windows, to stand and look out on the fog-shrouded garden. There was no moon, no distraction outside. She heard the door click shut, then felt Tristan approaching. Dragging in a breath, she swung to face him, put a palm to his chest to hold him back. "I want to discuss how you see me."

He didn't outwardly blink, but she'd obviously taken a tack he hadn't expected. "What—"

She stopped him with an upraised hand. "It's becoming increasingly clear that you view me as some sort of challenge. And men like you are constitutionally incapable of letting a challenge lie." She eyed him severely. "Am I right in thinking you view getting my agreement to marry you in such a light?"

Tristan returned her regard. Increasingly wary. It was difficult to think how else he would view it. "Yes."

"Ah-ha! That, you see, is our problem."

"Which problem is that?"

"The problem of you not being able to take my 'no' for an answer."

Propping his shoulder against the window frame, he looked down at her face, at her eyes glowing with zeal at her supposed discovery. "I don't follow."

She made a dismissive sound. "Of course you do, you just don't want to think about it because it doesn't fit your stated *intentions*."

"Bear with my muddled male mind and explain."

She threw him a long-suffering look. "You can hardly deny that any number of ladies have been—and more will be once the Season proper starts—throwing themselves at your head."

"No." It was one of the reasons he clung to her side, one of the reasons he wanted to gain her agreement to their wedding as soon as possible. "What have they to do with us?"

"Not us so much as *you*. You, like most men, have little appreciation for what you can have without a fight. You equate fighting for something with its value—the harder and more difficult the struggle, the more valuable the object attained. As with wars, so with women. The more a lady resists, the more desirable she becomes."

She fixed him with her clear, periwinkle blue gaze. "Am I right?"

He thought before nodding. "It's a reasonable hypothesis."

"Indeed, but you see where that leaves us?"

"No."

She gave an exasperated hiss. "You want to marry me because I won't marry you—not for any other reason. That"—she waved both hands—"primitive instinct of yours is what's driving you—and it's getting in the way of our attraction fading. It would be fading but—"

He reached out, caught one of her waving hands, and yanked her to him. She landed against his chest, gasped as his arms closed around her. He felt her body react as it always had, always did, to his. "Our mutual attraction hasn't faded."

She hauled in a tight breath. "That's because you're confusing it. . . ." Her words faded as he lowered his head. "I said we'd only talk!"

"That's illogical." He brushed her lips with his, pleased when hers clung. He shifted, settling her more comfortably in his arms. Setting her hips to his, the soft curve of her stomach cradling his erection. He looked down into her eyes, wide, darkening. His lips curved, but not in a smile. "You're right—it is a primitive instinct that's driving me. But you picked the wrong one."

"What—"

Her mouth was open—he filled it. Took possession in a long, slow, thorough kiss. She tried to resist, hold back, but then surrendered.

When, eventually, he lifted his head, she sighed, murmured, "What's illogical about talking?"

"It's not consistent with your conclusion."

"My conclusion?" She blinked at him. "I hadn't even got to my conclusion."

He brushed her lips again so she wouldn't see his wolfish grin. "Let me state it for you. If, as you hypothesize, the only reason I want to marry you—the only true reason driving our mutual attraction—is because you're resisting, why not try *not* resisting and see what happens?"

She stared dazedly up at him. "Not resisting?"

He shrugged lightly, his gaze falling to her lips. "If you're right, you'll prove your point." He took her lips, her mouth again, before she could consider what would happen if she was wrong.

His tongue stroked hers; she shivered delicately, then kissed him back. Stopped resisting, as she generally did when they'd reached this point; he wasn't fool enough to believe that meant anything more than that she'd inwardly shrugged and decided to take what she might, still firmly convinced the desire between them would wane.

He knew it wouldn't, at least on his part. What he felt for her was quite different from anything he'd felt before—not for any other woman, not for anyone at all. Protective, deeply to-his-bones possessive, and unquestionably right. It was that conviction of rightness that drove him to have her again and again, even in the teeth of her determined denials, to demonstrate the breadth and depth, the increasing power of all that was growing between them.

A stunning revelation in any circumstances, but he set himself to paint the sensual reality between them in bold and striking colors the better to impress her with its power, its potency, its undisguised truth.

She felt it, broke from the kiss, from beneath heavy lids met his eyes. Sighed. "I really did intend that tonight we would only dance."

There was no resistance, no reluctance, only acceptance.

He closed his hands about her bottom and shifted suggestively against her. Bent his head to brush her lips. "We are going to dance—it just won't be to a waltz."

Her lips curved. Her hand tightened on his nape and she drew him to her. "To our own music, then."

He took her mouth, caught their reins, and deliberately set them aside.

The daybed angled to the windows was the obvious place to

lay her, to lie alongside her and feast on her breasts. Until her soft gasps were urgent and needy, until she arched and her fingers clung to his skull.

Suppressing a triumphant smile, he slid farther down the daybed, raising her skirts, pressing them high about her waist to expose her hips, and her long slender legs. Tracing her curves, fingers first trailing, then gripping to part her thighs, opening her to him.

Then he bent his head and set his lips to her softness.

She cried out, tried to catch his shoulders, but they were beyond her reach. Her fingers tangled in his hair, clenched as he laved, licked, then lightly suckled.

"*Tristan!* No . . ."

"Yes." He held her down and pressed deeper, savoring the tart taste of her, step by step knowingly winding her tight . . .

She was quivering on the crest of climax when he shifted, freed his erection from the confines of his trousers, and rose over her. She gripped his forearms, nails sinking deep, her knees rising to grip his flanks. Sensual entreaty etched every line of her face; urgency drove her restless body, shifting wantonly, beckoning beneath his.

Her spine bowed as he entered her; he drove home and she climaxed, a glorious rippling release. He caught her up, drove her on. She clung, sobbed, and matched him, as committed as he as they swept up the mountain, with each forceful thrust climbed the jagged peaks, then tension splintered, fractured, fell away, and they soared into the void, into the sublime heat of their sharing.

Into that moment when all barriers fell away, and there was just him and her, joined in naked honesty, wrapped in that powerful reality.

Chests heaving, hearts thundering, heat coursing beneath their skins, they stilled, waited, locked intimately together, for the glory to wane. Their gazes touched, held—neither made any move to shift, to part.

She raised a hand, traced his cheek. Her eyes searched his, wondering . . .

He turned his head, pressed an openmouthed kiss to her palm.

Knew when she drew a deep breath that although her body and her senses were still sunk in the bliss, her mind had snapped free; she'd already resumed thinking.

Resigned, he looked into her eyes. Raised one brow.

"You said I'd picked the wrong primitive instinct—that it wasn't the response to a challenge that was driving you." She held his gaze. "If not that, then what? Why"—with one hand, she waved weakly—"are we here?"

He knew the answer, couldn't manage a smile. "We're here because I want you."

She made a derisive sound. "So it's just lust—"

"No." He pressed into her and gained her complete attention. "Not lust—not anything like it. But you're not hearing what I'm saying. I. Want. *You.* Not any other woman; no other will do. Only you."

She frowned.

His lips curved, not in a smile. "That's why we're here. That's why I'll pursue you no matter what comes until you agree to be mine."

Only you.

Sipping tea at the breakfast table the next morning, Leonora examined those words.

She wasn't at all sure she understood the implications, understood what Tristan had meant to convey. Men, at least those of his ilk, were a species unknown to her; she felt uneasy in attributing too much meaning—or the meaning she would have intended—to his phrase.

There were further complications.

The ease with which he'd subverted her determined intentions at Huntly House—just as he had on the evenings before that—made thinking she could stand against him and his practiced seduction a frankly ludicrous hope.

No more pretending on that front; if she seriously wanted to deny him, she'd have to unearth a chastity belt. And even then . . . he could almost certainly pick locks.

And there was more yet to consider.

While it was perfectly obvious that testing her hypothesis by not resisting would play into his hands, if she was right in her estimation of the reason behind his passion, then not resisting the notion of marrying him would indeed see his interest wane.

But what if it didn't?

She'd spent half the night wondering, imagining . . .

A gentle cough from Castor jerked her back to reality; she had no idea how long her mind had been wandering, caught by an unexpected vista, entranced by a prospect she'd long ago thought she'd turned her back on. Frowning, she pushed aside her uneaten toast and rose.

"When the footman takes Henrietta for her walk, please ask him to summon me—I'll accompany them today."

"Indeed, miss." Castor bowed as she left the room.

That evening, together with Mildred and Gertie, Leonora swept into Lady Catterthwaite's ballroom. They were neither early nor late. After greeting their hostess, they joined the fray. With every passing day, more of the fashionable returned to town and the balls grew commensurately more crowded.

Lady Catterthwaite's ballroom was small and cramped. Accompanying her aunts to where a grouping of chairs and chaises gave the older female guests a place to sit and watch their charges, and exchange all the latest news, Leonora was surprised to find no Trentham waiting for her—waiting to step out of the crowd and waylay her. Claim her.

She helped Gertie settle in an armchair, inwardly frowning at how accustomed to his attentions she'd grown. Straightening, she nodded to her aunts. "I'm going to mingle."

Mildred was already speaking with an acquaintance; Gertie nodded, then turned to join the circle.

Leonora glided into the already considerable crowd. Attracting a gentleman, joining a group of acquaintances would be easy enough, yet she had no desire to do either. She was . . . not precisely concerned, but certainly wondering over Tristan's nonappearance. Last night, after he'd so deliberately uttered the words "only you," she'd sensed a change in him, a sudden wariness, a watchfulness she'd been unable to interpret.

He hadn't cut himself off from her, hadn't precisely withdrawn, but she'd sensed a self-protective recoil on his part, as if he'd gone too far, said more than was safe . . . or, perhaps, true.

The possibility nagged; she was already having trouble enough trying to fathom his motives—coping with the fact that his motives had, entirely beyond her wishes or her will, become important to her—that the idea he might not be open with her, honest with her . . . that way lay a morass of uncertainty in which she had no intention of becoming mired.

It was precisely the sort of situation that most strongly supported her inflexible stance against marriage.

She continued drifting aimlessly, stopping here and there to exchange greetings, then, entirely unexpectedly, directly ahead of her in the crowd, she saw a pair of shoulders she recognized instantly.

They were clad in scarlet, as they had been years ago. As if sensing her regard, the gentleman glanced around and saw her. And smiled.

Delighted, he turned and held out his hands. "Leonora! How lovely to see you."

She returned his smile and gave him her hands. "Mark. I see you haven't sold out."

"No, no. A career soldier, that's me." Brown-haired, fair-skinned, he turned to include the lady standing by his side. "Allow me to present my wife, Heather."

Leonora's smile slipped a fraction, but Heather Whorton smiled sweetly and shook hands. If she recalled that Leonora was the lady her husband had been engaged to before he'd offered for her hand, she gave no sign. Relaxing, somewhat to her surprise Leonora found herself regaled with an account of the Whortons' life over the past seven or so years, from the birth of their first child to the arrival of their fourth, to the rigors of following the drum or alternatively the long separations imposed on military families.

Both Mark and Heather contributed; it was impossible to miss how dependent on Mark his wife was. She hung on his arm, but even more, seemed totally immersed in him and their children— indeed, she seemed to have no identity beyond that.

That was not the norm in Leonora's circle.

As she listened and smiled politely, commenting as appropriate, the truth of how badly she and Mark would have suited sank in. From his responses to Heather, it was patently clear that he rejoiced in her need of him—a need Leonora would never have had, would never have allowed herself to develop.

She'd long ago realized she hadn't loved Mark; at the time of their engagement she'd been a young and distinctly naive seventeen—she'd thought she wanted what all other young ladies wanted—lusted after—a handsome husband. Listening to him now, and remembering, she could admit that she hadn't been in love with him but with the idea of being in love, of getting married and having her own household. Of gaining what for girls of that age had been the Holy Grail.

She listened, observed, and sent up a heartfelt prayer; she truly had had a lucky escape.

Tristan strolled nonchalantly down the stairs of Lady Catterthwaite's ballroom. He was later than usual; a message received earlier in the day from one of his contacts had necessitated another visit to the docks—night had fallen before he'd returned to Trentham House.

Pausing two steps from the bottom, he scanned the room, but failed to find Leonora. He did, however, locate her aunts. A niggle of concern pricking his nape, he stepped down to the floor and headed their way.

Impelled by a need to find Leonora, an impulse whose strength unnerved him.

Their interlude the previous evening, the explanation he'd given her, that she and she alone could fulfill his need, had only served to underscore, to exacerbate, his growing sense of vulnerability. He felt as if he were going into battle missing part of his armor, that he was exposing himself, his emotions, in a reckless, foolish, wantonly idiotic fashion.

His intincts were to immediately and comprehensively guard

against any such weakness, to cover it up, shore it up with all speed.

He couldn't help being the type of man he was, had long ago accepted his nature. Knew there was no sense fighting his escalating need to secure Leonora, to make her unequivocally his.

To have her agree to marry him with all speed.

Reaching the gaggle of older ladies, he bowed before Mildred and shook hands with both her and Gertie. He then had to endure a round of introductions to the circle of eager, interested, matronly faces.

Mildred saved him by waving toward the crowd. "Leonora is here, somewhere in the melee."

"About time you got here!" Grumbling under her breath, Gertie, sitting to one side of the group, drew his attention. "She's over there." She pointed with her cane; Tristan turned, looked, and saw Leonora chatting with an officer from some infantry regiment.

Gertie snorted. "That blackguard Whorton's toadying up to her—can't imagine she's enjoying it. You'd best go and rescue her."

He'd never been one to rush in without understanding the game. Although the trio of which Leonora was one was at some distance, they were, from this angle, clearly visible. Although he could see only Leonora's profile, her stance and her occasional gesture assured him she was neither upset nor worried. She also showed no sign of wanting to slip away.

He looked back at Gertie. "Whorton—I assume he's the captain she's talking with?" Gertie nodded. "Why do you call him a blackguard?"

Gertie narrowed her old eyes at him. Her lips compressed in a tight line, she considered him closely; from the first, she'd been the less encouraging of Leonora's aunts, yet she hadn't attempted to thrust a spoke in his wheel. Indeed, as the days had passed, he thought she'd come to look on him more favorably.

He apparently passed muster, for she suddenly nodded and looked again at Whorton. Her dislike was evident in her face.

"He jilted her, that's why. They were engaged when she was seventeen, before he went away to Spain. He came back the next year, and came straightaway to see her—we were all expecting to learn when the wedding bells would ring. But then Leonora showed him out, and returned to tell us he'd asked her to release him. Seemed he'd found his colonel's daughter more to his liking."

Gertie's snort was eloquent. "That's why I call him a blackguard. Broke her heart, he did."

A complex swirl of emotions swept through Tristan. He heard himself ask, "She released him?"

"Of course she did! What lady wouldn't, in such circumstances? The bounder didn't want to marry her—he'd found a better billet."

Gertie's fondness for Leonora rang in her voice, colored her distress. Impulsively, he patted her shoulder. "Don't worry—I'll go and rescue her."

But he wasn't going to make Whorton into a martyr in the process. Aside from all else, he was damned glad the bounder hadn't married Leonora.

Eyes on the trio, he tacked through the crowd. He'd just been handed a vital piece of the jigsaw of Leonora and her attitude to marriage, but he couldn't yet spare the time to stop, consider, jiggle, and see exactly how it fitted, nor what it would tell him.

He came up beside Leonora; she glanced up at him, smiled.

"Ah—there you are."

Taking her hand, he raised it briefly to his lips, then placed it on his sleeve as was his habit. Her brows lifted faintly, in resignation, then she turned to the others. "Allow me to introduce you."

She did; he heard with a jolt that the other lady was Whorton's wife. His polite mask in place, he returned the greetings.

Mrs. Whorton smiled sweetly at him. "As I was saying, it's proved quite an effort to organize our sons' schooling . . ."

To his definite surprise, he found himself listening to a discussion of where to send the Whorton brats for their education. Leonora gave her opinion from her experience with Jeremy; Whorton quite clearly intended giving her advice due consideration.

Contrary to Gertie's supposition, Whorton made no attempt to attach Leonora, nor to evoke any long-ago sympathies.

Tristan watched Leonora closely, but could detect nothing beyond her customary serene confidence, her usual effortless social grace.

She wasn't a particularly good actress; her temper was too definite. Whatever her feelings over Whorton had been, they were no longer strong enough to raise her pulse. It beat steadily beneath his fingers; she was truly unperturbed.

Even discussing children who, had things been different, might have been hers.

He suddenly wondered how she felt about children, realized he'd been taking her views *vis à vis* his heir for granted.

Wondered if she was already carrying his child.

His gut clenched; a wave of possessiveness flowed over him. He didn't so much as flutter an eyelash, yet Leonora glanced at him, a faint frown—one of questioning concern—in her eyes.

The sight saved him. He smiled easily; she blinked, searched his eyes, then turned back to Mrs. Whorton's chatter.

Finally, the musicians tuned up. He seized the moment to part from the Whortons; he led Leonora directly to the floor.

Drew her into his arms, whirled her into the waltz.

Only then focused on her face, on the long-suffering look in her eyes.

He blinked, raised a brow.

"I realize you military men are accustomed to acting with dispatch, but within the ton's ballrooms, it's customary to *ask* a lady if she wishes to dance."

He met her gaze. After a moment, said, "My apologies."

She waited, then raised her brows high. "Aren't you going to ask me?"

"No. We're already waltzing—asking you is redundant. And you might refuse."

She blinked at him, then smiled, clearly amused. "I must try that sometime."

"Don't."

"Why not?"

"Because you won't like what happens."

She held his gaze, then sighed exaggeratedly. "You're going to have to work on your social skills. This dog-in-the-manger attitude won't do."

"I know. Believe me, I'm working on a solution. Your help would be appreciated."

She narrowed her eyes, then tipped up her nose and looked away. Feigning temper because he'd had the last word.

He swung her into a sweeping turn, and thought of the other little matter, a pertinent and possibly urgent matter, he now had to address.

Military men. Her memories of Whorton, no matter how ancient and buried, could not have been happy ones—and she almost certainly classed him and the captain as men of the same stamp.

"Excellent!" Leonora looked up as Tristan walked in. Quickly tidying her escritoire, she shut it and rose. "We can walk in the park with Henrietta, and I can tell you my news."

Tristan raised a brow at her, but obediently held the door and followed her back out into the hall. She'd told him last night that she'd received quite a few replies from Cedric's acquaintances; she'd asked him to call to discuss them—she'd made no mention of walking her hound.

He helped her into her pelisse, then shrugged on his greatcoat; the wind was chilly, whipping through the streets. Clouds hid the sun, but the day was dry enough. A footman arrived with Henrietta straining on a leash. Tristan fixed the hound with a warning glance, then took the leash.

Leonora led the way out. "The park is only a few streets away."

"I trust," Tristan said, following her down the garden path, "that you've been exercising with your dog?"

She shot him a glance. "If by that you mean to ask have I been strolling the streets without her, no. But it's definitely restricting. The sooner we lay Mountford by the heels, the better."

Bustling forward, she swung open the gate, held it while he and Henrietta passed through, then swung it shut.

He caught her hand, trapped her gaze as he wound her arm in his. "So cut line." Holding her beside him, he let Henrietta tow them in the direction of the park. "What have you learned?"

She drew breath, settled her arm in his, looked ahead. "I'd had great hopes of A. J. Carruthers—Cedric had communicated most frequently with Carruthers in the last few years. However, I didn't receive any reply from Yorkshire, where Carruthers lived, until yesterday. *Before* that, however, over the previous days, I received three replies from other herbalists, all scattered about the country. All three wrote that they believed Cedric *had* been working on some special formula, but none of them knew any details. Each of them, however, suggested I contact A. J. Carruthers, as they understood Cedric had been working most closely with Carruthers."

"Three independent replies, all believing Carruthers would know more?"

Leonora nodded. "Precisely. Unfortunately, however, A. J. Carruthers is dead."

"Dead?" Tristan halted on the pavement and met her gaze. The green expanse of the park lay across the street. "Dead how?"

She didn't misunderstand, but grimaced. "I don't know—all I do know is that he's dead."

Henrietta tugged; Tristan checked, then led both females across the street. Henrietta's huge and shaggy form, her gaping jaws filled with sharp teeth, gave him a perfect excuse to avoid the fashionable area thronging with matrons and their daughters;

he turned the questing hound toward the more leafy and over-grown region beyond the western end of Rotten Row.

That area was all but deserted.

Leonora didn't wait for his next question. "The letter I received yesterday was from the solicitor in Harrogate who acted for Carruthers and oversaw his estate. He informed me of Carruthers's demise, but said he couldn't otherwise help with my query. He suggested that Carruthers's nephew, who inherited all Carruthers's journals and so on, might be able to shed some light on the matter—the solicitor was aware that Carruthers and Cedric had corresponded a great deal in the months prior to Cedric's death."

"Did this solicitor mention exactly when Carruthers died?"

"Not exactly. All he said was that Carruthers died some months after Cedric, but that he'd been ill for some time before." Leonora paused, then added, "There's no mention in the letters Carruthers sent to Cedric of any illness, but they might not have been that close."

"Indeed. This nephew—do we have his name and direction?"

"No." Her grimace was frustration incarnate. "The solicitor advised that he'd forwarded my letter to the nephew in York, but that was all he said."

"Hmm." Looking down, Tristan walked on, assessing, extrapolating.

Leonora glanced at him. "It's the most interesting piece of information we've found yet—the most likely, indeed, the *only* possible link to something that might be what Mountford seeks. There's nothing specific in Carruthers's letters to Cedric, other than oblique references to something they were working on—no details at all. But we need to pursue it, don't you think?"

He looked up, met her eyes, nodded. "I'll get someone on it tomorrow."

She frowned. "Where? In Harrogate?"

"And York. Once we have the name and direction, there's no reason to wait to pay this nephew a visit."

His only regret was that he couldn't do so personally. Traveling to Yorkshire would mean leaving Leonora beyond his reach; he could surround her with guards, yet no amount of organized protection would be sufficient to reassure him of her safety, not until Mountford, whoever he was, was caught.

They'd been strolling, neither slowly nor briskly, towed along in Henrietta's wake. He realized Leonora was studying him, a rather odd look on her face.

"What?"

She pressed her lips together, her eyes on his, then she shook her head, looked away. "You."

He waited, then prompted, "What about me?"

"You knew enough to realize someone had taken an impression of a key. You waited for a burglar and closed with him without turning a hair. You can pick locks. Assessing premises for their ability to withstand intruders is something you've done before. You got access to special records from the Registry, records others wouldn't even know existed. With a wave of your hand"—she demonstrated—"you can have men watching my street. You dress like a navvy and frequent the docks, then change into an earl—one who somehow always knows where I'll be, one with exemplary knowledge of our hostesses' houses.

"And now, just like that, you'll arrange for people to go hunting for information in Harrogate and York." She pinned him with an intent but intrigued look. "You're the oddest ex-soldier-cum-earl I've ever met."

He held her gaze for a long moment, then murmured, "I wasn't your average soldier."

She nodded, looking ahead once more. "So I gathered. You were a major in the Guards—a soldier of Devil Cynster's type—"

"No." He waited until she met his gaze. "I—"

He broke off. The moment had come sooner than he'd anticipated. A rush of thoughts jostled through his mind, the most prominent being how a woman who'd been jilted by one soldier would feel about being lied to by another. Perhaps not quite lied to, but would she see the difference? His instincts were all for keeping her in the dark, for keeping his dangerous past and his equally dangerous propensities from her. For keeping her in sublime ignorance of that side of his life, and all it said of his character.

Her eyes on his face, she continued slowly strolling, head tilting as she studied him. And waited.

He drew breath, softly said, "I wasn't like Devil Cynster, either."

Leonora looked into his eyes; what she saw there she couldn't interpret. "What sort of soldier were you, then?"

The answer, she knew, held a vital key to understanding who the man beside her truly was.

His lips twisted wryly. "If you could get access to my record, it would say I joined the army at twenty and rose to the rank of major in the Guards. It would give you a regiment, but if you checked with soldiers in that regiment, you'd discover few knew me, that I hadn't been sighted since shortly after I first joined."

"So what sort of regiment were you in? Not the cavalry."

"No. Not the infantry, either, nor the artillery."

"You said you'd been at Waterloo."

"I was." He held her gaze. "I was on the battlefield, but not with our troops." He watched her eyes widen, then quietly added, "I was behind enemy lines."

She blinked, then stared at him, thoroughly intrigued. "You were a *spy?*"

He grimaced lightly, looked ahead. "An agent working in an unofficial capacity for His Majesty's government."

A host of impressions swamped her—observations that suddenly made sense, other things that were no longer so mysterious—yet she was far more interested in what the revelation meant, what it said of him. "It must have been terribly lonely, as well as being horrendously dangerous."

Tristan glanced at her; that wasn't what he'd expected her to say, to think of. His mind ranged back, over the years . . . he nodded. "Often."

He waited for more, for all the predictable questions. None came. They'd slowed; impatient, Henrietta woofed and tugged. He and Leonora exchanged a glance, then she smiled, tightened her hold on his arm and they stepped out more briskly, circling back toward the streets of Belgravia.

She had a pensive expression on her face, faraway and distant, yet not troubled, not irritated, not concerned. When she felt his gaze, she glanced at him, met his eyes, then smiled and looked ahead.

They crossed the thoroughfare and paced down the street, then turned into Montrose Place. Reaching her gate, he swung it wide, ushered her through, then followed her in. She was waiting to link her arm in his; she was still deep in thought.

He stopped before the steps. "I'll leave you here."

She glanced up at him, then inclined her head and reached for Henrietta's lead. She met his gaze; her eyes were a startling blue. "Thank you."

Those periwinkle blue eyes said she was speaking of much more than his help with Henrietta.

He nodded, thrust his hands into his pockets. "I'll have someone on their way to York tonight. I believe you'll be attending Lady Manivers' rout?"

Her lips lifted. "Indeed."

"I'll see you there."

Her eyes held his for a moment, then she inclined her head. "Until then."

She turned away. He watched her go inside, waited until the door shut, then turned and walked away.

Dealing with Tristan, Leonora decided, had become unbelievably complicated.

It was the following morning; she lolled in her bed and stared at the sunbeams making patterns on the ceiling. And tried to sort out what, exactly, was going on between them. Between Tristan Wemyss, ex-spy, ex–unofficial agent of His Majesty's government, and her.

She'd thought she'd known, but day by day, night by night, he kept . . . not so much changing as revealing greater and ever more intriguing depths. Facets of his character that she'd never imagined he might possess, aspects she found deeply appealing.

Last night . . . all had progressed as it usually did. She'd tried, not too hard, admittedly—she'd been distracted by all she'd learned that afternoon—but she nevertheless had made an effort to hold to a celibate line. He'd seemed even more determined, more ruthless than usual in storming her position—and taking her.

He'd whisked her off to a secluded room, one draped in shadows. There, on a daybed, he'd taught her to ride him—even now, just thinking of those moments made her blush. Remembered sensation sent warmth washing through her. The muscles in her thighs now ached, yet in that position she'd been better able to appreciate how much pleasure she gave him. How much sensual delight he took in her body. For the first time in all their interactions, she'd taken the lead, experimented, and gloried in her ability to pleasure him.

Addictive. Enthralling. Deeply satisfying.

That, however, had been the least of the revelations the evening had brought.

When, finally slumped in his arms, heated and replete, she'd nipped his shoulder and told him she liked the sort of soldier he was, he'd sent one hard palm stroking slowly, pensively, down her spine, then said, "I'm not like Whorton, I promise you."

She'd blinked, then struggled up onto her elbows to frown down into his face. "You're not anything like Mark." Her mind had been groggy; the rock-hard, tanned, scarred body beneath her was nothing like what she'd ever imagined Mark's might be, and as for the man within it . . .

Tristan's eyes had been dark pools, impossible to read. His hand had continued slowly, reassuringly stroking. He must have read her confusion in her face. "I want to marry you—I won't change my mind. You don't need to worry I'll hurt you like he did."

Realization had dawned. She'd pushed up, stared down at him. "Mark didn't hurt me."

He'd frowned. "He jilted you."

"Well, yes. But . . . I was actually quite happy to be jilted."

Of course, she'd had to explain. She'd done so with greater candor than she'd previously brought to the subject; stating the reality aloud had more clearly established the truth in her mind as well as his.

"So you see," she'd concluded, "it wasn't any deep and lasting slight—not in any way. I don't have any"—she'd waved—"adverse feelings toward soldiers because of it."

He'd considered her, searched her face. "So you don't hold my former career against me?"

"Because of what happened with Whorton? No."

His frown had only deepened. "If it wasn't Whorton jilting you that gave you a distaste for men and marriage, what did?" His gaze had sharpened; even in the shadows she'd been able to feel its edge. "Why haven't you married?"

She hadn't been ready to answer that.

She'd brushed it aside, clung to a more immediate point. "Is that why you told me about your career—to distinguish yourself from Whorton?"

He'd looked disgruntled. "If you hadn't asked, I wouldn't have told you."

"But I did ask. Is that why you answered?"

He'd hesitated, his reluctance clear, then admitted, "Partially. I would have had to tell you sometime . . ."

"But you told me this afternoon because you wanted me to see you as different from Whorton, different from how you imagined I saw him—"

He'd hauled her down and kissed her. Distracted her.

Effectively.

She hadn't known what to make of his reasoning—his motives, his reactions—last night. She still didn't. Yet . . . he'd obviously felt threatened enough by her experience with Whorton, and how he believed that affected her view of military men, to tell her the truth. To break with what she suspected was habit and neither hide nor conceal his past.

A past she felt sure none of his family knew. That few others of any sort knew.

He was a man with shadows behind him, yet circumstances had dictated he step into the light, and he needed someone— someone who understood, who could understand him, someone he could trust—beside him.

She could see that, acknowledge that much.

Slowly stretching under the covers, she sighed deeply. Because of his earlier suggestion, she'd allowed herself to imagine what being married to him would be like; her response to the vision had been completely different to what she'd expected. To what her response to all such thoughts of marriage had been in the past.

Now . . . now that she was imagining being *his* wife, the prospect enticed. With age and experience—maturity, perhaps— she'd come to value things—things like the gentle round of country life—far more than she had previously; she'd gradually come to realize such elements were important to her. They provided an outlet for her natural abilities—her organizational and managerial talents; without such outlets she'd feel stifled . . .

Just as, indeed, she felt increasingly stifled in her uncle's house.

The realization was not so much a shock as an earthquake, one that literally rocked the concepts she'd thought for so long were the foundations of her life. That realization was not a small thing to assimilate, to absorb.

The sunbeams danced on the ceiling; the household was awake—the day called to her. Yet she remained in the cocoon of her bed and instead opened her mind. Let her thoughts free.

Followed where they led.

The girlish dreams she'd buried long ago had revived, subtly re-created, altered so that this time they were attractive to the woman she now was—this time, they fitted her.

She could see, imagine—start to desire if she let herself—a future as Tristan's wife. His countess. His helpmate.

Swirling through those dreams, lending them greater fascination and power, was the enticement of being the one—the only one according to him—who could give him all he wanted. That, very possibly, he needed. When they were together, she could sense the power of what had grown between them, that welling emotion deeper than passion, stronger than desire. The emotion that in those quiet, intense and private moments wrapped them about.

The emotion they shared.

It was something ephemeral between them, something most easy to see in those heated moments when both their guards were completely down, yet it was also there, peeking through, like something caught from the corner of an eye in their more public exchanges.

He'd asked why she'd never married; the truth was, she'd never truly studied the reason. The instinctive, deeply held belief—the one that had made letting Whorton go so easy—was something so buried in her mind, so much a part of her, she'd never taken it out and examined it, never truly concerned herself with it before. It had simply been there, a certainty.

Until Tristan had appeared, and laid all he was before her.

He did, now, have the right to question, to ask for her reasons, to demand they were sound.

It was time to look deeper, into her heart, into her soul, and discover whether her old instincts were still relevant, whether they remained relevant to the new world on whose threshold she and Tristan now stood.

He'd seized her hand, dragged her to that threshold, forced her to open her eyes and truly see . . . and he wasn't going to go away. To simply draw back and leave her.

He'd been right; the attraction between them wouldn't fade.

It hadn't. It had grown.

Lips setting, she flung back the covers, got out of bed, and determinedly crossed to the bellpull.

Reexamining and possibly restructuring the basic tenets of one's life was not an undertaking that could be accomplished in a few rushed minutes.

Unfortunately, throughout that day and those following, rushed minutes were all Leonora could find. Yet as the events of each passing day strengthened and deepened the connection between her and Tristan, the need to revisit the reason underlying her aversion to marriage grew.

Their slow progress on the matter of Mountford, either locating the man masquerading by that name or identifying whatever it was he was after, only added pressure by way of Tristan's increasing protectiveness, which spilled over into a more primitive possessiveness.

Even though he battled to hide it, she saw. And understood.

Tried not to let it prod her temper; he couldn't, it seemed, help it.

February had finally given way to March; the first hint of spring blew in to soften winter's bleakness. The ton started to return to the capital in earnest, to prepare for the upcoming Season. While earlier the entertainments had been small, largely informal, the social calendar was growing ever more crowded, the events equally so.

Lady Hammond's ball bade fair to be the first acknowledged

crush of the year. Arriving with Mildred and Gertie, Leonora stood patiently on the stairs leading up to the ballroom together with half a hundred others all waiting to greet their hostess. Looking around, she noted familiar faces, nodded, exchanged smiles. There were weeks yet before the Season proper; in years past, she was sure town hadn't been so crowded so early in the year. Even in the park . . .

"My dear, of *course* we're here early."

The lady behind Leonora had just met an old friend.

"Everyone will be, mark my words. Or at least, every family with a daughter to bring out. It's quite criminal the number of gentlemen who were lost in all those wars . . ."

The lady continued; Leonora stopped listening—she'd seen the light. Pity the eligible gentlemen as yet unmarried.

Eventually, she, Mildred, and Gertie gained the ballroom door; after making her curtsy to Lady Hammond, an old acquaintance of her aunts', she followed Mildred and Gertie to one of the alcoves set with chairs and chaises to accommodate chaperones and the older generation.

Her aunts found seats among their cronies; after turning aside a number of arch queries, Leonora retreated.

Into the crowd. Tristan would have some difficulty locating her; he hadn't joined the queue to the ballroom by the time she'd gained the top of the stairs, which meant it would be some time before he could join her.

Tonight, the crowd was too dense to amble through with only nods and smiles; she had to stop and chat, to exchange greetings and opinions and social conversation. She'd never found that difficult, sometimes boring perhaps, but tonight so many were newly come to town that there was plenty to catch up with, to hear, to laugh at and be amused. Nevertheless, aware she was attracting a certain degree of attention from gentlemen too recently returned to the ballrooms to have registered Tristan's interest, she did not remain for too long within one group, but kept drifting.

Dealing with one wolf at a time seemed wise.

"Leonora!"

She turned, and smiled at Crissy Wainwright, a plump and these days somewhat buxom blond who had been presented in the same year she had. Crissy had quickly snared a lord and married; successive confinements had kept her away from London for some years. Crissy all but elbowed her way through the crowd. "Phew!" Reaching Leonora, she snapped open her fan. "It's a madhouse. And here I thought I was wise coming up to town early."

"Many had the same idea, it seems." Leonora took Crissy's hand; they pressed fingers, touched cheeks.

"Mama is going to be miffed." Eyes dancing, Crissy glanced at Leonora. "She was all for stealing a march on all others with daughters to establish this Season—she's got my youngest sister to puff off, and she's set her sights on this earl who has to marry."

Leonora blinked. "An earl who has to marry?"

Crissy leaned closer and lowered her voice. "It seems this poor soul has only recently inherited and has to marry before July or lose his wealth. But he'll retain his houses and his dependents, neither of which would be easy to maintain on a pauper's budget."

A chill touched Leonora's spine. "I hadn't heard. Which earl?"

Crissy waved. "Doubtless no one thought to mention it—you're not interested in a husband, after all." She grimaced. "I always thought you were quite touched, being so set against marriage, but now . . . I have to admit there are times I think you had it right." Her expression clouded briefly, but then brightened. "Indeed, I'm here determined to enjoy myself and not think about being married at all. If this poor earl is as hunted as it sounds he'll be, maybe I'll offer him a safe harbor? I've heard he's astonishingly handsome—so rare when combined with wealth and title—"

"What title?" Leonora broke in without compunction; Crissy could ramble for hours.

"Oh—didn't I say? It's Trillingwell, Trellham—something like that."

"Trentham?"

"Yes! That's it." Crissy swung to face her. "You have heard."

"I assure you I hadn't, but I do thank you for telling me."

Crissy blinked, then studied her face. "Why, you sly thing—you know him."

Leonora narrowed her eyes to slits—not at Crissy but at a dark head she could see tacking toward her through the crowd. "I do indeed know him." In the biblical sense, what was more. "If you'll excuse me . . . I daresay we'll meet again if you're to remain in town."

Crissy grabbed her hand as she stepped out.

"Just tell me—is he as handsome as they say?"

Leonora raised her brows. "He's too handsome for his own good." Twisting free of Crissy's slackening grip, she stalked into the crowd, on a direct collision course with the earl who had to marry.

Tristan knew something was wrong the instant Leonora appeared abruptly before him. The daggers stabbing from her eyes were difficult to miss; the fingertip she jabbed into his chest was even more pointed.

"I want to talk to you. Now!"

The words were hissed, her temper clearly seething.

He consulted his conscience; it remained clear. "What's happened?"

"I'll be delighted to tell you, but I suspect you'd prefer to hear me out in private." Her eyes bored into his. "What little nook have you found for us tonight?"

He held her gaze and considered the tiny servants' pantry, which, he'd been assured, was the only possible venue for totally private engagements in Hammond House. Unlit, it would be dark and closed in—perfect for what he'd had in mind . . . "There is no place in this house suitable for any private conversation."

Especially not if she lost her temper, the leash of which looked to be already fraying.

Her eyes snapped. "Now is the time to live up to your reputation. Find one."

His talents swung into action; he took her hand, set it on his sleeve, somewhat relieved that she permitted it. "Where are your aunts?"

She waved to the side of the room. "In the chairs over there."

He headed that way, his attention on her, avoiding all the glances cast his way. Bending close, he spoke softly. "You've developed a headache—a *migraine*. Tell your aunts you feel quite ill and must leave immediately. I'll offer to drive you home in my carriage—" He broke off, halted, beckoned a footman; when the footman arrived, he issued a terse order—the footman hurried off.

They resumed their progress. "I've already sent for my carriage." He glanced at her. "If you could soften your spine, wilt a little, we might have some chance of pulling this off. We have to ensure your aunts stay here."

That last wasn't easy, but whatever the particular bee Leonora had got stuck in her bonnet, she was bound and determined to have her moment with him; it wasn't so much her acting abilities that won the day as the impression she radiated that if people did not fall in with her stated wishes, she was liable to become violent.

Mildred cast him an anxious glance. "If you're sure . . . ?"

He nodded. "My carriage is waiting—you have my word I'll take her straight home."

Leonora glanced at him, eyes narrow; he kept his expression impassive.

With the air of females bowing to a stronger—and somewhat incomprehensible—will, Mildred and Gertie remained where they were and allowed him to escort Leonora from the room, and thence from the house.

As instructed, his carriage was waiting; he handed Leonora in, then followed. The footman shut the door; a whip cracked, and the carriage lurched forward.

In the dark, he caught her hand, squeezed it. "Not yet." He spoke softly. "My coachman doesn't need to hear, and Green Street is only around the corner."

Leonora glanced at him. "Green Street?"

"I promised to take you home. My home. Where else are we to find a private room with adequate lighting for a discussion?"

She had no argument with that; indeed, she was glad he recognized the need for lighting—she wanted to be able to see his face. Inwardly seething, she grudgingly waited in silence.

His hand remained closed about hers. As they rattled through the night, his thumb stroked, almost absentmindedly. She glanced at him; he was gazing out of the window—she couldn't tell if he even realized what he was doing, much less if he intended it to soothe her temper.

The touch was soothing, but it didn't dampen her ire.

If anything, it stoked it.

How dare he be so insufferably complacent, so confident and assured, when she'd just discovered his ulterior motive, which he must have guessed she'd learn?

The carriage turned, not into Green Street, but into a narrow lane, the mews serving a row of large houses. It rocked to a halt. Tristan stirred, opened the door, and descended.

She heard him speak to his coachman, then he turned to her, beckoned. She gave him her hand and alighted; he whisked her through a garden gate before she had a chance to get her bearings.

"Where are we?"

Tristan had followed her through the gate; he shut it behind them. On the other side of the high stone wall, she heard the carriage rumble off.

"My gardens." He nodded to the house on the other side of an expanse of lawn visible through a screen of bushes. "Arriving via the front door would necessitate explanations."

"What about your coachman?"

"What about him?"

She humphed. His hand touched her back and she started along the path through the bushes. As they stepped free of the concealing shadows, he took her hand and came up beside her. The narrow path followed the garden beds bordering that wing of the house; he led her past the conservatory, past what looked like a study, and on to the long room she recognized as the morning room where his old ladies had entertained her weeks earlier.

He halted before a pair of French doors. "You didn't see this." He placed his hand, palm flat, on the frame of the doors where they met, just where the lock linked them. He gave one sharp push, and the lock clicked; the doors swung inward.

"Good gracious!"

"Sssh!" He swept her in, then closed the doors. The morning room lay in darkness. At such a late hour, this wing of the house was deserted. Taking her hand, he drew her across the room to the steps leading up to the corridor. Pausing in the shadows on the steps, he looked to the left, to where the front hall was bathed in golden light.

Peeking past him, she could see no evidence of footmen or butler.

He turned and urged her to the right, along a short, unlighted corridor. Reaching past her, he opened the door at the end and pushed it wide.

She entered; he followed and quietly shut the door.

"Wait," he breathed, then moved past her.

Faint moonlight gleamed on a heavy desk, illuminated the large chair behind it and four other chairs placed around the room. A number of cabinets and chests of drawers lined the walls. Then Tristan drew the curtains and all light vanished.

An instant later came the scrape of tinder; flame flared, lighting his face, limning the austere planes as he adjusted the lamp's wick, then reset the glass.

The warm glow spread and filled the room.

He looked at her, then waved her to the two armchairs set before the hearth. When she reached them, he came up beside her and lifted her cloak from her shoulders. He laid it aside, then bent to the embers still glowing in the hearth; sinking into one of the armchairs, she watched as he efficiently restoked the fire until it was again an acceptable blaze.

Straightening, he looked down at her. "I'm going to have some brandy. Do you want anything?"

She watched him cross to a tantalus against the wall. She

doubted he would have sherry in his study. "I'll have a glass of brandy, too."

He glanced at her again, brows rising, but he poured brandy into two balloons, then returned and handed her one. She had to use both hands to hold it.

"Now." He sank into the other armchair, stretched his legs out before him, crossed his ankles, then sipped, and fixed his hazel gaze on her. "What is this all about?"

The brandy was a distraction; she set the balloon carefully on the small table beside the chair.

"This," she said, uncaring of how waspish she sounded, "is about you *needing* to marry."

He met her accusing gaze directly; he sipped again—the brandy balloon seemed a part of his large hand. "What of it?"

"*What of it?* You *have* to marry because of something to do with your inheritance. You'll lose it if you don't marry by July— is that right?"

"I'll lose the bulk of the funds but retain the title and every-thing entailed."

She dragged in a breath past the constriction suddenly grip-ping her lungs. "So—you have to marry. You don't actually *want* to marry, me or anyone else, but you have to, and so you thought I would suit. You need a wife, and I will do. Have I finally got that correct?"

He stilled. In a heartbeat changed from an elegant gentleman relaxed in the chair to a predator poised to react. All that truly changed was a sudden flaring tension, but the effect was pro-found.

Her lungs had locked tight; she could barely breathe.

She didn't dare take her eyes from his.

"No." When he spoke his voice had deepened, darkened. The

brandy balloon looked fragile in his grip; as if realizing, he eased his fingers. "That's not how it was—how it is."

She swallowed. And tipped up her chin. She was pleased when her voice remained steady—still haughty, disbelieving. Defiant. "How is it, then?"

His gaze didn't leave her. After a moment, he spoke, and there was that in his voice that warned her not even to entertain the notion that he wasn't speaking the absolute truth. "I have to marry, that much you have right. Not because I've any personal need for my great-uncle's funds, but because, without them, keeping my fourteen dependents in the manner to which they're accustomed would be impossible."

He paused, let the words and their meaning sink in. "So yes, I have to front the altar by the end of June. However, regardless, I had and have absolutely no intention of allowing my great-uncle, or the ton's matrons, to interfere in my life—to dictate whom I will take as my bride. It's obvious that, if I so wished, a wedding to some suitable lady could be arranged, signed, sealed, and consummated in less than a week."

He paused, sipped, his gaze locked with hers. He spoke slowly, distinctly. "June is still some months away. I saw no reason to rush. Consequently, I made no effort to consider any suitable ladies"—his voice deepened, strengthened—"and then I saw you, and all such considerations became redundant."

They were sitting feet apart, yet what had grown between them, what now existed between them sprang to life at his words—a palpable force, filling the space, all but shimmering in the air.

It touched her, held her, a web of emotion so immensely strong she knew she could never break free. And, very likely, nor could he.

His gaze had remained hard, openly possessive, unwavering. "I have to marry—I would at some point have been forced to seek a wife. But then I found you, and all searching became irrelevant. *You* are the wife I want. You are the wife I will have."

She didn't—couldn't—doubt what he was telling her; the proof was there, between them.

The tension grew, became unbearable. They both had to move; he did first, coming out of the chair in a fluid, graceful motion. He held out his hand; after a moment, she took it. He drew her to her feet.

Looked down at her, his face graven, hard. "Do you understand now?"

Tipping up her face, she studied his—his eyes, the harsh, austere planes that communicated so little. Drew breath, felt forced to ask, "Why? I still don't understand why you want to marry me. Why you want me, and me alone."

He held her gaze for a long moment; she thought he wasn't going to answer, then he did.

"Guess."

It was her turn to think long and hard, then she licked her lips and murmured, "I can't." After an instant, she added, with brutal honesty, "I don't dare."

Fourteen

໑ⓥ๑

He'd insisted on escorting her home. Only their hands had touched; she'd been intensely grateful. He'd been watching her; she'd sensed his need, so flagrantly possessive, had appreciated the fact he'd reined it in—that he seemed to understand that she needed time to think, to absorb all he'd said, all she'd learned.

Not just of him, but of herself.

Love. If that was what he'd meant, it changed everything. He hadn't said the word, yet standing close to him, she could feel it, whatever it was—not desire, not lust, but something much stronger. Something much finer.

If it was love that had grown between them, then walking away from him, from his proposal, was, perhaps, no longer an option. Walking away would be the coward's way out.

The decision was hers. Not just her happiness but his, too, hinged on it.

With the house silent and still about her, the clock on the landing ticking through the small hours, she lay in her bed and forced herself to face the reason that had kept her from marriage.

It wasn't an aversion—nothing so definite and absolute. An aversion she could have identified and assessed, convinced herself to set aside, or overcome.

Her problem lay deeper, it was much more intangible, yet all through the years time and again it had had her shying away from marriage.

And not just marriage.

Lying in her bed, staring up at the moon-washed ceiling, she listened to the telltale clicking on the polished boards outside her bedroom door as Henrietta stretched, then padded off downstairs to wander. The sound faded. No more distraction remained.

She drew breath, and forced herself to do what she had to. To take a long look at her life, to examine all the close friendships and relationships she'd not allowed to develop.

The only reason she'd ever considered marrying Mark Whorton was because she'd recognized from the first that she would never be close, emotionally close, to him. She would never have become to him what Heather, his wife, had—a woman dependent and happily so. He'd needed that, a dependent wife. Leonora had never been a candidate for supplying that need; she had simply not been capable of it.

Thanks be to all the gods he'd had the sense to, if not see the truth, then at least act on what he'd perceived to be a dissonance between them.

The same dissonance did not exist between her and Tristan. Something else did. Possibly love.

She had to face it—to face the fact that this time, with Tristan, she fitted the bill of his wife. Precisely, exactly, in every respect. He'd recognized it instinctively; he was the type of man accustomed to acting on his instincts—and he had.

He wouldn't—didn't—expect her to be dependent, to indeed

change in any way. He wanted her for what she was—the woman she was and could be—not to fulfill some ideal, some erroneous vision, but because he knew she was right for him. He was in absolutely no danger of setting her on any pedestal; conversely, through all their interactions, she'd realized he was not just capable of but disposed to worshiping her absolutely.

Her—the real her—not some figment of his imagination.

The thought—the reality—was so deeply, gut-wrenchingly attractive . . . she wanted it, could not let it go. But to grasp it, she would have to accept the emotional closeness that, with Tristan, would be—already was—a foregone conclusion, a vital part of what bound them.

She had to face what had kept her from allowing such a closeness with anyone else.

It wasn't easy going back through the years, forcing herself to strip away all the veils, all the facades she'd erected to hide and excuse the hurts. She hadn't always been as she now was—strong, capable, not needing others. Back then, she hadn't been self-sufficient, self-reliant, hadn't emotionally been able to cope, not with everything, not by herself. She'd been just like any other young girl, needing a shoulder to cry on, needing warm arms to hold her, to reassure her.

Her mother had been her touchstone, always there, always understanding. But then, one summer day, her mother and father both had died.

She still remembered the coldness, the icy loss that had settled about her, locking her in its prison. She hadn't been able to cry, had had no idea how to mourn, how to grieve. And there'd been no one to help her, no one who understood.

Her uncles and aunts—all the rest of the family—were older than her parents had been, and none had any children of their own. They'd patted her, praised her for being so brave; not one had glimpsed, had had any inkling of the anguish she'd hidden inside.

She'd kept hiding it; that was what had seemed expected of her. But every now and then, the burden had become too great, and she'd tried—*tried*—to find someone to understand, to help her find her way past it.

Humphrey had never understood; the staff at the house in Kent had no idea what was wrong with her.

No one had helped.

She'd learned to hide her need away. Step by step, incident by incident through the years of her girlhood, she'd learned *not* to ask help of anyone, not to open herself emotionally to anyone, not to trust any other person enough to ask for help—not to rely on them; if she didn't, they couldn't refuse her.

Couldn't turn her away.

The connections slowly clarified in her mind.

Tristan, she knew, wouldn't turn her away. Wouldn't refuse her. With him, she'd be safe.

All she had to do was find the courage to accept the emotional risk she'd spent the last fifteen years teaching herself never to take.

He called at noon the next day. She was arranging flowers in the garden hall; he found her there.

She nodded in greeting, conscious of his sharp gaze, of how closely he studied her before leaning his shoulder against the doorframe, only two feet away.

"Are you all right?"

"Yes." She glanced at him, then looked back at her flowers. "You?"

After a moment, he said, "I've just come from next door. You'll see more of us coming and going in future."

She frowned. "How many of you are there?"

"Seven."

"And you're all ex- . . . Guards?"

He hesitated, then replied. "Yes."

The idea intrigued. Before she could think of her next question, he stirred, shifted closer.

She was instantly aware of his nearness, of the flaring response that rushed through her. She turned her head and looked at him.

Met his gaze—fell into it.

Couldn't look away. Could only stand there, her heart thudding, her pulse throbbing in her lips as he leaned slowly closer, then brushed an achingly incomplete kiss over her mouth.

"Have you made up your mind yet?"

He breathed the words over her hungry lips.

"No. I'm still thinking."

He drew back enough to catch her eyes. "How much thinking does it take?"

The question broke the spell; she narrowed her eyes at him, then turned back to her flowers. "More than you know."

He resettled against the doorframe, his gaze on her face. After a moment, he said, "So tell me."

She pressed her lips tight, went to shake her head—then remembered all she'd thought of in the long watches of the night. She drew a deep breath, slowly let it out. Kept her eyes on the flowers. "It's not a simple thing."

He said nothing, just waited.

She had to draw another breath. "It's been a long time since I . . . trusted anyone, anyone at all to . . . do things for me. To help me." That had been one outcome, possibly the most outwardly obvious, of her shrinking from others.

"You came to me—asked for my help—when you saw the burglar at the bottom of your garden."

Lips tight, she shook her head. "No. I came to you because you were my only way forward."

"You saw me as a source of information?"

She nodded. "You did help, but I never asked you—you never offered, you simply gave. That"—she paused as it came clear in her mind, then went on—"that's what's been happening between us all along. I never asked for help—you simply gave it, and you're strong enough that refusing was never a real option, and there seemed no reason to fight you given we were seeking the same end . . ."

Her voice quavered and she stopped.

He moved closer, took her hand.

His touch threatened to shatter her control, but then his thumb stroked; an indefinable warmth flooded her, soothed, reassured.

She lifted her head, dragged in a shaky breath.

He stepped closer yet, slid his arms around her, drew her back against him.

"Stop fighting it." The words were dark, a sorceror's command in her mind. "Stop fighting me."

She sighed, long, deep; her body relaxed against the warm solid rock of his. "I'm trying. I will." She pressed her head back, looked up over her shoulder. Met his hazel eyes. "But it won't happen today."

He gave her time. Reluctantly.

She spent her days trying to decipher Cedric's journals, searching for any mention of secret formulae, or of work done in association with Carruthers. She'd discovered that the entries weren't in any chronological order; on any given topic they were almost random—first in one book, then in another—linked, it seemed, by some unwritten code.

Her nights she spent in the ton, at balls and parties, always with Tristan by her side. His attention, fixed and unwavering, was noted by all; the few brave ladies who had attempted to distract him were given short shrift. Extremely short indeed. Thereafter, the ton settled to speculate on their wedding date.

That evening, as they strolled about Lady Court's ballroom, she explained about Cedric's journals.

Tristan frowned. "What Mountford's after *must* be something to do with Cedric's work. There seems nothing else in Number 14 that might account for this much interest."

"How much interest?" She glanced at him. "What have you learned?"

"Mountford—I still don't have a better name—is still about London. He's been sighted, but keeps moving; I haven't been able to catch up with him yet."

She didn't envy Mountford when he did. "Have you heard anything from Yorkshire?"

"Yes and no. From the solicitor's files, we traced Carruthers's principal heir—one Jonathon Martinbury. He's a solicitor's clerk in York. He recently completed his articles, and was known to have been planning to travel to London, presumably to celebrate." He glanced at her, met her gaze. "It seems he received your letter, sent on from the solicitor in Harrogate, and brought his plans forward. He left on the mail coach two days later, but I've yet to locate him in town."

She frowned. "How odd. I would have thought, if he'd altered his plans in response to my letter, he would have called."

"Indeed, but one should never try to predict the priorities of young men. We don't know why he'd decided to visit London in the first place."

She grimaced. "True."

No more was said that night. Ever since their talk in his study, and their subsequent exchange in the garden hall, Tristan had refrained from arranging to indulge their senses beyond what could be achieved in the ballrooms. Even there, they were both intensely aware of each other, not just on the physical plane; each touch, each sliding caress, each shared glance, only added to the hunger.

She could feel it crawling her nerves; she didn't need to meet his often darkened eyes to know it rode him even harder.

But she had wanted time, and he gave her that.

One thing asked for—one thing received.

As she climbed the stairs to her bedroom that night, she acknowledged that, accepted it.

Once she was sunk in her bed, cozy and warm, returned to it.

She couldn't hesitate for forever. Not even for another day. It wasn't fair—not to him, not to her. She was toying with, tormenting, both of them. For no reason, not one that had relevance or power anymore.

Outside her door, Henrietta growled, then her nails scrabbled, clicked; the sound faded as the hound headed for the stairs. Leonora registered the fact, but distantly; she remained focused, undistracted.

Accept Tristan, or live without him.

Not a choice. Not for her. Not now.

She was going to take the chance—accept the risk and go forward.

The decision firmed in her mind; she waited, expecting some

pulling back, some instinctive recoil, but if it was there, it was swamped beneath an upwelling tide of certainty. Of sureness.

Almost of joy.

It suddenly occurred to her that deciding to accept that inherent vulnerability was at least half the battle. Certainly for her.

She suddenly felt lighthearted, immediately started plotting how to tell Tristan of her decision—how to most appropriately break the news . . .

She had no idea how much time had passed when the realization that Henrietta had not returned to her position before her door slid into her mind.

That distracted her.

Henrietta often wandered the house at night, but never for long. She always returned to her favorite spot on the corridor rug outside Leonora's door.

She wasn't there now.

Leonora knew it even before, tugging her wrapper around her, she eased open her door and looked.

At empty space.

Faint light from the stairhead reached down the corridor; she hesitated, then, pulling her wrapper firmly about her, headed for the stairs.

She remembered Henrietta's low growl before the hound had gone off. It might have been in response to a cat crossing the back garden. Then again . . .

What if Mountford was trying to break in again?

What if he harmed Henrietta?

Her heart leapt. She'd had the hound since she was a tiny scrap of fur; Henrietta was in truth her closest confidante, the silent recipient of hundreds of secrets.

Gliding wraithlike down the stairs, she told herself not to be silly. It would be a cat. There were lots of cats in Montrose Place. Maybe two cats, and that was why Henrietta hadn't yet come back upstairs.

She reached the bottom of the main stairs and debated whether to light a candle. Belowstairs would be black; she might even stumble over Henrietta, who would expect her to see her.

Stopping by the side table at the back of the front hall, she used the tinderbox left there to strike a match and light one of the candles left waiting. Picking up the simple candlestick, she pushed through the green baize door.

Holding the candle high, she walked down the corridor. The walls leapt out at her as the candlelight touched them, but all seemed familiar, normal. Her slippers slapping on the cold tile, she passed the butler's pantry and the housekeeper's room, then came to the short flight of stairs leading down to the kitchens.

She paused and looked down. All below was inky black, except for patches of faint moonlight slanting in through the kitchen windows and through the small fanlight above the back door. In the diffuse light from the latter, she could just make out the shaggy outline of Henrietta; the hound was curled up against the corridor wall, her head on her paws.

"Henrietta?" Straining her eyes, Leonora peered down.

Henrietta didn't move, didn't twitch.

Something was wrong. Henrietta wasn't that young. Greatly fearing the hound had suffered a seizure, Leonora grabbed up her trailing night rail and rushed down the stairs.

"Henriet—*oh!*"

She stopped on the last stair, mouth agape, face-to-face with the man who had stepped from the black shadows to meet her.

Candlelight flickered over his black-avised face; his lips curled in a snarl.

Pain exploded in the back of her skull. She dropped the candle, pitched forward as all light extinguished and everything went black.

For an instant, she thought it was simply the candle going out, then from a great distance she heard Henrietta start to howl. To bay. The most horrible, bloodcurdling sound in the world.

She tried to open her eyes and couldn't.

Pain knifed through her head. The black intensified and dragged her down.

Returning to consciousness wasn't pleasant. For some considerable time, she hung back, hovered in that land that was neither here nor there, while voices washed over her, concerned, some sharp with anger, others with fear.

Henrietta was there, at her side. The hound whined and licked her fingers. The rough caress drew her inexorably back, through the mists, into the real world.

She tried to open her eyes. Her lids were inordinately heavy; her lashes fluttered. Weakly, she raised a hand, and realized there was a wide bandage circling her head.

All talk abruptly ceased.

"She's awake!"

That came from Harriet. Her maid rushed to her side, took her hand, patted it. "Don't you fret. The doctor's been, and he says you'll be good as new in no time."

Leaving her hand limp in Harriet's clasp, she digested that.

"Are you all right, sis?"

Jeremy sounded strangely shaken; he seemed to be hovering close by. She was lying stretched out, her feet elevated higher than her head, on a chaise . . . she must be in the parlor.

A heavy hand awkwardly patted her knee. "Just rest, my dear,"

Humphrey advised. "Heaven knows what the world is coming to, but . . ." His voice quavered and trailed away.

An instant later came a rough growl, "She'll do better if you don't crowd her."

Tristan.

She opened her eyes, looked straight at him, standing beyond the end of the chaise.

His face was more rigidly set than she'd ever seen it; the cast of his patrician features screamed a warning to any who knew him.

His blazing eyes were warning enough to anyone at all.

She blinked. Didn't shift her gaze. "What happened?"

"You were hit on the head."

"That much I'd gathered." She glanced at Henrietta; the hound pushed closer. "I went down to look for Henrietta. She'd gone downstairs but hadn't come back. She usually does."

"So you went after her."

She looked back at Tristan. "I thought something might have happened. And it had." She looked back at Henrietta, frowned. "She was by the back door, but she didn't move . . ."

"She was drugged. Laudanum in port, trickled under the back door."

She reached for Henrietta, palmed the shaggy face, looked into the bright brown eyes.

Tristan shifted. "She's fully recovered—lucky for you, who-ever it was didn't use enough to do more than make her snooze."

She dragged in a breath, winced when her head ached sharply. Looked again at Tristan. "It was Mountford. I came face-to-face with him at the bottom of the stairs."

For one instant, she thought he would actually snarl; the vio-lence she glimpsed in him, that flowed across his features was frightening. Even more so because part of that aggression was directed, quite definitely, at her.

Her revelation had shocked the others; they were all looking at her, not Tristan.

"Who's Mountford?" Jeremy demanded. He looked from Leonora to Tristan. "What is this about?"

Leonora sighed. "It's about the burglar—he's the man I saw at the bottom of our garden."

That piece of information had Jeremy's and Humphrey's jaws dropping. They were horrified—doubly so because not even they could any longer close their eyes, pretend the man was a figment of her imagination. Imagination hadn't drugged Henrietta nor cracked Leonora's skull. Forced to acknowledge reality, they exclaimed, they declared.

The noise was all too much. She closed her eyes and slipped gratefully away.

Tristan felt like a violin string stretched to snapping point, but when he saw Leonora's eyes close, saw her brow and features smooth into the blankness of unconsciousness, he dragged in a breath, swallowed his demons, and got the others out of the room without roaring at them.

They went, but reluctantly. Yet after all he'd heard, all he'd learned, to his mind they'd forfeited any right they might have had to watch over her. Even her maid, devoted though she seemed.

He sent her to prepare a tisane, then returned to stand looking down at Leonora. She was still pale, but her skin was no longer deathly white as it had been when he'd first reached her side.

Jeremy, no doubt prodded by incipient guilt, had had the sense to send a footman next door; Gasthorpe had taken charge, send-

ing one footman flying to Green Street, and another for the doctor
he'd been instructed was the one always to summon. Jonas Pringle was a veteran of the Peninsula campaigns; he could treat knife
and gunshot wounds without turning a hair. A knock on the head
was a minor affair, but his assurance, backed by experience, had
been what Tristan had needed.

Only that had kept him marginally civilized.

Realizing Leonora might not wake for some time, he raised his
head and looked through the windows. Dawn was just starting to
streak the sky. The urgency that had propelled him through the
last hours started to ebb.

Pulling one of the armchairs around to face the chaise, he
dropped into it, stretched out his legs, fixed his gaze on Leonora's
face, and settled to wait.

She resurfaced an hour later, lids fluttering, then opening as
she drew in a sharp, pain-filled breath.

Her gaze fell on him, and widened. She blinked, glanced
around as well as she could without moving her head.

He lifted his jaw from his fist. "We're alone."

Her gaze returned to him; she studied his face. Frowned.
"What's wrong?"

He'd spent the last hour rehearsing how to tell her; now the
time had come, he was too tired to play any games. Not with her.
"Your maid. She was hysterical when I got here."

She blinked; when her lids lifted, he saw in her eyes that she'd
already jumped ahead, seen what must have happened, but when
she met his gaze, he couldn't interpret her expression. Surely she
couldn't have forgotten the earlier attacks. Equally, he couldn't
imagine why she'd be surprised at his reaction.

His voice was rougher than he intended when he said, "She

told me about two early attacks on you. Specifically on you. One in the street, one in your front garden."

Her eyes on his, she nodded, winced. "But it wasn't Mountford."

That was news. News that sent his temper soaring. He shot to his feet, unable any longer to pretend to a calmness that was far beyond him.

He swore, paced. Then swung to face her. *"Why didn't you tell me?"*

She met his gaze, didn't cower in the least, then quietly said, "I didn't think it was important."

"Not . . . important." Fists clenched, he managed to keep his tone reasonably even. "You were threatened, and you didn't think that was important." He locked his eyes on hers. "You didn't think *I* would think that important?"

"It wasn't—"

"No!" He cut off her words with a slicing motion. Felt compelled to pace again, glancing briefly at her, struggling to get his thoughts in order, in sufficient order to communicate to her.

Words burned his tongue, too heated, too violent to let loose. Words he knew he would regret the instant he uttered them.

He had to focus; he brought all his considerable training to bear, forcing himself to cut to the heart of the matter. Ruthlessly to strip away every last veil and face the cold hard truth—the central solid reality that was the only thing that truly mattered.

Abruptly, he halted, drew in a tense breath. Swung to face her, locked his eyes on hers. "I've come to care for you." He had to force the words out; low and gravelly, they grated. "Not just a little, but deeply. More deeply, more completely, than I've cared for anything or anyone in my life."

He drew a tight breath, kept his gaze on her eyes. "Caring for someone means, however reluctantly, giving some part of yourself into their keeping. They—the one cared for—becomes the repository of that part of you"—his eyes held hers—"of that something you've given that's so profoundly precious. That's so profoundly important. They, therefore, become *important*— deeply, profoundly important."

He paused, then more quietly stated, "As you are to me."

The clock ticked; their gazes remained locked. Neither moved.

Then he stirred. "I've done all I can to explain, to make you understand."

His expression closed; he turned to the door.

Leonora tried to rise. Couldn't. "Where are you going?"

Hand on the knob, he looked back at her. "I'm leaving. I'll send your maid to you." His words were clipped, but emotion, suppressed, seethed beneath them. "When you can cope with being important to someone, you know where to find me."

"Tristan . . ." With an effort, she swiveled, lifted her hand—

The door shut. Clicked with a finality that echoed through the room.

She stared at the door for a long moment, then sighed and sank back on the chaise. Closed her eyes. She comprehended perfectly what she'd done. Knew she would have to undo it.

But not now. Not today.

She was too weak even to think, and she would need to think, to plan, to work out exactly what to say to soothe her wounded wolf.

The next three days turned into a parade of apologies.

Forgiving Harriet was easy enough. The poor soul had been so overset on seeing Leonora lying senseless on the kitchen flags, she'd babbled hysterically about men attacking her; one minor comment had been enough to attract Tristan's attention. He'd ruthlessly extracted all the details from Harriet, and left her in an even more emotionally wrought state.

When Leonora retired to her bed after consuming a bowl of soup for luncheon—all she could imagine keeping down—Harriet helped her up the stairs and into her room without a word, without once looking up or meeting her eye.

Inwardly sighing, Leonora sat on her bed, then encouraged Harriet to pour out her guilt, her worries and concerns, then made peace with her.

That proved the easiest fence to mend.

Drained, still physically shaken, she remained in her room for the rest of the day. Her aunts called, but after one look at her face, kept their visit brief. At her insistence, they agreed to avoid all mention of the attack; to all who asked after her, she would be simply indisposed.

The next morning, Harriet had just removed her breakfast tray and left her sitting in an armchair before the fire, when a tap sounded on her door. She called, "Come in."

The door opened; Jeremy looked around it.

He spotted her. "Are you well enough to talk?"

"Yes, of course." She waved him in.

He came slowly, carefully shutting the door behind him, then walking quietly across to stand by the mantelpiece and look down at her. His gaze fastened on the bandage still circling her head. A spasm contorted his features. "It's my fault you got hurt. I should have listened—paid more attention. I knew it wasn't your imagination, what you said about the burglars, but it was so much easier to simply ignore it all—"

He was twenty-four, but suddenly he was, once again, her

little brother. She let him talk, let him say what he needed to.
Let him, too, make his peace, not just with her but himself. The
man he knew he should have been.

A draining twenty minutes later, he was sitting on the floor
beside her chair, his head leaning against her knee.

She stroked his hair, so soft yet as ever ruffled and unruly.

Suddenly, he shivered. "If Trentham hadn't come . . ."

"If he hadn't, you would have coped."

After a moment, he sighed, then rubbed his cheek against her
knee. "I suppose."

She remained in bed for the rest of that day, too. By the next
morning, she was feeling considerably better. The doctor called
again, tested her vision and her balance, probed the tender spot
on her skull, then pronounced himself satisfied.

"But I would advise you to avoid any activity that might ex-
haust you, at least for the next few days."

She was considering that—considering the apology *she* had
to make and how exhausting, mentally and physically, that was
likely to be—as she slowly, carefully, went down the stairs.

Humphrey was sitting on a bench in the hall; using his cane,
he slowly rose as she descended. He smiled, a little lopsidedly.
"There you are, my dear. Feeling better?"

"Indeed. A great deal better, thank you." She was tempted
to launch into questions about the household, anything to avoid
what she foresaw was to come. She put the urge from her as un-
worthy; Humphrey, like Harriet and Jeremy, needed to speak.
Smiling easily, she accepted his arm when he offered it and
steered him into the parlor.

The interview was worse—more emotionally involved—than
she'd expected. They sat side by side on the chaise in the parlor,
looking out over the gardens but seeing nothing of them. To her

surprise, Humphrey's guilt stretched back many more years than she'd realized.

He broached his recent shortcomings head-on, apologizing gruffly, but then he looked back, and she'd discovered he'd spent the last days thinking much more deeply than she'd guessed.

"I should have made Mildred come down to Kent more often—I knew it at the time." Staring through the window, he absentmindedly patted Leonora's hand. "You see, when your aunt Patricia died, I shut myself away—I swore I'd never care for anyone like that again, never leave myself open to so much hurt. I liked having you and Jeremy about the house—you were my distractions, my anchors to the daily round; with you two about, it was easy to forget my hurt and lead a normal enough life.

"But I was absolutely determined never to let any person get close, and become important to me. Not again. So I always kept myself distanced from you—from Jeremy, too, in many ways." His old eyes weary, half-filled with tears, he turned to her. Smiled weakly, wryly. "And so I failed you, my dear, failed to take care of you as I ought, and I'm immensely ashamed of that. But I failed myself, too, in more ways than one. I cut myself off from what might have been between us, you and me, and with Jeremy, too. I shortchanged us all in that regard. But I still didn't achieve what I wanted—I was too arrogant to see that caring about others is not wholly a conscious decision."

His fingers tightened about hers. "When we found you lying on the flags that night . . ."

His voice quavered, died.

"Oh, Uncle." Leonora raised her arms and hugged him. "It doesn't matter. Not anymore." She rested her head on his shoulder. "It's past."

He hugged her back, but brusquely replied, "It *does* matter, but we won't argue, because you're right—it's in the past. From now on, we go forward as we should have been." He ducked his head to look into her face. "Eh?"

She smiled, a trifle teary herself. "Yes. Of course."

"Good!" Humphrey released her and hauled in a breath. "Now—you must tell me all you and Trentham have discovered. I gather there's some question about Cedric's work?"

She explained. When Humphrey demanded to see Cedric's journals she fetched a few from the stack in the corner.

"Hmm . . . humph!" Humphrey read down one page, then eyed the stack of journals. "How far have you got with these?"

"I'm only onto the fourth, but . . ." She explained that the journals were not filled in chronological order.

"He'll have had some other order—a journal for each idea, for instance." Humphrey shut the book on his lap. "No reason Jeremy and I can't put our other work aside and give you a hand with these. Not your forte, but it is ours, after all."

She managed not to gape. "But what about the Mesapotamians—and the Sumerians?"

The work they were both engaged in was a commission from the British Museum.

Humphrey snorted, waved the protest aside as he levered to his feet. "The museum can wait—this patently can't. Not if some nefarious and dangerous bounder is after something here. Besides"—on his feet, he straightened and grinned at Leonora—"who else is the museum going to get to do such translations?"

An unarguable point. She rose and crossed to the bellpull. When Castor entered, she instructed him to move the stack of journals to the library. The journal he'd been looking at tucked under his arm, Humphrey shuffled out in that direction, Leonora assisting him; a footman carrying the journals passed them in the hall—they followed him into the library.

Jeremy looked up; as always open books covered his desk.

Humphrey waved his stick. "Clear a space. New task. Urgent matter."

"Oh?"

To Leonora's surprise, Jeremy obeyed, shutting books and moving them so the footman could set the towering stack of journals down.

Jeremy immediately took the top one and opened it. "What are they?"

Humphrey explained; Leonora added that they were assuming there was some valuable formula buried somewhere in the journals.

Already absorbed in the volume in his hands, Jeremy humphed.

Humphrey returned to his seat, and returned to the volume he'd carried from the parlor. Leonora considered, then left to check with the servants, and review all household matters.

An hour later, she reentered the library. Both Jeremy and Humphrey had their heads down; a frown was fixed on Jeremy's face. He looked up when she lifted the top volume off the pile of journals.

"Oh." He blinked somewhat myopically at her.

She sensed his instinctive wish to take the book back. "I thought I'd help."

Jeremy colored, glanced at Humphrey. "Actually, it's not going to be easy to do that, not unless you can stay here most of the day."

She frowned. "Why?"

"It's the cross-referencing. We've only just made a start, but it's going to be a nightmare until we discover the connection between the journals, and their correct sequence, too. We'll have to do it verbally—it's simply too big a job, and we need the answer too urgently, to attempt to write down connections." He looked at her. "We're used to it. If there are other avenues that need to be investigated, you might be better employed—we might get this mystery solved sooner if you gave your attention to them."

Neither wanted to exclude her; it was there in their eyes, in their earnest expressions. But Jeremy spoke the truth; they were the experts in this field—and she really did not fancy spending the rest of the day and the evening, too, squinting at Cedric's wavering script.

And there were numerous other matters on her plate.

She smiled benignly. "There are other avenues it would be worthwhile exploring, if you can cope without me?"

"Oh, yes."

"We'll manage."

Her smile widened. "Good, then I'll leave you to it."

Turning, she went to the door. Glancing back as she turned the knob, she saw both heads down again. Still smiling, she left.

And determinedly turned her mind to her most urgent task: tending to her wounded wolf.

Fifteen

୫⊙⌒⊙୫

Accomplishing that goal—making her peace with Tristan—arranging to do so, required a degree of ingenuity and bold-faced recklessness she'd never before had to employ. But she had no choice. She summoned Gasthorpe, boldly gave him orders, arranged to hire a carriage and be conveyed to the mews behind Green Street, the coachman to wait for her return.

All, of course, with the firm insistence that under no circum-stances was his-lordship-the-earl to be informed. She'd discov-ered a ready intelligence in Gasthorpe; although she hadn't liked subverting him from his loyalty to Tristan, when all was said and done, it was for Tristan's own good.

When, in the darkness of late evening, she stood in the bushes at the end of Tristan's garden and saw light shining from the win-dows of his study, she felt vindicated in every respect.

He hadn't gone out to any ball or dinner. Given her absence from the ton, the fact that he, too, wasn't attending the usual events would be generating intense speculation. Following the path through the bushes and farther to where it skirted the house, she wondered how immediate he would wish their wedding to be. For herself, having made her decision, she didn't truly care . . . or, if she did, she would rather it was sooner than later.

Less time to anticipate how things would work out—much better to take the plunge and get straight on with it.

Her lips lifted. She suspected he would share that opinion, if not for quite the same reasons.

Pausing outside the study, she stood on tiptoe and peeked in; the floor was considerably higher than the ground. Tristan was seated at his desk, his back to her, his head bent as he worked. A pile of papers sat on his right; on his left, a ledger lay open.

She could see enough to be sure he was alone.

Indeed, as he turned to check an entry in the ledger and she glimpsed his face, he *looked* very much alone. A lone wolf who'd had to change his solitary ways and live among the ton, with title, houses, and dependents, and all the associated demands.

He'd given up his freedom, his exciting, dangerous, and lonely life, and picked up the reins that had been left to his care without complaint.

In return, he'd asked for little, either in excuse, or as reward.

The one thing he had asked of this new life was to have her as his wife. He'd offered her all she could hope for, given her all she could and would accept.

In return, she'd given him her body, but not what he'd wanted most. She hadn't given him her trust. Or her heart.

Or rather, she had, but she'd never admitted it. Never told him.

She was there to rectify that omission.

Turning away, taking care to tread silently, she continued toward the morning room. She'd guessed he would stay in and work at estate matters, all the matters he'd no doubt been neglecting while concentrating on catching Mountford. The study was where she'd hoped he'd be; she'd seen both library and study, and it was the study that held the most definite impression of him, of being the room to which he would retreat. His lair.

She was glad to have been proved right; the library was in the other wing, across the front hall.

Reaching the French doors through which they'd entered on her previous visit, she placed herself squarely before them, braced her hands on the frame as he had—using both hands rather than just one—and pushed sharply.

The doors rattled, but remained closed.

"Damn!" She frowned at them, then stepped close and put her shoulder to the spot. She counted to three, then flung her weight against the doors.

They popped open; she only just saved herself from sprawling on the floor.

Regaining her balance, she whirled and closed the doors, then, catching her cloak about her, slunk silently into the room. She waited, breath bated, to see if anyone had been alerted; she didn't think she'd made much noise.

No footsteps sounded; no one came. Her heartbeat gradually slowed.

Cautiously, she went forward. The last thing she wished was to be discovered breaking into this house in order to meet illicitly with its master; if she were caught, once they wed, she'd have to dismiss, or bribe, the entire staff. She didn't want to have to face the choice.

She checked the front hall. As before, at this time of night there were no footmen hovering; Havers, the butler, would be belowstairs. Her way was clear; she slipped into the shadows of the corridor leading to the study with a prayer on her lips.

In thanks for what she'd thus far received, and with hope that her luck would hold.

Halting outside the study door, she faced the panels, and tried to imagine, in a last-minute rehearsal, how their conversation would go . . . but her mind stubbornly remained blank.

She had to get on with it, with her apology and her declaration. Drawing in a deep breath, she grasped the doorknob.

It jerked out of her grip; the door was flung wide.

She blinked, and found Tristan beside her. Towering over her.

He looked past her, down the corridor, then seized her hand and pulled her into the room. Lowering the pistol he held in his other hand, he released her and closed the door.

She stared at the pistol. "Good heavens!" She lifted stunned eyes to his face. "Would you have shot me?"

His eyes narrowed. "Not you. I didn't know who . . ." His lips thinned. He turned away. "Creeping up on me is never wise."

She opened her eyes wide. "I'll remember that in future."

He prowled to a sideboard and laid the pistol in the display case atop it. His gaze was dark as he glanced back at her, then returned to stand by the desk.

She remained where she'd halted, more or less in the middle of the room. It wasn't a big room, and he was in it.

His gaze rose to her face. Hardened. "What are you doing here? No—wait!" He held up a hand. "First tell me how you got here."

She'd expected that tack. Clasping her hands, she nodded. "You didn't call—not that I'd expected it"—she had, but had realized her error—"so I had to call here. As we've previously discovered, me calling during the customary visiting hours is unlikely to provide us with much chance of private conversation, so . . ." She dragged in a huge breath and rushed on, "I summoned Gasthorpe, and hired a coach through him—I insisted he keep the matter strictly private, so you mustn't hold that against him. The coach—"

She told him all, stressing that the coach with coachman and footman was waiting in the mews to take her home. When she came to the end of her recitation, he let a moment pass, then faintly raised his brows—the first change in his expression since she'd entered the room.

He shifted and leaned back against the edge of the desk. His gaze remained on her face. "Jeremy—where does he think you are?"

"He and Humphrey are quite sure I'm asleep. They've thrown themselves into making sense of Cedric's journals; they're engrossed."

A subtle change rippled across his features, sharpening, hardening; she quickly added, "Despite that, Jeremy did make sure the locks were all changed, as you suggested."

He held her gaze; a long moment passed, then he inclined his head fractionally, acknowledging she'd read his thoughts accurately. Dampening an urge to smile, she went on, "Regardless, I've been keeping Henrietta in my room at night, so she won't wander . . ." And disturb her, worry her. She blinked, and continued, "So I had to take her with me when I left this evening— she's with Biggs in the kitchen at Number 12."

Tristan considered. Inwardly humphed. She'd covered all the necessary details; he could rest easy on that score. She was there, safe; she'd even arranged her safe return. He settled against the desk, crossed his arms. Let his gaze, fixed on her face, grow even more intent. "So why are you here?"

She met his gaze directly, steadily, perfectly calm. "I've come to apologize."

He raised his brows; she went on, "I should have remembered

about those first attacks, and told you of them, but what with all that's happened more recently, they'd drifted to the back of my mind." She studied his eyes, considering rather than searching; he realized she was assembling her words as she went—this was no rehearsed speech.

"Nevertheless, at the time the attacks occurred, we hadn't met, and there was no other who considered me important in that vein, such that I would feel obliged to inform them. Warn them."

She lifted her chin, still held his eyes. "I accept and concede that the situation has now changed, that I'm important to you, and that you therefore need to know. . . ." She hesitated, frowned at him, then reluctantly amended, "Perhaps even have a right to know, of anything that constitutes a threat to me."

Again she paused, as if reviewing her words, then straightened and nodded, her eyes refocusing on his. "So I apologize unequivocally for not telling you of those incidents, for not recognizing that I should."

He blinked, slowly; he hadn't expected an apology in such thorough and crystal-clear terms. His nerves started tingling; a nervous eagerness gripped him. He recognized his typical reaction to being on the brink of success. To having victory—complete and absolute—within his grasp.

Of being only one step away from seizing it.

"You agree that I have a right to know of any threat to you?"

She met his gaze, nodded decisively. "Yes."

He considered for only a heartbeat, then asked, "Do I take it you agree to marry me?"

She didn't hesitate. "Yes."

A tight knot of tension he'd carried for so long he'd become unaware of it unraveled and fell from him. The relief was immense. He drew in a huge breath, felt as if it was the first truly free breath he'd had in weeks.

But he wasn't finished with her—hadn't finished extracting promises from her—yet.

Straightening from the desk, he trapped her gaze. "You agree to be my wife, to act in all ways as my wife, and obey me in all things?"

This time she hesitated, frowned. "That's three questions. Yes, yes, and in all things reasonable."

He raised one brow. " 'In all things reasonable.' It seems we need some definitions." He closed the distance between them, halted directly before her. Looked into her eyes. "Do you agree that wherever you go, whatever you do, should any activity involve the smallest degree of danger to you, then you will inform me of it first, before you undertake it?"

Her lips compressed; her eyes were locked on his. "If possible, yes."

He narrowed his eyes. "You're quibbling."

"You're being unreasonable."

"It's unreasonable for a man to want to know his wife is safe at all times?"

"No. But it's unreasonable to wrap her in some protective cocoon to achieve that."

"That's a matter of opinion."

He growled the words *sotto voce*, but Leonora heard them. He shifted intimidatingly closer; her temper started to rise. She determinedly reined it in. She hadn't come to war with him. He was far too used to conflict; she was determined to have none of it between them. She held his hard gaze, as definite as he. "I'm perfectly willing to do everything possible—everything within reason—to accommodate your protective tendencies."

She invested the words with every ounce of her determination, her commitment. He heard it ring; she saw understanding—and acceptance—flow behind his eyes.

They sharpened until his gaze was crystalline hazel, intent on her. "If that's the best offer you're prepared to make . . . ?"

"It is."

"Then I accept." His gaze dropped to her lips. "Now . . . I want to know to what lengths you're prepared to go to accommodate my other tendencies."

It was as if he'd lowered a shield, abruptly dropped a barrier between them. A wave of sexual heat washed over her; she suddenly remembered he was a wounded wolf—a wild wounded wolf—and she'd yet to appease him. At least on that level. Logically, rationally—in words—she'd made amends, and he'd accepted. But that wasn't the only plane on which they interacted.

Her breath slowly strangled. "What other tendencies?" She got the words out before her voice grew too weak—anything to gain a few more seconds . . .

His gaze drifted lower; her breasts swelled, ached. Then he raised his lids, looked into her face. "Those tendencies you've been running from, trying to avoid, but nevertheless enjoying for the past several weeks."

He shifted closer; his coat brushed her bodice, his thigh touched hers.

Her heart thudded in her throat; desire spread like wildfire beneath her skin. She looked into his face, at his thin, mobile lips, felt her own throb. Then she lifted her gaze to his mesmeric hazel eyes—and the truth broke over her. In all that had passed between them, all they'd shared to date, he hadn't yet shown her, revealed to her, all.

Revealed, let her see, the depths, the true breadth of his possessiveness. Of his passion, his desire to possess her.

He reached for the ties of her cloak, with one tug had them free; the garment slid to the floor, pooling behind her. She'd worn a simple, deep blue evening gown; she watched his gaze roam her shoulders, frankly possessive, frankly hungry, then once more he met her gaze. Raised one brow. "So . . . what will you give me? How much will you yield?"

His eyes were locked with hers; she knew what he wanted.

All.

No reservations, no restrictions.

Knew in her heart, knew by the leaping of her senses that in that they were matched, that regardless of any ideas to the contrary, she was and would always be incapable of denying him exactly what he wanted.

Because she wanted it, too.

Despite his aggressiveness, despite the dark desire that smoldered in his eyes, there was nothing here for her to fear.

Only enjoy.

While she finished paying his price.

She moistened her lips, glanced at his. "What do you want me to say?" Her voice was low, her tone unashamedly sultry. Meeting his eyes, she arched a haughty brow. "Take me, I'm yours?"

A spark to tinder; the flames flared in his eyes. Crackled between them.

"That"—he reached for her; hands spanning her waist, he drew her uncompromisingly flush against him—"will do nicely."

Bending his head, he set his lips to hers, and whirled them straight into the fire.

She parted her lips to him, welcomed him in, gloried in the heat he sent pouring through her veins.

Gloried in his possession of her mouth, slow, thorough, powerful, a warning of all that was to come.

Lifting her arms, she wound them about his neck, and aban-
doned herself to her fate.

He seemed to know, to sense her total and complete surrender—
to him, to this, to the heated moment.

To the passion and desire that spilled through them.

He raised his hands and framed her face, anchored her as he
deepened the kiss. Melding their mouths until they breathed as
one, until the same pounding rhythm had laid siege in their veins.

With a low murmur, she pressed to him, wantonly inciting.
His hands left her face, drifted down, curving about her shoulders, then boldly tracing her breasts. He closed his fingers, and
the flames leapt. She shuddered, and urged him on. Kissed him as
hungrily, as demanding as he was. He obliged, his fingers finding
the tight peaks of her nipples and squeezing slowly, excruciat-
ingly, tight.

She broke from the kiss on a gasp. His hands didn't stop; they
were everywhere, kneading, stroking, caressing. Possessing.

Heating her. Setting fires beneath her skin, making her pulse
rage.

"This time, I want you naked."

She could barely make out the words.

"With not a stitch to hide behind."

She couldn't imagine what he thought she might hide. Didn't
care. When he turned her and set his fingers to her laces, she
waited only until she felt the bodice loosen to slip the gown from
her shoulders. She went to slide her arms from the tiny sleeves—

"No. Wait."

A command she was in no position to disobey; her wits were
whirling, her senses in eager tumult, anticipation building with

every breath, with every possessive touch. But he wasn't touching her now. Lifting her head, she drew in a shaky, broken breath.

"Turn around."

She did, just as the level of light in the small room increased. Two heavy lamps sat on either end of the huge desk. He'd turned the wicks high; as she faced him he settled, sitting propped against the front edge of the desk midway between the lamps.

He met her gaze, then his lowered. To her breasts, still concealed behind the gauzy shimmer of her silk chemise.

He raised a hand, beckoned. "Come here."

She did, through the tumbling cascade of her thoughts recalled that despite the fact they'd been intimate on numerous occasions, he'd never seen her naked in any degree of light.

One glance at his face confirmed that he intended to see all tonight.

His hand slid about her hip; he drew her to stand before him, between his legs. Took her hands, one in each of his, and laid them, palms flat, on his thighs. "Don't move them until I tell you."

Her mouth was dry; she didn't answer. Just watched his face as he slid the sleeves of her bodice farther down her arms, then reached—not for the ties of her chemise as she'd expected—but for the silk-screened mounds of her breasts.

What followed was a delicious torment. He traced, fondled, weighed, kneaded—all the time watching her, gauging her reactions. Under his practiced ministrations, her breasts swelled, grew heavy and tight. Until they ached. The fine film of silk was just enough to taunt, to tease, to have her gasping with need—the need to have his hands on her.

Skin to burning skin.

"Please . . ." The plea fell from her lips as she looked up at the ceiling, trying to cling to sanity.

His hands left her; she waited, then felt his fingers close about her wrists. He lifted her hands as she lowered her head and looked at him.

His eyes were dark pools lit by golden flames. "Show me."

He guided her hands to the ribbon ties.

Her gaze merged with his, she gripped the ends of the ribbons, and tugged, then, totally enthralled by what she could see in his face, the naked passion, the driving need, she slowly peeled the fine fabric down, exposing her breasts to the light.

And to him. His gaze felt like flame, licking, heating. Without looking up, he caught her hands and drew them back to his thighs. "Leave them there."

Releasing her hands, he raised his to her breasts.

The real torture began. He seemed to know just how much she could take, then he bent his head, soothed an aching nipple with his tongue, then took it into his mouth.

Feasted.

Until she cried out. Until her fingertips clung to the iron muscles of his thighs. He suckled, and her knees quaked. He locked one arm beneath her hips and supported her, held her steady while he did as he wished, imprinted himself on her skin, on her nerves, on her senses.

She cracked open her lids; panting, glanced down. Watched and felt his dark head move against her as he pandered to his desires—and hers.

With each touch of his lips, each swirl of his tongue, each dragging nerve-tingling suction, he ruthlessly, relentlessly stoked the fire within her.

Until she burned. Until, incandescent and empty, she felt like a glowing void, one she yearned for, ached for, desperately needed him to fill. To complete.

She lifted her hands, with a wriggle slid her arms free of her sleeves, then reached for him, traced his jaw with her palms, felt them work as he suckled. She slid her fingers back into his hair; reluctantly, he eased back, released her soft flesh.

Looked into her face, met her eyes, then he set her on her feet. His large palms stroked up, tracing the heated swollen curves, then stroked down, over her waist, possessively following her contours, pushing her gown and chemise down, over the swell of her hips, until with a soft whoosh they fell, puddling about her feet.

His gaze had followed the fabric to her knees. He studied them, then slowly, deliberately, lifted his gaze, past her thighs, lingering on the dark curls at their apex before moving slowly on, upward, over the gentle swell of her stomach, over her navel, her waist, to her breasts, eventually to her face, her lips, her eyes. A long comprehensive survey, one that left her in no doubt that he considered all he saw, all she was, to be his.

She shivered, not with cold but with burgeoning need. She reached for his cravat.

He caught her hands. "No. Not tonight."

Despite the grip of desire, she managed a faint frown. "I want to see you, too."

"You'll see enough of me over the years." He stood; still holding her hands, he stepped to the side. "Tonight . . . I want you. Naked. Mine." He trapped her gaze. "On this desk."

The desk? She looked at it.

He released her hands, locked his about her waist and lifted her, placed her sitting on the front of the desk where he'd been leaning.

The sensation of polished mahogany beneath her bare bottom temporarily distracted her.

Tristan gripped her knees, spread them wide and stepped between. Caught her face in his hands as she looked up, surprised—and kissed her.

Let his reins slide, simply let go, let desire rage and pour through him, and her. Their mouths melded, tongues tangled. Her hands framed his jaw as his drifted lower, needing to find her soft flesh again, needing to feel her urgency, her flaring response to his touch—all the evidence that she truly was his.

Her body was liquid silk under his hands, passion hot and urgent. He gripped her hips and leaned into her, gradually eased her back, at the last pressing her down to lie across his great-uncle's desk.

He drew back from the kiss, half straightened, seized the moment to look down on her, lying naked, heated, and panting, across the gleaming mahogany. The wood was no richer than her hair, still anchored in a knot atop her head.

He thought of that as he set a hand to one bare knee and slowly slid it upward, tracing the firm muscle of her thigh as he leaned down to her and took her mouth again.

Filled it, claimed like a conqueror, then set up a rhythm of thrust and retreat she and her body knew well. She was with him in thought and deed, in desire and urgency. She shifted beneath his hands; locking one about her hip, anchoring her, he trailed the fingers of the other from the spot between her breasts down over her waist, over her stomach to tantalizingly caress the damp curls covering her mons.

She gasped through their kiss. He broke from it, drew back enough to catch her eyes, gleaming an intense violet blue beneath her lashes. "Let down your hair."

Leonora blinked, acutely conscious of his fingertips idly stroking through her curls. Not quite touching her aching flesh. It throbbed; all of her pulsed with longing. With a sensual need impossible to deny.

She lifted her arms, eyes locked with his, and slowly reached for the pins holding her long locks. As she grasped the first, he touched her, set one blunt fingertip to her.

Her body tensed, lightly bowed; she closed her eyes, gripped the pin, and pulled it loose. Sensed his satisfaction in his touch, in his slow, teasing caress. Cracking open her lids, she watched him watching her; fingers searching, she found another pin.

Had to close her eyes again as she pulled it free—and he made free with her body. Touched, stroked.

Then delicately probed.

Just a gentle pressure at the entrance to her body.

Enough to tantalize, not enough to slake.

Eyes closed, she pulled another pin; one large finger glided in a fraction farther.

She was swollen, throbbing, wet. Dragging in a breath, with both hands she searched, pulled, let the pins fall in a rain on the desk.

By the time her hair tumbled loose, he'd buried his fingers in her sheath, penetrating, stroking, stoking. She was gasping for breath, her nerves alive, her body writhing against his hold. Her long hair spread about her shoulders, across the desk. She looked up at him, and saw his gaze drifting over her, taking in her abandonment; stark possession stamped his features.

He caught her gaze, studied her, then leaned down, and kissed her. Took her mouth, captured her senses in a drugging kiss. Then his lips left hers; he nudged her jaw higher, dipped his head to trail hot, openmouthed kisses down the taut line of her throat, down over the swell of her breasts. He lingered there, licking, laving, suckling, but lightly, then his hair brushed the soft undersides as he followed the line of her body lower. She was struggling for breath, far past wanton abandon; feelings, sensations, poured irresistibly through her, filling her, sweeping her on.

Her hands had come to rest on his shoulders; he was still clad in his coat. The tactile reminder emphasized her vulnerability; he had her completely naked, writhing before him, displayed on his desk like a houri . . . she gasped as his lips cruised over her stomach.

He didn't stop.

"Tristan . . . *Tristan!*"

He paid no heed; she had to swallow her screams as he pressed her thighs wider and sank between. Settled to feast as he had once before, but that time she hadn't been naked, exposed. So vulnerable.

She closed her eyes. Tight. Tried to hold back the welling tide . . .

It rose inexorably, lick by lick, subtle flick by flick, until it caught her. Gripped her.

She fractured.

Her body arched.

Her senses shattered. The world disappeared into shards of bright light, into a pulsing radiance that surrounded her, sank into her, through her. Left her bones melted, her muscles limp, left a deep well of heat within her, still empty.

Incomplete.

She was giddy, all but incapable, but she forced her lids up. Glanced at him as he straightened.

His large frame thrummed with restrained aggression, with a finely tuned, powerful tension. His hands gripping her naked thighs, he stood looking down at her, hazel eyes burning as they roamed her body.

What she saw in his face made her lungs seize, her heart hitch, then beat more strongly.

Naked desire etched his features, harshly delineated every line of his face.

Yet there was an aloneness there, too, a vulnerability, a hope.

She saw it, understood it.

Then his eyes met hers. For an instant, time stood still, then she lifted her arms, weak though they were, and beckoned him to her.

He stirred. His eyes locked on hers, he shrugged out of his coat, stripped off his cravat, opened his shirt, baring the muscled contours of his chest, lightly dusted with dark hair. Recollected sensation, of feeling that hair rasp against her sensitized skin as he moved within her, had her breasts swelling to aching fullness, her nipples puckering tight. He saw. Reached for his waistband. Flicked the buttons undone, freed his erection.

He glanced down only briefly, fitting himself to her, then he nudged in, just a fraction.

And looked up. Caught her gaze again, then leaned down, bracing his hands on the table on either side of her head, flicking his fingers through her hair. He leaned closer, brushed her lips.

Eyes locking on hers once more, he pressed into her.

She rose beneath him. Their breaths mingled as she arched, adjusted, took him in. At the last, he thrust deep and filled her. Her breath fell from her lips; she closed her eyes, luxuriating in the feel of him buried inside her. Then she lifted one hand, speared her fingers into his hair, drew his head to hers, and set her lips to his. Opened her mouth to him, invited him in.

Flagrantly invited him to plunder.

And he did.

Each powerful stroke lifted her, shifted her.

They broke from the kiss. Without waiting for instructions, she raised her legs and wrapped them about his hips. Heard him groan, saw blankness sweep his face as he took advantage and sank deeper, thrust harder, farther. Sheathed himself in her.

He closed one hand about her hip, anchoring her against his repetitive invasions. As the tempo mounted, he leaned down to her again, let his lips brush hers, then plunged into her mouth as his body plunged wildly into hers.

As all restraint broke and he gave himself to her.

As she had already given herself, body and soul, mind and heart, to him.

She let go, truly let herself free, let him take her with him as he wished.

Even locked in the throes of an impossibly powerful passion, Tristan sensed her decision, her total surrender to the moment— her surrender to him. She was with him, not just locked together physically but in some other place, in some other way, on some other plane.

He'd never reached that mystical place with any other woman; he'd never dreamed such a soul-searing experience would ever be his. Yet she took him in, rode his every thrust, wrapped him in the heat of her body—and joyously, with true abandonment, gave him all he could wish for, all he had yearned for.

Unconditional surrender.

She had said she would be his. Now she was. Forever.

He needed no further reassurance, no evidence beyond the tight clasp of her body, the supple writhing of her naked curves beneath him.

But he'd always wanted more, and she'd given without him asking.

Not just her body, but this—an unfettered commitment to him, to her, to what lay between them.

It rose up in a tide, impossible to control. It rolled over them both, crashed, swirled, made them gasp, cling. Fight for air. Fight for their hold on life, then lose it as brilliance swamped them, as their bodies clutched, clung, shuddered.

He spilled his seed deep within her, held tight, immobile, as ecstasy drenched them.

Filled them, sank deep, then slowly ebbed and faded.

He let go, felt his muscles relax, let her hold him, cradle him, his forehead bowed to hers.

Wrapped together, lips brushing, together they surrendered to their fate.

She stayed for hours. Few words were spoken. There was no need between them to explain; neither needed nor wanted inadequate words to intrude.

He'd restoked the fire. Slumped in an armchair before it with her curled in his lap, still naked, with her cloak thrown over her to keep her warm, his arms beneath it, his hands on her bare skin, her hair like wild silk clinging to them both . . . he would have happily remained so forever.

He glanced down at her. The firelight gilded her face. It had earlier gilded her body when she'd stood unabashed before the flames and let him examine each curve, each line. This time, he'd left her largely unmarked; only the imprints of his fingers at her hip where he'd anchored her were visible.

Leonora looked up, caught his eye, smiled, then laid her head back on his shoulder. Under her palm, spread across his bare chest, his heart beat steadily. The beat echoed in her blood. Throughout her body.

Closeness wrapped them about, linked them in a way she couldn't define, certainly hadn't expected.

He hadn't either, yet they'd both accepted it.

Once accepted, it couldn't be denied.

It had to be love, but who was she to say? All she knew was that for her it was immutable. Unchanging, fixed, and forever.

Whatever the future held—marriage, family, dependents, and all—she would have that, that strength, to call on.

It felt right. More right than she'd imagined anything could feel.

She was where she belonged. In his arms. With love between them.

Sixteen

୬ⓒ⊘ঔ

The next morning, Leonora breezed down to the breakfast parlor somewhat later than usual; she was normally the first of the family up and about, but this morning she'd slept in. With a definite spring in her step and a smile on her lips, she swept over the threshold—and came to an abrupt halt.

Tristan sat beside Humphrey, listening intently while calmly demolishing a plate of ham and sausages.

Jeremy sat opposite; all three men looked up, then Tristan and Jeremy rose.

Humphrey beamed at her. "Well, my dear! Congratulations! Tristan has told us your news. I have to say I'm utterly delighted!"

"Indeed, sis. Congratulations." Leaning over the table, Jeremy caught her hand and drew her across to plant a kiss on her cheek. "Excellent choice," he murmured.

Her smile became a trifle fixed. "Thank you."

She looked at Tristan, expecting to see some degree of apology. Instead, he met her gaze with a steady, assured—confident—expression. She took due note of that last, inclined her head. "Good morning."

The "my lord" stuck in her throat. She would not soon forget his notion of an appropriate finale to their reconciliation the previous evening. Later, he'd dressed her, then carried her out to the carriage, overridden her by then thoroughly weak protest, and accompanied her to Montrose Place, leaving her in the tiny parlor of Number 12 while he collected Henrietta, then escorting them both to her front door.

Suavely, he took her hand, raised it briefly to his lips, then held her chair for her. "I trust you slept well?"

She glanced at him as he resumed his seat beside her. "Like one dead."

His lips twitched, but he merely inclined his head.

"We've been telling Tristan here that Cedric's journals do not, at first glance, fall into any of the customary patterns." Humphrey paused to eat a mouthful of egg.

Jeremy took up the tale. "They're not organized by subject, which is most usual with such things, and as you'd found"—he dipped his head to Leonora—"the entries are not in any type of chronological order."

"Hmm." Humphrey chewed, then swallowed. "There has to be some key, but it's perfectly possible Cedric kept it in his head."

Tristan frowned. "Does that mean you won't be able to make sense of the journals?"

"No," Jeremy answered. "It just means it'll take us rather longer." He glanced at Leonora. "I vaguely recall you mentioned letters?"

She nodded. "There are lots. I've only looked at the ones in the past year."

"You'd better give them to us," Humphrey said. "All of them. In fact, any scrap of paper of Cedric's you can find."

"Scientists," Jeremy put in, "especially herbalists, are renowned for writing vital information on scraps of whatever comes to hand."

Leonora grimaced. "I'll have the maids gather up everything from the workshop. I've been meaning to search Cedric's bedchamber—I'll do that today."

Tristan glanced at her. "I'll help you."

She turned her head to check his expression to see what he really intended—

"Aaaah! Aieee-ah!"

The hysterical wails came from a distance. They all heard them. The cries continued clearly for an instant, then were muted—by the green baize door, they all realized, when a footman, startled and pale, skidded to a halt in the parlor doorway. "Mr. Castor! You got to come quick!"

Castor, a serving dish in his ancient hands, goggled at him.

Humphrey stared. "What the devil's the matter, man?"

The footman, completely shaken out of his habitual aplomb, bowed and bobbed to those around the table. "It's Daisy, sir. M'lord. From next door." He fixed on Tristan, who was rising to his feet. "She's just rushed in wailing and carrying on. Seems Miss Timmins has fallen down the stairs and . . . well, Daisy says as she's dead, m'lord."

Tristan tossed his napkin on the table and stepped around his chair.

Leonora rose at his shoulder. "Where is Daisy, Smithers? In the kitchen?"

"Yes, miss. She's taking on something terrible."

"I'll come and see her." Leonora swept out into the hall, conscious of Tristan following at her heels. She glanced back at him, took in his grim expression, met his eyes. "Will you go next door?"

"In a minute." His hand touched her back, a curiously comforting gesture. "I want to hear what Daisy has to say first. She's no fool—if she says Miss Timmins is dead, then she probably is. She won't be going anywhere."

Leonora inwardly grimaced and pushed through the door into the corridor leading to the kitchen. Tristan, she reminded herself, was much more accustomed to dealing with death than she was. Not a nice thought, but in the circumstances it held a certain comfort.

"Oh, miss! Oh, *miss!*" Daisy appealed to her the instant she saw her. "I don't know what to do. I couldn't do nothing!" She sniffed, wiped her eyes with the dishcloth Cook pressed into her hand.

"Now, Daisy." Leonora reached for one of the kitchen chairs; Tristan anticipated her, lifting it and setting it for her to sit facing Daisy. Leonora sat, felt Tristan lean his hands on the chair's back. "What you must do now, Daisy—what would be most help to Miss Timmins now—is to compose yourself—just take deep breaths, there's a good girl—and tell us—his-lordship-the-earl and me—what happened."

Daisy nodded, dutifully gulped in air, then blurted out, "Everything started out normal this morning. I came down from my room by the back stairs, riddled the grate and got the kitchen fire going, then got Miss Timmins's tray ready. Then I went to take it up to her . . ." Daisy's huge eyes clouded with tears. "Swept through the door I did, as usual, and plonked the tray on the hall table to tidy my hair and straighten up before I went up—and there she was."

Daisy's voice quavered and broke. Tears gushed, she mopped them furiously. "She was lying there—at the bottom of the stairs—like a little broken bird. I rush over, o'course, and checked, but there was no point. She was gone."

For a moment, no one said anything; they'd all known Miss Timmins.

"Did you touch her?" Tristan asked, his tone quiet, almost soothing.

Daisy nodded. "Aye—I patted her hand, and her cheek."

"Her cheek—was it cold? Do you remember?"

Daisy looked up at him, frowning as she thought. Then she nodded. "Aye, you're right. Her cheek was cold. Didn't think anything of her hands—they always were cold. But her cheek . . . yeah, it was cold." She blinked at Tristan. "Does that mean she'd been dead for a while?"

Tristan straightened. "It means it's likely she died some hours ago. Sometime in the night." He hesitated, then asked, "Did she ever wander at night? Do you know?"

Daisy shook her head. She'd stopped crying. "Not that I ever knew. She never mentioned such a thing."

Tristan nodded, stepped back. "We'll take care of Miss Timmins."

His gaze included Leonora. She stood, too, but glanced back at Daisy. "You'd best stay here. Not just for today, but tonight, too." She saw Neeps, her uncle's valet, hovering, concerned. "Neeps, you can help Daisy get her things after luncheon."

The man bowed. "Indeed, miss."

Tristan waved Leonora before him; she led him out of the kitchen. In the front hall they found Jeremy waiting.

He looked distinctly pale. "Is it true?"

"It must be, I'm afraid." Leonora went to the hall stand and lifted down her cloak. Tristan had followed her; he took it from her hands.

He held it, and looked down at her. "I don't suppose I can convince you to wait with your uncle in the library?"

She met his gaze. "No."

He sighed. "I thought not." He draped the cloak about her shoulders, then reached around her to open the front door.

"I'm coming, too." Jeremy followed them out onto the porch, then down the winding path.

They reached the front door of Number 16; Daisy had left it on the latch. Pushing the door wide, they entered.

The scene was exactly as Leonora had imagined it from Daisy's words. Unlike their house with its wide front hall with the stairs at the rear facing the front door, here, the hall was narrow and the head of the stairs was above the door; the foot of the stairs was at the rear of the hall.

That was where Miss Timmins lay, crumpled like a rag doll. Just as Daisy had said, there seemed little doubt life had left her, but Leonora went forward. Tristan had halted ahead of her, blocking the hall; she put her hands on his back and gently pushed; after an instant's hesitation, he moved aside and let her through.

Leonora crouched by Miss Timmins. She was wearing a thick cotton nightgown with a lacy wrapper clutched around her shoulders. Her limbs were twisted awkwardly, but decently covered; a pair of pink slippers were on her narrow feet.

Her lids were closed, the fading blue eyes shut away. Leonora brushed back the thin white curls, noted the extreme fragility of the papery skin. Taking one tiny clawlike hand in hers, she looked up at Tristan as he paused beside her. "Can we move her? There seems no reason to leave her like this."

He studied the body for a moment; she got the impression he was fixing its position in his memory. He glanced up the stairs, all the way to the top. Then he nodded. "I'll lift her. The front parlor?"

Leonora nodded, released the bony hand, rose and went to open the parlor door. "Oh!"

Jeremy, who'd gone past the body, past the hall table with the breakfast tray and onto the kitchen stairs, came back through the swinging door. "What is it?"

Speechless, Leonora simply stared.

With Miss Timmins in his arms, Tristan came up behind her, looked over her head, then nudged her forward.

She came to with a start, then hurried to straighten the cushions on the chaise. "Put her here." She glanced around at the wreck of the once fastidiously neat room. Drawers were pulled out, emptied on the rugs. The rugs themselves had been pulled up, slung aside. Some of the ornaments had been smashed in the grate. The pictures on the walls, those still on their hooks, hung crazily. "It must have been thieves. She must have heard them."

Tristan straightened from laying Miss Timmins gently down. With her limbs extended and her head on a cushion, she looked to be simply fast asleep. He turned to Jeremy, standing in the open doorway, looking around in amazement. "Go to Number 12 and tell Gasthorpe that we need Pringle again. Immediately."

Jeremy lifted his gaze to his face, then nodded and left.

Leonora, fussing with Miss Timmins's nightgown, rearranging her wrapper as she knew she would have liked, glanced up at him. "Why Pringle?"

Tristan met her gaze, hesitated, then said, "Because I want to know if she fell, or was pushed."

"Fell." Pringle carefully repacked his black bag. "There's not a mark on her that can't be accounted for by the fall, and none that looks like bruises from a man's grip. At her age, there would be bruises."

He glanced over his shoulder at the tiny body laid out on the chaise. "She was fragile and old, not long for this world in any case, but even so. While a man could easily have grabbed her and flung her down the stairs, he couldn't have done it without leaving some trace."

His gaze on Leonora, tidying a vase on a table beside the chaise, Tristan nodded. "That's some small relief."

Pringle snapped his bag closed, glanced at him as he straightened. "Possibly. But there's still the question of why she was out of bed at that hour—somewhere in the small hours, say between one o'clock and three—and what so frightened her, and it was almost certainly fright, enough to make her faint."

Tristan focused on Pringle. "You think she fainted?"

"I can't prove it, but if I had to guess what happened . . ." Pringle waved at the chaos of the room. "She heard sounds from this, and came to see. She stood at the top of the stairs and peered down. And saw a man. Suddenly. Shock, faint, fall. And here we are."

Tristan, gazing at the chaise and Leonora beyond it, said nothing for a moment, then he nodded, looked at Pringle, and offered his hand. "As you say—here we are. Thank you for coming."

Pringle shook his hand, a grim smile flirting about his lips. "I thought leaving the army would mean a humdrum practice—with you and your friends about, at least I won't be bored."

With an exchange of smiles, they parted. Pringle left, closing the front door behind him.

Tristan walked around the back of the chaise to where Leonora stood, looking down at Miss Timmins. He put an arm around Leonora, lightly hugged.

She permitted it. Leaned into him for a moment. Her hands were tightly clasped. "She looks so peaceful."

A moment passed, then she straightened and heaved a huge sigh. Brushed down her skirts and looked around. "So—a thief broke in and searched this room. Miss Timmins heard him and got out of bed to investigate. When the thief returned to the hall, she saw him, fainted, and fell . . . and died."

When he said nothing, she turned to him. Searched his eyes. Frowned. "What's wrong with that as deduction? It's perfectly logical."

"Indeed." He took her hand, turned to the door. "I suspect that's precisely what we're supposed to think."

"Supposed to think?"

"You missed a few pertinent facts. One, there's not a single window lock or door lock forced or unexpectedly left open. Both Jeremy and I checked. Two"—stepping into the hall, ushering her ahead of him, he glanced back into the parlor—"no self-respecting thief would leave a room like that. There's no point, and especially at night, why risk the noise?"

Leonora frowned. "Is there a three?"

"No other room has been searched, nothing else in the house appears disturbed. *Except*"—holding the front door, he waved her ahead of him; she went out onto the porch, waited impatiently for him to lock the door and pocket the key.

"Well?" she demanded, linking her arm with his. "Except *what?*"

They started down the steps. His tone had grown much harder, much colder, much more distant when he replied, "Except for a few, very new, scrapes and cracks in the basement wall."

Her eyes grew huge. "The wall shared with Number 14?"

He nodded.

Leonora glanced back toward the parlor windows. "So this was Mountford's work?"

"I believe so. And he doesn't want us to know."

"What are we looking for?"

Leonora followed Tristan into the bedchamber Miss Timmins had used. They'd returned to Number 14 and broken the news to Humphrey, then gone to the kitchen to confirm for Daisy that her employer was indeed dead. Tristan had asked after relatives; Daisy hadn't known of any. None had called in the six years she'd worked in Montrose Place.

Jeremy had taken on the task of making the necessary arrangements; together with Tristan, Leonora had returned to Number 16 to try to identify any relative.

"Letters, a will, notes from a solicitor—anything that might lead to a connection." He pulled open the small drawer of the table by the bed. "It would be most unusual if she has absolutely no kin."

"She never mentioned any."

"Be that as it may."

They settled to search. She noticed he did things—looked in places—she'd never have thought of. Like the backs and undersides of drawers, the upper surface above a top drawer. Behind paintings.

After a while, she sat on a chair before the escritoire and applied herself to all the notes and letters therein. There was no sign of any recent or promising correspondence. When he glanced at her, she waved him on. "You're much better at that than I."

But it was she who found the connection, in an old, very faded and much creased letter lying at the back of the tiniest drawer.

"The Reverend Mr. Henry Timmins, of Shacklegate Lane, Strawberry Hills." Triumphant, she read the address to Tristan, who had paused in the doorway.

He frowned. "Where's that?"

"I think it's out past Twickenham."

He crossed the room, lifted the letter from her hand, scanned it. Humphed. "Eight years old. Well, we can but try." He glanced at the window, then pulled out his watch and checked it. "If we take my curricle . . ."

She rose, smiled, linked her arm in his. Very definitely approved of that "we." "I'll have to fetch my pelisse. Let's go."

The Reverend Henry Timmins was a relatively young man, with a wife and four daughters and a busy parish.

"Oh, dear!" He abruptly sat down in a chair in the small parlor to which he'd conducted them. Then he realized and started up.

Tristan waved him back, handed Leonora to the chaise, and sat beside her. "So you were acquainted with Miss Timmins?"

"Oh, yes—she was my great-aunt." Pale, he glanced from one to the other. "We weren't at all close—indeed, she always seemed most nervous when I called. I did write a few times, but she never replied . . ." He blushed. "And then I got my preferment . . . and married . . . that sounds so unfeeling, yet she wasn't at all encouraging, you know."

Tristan squeezed Leonora's hand, warning her to silence; he inclined his head impassively. "Miss Timmins passed away last night, but not, I fear, easily. She fell down the stairs sometime very early in the morning. While we have no evidence she was directly attacked, we believe that she came upon a thief in her house—her front parlor was ransacked—and because of the shock, fainted and fell."

Reverend Timmins's face was a study in horror. "Good gracious me! How dreadful!"

"Indeed. We have reason to believe that the burglar responsible is the same man intent on gaining entry into Number 14." Tristan glanced at Leonora. "The Carlings live there, and Miss Carling herself has been subject to several attacks, we presume intended to frighten the household into leaving. There have also been a number of attempts to break into Number 14, and also into Number 12, the house of which I am part owner."

Reverend Timmins blinked. Tristan calmly continued, explaining their reasoning that the burglar they knew as Mountford was attempting to gain access to something hidden in Number 14, and that his forays into Number 12 and last night into Number 16 were by way of seeking entry via the basement walls.

"I see." Frowning, Henry Timmins nodded. "I've lived in terraces like that—you're quite right. The basement walls are often a series of arches filled in. Quite easy to break through the archways."

"Indeed." Tristan paused, then continued, in the same, authoritative tone, "Which is why we've been so set on finding you, why we've been speaking to you so frankly." He leaned forward; clasping his hands between his knees, he captured Henry Timmins's pale blue gaze. "Your great-aunt's death was deeply regrettable, and if Mountford is responsible, he deserves to be caught and brought to book. In the circumstances, I feel it would be poetic justice to use the situation as it now stands—the situation that has arisen because of Miss Timmins's demise—to set a trap for him."

"Trap?"

Leonora didn't need to hear the word to know that Henry Timmins was caught, hooked. So was she. She edged forward so she could watch Tristan's face.

"There's no reason for anyone beyond those who already know to imagine Miss Timmins died other than by natural causes. She'll be mourned by those who knew her, then . . . if I may suggest, you, as heir, should put Number 16 Montrose Place up for rent." With a gesture, Tristan indicated the house about them. "You're clearly not in any need of a house in town at present. On the other hand, being a prudent man, you will not wish to sell precipitously. Renting the property is the sensible course, and no one will wonder at it."

Henry was nodding. "True, true."

"If you're agreeable, I'll arrange for a friend to pose as a house agent and handle the rental for you. Of course, we won't be renting to just anyone."

"You think Mountford will come forward and rent the house?"

"Not Mountford himself—Miss Carling and I have seen him. He'll use an intermediary, but it will be he who wants access to the house. Once he has it, and enters . . ." Tristan sat back; a smile that was no smile curved his lips. "Suffice to say that I have the right connections to ensure he won't escape."

Henry Timmins, eyes rather wide, continued to nod.

Leonora was less susceptible. "Do you really believe that after all this, Mountford will dare show his face?"

Tristan turned to her; his eyes were cold, hard. "Given the lengths to which he's already gone, I'm prepared to wager he won't be able to resist."

They returned to Montrose Place that evening with Henry Timmins's blessings, and, more importantly, a letter to the family solicitor from Henry instructing said solicitor to act on Tristan's directions regarding Miss Timmins's house.

There were lights burning in the rooms on the first floor of the Bastion Club; handing Leonora to the pavement, Tristan saw them, wondered . . .

Leonora shook out her skirts, then slipped her hand in his arm.

He looked down at her, refrained from mentioning how much he liked the little gesture of feminine acceptance. He was learning that she often did small revealing things instinctively, without noticing; he saw no reason to bring such transparency to her attention.

They headed up the path of Number 14.

"Who will you get to play the part of house agent?" Leonora glanced at him. "You can't—he knows what you look like." She ran her gaze over his features. "Even with one of your disguises . . . there's no way of being sure he wouldn't see through it."

"Indeed." Tristan glanced across at the Bastion Club as they climbed the porch steps. "I'll see you in, speak with Humphrey and Jeremy, then I'm going next door." He met her gaze as the front door opened. "It's possible some of my associates are in town. If so . . ."

She arched a brow at him. "Your ex-colleagues?"

He nodded, following her into the hall. "I can't think of any gentlemen more suited to aid us in this."

Charles, predictably, was delighted.

"Excellent! I always knew this notion of a club was a brilliant idea."

It was nearly ten o'clock; having consumed a superb dinner in the elegant dining room downstairs, they—Tristan, Charles, and Deverell—were now seated, sprawled and comfortable, in the library, each cradling a balloon liberally supplied with fine brandy.

"Indeed." Despite his more reserved manner, Deverell looked

equally interested. He eyed Charles. "I think I should be the house agent—you've already played one part in this drama."

Charles looked aggrieved. "But I could always play another."

"I think Deverell's right." Tristan firmly took charge. "He can be the house agent—this is only his second visit to Montrose Place, so chances are Mountford and his cronies won't have spotted him. Even if they have, there's no reason he can't play totally vague and say he's handling the matter for a friend." Tristan glanced at Charles. "Meanwhile, there's something else I think you and I should take care of."

Charles instantly looked hopeful. "What?"

"I told you of this solicitor's clerk who inherited from Carruthers." He'd told them the entire story, all the pertinent facts, over dinner.

"The one who came to London and disappeared into the teeming throng?"

"Indeed. I believe I mentioned he'd originally planned to come to town? While searching for information in York, my operative learned that this Martinbury had earlier arranged to meet with a friend, another clerk from his office, here, in town; before he left unexpectedly, he confirmed the meeting."

Charles raised his brows high. "When, and where?"

"Noon tomorrow, at the Red Lion in Gracechurch Street."

Charles nodded. "So we nab him after the meeting—I assume you have descriptions?"

"Yes, but the friend has agreed to introduce me, so all we need do is be there, and then we'll see what we can learn from Mr. Martinbury."

"He couldn't be Mountford, could he?" Deverell asked.

Tristan shook his head. "Martinbury was in York for much of the time Mountford's been active down here."

"Hmm." Deverell sat back, rolled the brandy in his balloon. "If it won't be Mountford who approaches me—and I agree that's unlikely—then who do you think will try to rent the house?"

"My guess," Tristan said, "would be a scrawny, weasel-faced specimen, short to medium height. Leonora—Miss Carling—has seen him twice. He seems certain to be an associate of Mountford's."

Charles opened his eyes wide. "Leonora, is it?" Swiveling in his chair, he fixed Tristan with his dark gaze. "So tell us—how sits the wind in that quarter, hmm?"

Impassive, Tristan studied Charles's devilish face, and wondered what fiendish devilment Charles might concoct if he didn't tell them . . . "As it happens, the notice of our engagement will appear in the *Gazette* tomorrow morning."

"Oh-ho!"

"I see!"

"Well, that was quick work!" Rising, Charles grabbed the decanter and replenished their glasses. "We have to toast this. Let's see." He struck a pose before the fireplace, his glass held high. "Here's to you and your lady, the delightful Miss Carling. Let's drink in acknowledgment of your success in determining your own fate—to your victory over the meddlers—and to the inspiration and encouragement this victory will provide to your fellow Bastion Club members!"

"Hear! Hear!"

Charles and Deverell both drank. Tristan saluted them with his glass, then drank, too.

"So when's the wedding?" Deverell asked.

Tristan studied the amber liquid swirling in his glass. "As soon as we lay Mountford by the heels."

Charles pursed his lips. "And if that takes longer than expected?"

Tristan raised his eyes, met Charles's dark gaze. Smiled. "Trust me. It won't."

Early the next morning, Tristan visited Number 14 Montrose Place; he left before Leonora or any of the family came downstairs, confident he'd solved the riddle of how Mountford had got into Number 16.

As Jeremy had, at his direction, already had the locks on Number 16 changed, Mountford must have suffered another disappointment. All the better for driving him into their snare. He now had no option other than to rent the house.

Leaving Number 14 by the front gate, Tristan saw a workman busy setting up a sign atop the low front wall of Number 16. The sign announced that the house was for rent and gave details for contacting the agent. Deverell had wasted no time.

He returned to Green Street for breakfast, manfully waited until all six of the resident old dears were present before making his announcement. They were more than delighted.

"She's just the sort of wife we wished for you," Millicent told him.

"Indeed," Ethelreda confirmed. "She's such a sensible young woman—we were awfully afraid you might land us with some flibbertigibbet. One of those empty-headed gels who giggle all the time. The good Lord only knows how we would have coped then."

In fervent agreement, he excused himself and took refuge in the study. Ruthlessly blocking out the obvious distraction, he spent an hour dealing with the more urgent matters awaiting his attention, remembering to pen a brief letter to his great-aunts informing them of his impending nuptials. When the clock chimed eleven, he put down his pen, rose, and quietly left the house.

He met Charles at the corner of Grosvenor Square. They hailed a hackney; at ten minutes before noon, they pushed through the door of the Red Lion. It was a popular public house catering to a mixture of trades—merchants, agents, shippers, and clerks of every description. The main room was crowded, yet after one glance, most moved out of Tristan's and Charles's way. They went to the bar, were served immediately, then, ale mugs in hand, turned and surveyed the room.

After a moment, Tristan took a sip of his ale. "He's over there, one table from the corner. The one that keeps looking around like an eager pup."

"That's the friend?"

"Fits the description to a tee. The cap's hard to miss." A tweed cap was sitting on the table at which the young man in question waited.

Tristan considered, then said, "He won't recognize us. Why don't we just take the table next to him, and wait for the right moment to introduce ourselves?"

"Good idea."

Once again the crowd parted like the Red Sea; they installed themselves at the small table in the corner without attracting more than a quick glance and a polite smile from the young man.

He seemed terribly young to Tristan.

The young man continued to wait. So did they. They discussed various points—difficulties they'd both faced on taking up the reins of large estates. There was more than enough there to provide believable cover had the young man been listening. He wasn't; like a spaniel, he kept his eyes on the door, ready to leap up and wave when his friend entered.

Gradually, as the minutes ticked by, his eagerness ebbed. He nursed his pint; they nursed theirs. But when the clang from a nearby belltower sounded the half hour, it seemed certain that he for whom they all waited was not going to appear.

They waited some more, in growing concern.

Eventually, Tristan exchanged a glance with Charles, then turned to the young man. "Mr. Carter?"

The young man blinked, focused properly on Tristan for the first time. "Y-yes?"

"We've not met." Tristan reached for a card, handed it to Carter. "But I believe an associate of mine told you we were concerned to meet with Mr. Martinbury over a matter of mutual benefit."

Carter read the card; his youthful face cleared. "Oh, yes— of course!" Then he looked at Tristan and grimaced. "But as you can see, Jonathon hasn't come." He glanced around, as if to make sure Martinbury hadn't materialized in the last minute. Carter frowned. "I really can't understand it." He looked back at Tristan. "Jonathon's very punctual, and we're very good friends."

Worry clouded his face.

"Have you heard from him since he's been in town?"

Charles asked the question; when Carter blinked at him, Tristan smoothly added, "Another associate."

Carter shook his head. "No. No one at home—York, that is—has had any word from him. His landlady was surprised; she made me promise to tell him to write when I met him. It's odd— he's really a very reliable person, and he is fond of her. She's like a mother to him."

Tristan exchanged a glance with Charles. "I think it's time we searched more actively for Mr. Martinbury." Turning to Carter, he nodded at his card, which the young man still held in his hand. "If you do hear from Martinbury, any contact at all, I'd be obliged if you would send word immediately to that address. Likewise, if you furnish me with your direction, I'll make sure you're informed if we locate your friend."

"Oh, yes. Thank you." Carter dragged a tablet from his pocket, found a pencil, and quickly wrote down the address of his lodging house. He handed the sheet to Tristan. He read it, then nodded and put the note in his pocket.

Carter was frowning. "I wonder if he even reached London."

Tristan rose. "He did." He drained his tankard, set it on the table. "He left the coach when it reached town, not before. Unfortunately, tracing a single man on the streets of London is not at all easy."

He said the last with a reassuring smile. With a nod to Carter, he and Charles left.

They paused on the pavement outside.

"Tracing a single man walking the streets of London may not be easy." Charles glanced at Tristan. "Tracing a dead one is not quite so hard."

"No, indeed." Tristan's expression had hardened. "I'll take the watchhouses."

"And I'll take the hospitals. Meet at the club later tonight?"

Tristan nodded. Then grimaced. "I just remembered . . ."

Charles glanced at him, then hooted. "Just remembered you'd announced your engagement—of course! No longer a life of ease for you—not until you're wed."

"Which only makes me even more determined to find Martinbury with all speed. I'll send word to Gasthorpe if I find anything."

"I'll do the same." With a nod, Charles headed down the street.

Tristan watched him go, then swore, swung on his heel, and strode off in the opposite direction.

Seventeen

The day was fleeing, whipped away by grey squalls, as Tristan climbed the steps of Number 14 and asked to see Leonora. Castor directed him to the parlor; dismissing the butler, he opened the parlor door and went in.

Leonora didn't hear him. She was seated on the chaise, facing the windows, looking out at the garden, at the shrubs bowing before the blustering wind. Beside her, a fire burned brightly in the hearth, crackling and spitting cheerily. Henrietta lay stretched before the flames, luxuriating in their heat.

The scene was comfortable, cozy—warming in a way that had nothing to do with temperature, a subtle comfort to the heart.

He took a step, let his heel fall heavily.

She heard, turned . . . then she saw him and her face lit. Not just with expectation, not just with eagerness to hear what he had learned, but with an open welcome as if a part of her had returned.

He neared and she rose, held out her hands. He took them, raised first one, then the other to his lips, then drew her nearer and bent his head. Took her mouth in a kiss he struggled to keep within bounds, let his senses savor, then reined them in.

When he lifted his head, she smiled at him; their gazes touched, held for a moment, then she sank onto the chaise.

He crouched to pat Henrietta.

Leonora watched him, then said, "Now before you tell me anything else, explain how Mountford got into Number 16 last night. You said there were no forced locks, and Castor told me some tale about you asking after a drainage inspector. What has he to do with anything—or was he Mountford?"

Tristan glanced at her, then nodded. "Daisy's description tallies. It seems he posed as an inspector and talked her into letting him inspect the kitchen, scullery, and laundry drains."

"And when she wasn't looking, he took an impression of a key?"

"That seems most likely. No inspector called here or at Number 12."

She frowned. "He's a very . . . calculating man."

"He's clever." After a moment of studying her face, Tristan said, "Added to that, he must be getting desperate. I'd like you to bear that in mind."

She met his gaze, then smiled reassuringly. "Of course."

The look he cast her as he rose to his feet looked more resigned than reassured.

"I saw the sign outside Number 16. That was quick." She let her approval show in her face.

"Indeed. I've handed that aspect over to a gentleman by the name of Deverell. He's Viscount Paignton."

She opened her eyes wide. "Do you have any other . . . associates helping you?"

Sinking his hands into his pockets, the fire warm on his back, Tristan looked down into her face, into eyes that reflected an intelligence he knew better than to underestimate. "I have a small army working for me, as you know. Most of them, you'll never meet, but there is one other who's actively helping me—another part-owner of Number 12."

"As is Deverell?" she asked.

He nodded. "The other gentleman is Charles St. Austell, Earl of Lostwithiel."

"Lostwithiel?" She frowned. "I heard something about the last two earls dying in tragic circumstances . . ."

"They were his brothers. He was the third son and is now the earl."

"Ah. And what is he helping you with?"

He explained about the meeting they'd hoped to have with Martinbury, and their disappointment. She heard him out in silence, watching his face. When he paused after explaining the agreement they'd made with Martinbury's friend, she said, "You think he's met with foul play."

Not a question. His eyes on hers, he nodded. "Everything that was reported to me from York, everything his friend Carter said of him, painted Martinbury as a conscientious, reliable, honest man—not one to miss an appointment he'd taken care to confirm." Again he hesitated, wondering how much he should tell her, then pushed aside his reluctance. "I've started checking the watchhouses for reported deaths, and Charles is checking the hospitals in case he was brought in alive, but then died."

"He could still be alive, perhaps gravely injured, but without friends or connections in London . . ."

He considered the timing, then grimaced. "True—I'll put some others onto checking that. However, given how long it's been without any word from him, we need to check the dead. Unfortunately, that's not the sort of search anyone but Charles and I, or one like us, can undertake." He met her gaze. "Members of the nobility, especially ones with our background, can get answers, demand to see reports and records, that others simply can't."

"So I've noticed." She sat back, considering him. "So you'll be busy during the days. I spent today with the maids, searching every nook and cranny in Cedric's workshop. We found various scraps and jottings which are now with Humphrey and Jeremy in the library. They're still poring over the journals. Humphrey's increasingly certain there ought to be more. He thinks there are sections—pieces of records—missing. Not torn out but written down somewhere else."

"Hmm." Tristan stroked Henrietta's head with his boot, then glanced at Leonora. "What about Cedric's bedchamber? Have you searched there yet?"

"Tomorrow. The maids will help—there'll be five of us. If there's anything there, I assure you we'll find it."

He nodded, mentally running down his list of matters he'd wanted to discuss with her. "Ah, yes." He refocused on her face, caught her gaze. "I put the customary notice in the *Gazette* announcing our betrothal. It was in this morning's edition."

A subtle change came over her face; an expression he couldn't quite place—resigned amusement?—invested her blue eyes.

"I was wondering when you were going to mention that."

Suddenly, he wasn't sure of the ground beneath his feet. He shrugged, his eyes still on hers. "It was just the usual thing. The expected thing."

"Indeed, but you might have thought to warn me—that way, when my aunts descended in a swirl of congratulations a bare ten minutes before the first of a good two dozen callers, all wanting to congratulate me, I wouldn't have been caught like a deer in a hunter's sights."

He held her gaze; for a moment, silence reigned. Then he winced. "My apologies. With Miss Timmins's death and all the rest, it escaped my mind."

She considered him, then inclined her head. Her lips weren't quite straight. "Apology accepted. However, you do realize that, now the news is out, we'll need to make the obligatory appearances?"

He stared down at her. "What appearances?"

"The necessary appearances every engaged couple are expected to make. For instance, tonight, everyone will expect us to attend Lady Hartington's soirée."

"Why?"

"Because it's the major event tonight, and so they can congratulate us, watch us, analyze and dissect, assure themselves it will be a good match, and so on."

"And this is obligatory?"

She nodded.

"Why?"

She didn't misunderstand. "Because if we don't give them that chance, it will fix unwarranted—and quite staggeringly intrusive—attention on us. We won't have a moment's peace. They'll call constantly, and not just within the accepted hours; if they're in the neighborhood, they'll drive down the street and peer out of their carriages. You'll find a couple of giggling girls on the pavement every time you step out of your house, or your club next door. And you won't dare appear in the park, or on Bond Street."

She fixed him with a direct look. "Is that what you want?"

He read her eyes, confirmed she was serious. Shuddered. "Good Lord!" He sighed; his lips thinned. "All right. Lady Hartington's. Should I meet you there, or call for you in my carriage?"

"It would be most appropriate for you to escort my aunts and

me. Mildred and Gertie will be here by eight. If you arrive a little
after, you can accompany us there, in Mildred's carriage."

He humphed, but nodded curtly. He didn't take orders well,
but in this sphere . . . that was one reason he needed her. He
cared very little for society, knew both enough and too little of
its tortuous ways to feel totally comfortable in its glare. While
he had every intention of spending as little time in it as possible, given his title, his position, if a quiet life was his aim, it
would never do to thumb his nose openly at the ladies' sacred
rites.

Such as passing judgment on newly affianced couples.

He refocused on Leonora's face. "How long do we have to
pander to prurient interest?"

Her lips twitched. "For at least a week."

He scowled, literally growled.

"Unless some scandal intervenes, or unless . . ." She held his
gaze.

He thought, then, still at sea, prompted, "Unless what?"

"Unless we have some serious excuse—like being actively involved in catching a burglar."

He left Number 14 half an hour later, resigned to attending the
soirée. Given Mountford's increasingly risky actions, he doubted
they'd have long to wait before he made his next move, and
stepped into their snare. And then . . .

With any luck, he wouldn't have to attend all that many more
of society's events, at least not as an unmarried man.

The thought filled him with grim determination.

He strode along purposefully, mentally planning his morrow
and how he'd extend the search for Martinbury. He'd turned

into Green Street, was nearly at his front door when he heard himself hailed.

Halting, turning, he saw Deverell descending from a hackney. He waited while Deverell paid off the jarvey, then joined him.

"Can I offer you a drink?"

"Thank you."

They waited until they were comfortable in the library, and Havers had withdrawn, before getting down to business.

"I've had a nibble," Deverell replied in response to Tristan's raised brow. "And I'd swear it's the weasel you warned me of—he slunk up just as I was about to leave. He'd been keeping watch for about two hours. I'm using a small office that's part of a property I own in Sloane Street. It was empty and available, and the right sort of place."

"What did he say?"

"He wanted details of the house at Number 16 for his master. I ran through the usual, the amenities and so on, and the price." Deverell grinned. "He led me to hope his master would be interested."

"And?"

"I explained how the property came to be for rent, and that, in the circumstances, I had to warn his master that the house may only be available for a few months, as the owner might decide to sell."

"And he wasn't put off?"

"Not in the least. He assured me his master was only interested in a short let, and didn't want to know what had happened to the last owner."

Tristan smiled, grim, wolfish. "It sounds like our quarry."

"Indeed. But I don't think Mountford's going to show himself to me. The weasel asked for a copy of the lease agreement and took it away with him. Said his master would want to study it. If Mountford signs it and sends it back with the first month's rent—well, what house agent would quibble?"

Tristan nodded; his eyes narrowed. "We'll let the game play out, but that certainly sounds promising."

Deverell drained his glass. "With luck, we'll have him within a few days."

Tristan's evening started badly and grew progressively worse.

He arrived in Montrose Place early; he was standing in the hall when Leonora came down the stairs. He turned, saw, froze; the vision she presented in a watered-silk gown of deep blue, her shoulders and throat rising like fine porcelain from the wide neckline, her hair glossy, garnet-shot, piled on her head, ripped his breath away. A gauzy shawl concealed and revealed her arms and shoulders, shifting and sliding over the svelte curves; his palms tingled.

Then she saw him, met his eyes, and smiled.

Blood drained from his head; he felt dizzy.

She crossed the hall toward him, the periwinkle blue hue of her eyes lit by that welcoming expression she seemed to save just for him. She gave him her hands. "Mildred and Gertie should be here any minute."

A commotion at the door proved to be her aunts; their advent saved him from having to formulate any intelligent response. Her aunts were full of congratulations and myriad social instructions; he nodded, trying to take them all in, trying to orient himself in this battlefield, all the while conscious of Leonora and that, very soon, she would be all his.

The prize was definitely worth the battle.

He escorted them out to the carriage. Lady Hartington's house wasn't far. Her ladyship, of course, was beyond thrilled to receive them. She exclaimed, twittered, gushed, and archly asked after their wedding plans; impassive, he stood beside Leonora, and listened while she calmly deflected all her ladyship's queries without answering any of them. From her ladyship's expression, Leonora's responses were perfectly acceptable; it was all a mystery to him.

Then Gertie stepped in and ended the inquisition. At a nudge from Leonora, he led her away. As usual, he made for a chaise by the wall.

Her fingertips sank into his arm. "No. No point. Tonight we'd be better served by taking center stage."

With a nod, she directed him to a position almost in the center of the large drawing room. Inwardly frowning, he hesitated, then complied; his instincts were twitching—the spot was so open, they would be easily flanked, even surrounded. . . .

He had to trust her judgment; in this theater, his own was severely underdeveloped. But even in this, being guided by another did not come easily.

Predictably, they were quickly surrounded by ladies young and old wanting to press their congratulations and hear their news. Some were sweet, pleasant, innocent of guile, ladies for whom he deployed his charm. Others set his back up; after one such encounter, brought to a close by Mildred cutting in and all but physically towing the old battle-ax away, Leonora glanced up at him, with her elbow surreptitiously jabbed him in the ribs.

He looked down at her, frowned with his eyes. She smiled serenely back. "Stop looking so grim."

He realized his mask had slipped, quickly reinstalled his charming facade. Meanwhile, *sotto voce*, informed her, "That harridan made me feel murderous, so grim was a mild response." He met her eyes. "I don't know how you can stand such as she— they're so patently insincere, and don't even try to hide it."

Her smile was both understanding and teasing; briefly she leaned more heavily on his arm. "You get used to it. When they become difficult, just let it wash over you, and remember that what they're after is a reaction—deny them that, and you've won the exchange."

He could see what she meant, tried to follow that line, but the situation itself abraded his temper. For the last decade, he'd eschewed any situation that focused attention on him; to stand there, in a ton drawing room, the cynosure of all eyes and at least half the conversations, ran directly counter to what had become ingrained habit.

The evening wore on, for him far too slowly; the number of ladies and gentlemen waiting to speak with them did not appreciably decrease. He continued to feel off-balance, exposed. And out of his depth in dealing with some of the more dangerous specimens.

Leonora took care of them with a sure touch he had to admire. Just the right amount of haughtiness, the right amount of confidence. Thank God he'd found her.

Then Ethelreda and Edith came up; they greeted Leonora as if she was already a member of the family, and she responded in kind. Mildred and Gertie touched fingers; he saw a brief question put by Edith, to which Gertie replied with a short word and a snort. Then glances were exchanged between the older ladies, succeeded by conspiratorial smiles.

Passing before them, Ethelreda tapped his arm. "Bear up, dear boy. We're here, now."

She and Edith moved on, but only as far as Leonora's side.

Over the next fifteen minutes, his other cousins—Millicent, Flora, Constance, and Helen—arrived, too. Like Ethelreda and Edith, they greeted Leonora, exchanged pleasantries with Mildred and Gertie, then joined Ethelreda and Edith in a loose gathering alongside Leonora.

And things changed.

The crowd in the drawing room had grown to uncomfortable proportions; there were even more people hovering, waiting to speak with them. It was a crush, and he'd never liked being hemmed in, yet Leonora continued to greet those who pressed forward, introducing him, deftly managing the interactions, but if any lady showed a tendency to spite or coldness, or simply a wish to monopolize, either Mildred and Gertie or one of his cousins would step in and, with a rush of seemingly inconsequential observations, draw such persons away.

In short order, his view of his old dears was shattered and reformed; even the retiring Flora displayed remarkable determination in distracting and removing one persistent lady. Gertie, too, left no doubt as to which mast her flag was pinned.

The reversal of roles kept him off-balance; in this arena, they were the protectors, sure and effective, he the one needing their protection.

Part of that protection was to prevent him from reacting to those who saw his and Leonora's engagement as a loss to themselves, who viewed her as having in some way snared him, when the truth was the exact opposite. It hadn't occurred to him just how real, how strong and powerful, the feminine competition in the marriage mart was, or that Leonora's apparent success in capturing him would make her the focus of envy.

His eyes were now open.

Lady Hartington had chosen to enliven her soirée with a

short spell of dancing. As the musicians set up, Gertie turned to him. "Grab the opportunity while you may." She poked his arm. "You've got another hour or more to endure before we can leave."

He didn't wait; he reached for Leonora's hand, smiled charmingly, and excused them to the two ladies with whom they'd been conversing. Constance and Millicent stepped in, smoothly covering his and Leonora's retreat.

Leonora sighed and went into his arms with real relief. "How exhausting. I had no idea it would be this bad, not so early in the year."

Whirling her down the room, he met her gaze. "You mean it could be worse?"

She looked into his eyes, and smiled. "Not everyone's in town yet."

She said no more; he studied her face as they twirled, turned, and precessed back up the room. She seemed to have given herself, her senses, over to the waltz; he followed her lead.

And found a degree of comfort. Of soothing reassurance in the feel of her in his arms, in the reality of her under his hands, in the brush of their thighs as they went through the turns, the flowing harmony with which their bodies moved, in tune, attuned. Together.

When the music finally ended, they were at the other end of the room. Without asking, he set her hand on his sleeve and guided her back to where their supporters waited, a small island of relative safety.

She slanted him a glance, a smile on her lips, understanding in her eyes. "How are you faring?"

He glanced at her. "I feel like a general surrounded by a bevy of personal guards well equipped with initiative and experience." He drew breath, looked ahead to where their group of sweet old ladies were waiting. "The fact they're female is a trifle unsettling, but I have to admit I'm humbly grateful."

A chortle, smothered, answered him. "Indeed, you should be."

"Believe me," he murmured as they neared the others, "I know my limitations. This is a female theater dominated by female strategies too convoluted for any male to fathom."

She threw him a laughing glance, one wholly personal, then they resumed their public personas and went forward to deal with the small horde still waiting to congratulate them.

The night, predictably but to his mind regrettably, ended without affording him and Leonora any opportunity to slake the physical need that had burgeoned, fed by close contact, by the promise of the waltz, by his inevitable reaction to the evening's less civilized moments.

Mine.

That word still rang in his head, prodded his instincts whenever she was close, most especially whenever others seemed not to comprehend that fact.

Not a civilized response but a primitive one. He knew it, and didn't care.

The next morning, he left Green Street restless and unfulfilled, and threw himself into the search for Martinbury. They were all increasingly convinced the object of Mountford's search was something buried in Cedric's papers; A. J. Carruthers had been Cedric's closest confidant, Martinbury was by all accounts the heir to whom Carruthers had entrusted his secrets—and Martinbury had unexpectedly disappeared.

Locating Martinbury, or discovering what they could of his fate, seemed the likeliest route to learning Mountford's aim and dealing with his threat.

The fastest way to end the business so he and Leonora could wed.

But entering watchhouses, gaining men's trust, accessing records in search of the recently deceased, took time. He'd started with those watchhouses closest to the coaching inn where Martinbury had alighted. As, in a hackney, he rumbled home in the late afternoon, no further forward, he wondered if that wasn't a false assumption. Martinbury could have been in London for some days before disappearing.

He entered his house to discover Charles waiting in his library to report.

"Nothing," Charles said the instant he'd shut the door. In one of the armchairs before the hearth, he swiveled to look up at him. "What about you?"

Tristan grimaced. "Same story." He picked up the decanter from the sideboard, filled a glass, then crossed to top up Charles's glass before sinking into the other armchair. He frowned at the fire. "Which hospitals have you checked?"

Charles told him—the hospitals and hospices closest to the inn where the mail coaches from York terminated.

Tristan nodded. "We need to move faster and widen our search." He explained his reasoning.

Charles inclined his head in agreement. "The question is, even with Deverell helping, how do we widen our search and simultaneously go faster?"

Tristan sipped, then lowered his glass. "We take a calculated risk and narrow the field. Leonora mentioned that Martinbury may still be alive, but if he's injured, with no friends or relatives in town, he may simply be lying in a hospital bed somewhere."

Charles grimaced. "Poor bugger."

"Indeed. In reality, that scenario is the only one that's going to advance our cause quickly. If Martinbury's dead, then it's unlikely whoever did the deed will have left any useful papers behind, ones that will point us in the right direction."

"True."

Tristan sipped again, then said, "I'm swinging my people on to searching the hospitals for any gentleman matching Martinbury's description who's still alive. They don't need our authority to do that."

Charles nodded. "I'll do the same—I'm sure Deverell will, too. . . ."

The sound of a male voice in the hall outside reached them. They both looked at the door.

"Speak of the devil," Charles said.

The door opened. Deverell walked in.

Tristan rose and poured him a brandy. Deverell took it and sprawled elegantly on the chaise. In contrast to their sober expressions, his green eyes were alight. He saluted them with his glass. "I bring tidings."

"Positive tidings?" Charles asked.

"The only sort a wise man brings." Deverell paused to sip his brandy; lowering the glass, he smiled. "Mountford took the bait."

"He rented the house?"

"The weasel brought the lease back this morning along with the first month's rent. A Mr. Caterham has signed the lease and intends moving in immediately." Deverell paused, frowning slightly. "I handed over the keys and offered to show them around the property, but the weasel—he goes by the name of Cummings—declined. He said his master was a recluse and insisted on total privacy."

Deverell's frown grew. "I did think of following the weasel back to his hole, but decided the risk of scaring them off was too high." He glanced at Tristan. "Given Mountford, or whoever he is, seems set on going into the house forthwith, letting him pursue that aim and walk into our trap with all speed seemed the wisest course."

Both Tristan and Charles were nodding.

"Excellent!" Tristan stared at the fire, his gaze distant. "So we have him, we know where he is. We'll continue trying to solve the riddle of what he's after, but even if we don't succeed, we'll be waiting for his next move. Waiting for him to reveal all himself."

"To success!" Charles said.

The others echoed the words, then they drained their glasses.

After seeing Charles and Deverell out, Tristan headed for his study. Passing the arches of the morning room, he heard the usual babel of elderly feminine voices and glanced in.

He halted in midstride. He could barely believe his eyes.

His great-aunts had arrived, along with—he counted heads— his other six resident pensioners from Mallingham Manor. All fourteen of his dependent old dears were now gathered under his Green Street roof, scattered about the morning room, heads together . . . plotting.

Uneasiness filled him.

Hortense glanced up and saw him. "There you are, m'boy! *Wonderful* news about you and Miss Carling." She thumped the arm of her chair. "*Just* as we'd all hoped."

He went down the steps. Hermione flapped her hand at him. "Indeed, my dear. We are *excellently* pleased!"

Bowing over her hand, he accepted those and the others' murmured expressions of delight with a mild, "Thank you."

"Now!" Hermione turned to look up at him. "I hope you won't think we've taken too much on ourselves, but we've organized a family dinner for tonight. Ethelreda has spoken with Miss Carling's family—Lady Warsingham and her husband, the elder Miss Carling, and Sir Humphrey and Jeremy Carling—and they are all in agreement, as is Miss Carling, of course. Given there are so many of us, and some of us are getting on in years, and as the proper course would be for us to meet Miss Carling and her family formally at such a dinner, we hoped you, too, would agree to holding it tonight."

Hortense snorted. "Aside from all else, we're too fagged from driving up this afternoon to weather an outing to some other entertainment."

"And, dear," Millicent put in, "we should remember that Miss Carling and Sir Humphrey and young Mr. Carling had a funeral to attend this morning. A neighbor, I understand?"

"Indeed." A vision danced through Tristan's mind, of a comfortable if large dinner party, rather less formal than might be imagined—he knew his great-aunts and their companions quite well . . . He looked around, met their bright, transparently hopeful gazes. "Do I take it you're suggesting this dinner would be in lieu of any appearance in the ton tonight?"

Hortense pulled a face. "Well, if you really wish to attend some ball or other—"

"No, no." The relief that flooded him was very real; he smiled, struggling to keep his delight within bounds. "I see no reason at all your dinner can't go ahead, precisely as you've planned it. Indeed"—his mask slipped; he let his gratitude shine through—"I'll be grateful for any excuse to avoid the ton tonight." He bowed to his aunts, with a glance extended the gesture to the others, deploying his charm to maximum effect. "Thank you."

The words were heartfelt.

They all smiled, bobbed, delighted to have been of use.

"Didn't think you'd be all that enamored of the gadding throng," Hortense opined. She grinned up at him. "If it comes to it, neither are we."

He could have kissed them. Knowing how flustered that would make most of them, he contented himself with dressing with extra care, then being in the drawing room to greet them as they entered, bowing over their hands, commenting on their gowns and coiffures, on their jewels—deploying for them that irresistible charm he knew well how to use but rarely did without some goal in mind.

Tonight, his goal was simply to repay them for their kindness, their thoughtfulness.

He'd never been so thankful to hear of a family dinner in his life.

While they waited in the drawing room for their guests to arrive, he thought of how incongruous their gathering would appear—he standing before the mantelpiece, the sole male surrounded by fourteen elderly females. But they were his family; he did, in truth, feel more comfortable surrounded by them and their amiable chatter than he did in the more glittering, more exciting, but also more malicious world of the ton. They and he shared something—an intangible connection of place and people spread over time.

And into this, Leonora would now come—and she would fit.

Havers entered to announce Lord and Lady Warsingham and Miss Carling—Gertie. On their heels, Sir Humphrey, Leonora, and Jeremy arrived.

Any thought that he would have to act as a formal host evaporated in minutes. Sir Humphrey was engaged by Ethelreda and

Constance, Jeremy by a group of the others, while Lord and Lady Warsingham were treated to the Wemyss charm as dispensed by Hermione and Hortense. Gertie and Millicent, who had met the previous evening, had their heads together.

After exchanging a few words with the other old dears, Leonora joined him. She gave him her hand, her special smile—the one she reserved just for him—curving her lips. "I have to say I was extremely glad of your great-aunts' suggestion. After attending Miss Timmins's funeral this morning, attending Lady Willoughby's ball tonight and dealing with the—as you described it—prurient interest, would have severely tried my temper." She glanced up, met his eyes. "And yours."

He inclined his head. "Even though I didn't attend the funeral. How was it?"

"Quiet, but sincere. I think Miss Timmins would have been pleased. Henry Timmins shared the service with the local vicar, and Mrs. Timmins was there, too—a nice woman."

After an instant, she turned to him and lowered her voice. "We found some papers in Cedric's room, hidden in the bottom of his woodbasket. They weren't letters, but sheets of entries similar to those in the journals but most importantly, they weren't in Cedric's hand—they were written by Carruthers. Humphrey and Jeremy are concentrating on those now. Humphrey says they're descriptions of experiments, similar to those in Cedric's journal, but there's still no way to make any sense of them, to know if they mean anything at all. It seems all we've discovered so far contains only part of whatever they were working on."

"Which suggests even more strongly that there is some discovery, one Cedric and Carruthers thought it worthwhile to deal with carefully."

"Indeed." Leonora searched his face. "In case you're wondering, the staff at Number 14 are very much on alert, and Castor will send to Gasthorpe should anything untoward occur."

"Good."

"Have you learned anything?"

He felt his jaw start to set; he pulled his charming mask back into place. "Nothing about Martinbury, but we're trying a new tack that might get us further faster. However, the big news is that Mountford—or whoever he is—has taken the bait. He, acting via the weasel, rented Number 16 late this afternoon."

Her eyes widened; she kept them fixed on his. "So things are starting to happen."

"Indeed."

He turned, smiling, as Constance joined them. Leonora stood by his side and chatted with the ladies as they came up. They told her of the church fete, and of the little routine day-to-day changes, the alterations the seasons brought to the manor. They told her of this and that, remembered snippets of Tristan's early life, of his father and grandfather.

She occasionally glanced at him, saw him extend that ready charm—also saw beneath it. Having met Lady Hermione and Lady Hortense, she could see from where he'd got it; she wondered what his father had been like.

Yet in this sphere Tristan's manners were more genuine; the real man showed through, not just with his strengths but with his weaknesses, too. He was comfortable, relaxing; she suspected that previously, he might well have gone for years without lowering his guard. Even now, the drawbridge chains were rusty.

She moved around the room, chatting here, chatting there, always conscious of Tristan, that he watched her as she watched him. Then Havers announced dinner, and they all went in, she on Tristan's arm.

He sat her beside him at one end of the table; Lady Hermione was at the other end. She made a neat speech expressing her pleasure at the prospect of shortly yielding her chair to Leonora, and led a toast to the affianced couple, then the first course was served. The gentle hum of conversation rose and engulfed the table.

The evening passed pleasantly, truly enjoyably. The ladies repaired to the drawing room, leaving the gentlemen to their port; it wasn't long before they rejoined them.

Her uncle Winston, Lord Warsingham, Mildred's husband, stopped by her side. "An excellent choice, my dear." His eyes twinkled; he'd been concerned by her lack of interest in marriage, but had never sought to interfere. "Might have taken you an unconscionable time to make up your mind, but the result's the thing, heh?"

She smiled, inclined her head. Tristan joined them, and she directed the conversation to the latest play.

And continued, at some level she wasn't sure she understood, to watch Tristan. She didn't always keep her eyes on him, yet she was wholly aware—an emotional watching if such a thing could be, a focusing of the senses.

She'd noticed, again and again, his momentary hesitations when, discussing something with her, he would check, pause, consider, then go on. She'd started to identify the patterns that told her what he was thinking, when and in what vein he was thinking of her. The decisions he was making.

The fact he'd made no move to exclude her from their active investigations heartened her. He could have been much more difficult; indeed, she'd expected it. Instead, he was feeling his way, accommodating her as he could; that bolstered her hope that in the future—the future they'd both committed themselves to—they would rub along well together.

That they would be able to accommodate each other's natures and needs.

His, both nature and needs, were more complex than most; she'd realized that sometime ago—it was part of the attraction he held for her, that he was different from others, that he needed and wanted on a somewhat different scale, on a different plane.

Given his dangerous past, he was less disposed to excluding women, infinitely more disposed to using them. She'd sensed that from the first, that he was less inclined than his less adventurous brethren to coddle females; she now knew him well enough to guess that in pursuit of his duty he would have been coldly ruthless. It was that side of his nature that had allowed her to become as involved as she was in their investigations with only relatively minor resistance.

However, with her, that more pragmatic side had come into direct conflict with something much deeper. With more primitive impulses, all-but-primal instincts, the imperative to keep her forever shielded, tucked away from all harm.

Again and again, that conflict darkened his eyes. His jaw would set, he would glance at her briefly, hesitate, then leave matters as they were.

Adjustment. Him to her, her to him.

They were meshing together, step by step learning the ways in which their lives would interlock. Yet that fundamental clash remained; she suspected it always would.

She would have to bear with it, adjust to it. Accept but not react to his repressed but still present instincts and suspicions.

She didn't believe he'd put the latter into words, not even to himself, yet they remained, beneath all his strengths, the weaknesses she'd brought forth. She'd told him, admitted why she didn't easily accept help, could not easily trust him or anyone with things that mattered to her.

Logically, consciously, he believed in her decision to trust him, to accept him into the innermost sphere of her life. At a deeper, instinctive level, he kept watching for signs she would forget.

For any sign she was excluding him.

She'd hurt him once in precisely that way. She wouldn't do so again, but only time would teach him that.

His gift to her had been, from the first, to accept her as she was. Her gift in return would be to accept all he was and give him the time to lose his suspicions.

To learn to trust her as she did him.

Jeremy joined them; her uncle seized the moment to talk estates with Tristan.

"Well, sis." Jeremy glanced around at the company. "I can see you here, with all these ladies, organizing them, keeping the whole household ticking smoothly along." He grinned at her, then sobered. "Their gain. We'll miss you."

She smiled, put her hand on his arm, squeezed. "I haven't left you yet."

Jeremy lifted his gaze to Tristan, beyond her. Half smiled as he looked back at her. "I think you'll find you have."

Eighteen

⊱◈⊰

For all his relative naïveté, Jeremy was correct in one respect—Tristan clearly considered their union already accepted, established, acknowledged.

The Warsinghams were the first to leave, Gertie with them. When Humphrey and Jeremy prepared to follow them, Tristan trapped her hand on his sleeve and declared that he and she had matters pertaining to their future that they needed to discuss in private. He would see her home in his carriage in half an hour or so.

He stated it so glibly, with such complete assurance, everyone meekly nodded and fell into line. Humphrey and Jeremy departed; his great-aunts and cousins bade them good night and retired.

Leaving him to usher her into the library, alone at last.

He paused to give Havers instructions for the carriage. Leonora went to stand before the fire, a goodly blaze throwing heat into the room. Outside, a chill wind blew and heavy clouds blocked the moon; not a pleasant evening.

Holding out her hands to the flames, she heard the door click softly shut, sensed Tristan draw near.

She turned; his hands slid about her waist as she did. Her palms came to rest on his chest. She locked her eyes on his. "I'm glad you arranged this—there are a number of matters we should talk about."

He blinked. He didn't let her go, yet he didn't draw her closer. Their hips and thighs were lightly, teasingly, brushing; her breasts were just touching his chest. His hands spanned her waist; she was neither in his arms nor out of them, yet wholly within his control. He looked down into her eyes. "What matters are those?"

"Matters such as where we'll live—how you imagine our life should run."

He hesitated, then asked, "Do you want to live here, in London, among the ton?"

"Not especially. I've never felt any great attraction to the ton. I'm comfortable enough in it, but I don't crave its dubious excitements."

His lips twitched. He lowered his head. "Thank heaven for that."

She laid a finger across his lips before they could capture hers. Felt his hands release her waist, his palms slide over her silk-clad back. From beneath her lashes, she met his eyes, drew a quick breath. "So we'll live at Mallingham Manor?"

Against her finger, his lips curved distractingly. "If you can bear to live buried in the country."

"Surrey is hardly the depths of buccolic rusticity." She lowered her hand.

His lips came nearer, hovered an inch from hers. "I meant the old dears. Can you cope with them?"

He waited; she struggled to think. "Yes." She understood the old ladies, recognized their ways, foresaw no difficulty dealing with them. "They're well-disposed—I understand them, and they understand us."

He made a derisive sound; it feathered over her lips, made them throb. "You may understand them—they frequently leave me at a total loss. There was something a few months ago about the vicarage curtains that completely passed me by."

She was finding it hard not to laugh; his lips were so close, it seemed terribly dangerous, like letting her guard down with a wolf about to pounce.

"So you truly will be mine?"

She was about to laughingly offer her mouth and herself in proof when something in his tone struck her; she met his eyes—realized he was deadly serious. "I'm already yours. You know it."

His lips, still distractingly near, twisted; he shifted, easing her closer—his restlessness reached her, washed over her in a wave of tangible, shifting uncertainty. With the fuller touch of their bodies heat flared; he bent his head and set his lips to the corner of hers.

"I'm not your average gentleman."

The words whispered over her cheek.

"I know." She turned her head and their lips met.

After a brief exchange, he drew away, sent his lips tracing upward, over her cheekbone to her temple, then down until his breath warmed the hollow beneath her ear.

"I've lived dangerously, beyond all laws, for a decade. I'm not as civilized as I ought to be. You know that, don't you?"

She did, indeed, know that; the knowledge was crawling her nerves, anticipation sliding like heated silk down her veins. More to the immediate point, amazing though it seemed, she realized he was still unsure of her. And that whatever the matter he'd wanted to discuss, it was still on his mind, and she'd yet to hear of it.

Pushing up her hands, she caught and framed his face, and boldy kissed him. Trapped him, caught him, drew him in. Moved into him. Felt his response, felt his hands spread over her back, firm, then mold her to him.

When she finally consented to let him free, he raised his head and looked down at her; his eyes were dark, turbulent.

"Tell me." Her voice was husky, but commanding. Demanding. "What is it you wanted to say?"

A long moment passed; she was conscious of their breaths, of their pulses throbbing. She thought he wasn't going to answer, then he drew a short breath. His eyes had never left hers.

"*Don't*. Go. Into. Danger."

He didn't have to say more, it was there in his eyes. There for her to see. A vulnerability so deeply enmeshed in him, in who he was, that he could never not have it, and still have her.

A dilemma, one he could never resolve, but could only accept. As, in taking her as his wife, he'd chosen to do.

She leaned into him; her hands were still bracketing his face. "I will never willingly place myself in danger. I've decided to be yours—I intend to continue in that role, to remain important to you." She held his gaze. "Believe that."

His features hardened; he ignored her hands and lowered his head. Took her lips, her mouth in a searing kiss that bordered on the wild.

Drew back to whisper against her lips. "I'll try to, if you'll remember this. If you fail, we both will pay the price."

She traced his lean cheek. Waited until he met her eyes. "I won't fail. And neither will you."

Their hearts were thudding; familiar flames licked hungrily

over their skins. She searched his eyes. *"This"*—she shifted sinu-
ously against him, felt his breath hitch—"was meant to be. We
didn't decree it, you or I, it was there, waiting to snare us. Now
the challenge is to make all the rest work—it's not an endeavor
we can escape or decline, not if we want this."

"I definitely want this, and more. I'm not letting you go. Not
for any reason. Not ever."

"So we're committed, you and I." She held his darkened gaze.
"We'll make it work."

Two heartbeats passed, then he bent his head; his hands
firmed, lifting her against him.

She dropped her hands to his shoulders, pressed back.
"But . . ."

He paused, met her eyes. "But what?"

"But we've run out of time tonight."

They had. Tristan tightened his arms, kissed her witless, then
shackled his demons, clamoring for her, and, grim-faced, set her
on her feet.

She looked as chagrined as he felt—a minor consolation.

Later.

Once they had Mountford by the heels, nothing was going to
get in their way.

His carriage was waiting; he escorted Leonora out to it, helped
her in, and followed. As the carriage rattled off over the now
wet cobbles, he returned to something she'd mentioned earlier.
"Why does Humphrey think pieces of Cedric's puzzle are missing? How can he know?"

Leonora settled back beside him. "The journals are details
of experiments—what was done and the results, nothing more.
What's missing is the rationale that makes sense of them—the

hypotheses, the conclusions. Carruthers's letters refer to some of Cedric's experiments, and others which Humphrey and Jeremy reason must be Carruthers's own, and the sheets of descriptions from Carruthers we found in Cedric's room—Humphrey thinks at least some of those match some of the experiments referred to in Carruthers's letters."

"So Cedric and Carruthers appear to have been exchanging details of experiments?"

"Yes. But as yet Humphrey can't be certain whether they were working on the same project together, or whether they were simply exchanging news. Most pertinently, he hasn't found anything to define what their mutual project, assuming there was one, was."

He juggled the information, debating whether it made Martinbury, Carruthers's heir, more or less important. The carriage slowed, then halted. He glanced out, then climbed out before Number 14 Montrose Place and handed Leonora down.

Overhead, the clouds were scudding, the dark pall breaking up before the wind. She tucked her hand into his arm; he glanced at her as he swung the gate wide. They walked up the winding path, both distracted by the eccentric world of Cedric's creation gleaming in the fitful moonlight, the odd-shaped leaves and bushes embroidered with droplets of rain.

Light beamed from the front hall. As they climbed the porch steps the door swung open.

Jeremy looked out, his face tense. He saw them and his features eased. "About time! The blackguard's already started tunneling."

In absolute silence, they faced the wall beside the laundry trough in the basement of Number 14 and listened to the stealthy *scritch-scritch* of someone scraping away mortar.

Tristan motioned Leonora and Jeremy to stillness, then put out a hand, and laid it on the bricks from behind which the noise was emanating.

After a moment, he removed his hand and signaled them to retreat. At the entrance to the laundry, a footman stood waiting. Leonora and Jeremy went silently past him; Tristan paused. "Good work." His voice was just loud enough to reach the footman. "I doubt they'll get through tonight, but we'll organize a watch. Close the door and make sure no one makes any unusual sound in this area."

The footman nodded. Tristan left him and followed the others into the kitchen at the end of the corridor. From their faces, both Leonora and Jeremy were bursting with questions; he waved them to silence and addressed Castor and the other footmen, all gathered and waiting with the rest of the staff.

In short order he organized a rotating watch for the night, and reassured the housekeeper, cook, and maids that there was no likelihood of the villains breaking in undetected while they slept.

"At the rate they're going—and they'll have to go slowly—they can't risk a hammer and chisel—they'll take at least a few nights to loosen enough bricks to let a man through." He glanced around the company gathered about the kitchen table. "Who noticed the scratching?"

A tweeny colored and bobbed. "Me, sir—m'lord. I went in to get the second hot iron and heard it. Thought it was a mouse at first, then I remembered what Mr. Castor had said about odd noises and such, so I came straightaway and told him."

Tristan smiled. "Good girl." His gaze rested on the baskets piled high with folded sheets and linens set between the maids and the stove. "Was it washing day today?"

"Aye." The housekeeper nodded. "We always do our main wash on a Wednesday, then a small wash on Mondays."

Tristan looked at her for a moment, then said, "I have one last question. Have any of you, at any time in the last several months, going back to November or so, seen or been spoken to by either of these two gentlemen?" He proceeded to give quick word sketches of Mountford and his weasely accomplice.

"How did you guess?" Leonora asked when they were back in the library.

The two older maids and two of the footmen had been approached independently at various times in November, the maids by Mountford himself, the footmen by his accomplice. The maids had thought they'd found a new admirer, the footmen a new and unexpectedly well-heeled acquaintance always ready to buy the next pint.

Tristan dropped onto the chaise beside Leonora and stretched out his legs. "I always wondered why Mountford tried first to buy the house. How did he know Cedric's workshop had been locked up and left essentially undisturbed? He couldn't see in—the windows are so old, so fogged and crazed, it's impossible to see anything through them."

"He knew because he'd cozened the maids." Jeremy sat in his usual place behind his desk. Humphrey was in his chair before the hearth.

"Indeed. And that's how he's known other things"—Tristan glanced at Leonora—"like your propensity to walk alone in the garden. At what times you go out. He's been focused on this household for months, and he's done a decent job of reconnoitering."

Leonora frowned. "That begs the question of how he knew there's something here to be found." She looked at Humphrey, one of Cedric's journals open on his lap, a magnifying glass in his hand. "*We* still don't know there's anything valuable here—we're only surmising because of Mountford's interest."

Tristan squeezed her hand. "Trust me. Men like Mountford never are interested unless there's something to gain."

And the notice of foreign gentlemen was even less easy to attract. Tristan kept that observation to himself. He looked at Humphrey. "Any advance?"

Humphrey spoke at length; the answer was no.

At the end of his explanation, Tristan stirred. They were all keyed up; sleep would be difficult knowing that in the basement, Mountford was quietly excavating through the wall.

"What do you expect to happen now?" Leonora asked.

He glanced at her. "Nothing tonight. You can rest easy on that score. It'll take at least three nights of steady working to open a hole big enough for a man without alerting anyone on this side."

"I'm more worried about someone on this side alerting him."

He smiled his predator's smile. "I have men all around—they'll be there night and day. Now Mountford's in there, he won't get away."

Leonora looked into his eyes; her lips formed a silent O.

Jeremy humphed. He picked up a sheaf of the papers they'd found in Cedric's room. "We'd better get on with these. Somewhere here, there has to be a clue. Although why our dear departed relative couldn't use some simple, understandable cross-referencing system I don't know."

Humphrey's snort was eloquent. "He was a scientist, that's why. Never show any consideration for whoever might have to make sense of their works once they're gone. Never come across one who has in all my days."

Tristan stood, stretched. Exchanged a glance with Leonora. "I need to think through our plans. I'll call tomorrow morning and we'll make some decisions." He looked at Humphrey, included Jeremy when he said, "I'll probably bring some associates with me in the morning—can I ask you to give us a report on what you've discovered up to then?"

"Of course." Humphrey waved. "We'll see you at breakfast."

Jeremy barely glanced up.

Leonora saw him to the front door. They stole a quick, unsatisfying kiss before Castor, summoned by some butlerish instinct, appeared to open the door.

Tristan looked down into Leonora's shadowed eyes. "Sleep well. Believe me, you're at no risk."

She met his eyes, then smiled. "I know. I have proof."

Puzzled, he raised a brow.

Her smile deepened. "You're leaving me here."

He searched her face, saw understanding in her eyes. He saluted her, and left.

By the time he reached Green Street, his plan was clear in his mind. It was late; his house was quiet. He went straight to his study, sat at his desk, and reached for his pen.

The next morning, he, Charles, and Deverell met at the Bastion Club shortly after dawn. It was March; dawn wasn't that early, but they needed sufficient light to see by as they circled Number 16 Montrose Place. They checked every possible escape route, tested the guards Tristan already had in place, and arranged for reinforcements where needed.

At half past seven, they retreated to the club's meeting room to reassess and report all that each individually had done, had set in train since the previous evening. At eight o'clock, they repaired to Number 14, where Humphrey and Jeremy, weary after working most of the night, and an eager Leonora were waiting.

Along with a substantial breakfast. Leonora had clearly given orders that they were to be fed well.

Seated at one end of the table, Leonora sipped her tea; over the rim of her cup, she regarded the trio of dangerous men who had invaded her home.

It was the first time she'd met St. Austell and Deverell; one glance was enough for her to see the similarities between them and Tristan. Likewise, they both evoked the same wariness she'd initially felt with Tristan; she wouldn't trust them, not entirely, not as a woman trusts a man, not unless she came to know them much better.

She looked at Tristan, beside her. "You said you would discuss a plan."

He nodded. "A plan of how best to react to the situation as we currently know it." He glanced at Humphrey. "Perhaps, if I outline the situation, you would correct me if you have more recent information."

Humphrey inclined his head.

Tristan looked down at the table, clearly gathering his thoughts. "We know that Mountford is searching for something he believes hidden in this house. He's been intent, persistent, unswervingly fixed on his goal for months. He seems increasingly desperate, and clearly will not cease until he finds what he's after. We have a connection between Mountford and a foreigner, which may or may not be pertinent. Mountford is now on the scene, trying to gain access to the basement here. He has one known accomplice, a weasel-faced man." Tristan paused to sip his coffee. "That's the opposition as we know it.

"Now, to the something they're after. Our best guess is that it's something the late Cedric Carling, the previous owner of this house and a renowned herbalist, discovered, possibly working with another herbalist, A. J. Carruthers, unfortunately now also deceased. Cedric's journals, and Carruthers's letters and notes, all we've found so far, suggest a collaboration, but the project itself remains unclear." Tristan looked at Humphrey.

Humphrey glanced at Jeremy. Waved him on.

Jeremy met the others' eyes. "We have three sources of information—Cedric's journals, letters to Cedric from Carruthers, and a set of notes from Carruthers, which we believe were enclosures sent with the letters. I've been concentrating on the letters and notes. Some of the notes detail individual experiments discussed and referred to in the letters. From what we've been able to link together so far, it seems certain Cedric and Carruthers were working together on some specific concoction. They discuss the properties of some fluid they were trying to influence with this concoction." Jeremy paused, grimaced. "We have nothing where they state what the fluid is, but from various references, I believe it to be blood."

The effect of that pronouncement on Tristan, St. Austell, and Deverell was marked. Leonora watched them exchange significant glances.

"So," St. Austell murmured, his gaze locked with Tristan's, "we have two renowned herbalists working on something to affect blood, and a possible foreign connection."

Tristan's expression had hardened. He nodded to Jeremy. "That clarifies the one uncertainty I had regarding our way forward. Clearly, Carruthers's heir, Jonathon Martinbury, an upright and honest young man who has mysteriously disappeared after reaching London, apparently coming down in response to a letter regarding Carruthers's and Cedric's collaboration, is a potentially critical pawn in this game."

"Indeed." Deverell looked at Tristan. "I'll swing my people on to that line, too."

Leonora glanced from one to the other. "What line?"

"It's now imperative we locate Martinbury. If he's dead, that will take some time—probably more time than we have with Mountford working downstairs. But if Martinbury's alive, there's a chance we can scour the hospitals and hospices sufficiently well to locate him."

"Convents." When Tristan glanced at her, Leonora elaborated. "You didn't mention them, but there are quite a lot in the city, and most take in the sick and injured as they're able."

"She's right." St. Austell looked at Deverell.

Who nodded. "I'll direct my people that way."

"What people?" Jeremy frowned at the trio. "You talk as if you have troops at your disposal."

St. Austell raised his brows, amused. Tristan straightened his lips and replied, "In a way, we do. In our previous calling, we had need of . . . connections at all levels of society. And there are a lot of ex-soldiers we can call on for assistance. We each know people who are used to going out and looking for things for us."

Leonora frowned Jeremy down when he would have asked more. "So you've combined your troops and sent them out to search for Martinbury. What does that leave us to do? What's your plan?"

Tristan met her eyes, then glanced at Humphrey and Jeremy.

"We still don't know what Mountford's after—we could simply sit back and wait for him to break in, then see what he goes for. That, however, is the more dangerous course. Letting him into this house, letting him at any stage get his hands on what he's after, should be our last resort."

"The alternative?" Jeremy asked.

"Is to go forward following the lines of inquiry we already have. One, seek Martinbury—he may have more specific information from Carruthers. Two, continue to piece together what we can from the three sources we have—the journals, letters, and notes. It's likely those are at least part of what Mountford is after. If he has access to the pieces we're missing, that would make sense.

"Three." Tristan glanced at Leonora. "We've assumed that the something—let's call it a formula—was hidden in Cedric's workshop. That may still be the case. We've only removed all the obvious written materials—if there's something specificially concealed in the workshop, it may still be there. Lastly, the formula may be completed, written down and hidden elsewhere in this house." He paused, then continued, "The risk of letting something like that fall into Mountford's hands is too great to take. We need to search this house."

Recalling how he'd searched Miss Timmins's rooms, Leonora nodded. "I agree." She glanced around the table. "So Humphrey and Jeremy should continue with the journals, letters, and notes in the library. Your people are scouring London for Martinbury. That leaves you three, I take it?"

Tristan smiled at her, one of his charming smiles. "And you. If you could warn your staff and clear the way for us, we three will search. We may need to search from attics to basement, and this is a large house." His smile took on an edge. "But we're very good at searching."

They were.

Leonora watched from the doorway of the workshop as, silent as mice, the three noblemen pried, poked, and prodded into every last nook and cranny, climbed about the heavy shelving, squinting down the backs of cupboards, whisked hidden crevices with canes, and lay on the floor to inspect the undersides of desks and drawers. They missed nothing.

And found nothing but dust.

From there, they worked steadily outward and upward, going through kitchen and pantries, even the now silent laundry, through every room on the lower floor, then they climbed the stairs and, quietly determined, set about applying their unexpected skills to the rooms on the ground floor.

Within two hours, they'd reached the bedchambers; an hour later, they broached the attics.

The luncheon gong was clanging when Leonora, seated on the stairs leading up to the attics—into which she'd flatly refused to venture—felt the reverberations of their descent.

She stood and swung around. Their footfalls, heavy, slow, told her they'd found nothing at all. They came into view, brushing cobwebs from their hair and coats—Shultz would not have approved.

Tristan met her eyes, somewhat grimly concluded, "If any precious formula is secreted in this house, it's in the library."

In Cedric's journals, Carruthers's letters and notes.

"At least we're now sure of that much." Turning, she led them back to the main stairs and down to the dining room.

Jeremy and Humphrey joined them there.

Jeremy shook his head as he sat. "Nothing more, I'm afraid."

"Except"—Humphrey frowned as he shook out his napkin—"that I'm increasingly certain Cedric did not keep any record of his own as to the rationale and conclusions he drew from his experiments." He grimaced. "Some scientists are like that—keep it all in their head."

"Secretive?" Deverall asked, starting on his soup.

Humphrey shook his head. "Not usually. More a case of they don't want to waste time writing down what they already know."

They all started eating, then Humphrey, still frowning, continued, "If Cedric didn't leave any record—and most of the books in the library are ours—there were only a handful of ancient texts in there when we moved in."

Jeremy nodded. "And I went through all of those. There were no records stuck in them, or written in them."

Humphrey continued, "If that's so, then we're going to have to pray Carruthers left some more detailed account. The letters and notes give one hope—and I'm not saying we won't ever get the answer if that's all there is for us to work with—but a properly kept journal with a *consecutive* listing of experiments . . . if we had that, we could sort out which recipes for this concoction were the later ones. Especially which was the final version."

"There are any number of versions, you see." Jeremy took up the explanation. "But there's no way to tell from Cedric's journal which came after which, let alone why. Cedric must have known, and from comments in the letters, Carruthers knew, too, but . . . so far, we've only been able to match a handful of Carruthers's experimental notes with his letters, which are the only things that are dated."

Humphrey chewed, nodded morosely. "Enough to make you tear out your hair."

In the distance, the front doorbell pealed. Castor left them, reappearing a minute later with a folded note on a salver.

He walked to Deverell's side. "A footman from next door brought this for you, my lord."

Deverell glanced at Tristan and Charles as he set down his fork and reached for the note. It was a scrap of plain paper, the writing an ill-formed scrawl in pencil. Deverell scanned it, then looked at Tristan and Charles across the table.

They both sat up.

"What?"

Everyone looked at Deverell. A slow smile curved his lips.

"The good sisters of the Little Sisters of Mercy off the Whitechapel Road have been caring for a young man who answers to the name of Jonathon Martinbury." Deverell glanced at the note; his face hardened. "He was brought to them two weeks ago, the victim of a vicious beating left to die in a gutter."

Arranging to fetch Martinbury—they all agreed he had to be fetched—was an exercise in logistics. In the end, it was agreed that Leonora and Tristan would go; neither St. Austell nor Deverell wanted to risk being seen leaving or returning to Number 14. Even Leonora and Tristan had to be cautious. They left the house via the front door, with Henrietta on her lead.

Once on the street, the line of trees along the boundary of Number 12 screened them from anyone watching from Number 16. They turned in at the gate of the club and, much to Henrietta's disgruntlement, left her in the kitchens there.

Tristan hurried Leonora down the back path of the club, then out into the alleyway behind. From there it was easy to reach the next street, where they hired a hackney and headed with all speed for the Whitechapel Road.

In the infirmary at the convent, they found Jonathon Martin-bury. He looked to be a stalwart young man, squarish of both build and countenance, with brown hair visible through the breaks in the bandages wrapping his head. Much of him seemed bandaged; one arm rested in a sling. His face was badly bruised and cut, with a massive contusion above one eye.

He was lucid, if weak. When Leonora explained their presence by saying they'd been searching for him in relation to Cedric Carling's work with A. J. Carruthers, his eyes lit.

"Thank God!" Briefly, he closed his eyes, then opened them. His voice was rough, still hoarse. "I got your letter. I came down to town early, intending to call on you—" He broke off, his face clouding. "Everything since has been a nightmare."

Tristan talked to the sisters. Although concerned, they agreed that Martinbury was well enough to be moved, given he was now with friends.

Between them, Tristan and the convent's gardener supported Jonathon out to the waiting hackney. Leonora and the sisters fussed. Climbing into the carriage severely tried the young man's composure; he was tight-lipped and pale when they had him finally settled on the seat, wrapped in a blanket and cushioned by old pillows. Tristan had given Jonathon his greatcoat; Jonathon's coat had been ripped beyond redemption.

Together with Leonora, Tristan repeated Jonathon's thanks to the sisters and promised a much-needed donation as soon as he could arrange it. Leonora gave him an approving look. He handed her up into the carriage, and was about to follow when a motherly sister came hurrying up.

"Wait! Wait!" Lugging a large leather bag, she huffed out of the convent gate.

Tristan stepped forward and took the bag from her. She beamed in at Jonathon. "A pity after all you've been through to lose that one little piece of good luck!"

As Tristan hoisted the bag onto the carriage floor, Jonathon leaned down, reaching to touch it as if to reassure himself. "Indeed," he gasped, nodding as well as he could. "Many thanks, Sister."

The sisters waved and called blessings; Leonora waved back. Tristan climbed up and closed the door, settling beside Leonora as the carriage rumbled off.

He looked at the large leather traveling bag sitting on the floor between the seats. He glanced at Jonathon. "What's in it?"

Jonathon laid his head back against the squabs. "I think it's what the people who did this to me were after."

Both Leonora and Tristan looked at the bag.

Jonathon drew a painful breath. "You see—"

"No." Tristan held up a hand. "Wait. This journey's going to be bad enough. Just rest. Once we've got you settled and comfortable again, then you can tell us all your story."

"All?" Through half-closed lids Jonathon regarded him. "How many of you are there?"

"Quite a few. Better if you have to tell your tale only once."

A fever of impatience gripped Leonora, centered on Jonathon's black leather bag. A perfectly ordinary traveling bag, but she could imagine what it might contain; she was almost beside herself with frustrated curiosity by the time the carriage finally rolled to a halt in the alleyway alongside the back gate of Number 14 Montrose Place.

Tristan had first halted the carriage in a street closer to the park; he'd left them there, saying he needed to get things in place.

He'd returned more than half an hour later. Jonathon had been sleeping; he was still groggy when they stopped for the last time, and Deverell opened the carriage door.

"Go." Tristan gave her a little push.

She gave Deverell her hand and he helped her down; behind him, the garden gate stood open, with Charles St. Austell beyond—he beckoned her through.

Their largest footman, Clyde, was standing behind Charles with what Leonora realized was a makeshift stretcher in his hands.

Charles saw her looking. "We're going to carry him in. Too slow and painful otherwise."

She glanced at him. "Slow?"

With his head, he indicated the house next door. "We're trying to minimize the chance of Mountford seeing anything."

They'd assumed Mountford or more likely his accomplice would be watching the comings and goings at Number 14.

"I thought we'd have taken him to Number 12." Leonora glanced toward their club.

"Too difficult to disguise getting all of us over there to hear his story." Gently, Charles eased her aside as Tristan and Deverell helped Jonathon through the gate. "Here we are."

Between the four of them, they got Jonathon settled in the stretcher, constructed from folded sheets and two long broom poles. Deverell went ahead, leading the way. Clyde and Charles followed, carrying the stretcher. Carrying Jonathon's bag in one hand, Tristan brought up the rear, Leonora before him.

"What about the hackney?" Leonora whispered.

"Taken care of. I've paid him to rest there for another ten minutes before rumbling off, just in case the sound as he passes behind next door alerts them."

He'd thought of everything—even cutting a new, narrow arch in the hedge dividing the well-screened kitchen garden from the more open lawn. Instead of going up the central path and on through the central archway and then having to cross a wide expanse of lawn, they headed up a narrow side path following the boundary wall with Number 12, then through the newly hacked breach in the hedge, emerging hard by the garden wall, largely concealed in its shadow.

They only had a short distance to cover until the jut of the kitchen wing hid them from Number 16. Then they were free to climb the steps to the terrace and go in through the parlor doors.

When Tristan closed the French doors behind her, she caught his eye. "Very neat."

"All part of the service." His gaze went past her. She turned to see Jonathon being helped out of the stretcher and onto a daybed, already made up.

Pringle was hovering. Tristan caught his eye. "We'll leave you to your patient. We'll be in the library—join us when you're finished."

Pringle nodded, and turned to Jonathon.

They all filed out. Clyde took the stretcher and headed for the kitchens; the rest of them trooped into the library.

Leonora's eagerness to see what Jonathon had in his bag was nothing to Humphrey's and Jeremy's. If Tristan and the others had not been there, she doubted she would have been able to prevent them having the bag fetched and "just checking" what it contained.

The comfortable old library had rarely seemed so full, and even more rarely so alive. It wasn't just Tristan, Charles, and Deverell, all pacing, waiting, hard-faced and intent; their repressed energy seemed to infect Jeremy and even Humphrey.

This, she thought, sitting feigning patience on the chaise and with Henrietta, sprawled at her feet, watching them all, must be what the atmosphere in a tent full of knights had felt like just before the call to battle.

Finally, the door opened and Pringle entered. Tristan splashed brandy into a glass and handed it to him; Pringle took it with a nod, sipped, then sighed appreciatively. "He's well enough, certainly well enough to talk. Indeed, he's eager to do so, and I'd suggest you hear him out with all speed."

"His injuries?" Tristan asked.

"I'd say those who attacked him were coldly intent on killing him."

"Professionals?" Deverall asked.

Pringle hesitated. "If I had to guess, I'd say they were professionals, but more used to knives or pistols, yet in this case they were trying to make the attack look like the work of local thugs. However, they failed to take Mr. Martinbury's rather heavy bones into account; he's very bruised and battered, but the sisters have done well, and with time he'll be as good as new. Mind you, if some kind soul hadn't taken him to the convent, I wouldn't have given much for his chances."

Tristan nodded. "Thank you once again."

"Think nothing of it." Pringle handed back his empty glass. "Every time I hear from Gasthorpe, I at least know it'll be something more interesting than boils or carbuncles."

With nods all around, he left them.

They all exchanged glances; the excitement leapt a notch.

Leonora rose. Glasses were quickly drained and set down. She shook out her skirts, then swept to the door, and led them all back to the parlor.

Nineteen

"It's all still a mystery to me. I can't make head or tail of it—if you can shed any light on the affair I'd be grateful." Jonathon settled his head against the back of the chaise.

"Start at the beginning," Tristan advised. They were all gathered around—in chairs, propped against the mantelpiece—all keenly focused. "When did you first hear of anything to do with Cedric Carling?"

Jonathon's gaze fixed, grew distant. "From A. J.—on her deathbed."

Tristan, and everyone else, blinked. "*Her* deathbed?"

Jonathon looked around at them. "I thought you knew. A. J. Carruthers was my aunt."

"*She* was the herbalist? A. J. Carruthers?" Humphrey's disbelief rang in his tone.

Jonathon, somewhat grim-faced, nodded. "Yes, she was. And that was why she liked living hidden away in north Yorkshire. She had her cottage, grew her herbs and conducted her experiments and no one bothered her. She collaborated and corresponded with a large number of other well-respected herbalists, but they all knew her only as A. J. Carruthers."

Humphrey frowned. "I see."

"One thing," Leonora put in. "Did Cedric Carling, our cousin, know she was a woman?"

"I honestly don't know," Jonathon replied. "But knowing A. J., I doubt it."

"So when did you first hear of Carling or anything to do with this business?"

"I'd heard Carling's name from A. J. over the years, but only as another herbalist. The first I knew of this business was just a few days before she died. She'd been failing for months—her death was no surprise. But the story she told me then—well, she was starting to drift away, and I wasn't sure how much to credit."

Jonathon drew breath. "She told me she and Cedric Carling had gone into partnership over a particular ointment they'd both been convinced would be eminently useful—she was a great one for working on *useful* things. They'd been working on this ointment for over two years, quite doggedly, and from the first they'd made a solemn and binding agreement to share in any profits from the discovery. They'd enacted a legal document—she told me I'd find it in her papers, and I did, later. However, the thing she was most urgent to tell me then was that they'd succeeded in their quest. Their ointment, whatever it was, was effective. They'd reached that point some two months or so before, and then she'd heard no more from Carling. She'd waited, then written to other herbalists she knew in the capital, asking after Carling, and she'd only just heard back that he'd died."

Jonathon paused to look at their faces, then continued, "She was too old and frail to do anything about it then, and she assumed that with Cedric's death, it would take his heirs some time to work through his effects and contact her, or her heirs, about the matter. She told me so I'd be prepared, and know what it was about when the time came."

He dragged in a breath. "She died shortly after, and left me all her journals and papers. I kept them, of course. But what with one thing and another, my work for my articles, and not hearing anything from anyone about the discovery, I more or less forgot about it, until last October."

"What happened then?" Tristan asked.

"I had all her journals in my rooms, and one day I picked one up, and started to read. And that's when I realized she might have been right—that what she and Cedric Carling had discovered might, indeed, be very useful." Jonathon shifted awkwardly. "I'm no herbalist, but it seemed like the ointment they'd created would help to clot blood, especially in wounds." He glanced at Tristan. "I could imagine that that might have quite definite uses."

Tristan stared at him, knew Charles and Deverell were doing the same, and they were all reliving the same day, reliving the carnage on the battlefield at Waterloo. "An ointment to clot blood." Tristan felt his face set. "Very useful indeed."

"We should have kept Pringle," Charles said.

"We can ask his advice fast enough," Tristan answered. "But first let's hear the rest. There's a lot we don't yet know—like who Mountford is."

"Mountford?" Jonathon looked blank.

Tristan waved. "We'll get to him—whoever he is—in time. What happened next?"

"Well, I wanted to come down to London and follow things up, but I was right in the middle of my final examinations—I couldn't leave York. The discovery had sat around doing nothing for two years—I reasoned it could wait until I was finished with my articles and could devote proper time to it. So that's what I did. I discussed it with my employer, Mr. Mountgate, and also with A. J.'s old solicitor, Mr. Aldford."

"Mountford," Deverell put in.

They all looked at him.

He grimaced. "Mountgate plus Aldford equals Mountford."

"Good heavens!" Leonora looked at Jonathon. "Who else did you tell?"

"No one." He blinked, then amended, "Well, not initially."

"What does that mean?" Tristan asked.

"The only other person who was told was Duke—Marmaduke Martinbury. He's my cousin and A. J.'s other heir—her other nephew. She left me all her journals and papers and herbalist things—Duke never had a moment for her interest in herbs— but her estate was otherwise divided between the two of us. And, of course, the discovery as such was part of her estate. Aldford felt duty-bound to tell Duke, so he wrote to him."

"Did Duke reply?"

"Not by letter." Jonathon's lips thinned. "He came to visit me to ask about the matter." After a moment, he went on, "Duke is the black sheep of the family, always has been. As far as I know, he has no real fixed abode, but is usually to be found at whatever racecourse is holding a carnival.

"Somehow—probably because he was strapped for cash and so at home at his other aunt's house in Derby—Aldford's letter found him. Duke came around wanting to know when he could expect his share of the cash. I felt honor-bound to explain the whole to him—after all, A. J.'s share of the discovery was half his." Jonathon paused, then went on, "Although he was his usual obnoxious self, he didn't, once he understood what the legacy was, seem all that interested."

"Describe Duke."

Jonathon glanced at Tristan, noting his tone. "Leaner than me, a few inches taller. Dark hair—black, actually. Dark eyes, pale skin."

Leonora stared at Jonathon's face, did a little mental rearranging, then nodded decisively. "That's him."

Tristan glanced at her. "You're sure?"

She looked at him. "How many lean, tallish, black-haired young men with"—she pointed at Jonathon—"a nose like that do you expect to stumble over in this affair?"

His lips twitched, but thinned immediately. He inclined his head. "So Duke is Mountford. Which explains a few things."

"Not to me," Jonathon said.

"All will be made clear in time," Tristan promised. "But carry on with your tale. What happened next?"

"Nothing immediately. I finished my exams and arranged to come down to London, then I received that letter from Miss Carling, via Mr. Aldford. It seemed clear that Mr. Carling's heirs knew less than I did, so I brought forward my visit . . ." Jonathon stopped, puzzled, looked at Tristan. "The sisters said you'd sent people asking after me. How did you know I was in London, let alone hurt?"

Tristan explained, succinctly, from the beginning of the odd happenings in Montrose Place to their realization that A. J. Carruthers's work with Cedric held the key to the mysterious Mountford's desperate interest, to how they had tracked and finally found Jonathon himself.

He stared at Tristan, dazed. "Duke?" He frowned. "He is the

black sheep, but although he's nasty, mean-tempered, even something of a brute, it's a bully's facade—I'd have said he was something of a coward beneath his bluster. I can imagine he might have done *most* of what you say, but I honestly can't see him arranging to have me beaten to death."

Charles smiled that deadly smile he, Tristan, and Deverell all seemed to have in their repertoires. "Duke might not have—but the people he's very likely now dealing with would have no scruples in disposing of you if you threatened to butt in."

"If what you say is true," Deverell put in, "they're probably having trouble keeping Duke up to scratch. That would certainly fit."

"The weasel," Jonathon said. "Duke has a . . . well, a valet I suppose. A manservant. Cummings."

"That's the name he gave me." Deverell raised his brows. "About as clever as his master."

"So," Charles said, straightening away from the mantelpiece, "what now?"

He looked at Tristan; they all looked at Tristan. Who smiled, not nicely, and rose. "We've learned all we need to this point." Settling his sleeves, he glanced at Charles and Deverell. "I rather think it's time we invited Duke to join us. Let's hear what he has to say."

Charles's grin was diabolical. "Lead the way."

"Indeed." Deverell was already at Tristan's heels as he turned for the door.

"Wait!" Leonora looked at the black bag, sitting beside the chaise, then raised her gaze to Jonathon's face. "Please tell me you have all of A. J.'s journals and her letters from Cedric in there."

Jonathon grinned, a trifle lopsidedly. He nodded. "The purest luck, but yes, I have them."

Tristan turned back. "That's one point we haven't covered. How did they catch you, and why didn't they take the letters and journals?"

Jonathon looked up at him. "Because it was so cold, there were hardly any passengers on the mail coach—it got in early." He glanced at Leonora. "I don't know how they knew I was on it—"

"They'd have had someone watching you in York," Deverell said. "I take it you didn't change your schedule immediately after you got Leonora's letter and rush off?"

"No. It took two days to organize bringing my time away forward." Jonathon sank back on the chaise. "When I got off the coach, there was a message waiting for me, telling me to meet a Mr. Simmons at the corner of Green Dragon Yard and Old Montague Street at six o'clock to discuss a matter of mutual interest. It was a nicely worded letter, well written, good quality paper— I thought it was from you, the Carlings, about the discovery. I didn't really think—you couldn't have known I was on the mail coach, but at the time it all seemed to fit.

"That corner is a few minutes from the coaching inn. If the mail had got in on schedule, I wouldn't have had time to organize a room before going to the meeting. Instead, I had an hour to look about, to find a clean room, and leave my bag there, before going to the rendezvous."

Tristan's unnerving smile remained. "They assumed you hadn't brought any papers with you. They would have searched."

Jonathon nodded. "My coat was ripped apart."

"So, finding nothing, they put you out of the picture and left you for dead. But they didn't check what time the coach pulled in—tsk, tsk. Very slapdash." Charles strolled toward the door. "Are we going?"

"Indeed." Tristan swung on his heel and headed for the door. "Let's fetch Mountford."

Leonora watched the door close behind them.

Humphrey cleared his throat, caught Jonathon's eye, then pointed to the black bag. "May we?"

Jonathon waved. "By all means."

Leonora was torn.

Jonathon was obviously drooping, exhaustion and his injuries catching up with him; she urged him to lie back and recoup. At her suggestion, Humphrey and Jeremy took themselves and the black bag off to the library.

Closing the parlor door behind her, she hesitated. Part of her wanted to hurry after her brother and uncle, to help with and share in the academic excitement of making sense of Cedric and A. J.'s discovery.

More of her was drawn to the real, more physical excitement of the hunt.

She debated for all of ten seconds, then headed for the front door. Opening it, she left it on the latch. Night had fallen, the darkness of evening closing in. On the porch, she hesitated. Wondered if she should take Henrietta. But the hound was still in the kitchens of the Club; she didn't have time to fetch her. She peered across at Number 16, but its front door was closer to the street; she couldn't see anything.

Don't. Go. Into. Danger.

There were three of them ahead of her; what danger could there be?

She hurried down the front steps and ran quickly down the front path.

They were, she assumed, going to pluck Mountford from his hole—she was curious, after all this time, to see what he was really like, what sort of man he was. Jonathon's description was ambivalent; yes, Mountford—Duke—was a violent bully, but not a murderous one.

He'd been violent enough where she was concerned. . . .

She approached the front door of Number 16 with appropriate caution.

It stood half-open. She strained her ears but heard nothing.

She peered past the door.

Faint moonlight threw her shadow deep into the hall. Caused the man framed in the doorway to the kitchen stairs to pause and turn around.

It was Deverell. He motioned her to silence, and to stay back, then he turned and melted into the shadows.

Leonora hesitated for a second; she'd stay back, just not this far back.

Her slippers silent on the tiles, she glided into the hall and followed in Deverell's wake.

The stairs leading down to the kitchens and the basement level were just beyond the hall door. From her earlier visit following Tristan around, Leonora knew that the double flight of stairs ended in a long corridor. The doors to the kitchens and scullery gave off it to the left; on the right lay the butler's pantry, followed by a long cellar.

Mountford was tunneling through from the cellar.

Pausing at the stairhead, she leaned over the banister and peered down; she could make out the three men moving below, large shadows in the gloom. Faint light shone from somewhere ahead of them. As they moved out of her sight, she crept down the stairs.

She paused on the landing. From there she could see the length of the corridor before and below her. There were two doors into the cellar. The nearer stood ajar; the faint light came from beyond it.

Even more faintly, like a *frisson* across her nerves, came a steady, *scritch-scratch*.

Tristan, Charles, and Deverell came together before the door; although she saw them move, assumed they were talking, she heard nothing, not the slightest sound.

Then Tristan turned to the cellar door, thrust it open and walked in.

Charles and Deverell followed.

The silence lasted for a heartbeat.

"*Hey!*"

"*What . . . ?*"

Thuds. Bangs. Stifled shouts and oaths. It was more than just a scuffle.

How many men had been in there? She'd assumed only two, Mountford and the weasel, but it sounded like more . . .

A horrendous *crash* shook the walls.

She gasped, stared down. The light had gone out.

In the gloom, a figure burst out of the second cellar door, the one at the end of the corridor. He turned, slammed the door, fiddled. She heard the grating sound of an old iron lock falling into place.

The man ran from the door, raced, hair and coat wildly flapping, up the corridor toward the stairs.

Startled, paralyzed by recognition—the man was Mountford—Leonora hauled in a breath. She forced her hands to her skirts, grasped them to turn and flee, but Mountford hadn't seen her—he skidded to a halt by the nearer cellar door, now wide-open.

He reached in, grabbed the door, and swung it shut, too. Grabbed the knob, desperately worked.

Into a sudden silence came a telltale grating, then the clunk as the heavy lock fell home.

Chest heaving, Mountford stepped back. The blade of a knife held in one fist gleamed dully.

A thud fell on the door, then the handle rattled.

A muffled oath filtered through the thick panels.

"Hah! Got you!" Face alight, Mountford turned.

And saw her.

Leonora whirled and fled.

She was nowhere near fast enough.

He caught her at the top of the stairs. Fingers biting into her arm, he swung her hard back against the wall.

"*Bitch!*"

The word was vicious, snarled.

Looking into the starkly pale face thrust close to hers, Leonora had a second to make up her mind.

Strangely, that was all it took—just a second for her emotions to guide her, for her wits to catch up. All she had to do was delay Mountford, and Tristan would save her.

She blinked. Wilted a fraction, lost a little of her starch. Infused her best imitation of Miss Timmins's vagueness into her manner. "Oh, dear—you must be Mr. Martinbury?"

He blinked, then his eyes blazed. He shook her. "How do you know that?"

"Well . . ." She let her voice quaver, kept her eyes wide. "You are the Mr. Martinbury who is related to A. J. Carruthers, aren't you?"

For all his reconnoitering, Mountford—Duke—would not

have learned what sort of woman she was; she was perfectly certain he wouldn't have thought to ask.

"Yes. That's me." Gripping her arm, he pushed her ahead of him into the front hall. "I'm here to get something of my aunt's that now belongs to me."

He didn't put away the knife, a dagger of sorts. A frenetic tension thrummed through him, about him; his manner was strained, nervous.

She let her lips part, striving to look suitably witless. "Oh! Do you mean the formula?"

She had to get him away from Number 16, preferably into Number 14. Along the way, she had to convince him she was so helpless and unthreatening that he didn't need to keep hold of her. If Tristan and the others came up the stairs now . . . Mountford had her and a dagger, not to her mind a helpful arrangement.

He was studying her through slitted eyes. "What do you know about the formula? Have they found it?"

"Oh, I believe so. At least, I think that's what they said. My uncle, you know, and my brother. They've been working on our late cousin Cedric Carling's journals, and I *think* they were saying only just a few hours ago that they believe they have the thing clear at last!"

Throughout her artless speech, she'd been drifting toward the front door; he'd been drifting with her.

She cleared her throat. "I realize there must have been some misunderstanding." With an airy wave, she dismissed whatever had occurred downstairs. "But I'm sure if you talk to my uncle and brother, they'd be happy to share the formula with you, given you are A. J. Carruthers's heir."

Emerging into the moonlight on the front porch, he stared at her.

She kept her expression as vacant as she could, tried not to react to his menace. The hand holding the knife was trembling; he seemed uncertain, off-balance, struggling to think.

He looked across at Number 14. "Yes," he breathed. "Your uncle and brother are very fond of you, aren't they?"

"Oh, yes." She gathered her skirts and with absolutely no hurry, descended the steps; he still did not let go of her arm but descended alongside her. "Why, I've kept house for them for more than a decade, you know. Indeed, they'd be lost without me——"

She continued in airy, totally vacuous vein as they went down the path, turned into the street, walked the short distance to the gate of Number 14, and went in. He walked beside her, still holding her arm, not saying anything; he was so tense, nervously starting, twitching, if he'd been a woman she'd have diagnosed incipient hysteria.

When they reached the front steps, he pulled her roughly closer. Held the dagger up for her to see. "We don't need any interference from your servants."

She blinked at the dagger, then, forcing her eyes wide, stared blankly up at him. "The door's on the latch—we won't need to disturb them."

His tension eased a notch. "Good." He propelled her up the steps. He seemed to be trying to look in every direction at once.

Leonora reached for the door; she glanced at Duke's white face, tight, taut, wondered for one instant if she was wise to trust in Tristan . . .

Hauling in a breath, she lifted her head and opened the door. Prayed Castor wouldn't appear.

Duke stepped inside with her, keeping close beside her. His grip on her arm eased as he scanned the empty hall.

Quietly closing the door, she said, her tone easy and light, inconsequential, "My uncle and brother will be in the library. It's this way."

He kept his hand on her arm, still looked this way and that, but went with her quickly and quietly through the hall and into the corridor leading to the library.

Leonora thought furiously, tried to plan what she should say. Duke's nerves were strung tight, any tighter and they'd snap. God only knew what he might do then. She hadn't dared look to see if Tristan and the others were following, but the old locks on the cellar doors might take longer to pick than less heavy modern locks.

She still didn't feel that she'd made the wrong decision—Tristan *would* rescue her, and Jeremy and Humphrey, soon. Until then, it was up to her to keep them all—Jeremy, Humphrey, and herself—safe.

Her ploy had worked so far; she couldn't think of anything better than to continue in that vein.

Opening the library door, she sailed in. "Uncle, Jeremy—we have a guest."

Duke kept pace with her, kicking the door shut behind them.

Inwardly muttering—*when* would he let her go?—she kept a silly, innocuous expression plastered on her face. "I found Mr. Martinbury next door—it seems he's been looking for that formula of Cousin Cedric's. He seems to think it belongs to him—I told him you wouldn't mind sharing it with him . . . ?"

She infused every ounce of quavering helplessness into her voice, every last iota of intent into her eyes. If anyone could confuse and obstruct someone with words written on a page, it was her brother and uncle.

Both were in their usual places; both had glanced up, then remained frozen.

Jeremy met her gaze, read the message in her eyes. His desk was awash with papers; he started to rise from his chair behind it.

Mountford panicked. "Wait!" His fingers tightened on Leonora's arm; he hauled her to him, jerking her off-balance so she fell against him. He brandished his dagger before her face.

"Don't do anything rash!" Wildly, he looked from Jeremy to Humphrey. "I just want the formula—just give it to me, and she won't get hurt."

She felt his chest heave as he dragged in a breath.

"I don't want to hurt anyone, but I *will*. I want that formula."

The sight of the knife had shocked Jeremy and Humphrey; Duke's rising tones were scaring her.

"I say, see here!" Humphrey struggled up out of his chair, uncaring of the journal that slid to the floor. "You can't just come in here and—"

"Shut *up!*" Mountford was dancing with impatience. His eyes kept flicking to Jeremy's desk.

Leonora couldn't help but focus on the blade, waltzing before her eyes.

"Listen, you can have the formula." Jeremy started to come around his desk. "It's here." He waved at the desk. "If you'll—"

"Stop right there! Not one more step, or I'll slice her cheek!"

Jeremy paled. Halted.

Leonora tried not to think about the knife slicing into her cheek. She closed her eyes briefly. She had to think. Had to find a way . . . a way to take control . . . to waste time, to keep Jeremy and Humphrey safe . . .

She opened her eyes and focused on her brother. "Don't come any closer!" Her voice was weak and wavery, totally unlike her. "He might lock you up somewhere, and then I'll be alone with him!"

Mountford shifted, dragging her so he could keep both Humphrey and Jeremy in view but was no longer standing directly before the door. "Perfect," he hissed. "If I lock you two up, just like I locked the others up, then I can take the formula and be on my way."

Jeremy stared at her. "Don't be stupid." He meant every word. Then he glanced at Mountford. "Anyway, there's nowhere he could lock us up—this is the only room on this floor with a lock."

"Indeed!" Humphrey puffed. "A nonsensical suggestion."

"Oh, no," she warbled, and prayed Mountford would believe her act. "Why, he could lock you in the broom closet across the hall. You'd both fit."

The look Jeremy sent her was furious. "You *fool!*"

His reaction played into her hands. Mountford, so nervous he was jigging, jumped on the idea. "Both of you—now!" He waved with the knife. "You"—he pointed at Jeremy—"get the old man and help him to the door. You don't want your sister's lovely face scarred, do you?"

With a final glare at her, Jeremy went and took Humphrey's arm. He helped Humphrey to the door.

"Stop." Mountford pulled her around so they were directly behind the other two, facing the door. "Right—no noise, no nonsense. Open the door, walk to the broom closet, open its door and walk in. Close the door quietly behind you. Remember—I'm watching every move, and my dagger is at your sister's throat."

She saw Jeremy haul in a breath, then he and Humphrey did exactly as Mountford had ordered. Mountford edged forward as they went into the broom closet directly across the wide corridor; he glanced down the corridor toward the front hall, but no one came from that direction.

The instant the broom closet door shut, Mountford pushed her forward. The key was in the lock. Without releasing her, he turned it.

"Excellent!" He turned to her, eyes feverishly bright. "Now you can get me the formula, and I'll be on my way."

He pushed her back into the library. He closed the door and hurried her to the desk. "Where is it?"

Leonora spread her hands and shuffled papers, confusing what little order there had been. "He said it was here . . ."

"Well find it, damn you!" Mountford released her, ran his fingers through his hair.

Frowning as if concentrating, disguising her sudden spurt of relief, Leonora drifted around the large desk, spreading and sorting papers. "If my brother said it was here, I can assure you it will be . . ." She continued rambling, just like any of the dithery old dears she'd helped over the years. And steadily, paper by paper, worked her way around the desk.

"Is this it?" Finally opposite Mountford, she picked up one sheet, squinted at the receipe, then shook her head. "No. But it must be here . . . perhaps it's this one?"

She felt Mountford quiver, made the mistake of glancing up— he caught her eye. Saw . . .

His face blanked, then rage poured into his expression. "Why *you*—!"

He lunged for her.

She weaved back.

"This was a trick, wasn't it? I'll teach you—"

He would have to catch her first. Leonora wasted no time arguing; she put her mind to dodging him, darting this way, then that. The desk was big enough that he couldn't reach her over it.

"*Ah!*" He launched himself over the desk at her.

With a shriek, she whisked out of his reach. She glanced at the door but he was already scrambling to his feet, his face a mask of fury.

He raced at her. She ran.

Around and around.

The door opened.

She rounded the desk and fled straight for the tall figure who walked in.

Flung herself at him and clutched.

Tristan caught her, then caught her hands, pushed her behind him.

"Out."

One word, but the tone was not one to disobey. Tristan didn't look at her. Out of breath, she followed his gaze to Mountford, leaning, panting, on the opposite side of the desk. He was still holding the dagger in one fist.

"Now."

A warning. She backed a few steps, then whirled. He didn't need her there to distract him.

She rushed out into the corridor, intending to summon help, only to realize Charles and Deverell were there, standing in the shadows.

Charles reached past her, caught the door, and pulled it shut. Then he leaned nonchalantly against the frame and grinned somewhat resignedly at her.

Deverell, his lips curved in the same, almost reminiscent wolf-ish smile, leaned back against the corridor wall.

She stared at them. Pointed to the library. "Mountford's got a dagger!"

Deverell raised his brows. "Only one?"

"Well, yes . . ." A thud reverberated from behind the door. She started, swung around and stared at it—as much of it as she could see past Charles's shoulders. She glared at him. "Why aren't you helping him?"

"Who? Mountford?"

"*No!* Tristan!"

Charles screwed up his face. "I doubt he needs help." He glanced at Deverell.

Who grimaced. "Unfortunately." The word "pity" danced in the air.

Thuds and grunts issued from the library, then a body hit the floor. Hard.

Leonora winced.

Silence reigned for a moment, then Charles's expression changed and he straightened away from the door.

It opened. Tristan stood framed in the doorway.

His gaze locked on Leonora, then flicked to Charles and Deverell. "He's all yours." Reaching out, he took Leonora's arm, pushing her down the corridor. "If you'll excuse us for a moment?"

A rhetorical question; Charles and Deverell were already slipping past him into the library.

Leonora felt her heart thudding; it still hadn't slowed. Swiftly she scanned Tristan, all of him she could see as he drew her down the corridor. His face was set and definitely grim. "Did he hurt you?"

She could barely keep the panic from her voice. Daggers could be deadly.

He flicked her a narrow-eyed glance; if anything his jaw set harder. "Of course not."

He sounded insulted. She frowned at him. "Are you all right?"

His eyes flared. "No!"

They'd reached the front hall; Tristan threw open the morning room door and propelled her in. He followed on her heels, all but slamming the door. "Now! Just refresh my memory—what was it I warned you—only yesterday, I seem to recall—never, *ever* to do?"

She blinked, met his barely restrained fury with her usual steady gaze. "You told me never to go into danger."

"*Don't. Go. Into. Danger.*" He stepped closer, deliberately intimidating. "Precisely. *So*"—his chest swelled as he dragged in a desperate breath, felt the reins of his temper slither free regardless—"*what the devil did you think you were doing by following us next door?*"

He didn't raise his voice, rather, he lowered it. Infused every last ounce of power into his diction so the words cracked like a whip. Stung like one, too.

"I—"

"If that's an example of how you intend obeying me in future, of how you intend going on, despite my clear warning, I take leave to tell you that it *won't do!*" He ran a hand through his hair.

"If—"

"*God!* I aged a decade and more when Deverell told me he'd seen you out there. And *then* we had to subdue Mountford's cronies before we could get at the locks, and *they* were ancient and stiff! I can't remember feeling so damned desperate in my life!"

"I under—"

"No, you *don't!*" He pinned her with a glare. "And don't think this means we're not going to get married, because we are—that's final!"

He emphasized how final with a swift motion of his hand. "But as you can't be trusted to pay attention, to behave with a modicum of common sense—to exercise those wits God definitely gave you and spare me this torment—be damned if I don't have a bloody tower built at Mallingham and *lock you in it!*"

He stopped to drag in a breath, noticed her eyes were glittering strangely. Warningly.

"If you're quite finished?" Her tone was considerably more glacial than his.

When he didn't immediately respond, she went on, "For your information, you have what happened here this evening entirely wrong." She lifted her chin, met his gaze defiantly. "I didn't go into danger—*not at all!*" Her eyes snapped; she held up a finger to stop him from erupting—interrupting.

"What happened was this. I followed you and Charles and Deverell—three gentlemen of not inconsiderable experience and abilities—into a house we all believed held only two far less able men." Her eyes bored into his, defying him to contradict her. "We *all* believed there was no great danger. As it happened, fate took a hand, and the situation became *unexpectedly* dangerous.

"*However!*" She fixed him with a look as furious as any of his had been. "What you are doggedly failing to see in all this is what to me is the most crucial point!" She flung her hands outward. "*I trusted you!*"

She turned, paced, then with an angry swish faced him and drilled a finger into his chest. "I *trusted* you to get yourself free and come after me and rescue me—*and you did.* I *trusted* you to save me, and yes, you turned up and dealt with Mountford.

In typical blinkered male fashion, you're refusing to see this!"

He caught her finger. She locked her eyes on his. Her chin set. "I trusted in you, and you *didn't* fail me. I got it—*we* got it—right."

She held his gaze; a faint sheen invested her blue eyes. "I have a warning for you," she said, her voice low. *"Don't. Spoil. It."*

If he'd learned anything in his long career, it was that, in certain circumstances, retreat was the wisest option.

"Oh." He searched her eyes, then nodded and released her hand. "I see. I didn't realize."

"Humph!" She lowered her hand. "Just as long as you do now . . ."

"Yes." A sense of euphoria was welling inside him, threatening to spill over and sweep him away. "I do see . . ."

She watched him, waited, unconvinced by his tone.

He hesitated, then asked, "You really did *mean* to trust me with your life?"

Her eyes were definitely glittery now, but not with anger. She smiled. "Yes, I definitely did. If I hadn't had you to trust in, I don't know what I would have done."

She moved into his arms; he closed them around her. She tipped up her face to look into his. "With you in my life, the decision was easy." Raising her arms, she draped them over his shoulders. Looked into his eyes. "So now all is well."

He studied her face, then nodded. "Indeed." He was lowering his head to kiss her when his strategist's brain, routinely checking that all was indeed well in their world, snagged on one point.

He hesitated, lifted his lids, waited until she did the same. He frowned. "I assume Jonathon Martinbury's still in the parlor, but what happened to Humphrey and Jeremy?"

Her eyes widened; her expression dissolved into one of mild horror. "Oh, great heavens!"

"I'm so sorry!" Leonora helped Humphrey out of the closet. "Things . . . just happened."

Jeremy followed Humphrey out, kicking aside a mop. He glowered at her. "That was the most hopeless piece of acting I've ever witnessed—and that dagger was *sharp*, for heaven's sake!"

Leonora looked into his eyes, then quickly hugged him. "Never mind—it worked. That's the important thing."

Jeremy humphed and looked at the closed library door. "Just as well. We didn't want to knock and draw attention to ourselves—didn't know if it would distract someone at the wrong moment." He looked at Tristan. "I take it you caught him?"

"Indeed." Tristan waved to the library door. "Let's go in—I'm sure St. Austell and Deverell will have explained his position to him by now."

The scene that met their eyes as they filed into the library suggested that was the case; Mountford—Duke—sat slumped, head and shoulders drooping, in a straight-backed chair in the middle of the library. His hands, hanging limp between his knees, were bound with curtain cord. One booted ankle was lashed to a chair leg.

Charles and Deverell were propped side by side against the front edge of the desk, arms folded, eyeing their prisoner as if imagining what they might do to him next.

Leonora checked, but could see only a graze on one of Duke's cheekbones; nevertheless, despite the lack of outward damage, he didn't look at all well.

Deverell looked up as they headed toward their usual places. Leonora helped Humphrey into his chair. Deverell caught Tristan's eye. "Might be an idea to get Martinbury in to hear this." He glanced around at the limited seating. "We could carry his chaise in."

Tristan nodded. "Jeremy?"

The three of them went out, leaving Charles on watch.

A minute later, a deep woof sounded from the front of the house, followed by the click of Henrietta's claws as she loped toward them.

Surprised, Leonora glanced at Charles.

He didn't shift his gaze from Mountford. "We thought she might prove helpful in persuading Duke to see the error of his ways."

Henrietta was already growling when she appeared in the doorway. Her hackles had risen; she fixed glowing amber eyes on Duke. Rigid, frozen, lashed to the chair, he stared, horrified, back.

Henrietta's growl dropped an octave. Her head lowered. She took two menacing steps forward.

Duke looked ready to faint.

Leonora clicked her fingers. "Here, girl. Come here."

"Come on, old girl." Humphrey tapped his thigh.

Henrietta looked again at Mountford, then snuffled and ambled over to Leonora and Humphrey. After greeting them, she circled, then collapsed in a shaggy heap between them. Resting her huge head on her paws, she fixed an implacably hostile gaze on Duke.

Leonora glanced at Charles. He looked well pleased.

Jeremy reappeared and held the library door wide; Tristan and Deverell carried the chaise from the parlor with Jonathon Martinbury reclining on it into the room.

Duke gasped. He stared at Jonathon; the last vestige of color drained from his face. "Good Lord! What happened to you?"

No actor could have given such a performance; he was transparently shocked by his cousin's state.

Tristan and Deverell set the chaise down; Jonathon met Duke's eyes steadily. "I gather I met some friends of yours."

Duke looked ill. His face waxen, he stared, then slowly shook his head. "But how did they know? *I* didn't know you were in town."

"Your *friends* are determined, and they have very long arms." Tristan sank onto the chaise beside Leonora.

Jeremy closed the door. Deverell had returned to his position beside Charles. Crossing the room, Jeremy pulled out his chair from behind the desk and sat.

"Right." Tristan exchanged glances with Charles and Deverell, then looked at Duke. "You're in a serious and dire position. If you have any wits at all, you'll answer the questions we put to you quickly, straightforwardly, and honestly. And, most importantly, accurately." He paused, then went on, "We're not interested in hearing your excuses—justifications would be wasted breath. But for understanding's sake, what started you off on this tack?"

Duke's dark eyes rested on Tristan's face; from her position beside Tristan, Leonora could read their expression. All Duke's violent bravado had deserted him; the only emotion now investing his eyes was fear.

He swallowed. "Newmarket. It was last year's Autumn Carnival. I hadn't before dealt with the London cent-per-cents, but there was this nag . . . I was certain . . ." He grimaced. "Anyway, I got in deep—deeper than I've ever been. And those sharks—they have thugs who act as collectors. I went up north, but they followed. And then I got the letter about A. J.'s discovery."

"So you came to see me," Jonathon put in.

Duke glanced at him, nodded. "When the collectors caught up with me a few days later, I told them about it—they made me write it all down and took it back to the cent-per-cent. I thought the promise would hold him for a while . . ." He glanced at Tristan. "That's when things went from bad to hellish."

He drew breath; his gaze fixed on Henrietta. "The cent-per-cent sold my vowels on, on the strength of the discovery."

"To a foreign gentleman?" Tristan asked.

Duke nodded. "At first it seemed all right. He—the foreigner—encouraged me to get hold of the discovery. He told me how there was clearly no need to include the others"—Duke flushed—"Jonathon and the Carlings, as they hadn't bothered about the discovery for all this time—"

"So you attempted by various means to get into Cedric Carling's workshop, which by asking the servants you'd learned had been closed up since his death."

Again Duke nodded.

"You didn't think to check your aunt's journals?"

Duke blinked. "No. I mean . . . well, she was a woman. She

could only have been helping Carling. The final formula had to be in Carling's books."

Tristan glanced at Jeremy, who returned a wry look. "Very well," Tristan continued. "So your new foreign backer encouraged you to find this formula."

"Yes." Duke shifted on the chair. "At first, it seemed quite a lark. A challenge to see if I could get the thing. He was even willing to underwrite buying the house." His face clouded. "But things kept going wrong."

"We can dispense with a list—we know most of it. I take it your foreign friend became more and more insistent?"

Duke shivered. His eyes, when they met Tristan's, looked haunted. "I offered to find the money, buy back my debt, but he wouldn't have it. He wanted the formula—he was willing to give me as much money as it took to get it, but it was get the damned thing for him—or die. He *meant* it!"

Tristan's smile was cold. "Foreigners of his ilk generally do." He paused, then asked, "What's his name?"

What little color had returned to Duke's face fled. A moment passed, then he moistened his lips. "He told me if I told anyone at all about him, he'd kill me."

Tristan inclined his head, gently said, "And what do you imagine will happen to you if you don't tell us about him?"

Duke stared, then glanced at Charles.

Who met his gaze. "Don't you know the punishment for treason?"

A moment passed, then Deverell quietly added, "That's assuming, of course, that you make it to the scaffold." He shrugged. "What with all the ex-soldiers in the prisons these days . . ."

Eyes huge, Duke dragged in a breath and looked at Tristan. "I didn't know it was *treason!*"

"I'm afraid what you've been doing definitely qualifies."

Duke hauled in another breath, then blurted out, "But I don't *know* his name."

Tristan nodded, accepting. "How do you contact him?"

"I don't! He set it up at the beginning—I have to meet him in St. James's Park every third day and report what's happened."

The next meeting was to occur the following day.

Tristan, Charles, and Deverell grilled Duke for a further half hour, but learned little more. Duke was patently cooperating; recalling how keyed up—how panic-stricken, she now realized—he'd been earlier, Leonora suspected he'd realized that they were his only hope, that if he helped, he might escape a situation that had transformed into a nightmare.

Jonathon's assessment had been accurate; Duke was a black sheep with few morals, a cowardly and violent bully, untrustworthy and worse, but he wasn't a killer, and he'd never meant to be a traitor.

His reaction to Tristan's questions about Miss Timmins was revealing. His face a ghastly hue, Duke falteringly recounted how he'd gone up to check on the ground-floor walls, heard a choking sound in the dimness, and looked up, to see the fragile old woman come tumbling down the stairs to land, dead, at his feet. His horror was unfeigned; it was he who had closed the old lady's eyes.

Watching him, Leonora grimly concluded justice of a sort had been served; Duke would never forget what he'd seen, what he'd inadvertently caused.

Eventually, Charles and Deverell hauled Duke off to the club, there to be held in the basement under the watchful eyes of Biggs and Gasthorpe, together with the weasel and the four thugs Duke had hired to help with the excavations.

Tristan glanced at Jeremy. "Have you identified the final formula?"

Jeremy grinned. He picked up a sheet of paper. "I'd just copied it out. It was in A. J.'s journals, all neatly noted. Anyone could have found it." He handed the sheet to Tristan. "It was definitely half Cedric's work, but without A. J. and her records, it would have been the devil to piece together."

"Yes, but will it work?" Jonathon asked. He'd remained silent throughout the interrogation, quietly taking things in. Tristan handed the paper to him; he scanned it.

"I'm no herbalist," Jeremy said. "But if the results as laid out in your aunt's journals are correct, then yes, their concoction will definitely aid clotting when applied to wounds."

"And it was lying there in York for the past two years." Tristan thought of the battlefield at Waterloo, then banished the vision. Turned to Leonora.

She met his eyes, squeezed his hand. "At least we have it now."

"One thing I don't understand," Humphrey put in. "If this foreigner was so set on finding the formula, and he was able to order Jonathon here killed, why didn't he come after the formula himself?" Humphrey raised his shaggy brows. "Mind you, I'm deuced glad he didn't. Mountford was bad enough, but at least we survived him."

"The answer's one of those diplomatic niceties." Tristan rose and resettled his coat. "If a foreigner from one of the embassies was implicated in an attack on, even the death of, an unknown young man or even two from the north, the government would frown, but largely ignore it. However, if the same foreigner was implicated in burglarly and violence in a house in a wealthy part of London, the house of distinguished men of letters, the government would assuredly be most displeased and not at all inclined to ignore anything."

He glanced at them all, his smile coolly cynical. "An attack on property close to the government's heart would create a diplomatic incident, so Duke was a necessary pawn."

"So what now?" Leonora asked.

He hesitated, looking down into her eyes, then smiled faintly, just for her. "Now we—Charles, Deverell, and I—need to take this information to the proper quarters, and see what they want done."

She stared at him. "Your erstwhile employer?"

He nodded. Straightened. "We'll meet again here for breakfast if you're agreeable and make whatever plans we need to make."

"Yes, of course." Leonora reached out and touched his hand in farewell.

Humphrey nodded magnanimously. "Until tomorrow."

"Unfortunately, your meeting with your government contact will have to wait until morning." Jeremy nodded at the clock on the mantelpiece. "It's past ten."

Tristan, heading for the door, turned, smiling, as he reached it. "Actually, no. The State never sleeps."

The State for them meant Dalziel.

They sent word ahead; nevertheless, the three of them had to cool their heels in the spymaster's anteroom for twenty minutes before the door opened, and Dalziel waved them in.

As they sank onto the three chairs set facing the desk, they glanced around, then met each other's eyes. Nothing had changed.

Including Dalziel. He rounded the desk. He was dark-haired,

dark-eyed and always dressed austerely. His age was unusually difficult to gauge; when he'd first started working through this office, Tristan had assumed Dalziel to be considerably his senior. Now . . . he was starting to wonder if there were all that many years between them. He had visibly aged; Dalziel had not.

As cool as ever, Dalziel sat behind the desk, facing them. "Now. Explain, if you please. From the beginning."

Tristan did, severely editing his account as he went, leaving out much of Leonora's involvement; Dalziel was known to disapprove of ladies dabbling in the game.

Even so, how much missed that steady dark gaze was a matter for conjecture.

At the end of the tale, Dalziel nodded, then looked at Charles and Deverell. "And how is it you two are involved?"

Charles grinned wolfishly. "We share a mutual interest."

Dalziel held his gaze for an instant. "Ah, yes. Your club in Montrose Place. Of course."

He looked down; Tristan was sure it was so they could blink in comfort. The man was a menace. They weren't even part of his network anymore.

"So"—looking up from the notes he'd scrawled while listening, Dalziel leaned back and steepled his fingers; he fixed them all with his gaze—"we have an unknown European intent—seriously intent—on stealing a potentially valuable formula for aiding wound healing. We don't know who this gentleman might be, but we have the formula, and we have his local pawn. Is that correct?"

They all nodded.

"Very well. I want to know who this European is, but I don't want him to know I know. I'm sure you follow me. What I want you to do is this. First, tamper with the formula. Find someone who can make it look believable—we have no idea what training this foreigner might have. Second, convince the pawn to keep his next meeting and hand over the formula—make sure he understands his position, and that his future hangs on his performance. Third, I want you to follow the gentleman back to his lair and identify him for me."

They all nodded. Then Charles grimaced. "Why are we still doing this—taking orders from you?"

Dalziel looked at him, then softly said, "For the same reason I'm giving those orders with every expectation of being obeyed. Because we are who we are." He raised one dark brow. "Aren't we?"

There was nothing else to say; they understood one another all too well.

They rose.

"One thing." Tristan caught Dalziel's questioning look. "Duke Martinbury. Once he has the formula, this foreigner is liable to want to tie up loose ends."

Dalziel nodded. "That would be expected. What do you suggest?"

"We can make sure Martinbury walks away from the meeting, but after that? In addition, he's due some punishment for his part in this affair. All things considered, impression into the army for three years would fit the bill on both counts. Given he's from Yorkshire, I thought of the regiment near Harrogate. Its ranks must be a little thin these days."

"Indeed." Dalziel made a note. "Muffleton's colonel there. I'll tell him to expect Martinbury—Marmaduke, wasn't it?—as soon as he's finished being useful here."

With a nod, Tristan turned; with the others, he left.

"A fake formula?" His gaze on the sheet containing Cedric's formula, Jeremy grimaced. "I wouldn't know where to start."

"Here! Let me see." Seated at the end of the breakfast table, Leonora held out her hand.

Tristan paused in consuming a mound of ham and eggs to pass the sheet to her.

She sipped her tea and studied it while the rest of them applied themselves to their breakfasts. "Which are the critical ingredients, do you know?"

Humphrey glanced down the table at her. "From what I gathered from the experiments, shepherd's purse, moneywort, and comfrey were all crucial. As to the other substances, it was more a matter of enhancement of action."

Leonora nodded, and set down her cup. "Give me a few minutes to consult with Cook and Mrs. Wantage. I'm sure we can concoct something believable."

She returned fifteen minutes later; they were sitting back, replete, enjoying their coffee. She laid a neatly written formula in front of Tristan and retook her seat.

He picked it up, read it, nodded. "Looks believable to me." He passed it to Jeremy. Looked at Humphrey. "Can you recopy that for us?"

Leonora stared at him. "What's wrong with my copy?"

Tristan looked at her. "It wasn't written by a man."

"Oh." Mollified, she poured herself another cup of tea. "So what's your plan? What do we have to do?"

Tristan caught the inquiring gaze she directed at him over the rim of her cup, inwardly sighed, and explained.

As he'd anticipated, no amount of argument had swayed Leonora from joining him on the hunt.

Charles and Deverell had thought it a great joke, until Humphrey and Jeremy also insisted on playing a part.

Short of tying them up and leaving them in the club under Gasthorpe's eye—something Tristan actually considered—there was no way to prevent them appearing in St. James's Park; in the end, the three of them decided to make the best of it.

Leonora proved surprisingly easy to disguise. She was the same height as her maid Harriet, so could borrow her clothes; with the judicious application of some soot and dust, she made a passable flowerseller.

They decked Humphrey out in some of Cedric's ancient clothes; by disregarding every edict of elegance, he was transformed into a thoroughly disreputable specimen, his thinning white hair artfully straggling, apparently unkempt. Deverell, who'd returned to his house in Mayfair to assume his own disguise, returned, approved, then took Humphrey in charge. They set out in a hackney to take up their positions.

Jeremy was the hardest to easily disguise; his slender length and clear-cut, well-defined features screamed "well-bred." In the end, Tristan took him with him back to Green Street. They returned half an hour later as two rough-looking navvies; Leonora had to look twice before she recognized her brother.

He grinned. "This is almost worth being locked in the closet."

Tristan frowned at him. "*This* is no joke."

"No. Of course not." Jeremy tried to look suitably chastened, and failed miserably.

They bade Jonathon, unhappy but resigned to missing out on all the fun, farewell, promising to tell him all when they returned, then went to the club to check on Charles and Duke.

Duke was exceedingly nervous, but Charles had him in hand. They each had defined roles to play; Duke knew his—had had it explained to him in painstaking detail—but even more important, he'd been told very clearly what Charles's role was. They were all sure that come what may, knowing what Charles would do if he didn't behave as instructed would be enough to ensure Duke's continued cooperation.

Charles and Duke would be the last to leave for St. James's Park. The meeting was scheduled for three o'clock, close by Queen Anne's Gate. It was just after two when Tristan handed Leonora into a hackney, waved Jeremy in, then followed.

They left the hackney at the nearer end of the park. As they strolled onto the lawns, they separated, Tristan going ahead, striding easily, stopping now and then as if looking for a friend. Leonora followed a few yards behind, an empty trug hung over her arm—a flowerseller heading home at the end of a good day. Behind her, Jeremy slouched along, apparently sulking to himself and paying little attention to anyone.

Eventually Tristan reached the entrance known as Queen Anne's Gate. He slouched against the bole of a nearby tree and settled somewhat grumpily to wait. As per his instructions, Leonora angled deeper into the park. A wrought-iron bench sat beside the path wending in from Queen Anne's Gate; she sank onto it, stretched her legs out before her, balancing the empty trug against them, and fixed her gaze on the vista before her, of the treed lawns leading down to the lake.

On the next wrought-iron bench along the path sat an old, white-haired man weighed down by a veritable mountain of mismatched coats and scarves. Humphrey. Closer to the lake, but in line with the gate, Leonora could just see the old plaid cap Deverell had pulled low over his face; he was slumped down against the trunk of a tree, apparently asleep.

Without seeming to notice anyone, Jeremy slouched past; he made his way out of the gate, crossed the road, then stopped to peer into the window of a tailor's shop.

Leonora swung her legs and her trug slightly, and wondered how long they would have to wait.

It was a fine day, not sunny, but pleasant enough for there to be many others loitering, enjoying the lawns and the lake. Enough, at least, for their little band to be entirely unremarkable.

Duke had been able to describe his foreigner in only the most cursory terms; as Tristan had somewhat acidly commented, the majority of foreign gentlemen of Germanic extraction presently in London would fit his bill. Nevertheless, Leonora kept her eyes wide, scanning the strollers who passed before her, as an idle flowerseller with no more work for the day might do.

She saw a gentleman coming along the path from the direction of the lake. He was fastidiously turned out in a grey suit; he wore a grey hat and carried a cane, held rigidly in one hand. There was something about him that caught her eye, tweaked her memory, something odd about the way he moved . . . then she recalled Duke's landlady's description of his foreign visitor. *A poker strapped to his spine.*

This had to be their man.

He passed by her, then stepped to the verge, just short of where Tristan lounged, his gaze fixed on the gate, one hand tapping his thigh impatiently. The man pulled out his watch, checked it.

Leonora stared at Tristan; she was sure he hadn't seen the man. Angling her head as if she'd just noticed him, she paused as if debating with herself, then rose and sauntered, hips swinging in time with her trug, to his side.

He glanced at her, straightened as she came up beside him.

His gaze flicked beyond her, noted the man, then returned to her face.

She smiled, nudged him with her shoulder, angling closer, doing her best to mimic the encounters she'd occasionally witnessed in the park. "Pretend I'm suggesting a little dalliance to enliven the day."

He grinned at her, slowly, showing his teeth, but his eyes remained cold. "What do you think you're doing?"

"That's the man over there, and any minute Duke and Charles will arrive. I'm giving us a perfectly reasonable reason for following the man when he leaves, together."

His lips remained curved; he slid one arm about her waist and pulled her closer, bending his head to whisper in her ear, "You are not coming with me."

She smiled into his eyes, patted his chest. "Unless the man goes into the stews, and that hardly seems likely, I am."

He narrowed his eyes at her; she smiled more brightly, but met his gaze directly. "I've been a part of this drama from the beginning. I think I should be a part of its end."

The words gave Tristan pause. And then fate stepped in and took the decision from him.

The bell towers of London's churches tolled the hour—three clangs, echoed and repeated in multiple keys—and Duke came striding swiftly along the pavement and turned in at Queen Anne's Gate.

Charles, in the guise of a tavern brawler, came sauntering along a little way behind, timing his approach.

Duke halted, saw his man, and marched toward him. He looked neither right nor left; Tristan suspected Charles had drilled him until he was so focused on what he had to do, so desperate to get it right, that paying attention to anything else was presently beyond him.

The wind was in the right quarter; it wafted Duke's words to them.

"Do you have my vowels?"

The demand took the foreigner aback, but he recovered swiftly. "I might have. Have you got the formula?"

"I know where it is, and can get it for you in less than a minute, if you have my vowels to give me in return."

Through narrowing eyes, the foreign gentleman searched Duke's pale face, then he shrugged, and reached into his coat pocket.

Tristan tensed, saw Charles lengthen his stride; they both relaxed a fraction when the man drew out a small packet of papers.

He held them up for Duke to see. "Now," he said, his voice cold and crisply accented, "the formula, if you please."

Charles, until then apparently about to stroll past, changed direction and with one step joined the pair. "I have it here."

The foreigner started. Charles grinned, wholly evil. "Don't mind me—I'm just here to make sure my friend Mr. Martinbury comes to no harm. So"—he nodded at the papers, glanced at Duke—"they all there then?"

Duke reached for the vowels.

The foreigner drew them back. "The formula?"

With a sigh, Charles pulled out the copy of the altered formula Humphrey and Jeremy had prepared and made to look suitably aged. He unfolded it, held it up where the foreigner could see it but not quite read it. "Why don't I just hold it here, then as soon as Martinbury has checked over his vowels, you can have it."

The foreigner was clearly unhappy, but had little choice; Charles was intimidating enough in civilized garb—in his present guise, he exuded aggression.

Duke took the vowels, quickly checked, then looked at Charles and nodded. "Yes." His voice was weak. "They're all here."

"Right then." With a nasty grin, Charles handed the formula to the foreigner.

He seized it, pored over it. "This is the right formula?"

"That's what you wanted—that's what you've got. Now," Charles continued, "if you're done, my friend and I have other business to see to."

He saluted the foreigner, a parody of a gesture; taking Duke's arm, he turned. They marched straight out of the gate. Charles hailed a hackney, bundled a now trembling Duke in, and climbed in after him.

Tristan watched the carriage rumble off. The foreigner looked up, watched it go, then carefully, almost reverently, folded the formula and slipped it into his inner coat pocket. That done, he adjusted his grip on his cane, straightened his back, pivoted on his heel, and walked stiffly back toward the lake.

"Come on." His arm around Leonora, Tristan straightened away from the tree and started off in the man's wake.

They passed Humphrey; he didn't look up but Tristan saw that he'd produced a sketch pad and pencil and was rapidly drawing, a somewhat incongruous sight.

The foreigner didn't look back; he seemed to have swallowed their little charade. They'd hoped he would head straight back to his office rather than into any of the less salubrious areas not far from the park. The direction he was taking looked promising. Most of the foreign embassies were located in the area north of St. James's Park, in the vicinity of St. James's Palace.

Tristan released Leonora, then took her hand, glanced down at her. "We're out for a night of entertainment—we've decided to look in at one of the halls around Piccadilly."

She opened her eyes wide. "I've never been to one—I take it I should treat the prospect with enthusiam?"

"Precisely." He couldn't help but grin at her delight—nothing to do with any music hall but the result of pure excitement.

They passed Deverell, who'd got to his feet and was brushing himself down preparatory to joining them in following their quarry.

Tristan was an expert at trailing people through cities and crowds; so, too, was Deverell. They'd both worked primarily in the larger French cities; the best methods of the chase were second nature.

Jeremy would collect Humphrey and they'd return to Montrose Place to await developments; Charles would be there ahead of them with Duke. It was Charles's job to hold the fort until they returned with the last, vital piece of information.

Their quarry crossed the bridge over the lake and continued on toward the environs of St. James's Palace.

"Follow my lead in all things," Tristan murmured, his eyes on the man's back.

Just as he'd expected, the man paused just before the gate leading out of the park and bent down as if to ease a stone from his shoe.

Sliding his arm around Leonora, Tristan tickled her; she giggled, squirmed. Laughing, he settled her familiarly against him, and continued straight past the man without so much as a look.

Breathless, Leonora leaned close as they continued on. "Was he checking?"

"Yes. We'll stop a little way along and argue about which way to go so he can pass us again."

They did; Leonora thought they put on a creditable performance of a pair of lower-class lovers debating the merits of music halls.

When the man was once more ahead of them, striding along,

Tristan grasped her hand, and they followed, now rather more briskly as if they'd made up their minds.

The area surrounding St. James's Palace was riddled with tiny lanes and interconnecting alleyways and yards. The man turned into the labyrinth, striding along confidently.

"This won't work. Let's leave him to Deverell and go on to Pall Mall. We'll pick him up there."

Leonora felt a certain wrench as they left the man's trail, continuing straight on where he had turned left. A few houses along, she glanced back, and saw Deverell turn off in the man's wake.

They reached Pall Mall and turned left, ambling very slowly, scanning the openings of the lanes ahead. They didn't have long to wait before their quarry emerged, striding along even more quickly.

"He's in a hurry."

"He's excited," she said, and felt certain it was true.

"Perhaps."

Tristan led her on; they switched with Deverell again in the streets south of Piccadilly, then joined the crowds enjoying an evening stroll along that major thoroughfare.

"This is where we might lose him. Keep your eyes peeled."

She did, scanning the throng bustling along in the fine evening.

"There's Deverell." Tristan stopped, nudged her so she looked in the right direction. Deverell had just stepped into Pall Mall; he was looking about him. "Damn!" Tristan straightened. "We've lost him." He started openly searching the crowds before them. "Where the devil did he go?"

Leonora stepped closer to the buildings, looked along the narrow gap the crowds left. She caught a flash of grey, then it was gone.

"There!" She grabbed Tristan's arm, pointed ahead. "Two streets up."

They pushed through, tacked, ran—reached the corner and rounded it, then slowed.

Their quarry—she hadn't been wrong—was almost at the end of the short street.

They hurried along, then the man turned right and disappeared from view. Tristan signaled to Deverell, who started running along the street after the man. "Down the alley." Tristan pushed her toward the mouth of a narrow lane.

It cut straight across to the next street running parallel to the one they'd been on. They hurried along it, Tristan gripping her hand, steadying her when she slipped.

They reached the other street and turned up it, strolling once more, catching their breaths. The opening where the street the man had turned down joined the one they were now on lay ahead to their left; they watched it as they walked, waiting for him to reappear.

He didn't.

They reached the corner and looked down the short street. Deverell stood leaning against a railing at the other end.

Of the man they'd been following there was absolutely no sign.

Deverell pushed away from the railing and walked toward them; it only took a few minutes for him to reach them.

He looked grim. "He'd disappeared by the time I got here."

Leonora sagged. "So it's a dead end—we've lost him."

"No," Tristan said. "Not quite. Wait here."

He left her with Deverell and crossed the road to where a streetsweeper stood leaning on his broom midway down the short street. Reaching under his scruffy coat, Tristan located a sovereign; he held it between his fingers where the sweeper could see it as he lounged on the rails beside him.

"The gent in grey who went into the house across the way. Know his name?"

The sweep eyed him suspiciously, but the glimmer of gold spoke loudly. "Don't rightly know his name. Stiff-rumped sort he is. 'Ave 'eard the doorman call him Count something-unpronounceable-beginning-wif-an-eff."

Tristan nodded. "That'll do." He dropped the coin into the sweep's palm.

Strolling back to Leonora and Deverell, he made no effort to keep his self-satisfied smile from his lips.

"Well?" Predictably, it was the light of his life who prompted him.

He grinned. "The man in grey is known to the doorman of the house in the middle of the row as 'Count something-unpronounceable-beginning-wif-an-eff.' "

Leonora frowned at him, then looked past him at the house in question. Then she narrowed her eyes at him. *"And?"*

His smile broadened; it felt amazingly good. "The house is Hapsburg House."

At seven o'clock that evening, Tristan ushered Leonora into the anteroom of Dalziel's office, secreted in the depths of Whitehall.

"Let's see how long he keeps us waiting."

Leonora settled her skirts on the wooden bench Tristan had handed her to. "I would have assumed he'd be punctual."

Sitting beside her, Tristan smiled wryly. "Nothing to do with punctuality."

She studied his face. "Ah. One of those strange games men play."

He said nothing, simply smiled and leaned back.

They only had to wait five minutes.

The door opened; a darkly elegant man appeared. He saw them. A momentary hiatus ensued, then, with a graceful gesture, he invited them in.

Tristan rose, drawing her to her feet beside him, setting her hand on his sleeve. He led her in, halting before the desk and the chairs set before it.

After closing the door, Dalziel joined them. "Miss Carling, I presume."

"Indeed." She gave him her hand, met his gaze—as penetrating as Tristan's—coolly. "I'm pleased to make your acquaintance."

Dalziel's gaze flicked to Tristan's face; his thin lips were not quite straight when he inclined his head and waved them to the chairs.

Rounding the desk, he sat. "So—who was behind the incidents in Montrose Place?"

"A Count something-unpronounceable-beginning-wif-an-eff."

Unimpressed, Dalziel raised his brows.

Tristan smiled his chilly smile. "The Count is known at Hapsburg House."

"Ah."

"And—" From his pocket, Tristan withdrew the sketch Humphrey had, to everyone's surprise, made of the Count. "This should help in identifying him—it's a remarkable likeness."

Dalziel took it, studied it, then nodded. "Excellent. And he accepted the false formula?"

"As far as we could tell. He handed over Martinbury's vowels in exchange."

"Good. And Martinbury is on his way north?"

"Not yet, but he will be. He appears genuinely appalled by his cousin's injuries and will escort him back to York once he—Jonathon—is fit enough to travel. Until then, they'll remain at our club."

"And St. Austell and Deverell?"

"Both have been neglecting their own affairs. Pressing matters necessitated their return to their own hearths."

"Indeed?" One laconic brow rose, then Dalziel turned his dark gaze on Leonora. "I've made inquiries among government ranks, and there's considerable interest in your late cousin's formula, Miss Carling. I've been asked to inform your uncle that certain gentlemen would like to call on him at his earliest convenience. It would, of course, be helpful if their visit could take place before the Martinburys leave London."

She inclined her head. "I'll convey that message to my uncle. Perhaps your gentlemen could send a messenger tomorrow to set a time?"

Dalziel inclined his head in turn. "I'll advise them to do so."

His gaze, fathomless, lingered on her for a moment, then switched to Tristan. "I take it"—the words were even, yet gentler—"that this is farewell, then?"

Tristan held his gaze, then his lips quirked. He rose, and extended his hand. "Indeed. As close to farewell as those in our business ever get."

An answering smile fleetingly softened Dalziel's face as rising, too, he gripped Tristan's hand. Then he released it, and bowed to Leonora. "Your servant, Miss Carling. I won't pretend I would much rather you did not exist, but fate has clearly overruled me." His lazy smile robbed the words of any offense. "I sincerely wish you both well."

"Thank you." Feeling far more in charity with him than she had expected, Leonora politely nodded.

Then she turned. Tristan took her hand, opened the door, and they left the small office in the bowels of Whitehall.

"Why did you take me to meet him?"

"Dalziel?"

"Yes, Dalziel. He obviously wasn't expecting me—he clearly saw my presence as some message. What?"

Tristan looked into her face as the carriage slowed for a corner, then righted and rolled on. "I took you because seeing you, meeting you, was the one message he could neither ignore nor misconstrue. He is my past; you—" He lifted her hand, placed a kiss in her palm, then closed his hand about hers. "You," he said, his voice deep and low, "are my future."

She considered what little she could read in his shadowed face. "So all that"—with her other hand, she gestured back toward Whitehall—"is at an end—behind you?"

He nodded. Lifted her trapped fingers to his lips. "The end of one life—the beginning of another."

She looked into his face, into his dark eyes, then slowly smiled. Leaving her hand in his, she leaned closer. "Good."

His new life—he was impatient to get on with it.

He was a master of strategy and tactics, of exploiting situations for his own ends; by the next morning, he had his latest plan in place.

At ten, he called to take Leonora for a drive, and kidnapped her. He whisked her down to Mallingham Manor, currently devoid of old dears—they were all still in London, busily devoting themselves to his cause.

The same cause to which, after an intimate luncheon, he devoted himself with exemplary zeal.

When the clock on the mantelpiece of the earl's bedchamber chimed three o'clock, he stretched, luxuriating in the slide of the silk sheets over his skin, and even more in the warmth of Leonora slumped boneless against him.

He glanced down. The tumbled mahogany silk of her hair screened her face. Beneath the sheet, he curved a hand about her hip, possessively caressed.

"Hmm-mm." The sated sound was that of a woman well loved. After a moment, she mumbled, "You planned this, didn't you?"

He grinned; a touch of the wolf still remained. "I've been plotting for some time to get you into this bed." His bed, the earl's bed. Where she belonged.

"As distinct from all those nooks you were so successful in finding in all the hostesses's houses?" Lifting her head, she pushed back her hair, then rearranged herself against him, propping her arms on his chest so she could look into his face.

"Indeed—they were merely necessary evils, dictated by the vagaries of the battle."

She looked into his eyes. "I'm not a battle—I told you before."

"But you are something I had to win." He let a heartbeat pass, then added, "And I've triumphed."

Lips curving, Leonora searched his eyes and didn't bother to deny it. "And have you found victory to be sweet?"

He closed his hands over her hips, held her to him. "Sweeter than I'd expected."

"Indeed?" Ignoring the rush of warmth over her skin, she raised a brow. "Well, now you've plotted and planned and got me into your bed, what next?"

"As I aim to keep you here, I suspect we'd better get married." Lifting one hand, he caught and played with strands of her hair. "I wanted to ask—did you want a big wedding?"

She hadn't really thought. He was rushing her—calling the shots—yet . . . she didn't want to waste any more of their lives either.

Here—lying naked with him in his bed—the physical sensations underscored the real attraction, all that had tempted her into his arms. It wasn't just the pleasure that wrapped them about, but the comfort, the security, the promise of all their lives combined could be.

She refocused on his eyes. "No. A small ceremony with our families would suit very well."

"Good." His lashes flickered down.

She sensed the spurt of relief he tried to hide. "What is it?" She was learning; rarely did he not have some plan afoot.

His eyes flicked up to hers. He shrugged lightly. "I was hoping you'd agree to a small wedding. Much easier and faster to organize."

"Well, we can discuss the details with your great-aunts and my aunts when we return to town." She frowned, recollecting. "It's the De Veres' ball tonight—we have to attend."

"No. We don't."

His tone was firm—decided; she glanced at him, puzzled. "We don't?"

458 *Stephanie Laurens*

"I've had enough of the ton's entertainments to last me for a year. And when they hear our news, I'm sure the hostesses will excuse us—after all, they love that sort of gossip and should be grateful to those of us who supply it."

She stared at him. "What news? *What* gossip?"

"Why that we're so head over heels in love that we refused to countenance any delay and have organized to be married in the chapel here tomorrow, in the presence of our combined families and a few selected friends."

Silence reigned; she could barely take it in . . . then she did. "Tell me the details." With one finger, she prodded his bare chest. "All of them. How is this supposed to work?"

He caught her finger, dutifully recited, "Jeremy and Humphrey will arrive this evening, then . . ."

She listened, and had to approve. Between them, he, his old dears, and her aunts had covered everything, even a gown for her to wear. He had a special license; the reverend of the village church who acted as chaplain for the estate would be delighted to marry them . . .

Head over heels in love.

She suddenly realized he'd not only said it, but was living it. Openly, in a manner guaranteed to demonstrate that fact to all the ton.

She refocused on his face, on the hard angles and planes that hadn't changed, hadn't softened in the least, that were now, here with her, totally devoid of his charming social mask. He was still talking, telling her of the arrangements for the wedding breakfast. Her eyes misted; freeing her finger, she laid it across his lips.

He stopped talking, met her gaze.

She smiled down at him; her heart overflowed. "I love you. So yes, I'll marry you tomorrow."

He searched her eyes, then his arms closed around her. "Thank God for that."

She chuckled, sank down, laying her head on his shoulder. Felt his arms settle, holding her tight. "This is really all a plot to avoid having to attend any more balls and soirées, isn't it?"

"And musicales. Don't forget those." Tristan bent his head and brushed a kiss to her forehead. Caught her gaze, softly said, "I'd much rather spend my evenings here, with you. Attending to my future."

Her eyes, the periwinkle blue intense and brilliant, held his for a long moment, then she smiled, shifted, and drew his lips to hers.

He took what she offered, gave all he had in return.

Lust and a virtuous woman.

Fate had chosen his lady for him, and done a bloody good job.

The World of Stephanie Laurens

Enter the unforgettable world of
#1 *New York Times* bestselling author

STEPHANIE LAURENS

with a sneak peek at
The Bastion Club Novels

*London's most eligible bachelors band
together to form the Bastion Club, an elite
society dedicated to allowing these heroes of
the Crown the freedom to determine their
own fate where marriage is concerned.*

Read on for a look at the entire series!

The book that started it all ...

Captain Jack's Woman
A Bastion Club Prequel

They meet in a clash of swords, drenched in the moonlight of Britain's rugged eastern coast: Captain Jack, his handsome features etched in silver and shadow, his powerful physique compelling Kit Cranmer to surrender. He is her dream lover come vividly alive. Suddenly, Kit finds she's only too delighted to explore with Jack the pleasures normally reserved for married ladies . . . little knowing what dangerous forces she's unleashing.

The Lady Chosen
This volume

A Gentleman's Honor

When Anthony Blake, Viscount Torrington, discovers Alicia standing over a dead body in his godmother's garden, he knows she is innocent of the crime . . . and innocent of love. His connections allow him to take control of the investigation, his social prominence provides her public support, but it is more than honor that compels him to protect her . . . and to do everything in his seductive power to make her his.

A Lady of His Own

Charles St. Austell returns to Cornwall to investigate rumors of spies operating via smuggling gangs near his home. The first unusual thing he discovers is his former love, Lady Penelope Selbourne, marching through his house after midnight. What is she after? Charles has his hands full unravelling the truth while simultaneously convincing the independent lady that she and only she will do for him—and he for her.

A Fine Passion

Jack, Baron Warnefleet rescues the startlingly beautiful Lady Clarice Atwood from a menacing, unmanageable horse. Clarice is no meek and mild miss. She is the very antithesis of the woolly-headed young ladies Jack has rejected as not for him. So why is she rusticating in the country? It quickly becomes clear that Clarice is in danger. Jack must use every ounce of his cunning and wit to protect this highly independent and richly passionate woman . . .

To Distraction

Deverell, Viscount Paignton, is in desperate need of a wife. Dispatched to a country house party to look for the lady his aunt deems perfect for him, he discovers Phoebe Malleson with her nose buried in a book. She is tempted to distraction by Deverell, but marrying him isn't part of her plan. Telling Deverell to go away doesn't work, and he quickly learns her secret—though the cost to them both might be deadly.

Beyond Seduction

In a moment of recklessness, Gervase Tregarth, 6th Earl of Crowhurst, swears he'll marry the next eligible lady to cross his path. Cloistered at his ancestral castle in Cornwall, he never expects he'll have to fulfill his pledge . . . but then he meets his neighbor, the very appealing Madeline Gascoigne. From their very first kiss, Gervase discovers that the headstrong and independent Madeline is no meek country miss . . . and that the fire between them will burn long beyond that first seduction.

The Edge of Desire

When Christian Allardyce, 6th Marquess of Dearne, receives a note from Lady Letitia Randall begging for his help, his world turns upside down. The day he left her behind to fight for king and country was the most difficult of his life. To clear her brother's name, Letitia has sworn to use every weapon at her command, even if it means seducing her ex-lover. But Christian is waging a war of his own—one of pure pleasure and sweet revenge that will take them both beyond the edge of desire.

Mastered By Love

"Dalziel," Royce Varisey, 10th Duke of Wolverstone, served his country for decades, facing dangers untold. As the holder of one of England's most august noble titles, he must now take on that gravest duty of all: marriage. But most young ladies are predictably boring. Far more tempting is his castle's aloof chatelaine, Minerva Chesterton. Determined to claim her, he embarks on a seduction to prove his mastery over every inch of her body . . . and every piece of her heart.